THE MISADVENTURES OF NERO WOLFE

THE MISADVENTURES OF NERO WOLFE

PARODIES AND PASTICHES FEATURING THE GREAT DETECTIVE OF WEST 35TH STREET

EDITED BY JOSH PACHTER

MYSTERIOUSPRESS.COM

INTEGRATED MEDIA
NEW YORK

Cover design by Mauricio Díaz

978-1-5040-5986-2

Published in 2020 by MysteriousPress.com/Open Road Integrated Media, Inc.
180 Maiden Lane
New York, NY 10038
www.mysteriouspress.com
www.openroadmedia.com

CONTENTS

PART II: PARODIES

PART III: POTPOURRI

TRIBUTE IN TRIPLICATE

INTRODUCTIONS

At Wolfe's Door

by Otto Penzler

Sherlock Holmes was not the first detective, but he was the first fictional character to become more real than the flesh-and-blood personages of his time. The only other detective in literature about whom that is true is Nero Wolfe. A few other detectives may be greater in that they have solved more complex cases, a few may be more famous in distant regions of the world, and a few may even sell more books—but none has achieved an emotional rapport with readers to equal that of Rex Stout's fat man.

In book after book, from 1934 to 1975, Stout wove a pattern of intricate detail that brought the eccentric detective and his tough, wisecracking assistant Archie Goodwin to life. The old brownstone on West Thirty-Fifth Street exists, almost as clearly as 221B Baker Street.

Wolfe and Holmes follow paths that cross at more than one

point. Much like the greatest detective of them all, Wolfe has inspired a devout fandom that speculates on unrevealed details of his past, combing the books for evidence, filling in gaps with inferences, suffering frustration at the hands of an author who changed facts, dates, names, and other elements of his detective's history to suit the exigencies of the newest book.

Still, more is known about Wolfe's life than about most other detectives, thanks to the narrative efforts of his assistant and chronicler, Goodwin, who represents (particularly in the early books) the dominant form of the American detective story, the "hard-boiled" school, just as Wolfe represents the classic English form, the puzzle story solved by an eccentric armchair detective.

Archie is no mere stupid, worshipful acolyte, employed solely to feed the ego of the detective and ask foolish questions for the benefit of dull readers. Archie is an excellent detective in his own right, a tough, cynical man of action, able to do many things beyond Wolfe's power, just as Wolfe's intellect towers over Archie's. In an unusual and healthy relationship, the talents of the two men complement each other to produce the best detective agency in New York—and the best dialogue in mystery fiction.

Wolfe, of course, is still the mastermind, and Archie has no choice but to stumble blindly along, as much out of his depth as Holmes's Dr. Watson or Poirot's Captain Hastings. The difference is that Archie doesn't care for it very much and takes no pains to disguise the fact. He is not above calling Wolfe a "hippo" or a "rhinoceros," nor is he reluctant to quit when he has had too much. He once told Wolfe, "You are simply too conceited, too eccentric, and too fat to work for!" Not the reaction of the typical Boswell of crime literature.

Neither Wolfe nor Archie age during the forty-one-year history of their affairs, nor do the other recurring characters who populate their world.

Stout was a fast writer, completing a novel in four to six weeks, and he did not revise. Although his prose suffered not at all, his hard facts sometimes strayed, which may account for the ambiguity of Wolfe's and Archie's birthplaces, some fuzziness about Wolfe's early years, and some characters undergoing a name change from one book to another.

Other facts are deliberately—not inadvertently—obscured. These are not the lapses of Stout; they are the flummery of Wolfe himself, who prefers to remain reticent about his biography. Sometimes the confusion is Archie's, although it is impossible to deny that his memory is superb, and he is less susceptible to errors of omission or commission than Watson, Hastings, Polton, or Dupin's anonymous chronicler.

Little is revealed about Wolfe's ancestry, for example, but that is not Archie's oversight so much as it is Wolfe's sense of privacy. There is some evidence, and a widely held belief, that Wolfe is the illegitimate son of a liaison between Holmes and *the* woman in his life, Irene Adler. And knowledgeable students of detective fiction will have no difficulty in noting the striking physical similarities between Wolfe and Holmes's older brother, Mycroft.

Like most other creators of memorable detectives, Stout did not intend for his books to undergo intense scrutiny, or to serve as subjects for profound scholarship. His purpose in writing the books was more noble: they were conceived to give pleasure. "If I'm not having fun writing a book," he said, "no one's going to have any fun reading it."

There can be no doubt that Rex Stout had enormous fun writing his books about Nero Wolfe. And there can be no doubt that the authors represented in this collection had every bit as much fun paying homage to and/or poking respectful fun at Stout's most famous creations.

Excerpted and adapted from The Private Lives of Private Eyes, Spies, Crimefighters and Other Good Guys *(Grosset & Dunlap, 1977)*

A Family Affair

by Rebecca Stout Bradbury

My father died in 1975. I am indeed proud and appreciate that Rex Stout remains an active part of the literary world. His books have given many people many hours of pleasure.

Rex and Pola Stout were married for forty-three years. They had two daughters. We lived in a house my father built in 1930 on a hill in Connecticut with the help of seventeen farm boys. Harold Salmon, one of the farm boys, lived in a house at the bottom of our road and would bring us raw milk in a metal can every morning with delicious cream on the top. He spent all his days at High Meadow, actively helping, participating in our family life.

My father bought boxes of Fanny Farmer candy, would offer us a piece of candy when it arrived, then take the box to his bedroom. He would "hide" it in one of his bureau drawers. (He built his bureau so that it had cubbyholes for his socks and a separate little closet for his shirts—drawers that pulled out, each with a folded shirt on it.) My sister, Barbara, and I would find the candy and punch a hole in the bottom of a piece to see if we wanted to eat it. If not, we would put it back in the box. Dad never said anything to us about the punched candy.

My mother was a textile designer and had a mill in Philadelphia for fifteen years. Dad, Barbara, and I wore her fabrics often. We had a "Christmas" skirt—red and green—every year. My dad wore a red wool jacket to my wedding in June on the croquet court at High Meadow.

I didn't read my first Rex Stout book until I was thirty years old, but Nero and Archie were always part of our lives. Dad would come down to dinner and say "Nero just said to Archie" or vice versa . . . and we believed they were upstairs!

We had "misadventures" at High Meadow. Once Barbara drove the family car down the hill—which is what we called our long hilly dirt/gravel driveway—with her eyes closed. Going around the second curve, she landed in a field and had to walk back up the hill and tell Dad. He laughed his wonderful laugh and got into the Jeep and went to pull the car out. I also had a driving mishap. Dad was teaching me to drive. We drove down the hill, and he told me to turn right onto Milltown Road. I did—but I didn't let go of the steering wheel and ran into a telephone pole. Again, he laughed and said, "Next time, let go of the wheel, and the car will straighten out." And we walked up the hill to get Harold to help us.

Rex Stout wrote fiction. There were lessons in his books, as well as a slice of history. During World War II, from 1941 to 1945, we lived in New York City, so my father could devote his days to the Writers War Board, which he created to promote the sale of war bonds and to inform the citizens of the United States about what was taking place in Germany. *The Second Confession* spoke about totalitarianism and the role of government; *Too Many Cooks* and *A Right to Die* spoke about race relations; *The Doorbell Rang* was a strong statement about J. Edgar Hoover and the FBI. The issues he was concerned about during his lifetime remain important and relevant today.

When I was nine years old, I began to wonder what my father did for a living. My friends' fathers went off with briefcases on the commuter train or worked on farms, at stores, in offices. What I did know was that, several times a year, a scenario was repeated that started with my father moving through the house and doing his gardening, building furniture—I have three pieces that he built for me—or working on one of his activities, such as being president of the Authors' League and chairman of Freedom House, without really hearing what anyone was saying to him, though he was usually an alert listener. I realized that he was "working"—getting to know his characters, setting out the story in his mind. Then, when he began to write the book on his manual typewriter, each day he would disappear into his study precisely at noon and reappear for dinner promptly at six thirty until the new book was finished.

My father always took Nero and Archie quite seriously, but he found it amusing when other authors imitated or poked fun at them. I think he would be amused—and honored, and perhaps even touched—by the tributes included in the pages that follow.

I know that I certainly am!

San Diego, California
March 2019

Plot It Yourselves

by Josh Pachter

Many years ago, I suggested to Frederic Dannay—who with his cousin Manfred B. Lee created the character of Ellery Queen—that there ought to be a collection of EQ parodies and pastiches titled *The Misadventures of Ellery Queen.* He liked the idea but thought it would be inappropriate for him to edit such a volume himself, so he graciously suggested that I do it. I was a teenager at the time, though, and had no idea how to edit a book, so the idea lay dormant for decades. Then, one night in 2016, over dinner with my old friend Mike Nevins and new friend Dale Andrews—both of whom had written excellent Queen pastiches—the subject came up, and Dale and I decided it was time to put a *Misadventures of Ellery Queen* together at long last. We did, and it was published by Wildside Press early in 2018.

While Dale and I were gathering the material for that collection, I got an unrelated, out-of-the-blue e-mail from Rex Stout's daughter, Rebecca Stout Bradbury. Rebecca lives in California, but she was going to be visiting *her* daughter, who was living at the time in a Washington, DC, suburb—not far from where *I* live—and she invited me to have lunch with them. Why? Because she'd heard that, long ago, I'd written a loving *homage* to Nero Wolfe, her father's best-known creation. What she was referring to was a short story of mine called "Sam Buried Caesar," about a ten-year-old boy named Nero Wolfe Griffen. I was eighteen years old when I wrote it, nineteen when it was published in the May 1971 issue of *Ellery Queen's Mystery Magazine.*

Rebecca and her daughter and I had a very pleasant lunch, and out of that came an invitation to address the annual Assembly of the Wolfe Pack, which is to Nero Wolfe what the Baker Street Irregulars are to Sherlock Holmes: a gathering of fans, as dedicated to fellowship as they are to scholarship. The group, under the direction of its leader, Ira B. Matetsky—who is officially known as the Wolfe Pack's werowance (an Algonquian word meaning a leader of the Powhatan Confederacy of Native Americans)—meets at regular intervals to eat meals that would have made Fritz Brenner proud, invent and sing song parodies with Wolfean content, and discuss in detail what Sherlockians call the Canon and Wolfe Packians call the Corpus, which is to say the thirty-three novels and forty-one novellas and short stories narrated by Archie Goodwin and devoted to the genius of that seventh-of-a-ton orchid fancier, Nero Wolfe.

In December of 2016, I took the train up to New York and addressed the Assembly, which was enormous fun—and during the course of the evening Rebecca pulled me aside and asked if I might consider editing a *Misadventures of Nero Wolfe*.

As you can see from the volume you now hold in your hands, my answer was yes.

Although I've edited this one on my own and it's being released by a different publisher, I've followed the same basic format Dale and I used for *The Misadventures of Ellery Queen*, dividing the book into three sections: pastiches (which are respectful imitations of the original, making use of the Nero and Archie characters), parodies (which are exaggerated imitations, often punning on the names of the original characters and intended to poke fun at the source material), and potpourri (which are stories inspired in some way by Rex Stout and/or his characters but written neither to re-create them nor mock them).

In addition to the formatting similarity, some of the same authors appear in both collections: Thomas Narcejac is back with another pastiche from his 1947 *Usurpation d'identité* collection, William Brittain with another story from his "Man Who Read" series (although, as you'll see, in this case the man is a woman), and Lawrence Block with the other of his two Chip Harrison stories. Joseph Goodrich is represented this time, not by a story, but by a scene from his stage adaptation of *Might as Well Be Dead*, Jon L. Breen dug up a fifty-year-old pastiche that has never before been published, there's another of Norma Schier's delightful anagram stories, and I've included my own "Sam Buried Caesar."

On the other hand, many of the authors represented here were *not* part of *The Misadventures of Ellery Queen*: in these pages, you'll find the first chapter of Robert Goldsborough's first novel-length continuation of the Corpus, one of Marvin Kaye's estate-sanctioned short stories, a Claudius Lyon story by Loren D. Estleman and a Julius Katz story by Dave Zeltserman, a science-fictional Nero from the pen of the late Mack Reynolds, two vignettes from the pages of the *Saturday Review of*

Literature, a chapter from John Lescroart's *Rasputin's Revenge*, and brand-new stories written especially for this collection by Michael Bracken and Robert Lopresti.

Before I turn you over to the stories themselves, I'd like to mention some of the material I chose *not* to include in this collection, to give you a sense of what else is out there:

• Viola Brothers Shore's "A Case of Facsimile" (*EQMM*, October 1948) is a whirlwind of a story, in which the daughters of famous fictional detectives (Shirley Holmes, Samantha Spade, Elsie Queen, Charlotte Chan, and so on) are students at the Edgar Allan Poe School, but the sole reference relevant to us is a parenthetical mention of "Nerissa Wolfe, who will be a perfect elephant some day."

• W. Heidenfeld's "The Unpleasantness at the Stooges' Club" (*EQMM*, February 1953) has a lovely premise—a locked-room murder is committed not far from the English country estate where the second bananas of great fictional detectives can get away from their stooging responsibilities for a bit of R and R—but the solution to the crime is hackneyed, Nero Wolfe is mentioned only once, in passing, and Archie Goodwin is conspicuously absent.

• At one point in Maurice Richardson's "The Last Detective Story in the World" (*EQMM*, February 1947), "Nero Wolfe's man-eating orchid snapped at Ellery Queen," but there was otherwise no reference to Wolfe.

• The February 1976 issue of *The Magazine of Fantasy and Science Fiction* includes a story titled "The Volcano," published by Paul Chapin. An "Editorial Preface" to the story includes these sentences: "Though no biography of Paul Chapin has yet been published, millions know of the man and his works. The most complete account of him is given in *The League of*

Frightened Men, the second volume in the biography of the great detective, Nero Wolfe. . . . [H]e became a murder suspect but was proved innocent by Wolfe. Chapin repaid Wolfe by putting him in his next novel under the name of Nestor Whale and killing him off in a particularly gruesome fashion." Both this preface and the story that follows were in fact written by noted science-fiction writer Philip José Farmer, the fourth entry in what has become known as his "Fictional Author Series," which began two years earlier when Farmer, afflicted with a bad case of writer's block, decided to write a novel as by Kurt Vonnegut's Kilgore Trout. "The Volcano" features a private investigator named Curtius Parry, who lives in an apartment on East Forty-Fifth Street in New York, but neither the character nor the case have any real connection to the world of Nero Wolfe.

• The first half of my old friend Marvin Lachman's "The Real Fourth Side of the Triangle" (*The Mystery Nook*, August 1976) is a nonfiction article about the relationship between Perry Mason and his secretary, Della Street, but the piece then morphs into a fictional account of Mason's and Ellery Queen's rivalry for Della's attentions before winding up at "the old four-story brownstone on West 35th Street," where the reader learns that Della has ultimately opted to run off with . . . not Archie Goodwin, but Nero Wolfe!

• David Langford's "If Looks Could Kill," which appeared in the 1992 anthology *EuroTemps* (edited by Alex Stewart and Neil Gaiman), features a British detective named Caligula Foxe in a fantasy world in which paranormal powers exist. Interesting, especially due to the Stout-inspired character names (narrator Charlie Goodman, Franz the chef, and others), but not enough to my liking to include.

• Alan Vanneman has written several novella-length pastiches that have much to recommend them, but they're too long to have included here. Vanneman has collected them as *Three Bullets*, and some careful websurfing should allow you to download them for free, courtesy of Mr. Vanneman.

So there's certainly more at least tangentially relevant material out there, but in this volume you'll find what I believe to be the cream of the crop.

As Rex Stout put it in *Plot It Yourself*: "Any writer that's any good can imitate a style. They do it all the time. Look at all the parodies."

That's excellent advice. So "pfui!" to further comment from me. It's time to lean back in a red armchair, ring for beer, and commence our journey into the wonderful world of Wolfean misadventures.

Bon voyage!

Herndon, Virginia
March 2020

PART I

PASTICHES

The Red Orchid

by Thomas Narcejac

(translated from the French by Rebecca K. Jones)

EDITOR'S NOTE: Thomas Narcejac, together with his longtime collaborator Pierre Boileau, wrote several dozen crime novels from the early 1950s through Boileau's death in 1989, including the 1954 thriller D'entre les morts, *which was filmed four years later by Alfred Hitchcock as* Vertigo. *Prior to the beginning of their collaboration, Narcejac wrote numerous novels on his own. And in the late '40s, he also wrote eighteen pastiches featuring fictional detectives, including Conan Doyle's Sherlock Holmes, G. K. Chesterton's Father Brown, Dorothy L. Sayers's Peter Wimsey, Leslie Charteris's The Saint, Ellery Queen's Ellery Queen . . . and Rex Stout's Nero Wolfe, which were collected and published as* Usurpation d'identité. *I'm delighted to open this volume with*

Narcejac's Wolfean pastiche, "L'Orchidée rouge." Written in 1947, it was translated into English and published in Ellery Queen's Mystery Magazine *in 1961. What follows is a new translation by Rebecca Jones, who also translated Narcejac's "Le mystère de ballons rouges" for* The Misadventures of Ellery Queen *(Wildside Press, 2018).*

"You're mistaken," Nero Wolfe said. "There are no red orchids."

"I'm sorry, sir, but I assure you that it is red."

"Impossible!" Wolfe scoffed.

"It's a *Coelogyne pandurata*."

"Your uncle has been cheated."

"I've *seen* the flower."

"Well, then, you lie," Wolfe barked, losing his patience. "Help me, Archie!"

He heaved himself out of his chair and headed for the elevator. Isabella Tyndall ran after him.

"I beg you, Mr. Wolfe."

"Don't beg," I said. "He's an insensitive monster. If you offer him enough money, then maybe. . . ."

"Two thousand dollars," she said.

Wolfe turned back and pointed a finger at her.

"The *Coelogyne* is pink," he growled. "I have been trying for two years to breed one in red, and I cannot do it. I refuse to believe that your uncle—"

"You haven't tried ultrasound," I protested. "I think she's telling the truth. And she came here to offer you three thousand dollars . . . I heard that right, didn't I, Miss Tyndall, it was three thousand dollars?"

"Yes, yes," the young blonde stammered, but Wolfe was already boarding the elevator that would take him to the plant rooms.

"Well, then," I murmured, "he'll have to decide."

I was ready to fly to Isabella's aid. So young, so fragile, so blond, so—you'd have to have the heart of a tiger in the stomach of a whale, like Wolfe, not to be moved by her predicament. I took her hand and invited her to sit.

"Is he angry?" she asked.

"Him? He's already forgotten you. From nine to eleven every morning, he's upstairs with his orchids. He thinks he's God Almighty—only, instead of creating the stars, he invents flowers."

"Is he a poet?"

What a babe! I sat on the arm of her chair and stroked her hair.

"He's an executioner," I said. "He torments flowers because they can't defend themselves—flowers and young girls. But, as you've guessed, I am Wolfe's guardian angel. He thinks I'm a detective. I'm twenty-eight, a hundred and sixty pounds, with plenty of muscle and a miniature brain. He doesn't suspect that, under that deceptive exterior, I am a pure spirit. Now don't worry: I'm going to take your case."

I leaned down, brushed the nape of her neck with a kiss, and returned to my desk.

"Tell me again, Isabella. I forget everything when you look at me."

She smiled. "I thought you were a pure spirit?"

"We spirits are enamored with beauty and innocence."

That smile could blow fuses.

"Shall I begin from the beginning, Mr. Goodwin?"

"Call me Archie. Spirits don't have surnames."

"Well, then . . . I am the niece of Sir Lawrence Tyndall. My uncle is a savant who has been experimenting with ultrasound for the past ten years. He works in absolute secrecy. Glory and honor mean nothing to him, so he has never published his results. No one knows his name. And yet he has developed a simple machine that allows the user to stop engines from miles away. His experiments are conclusive, and my uncle was about to turn his invention over to the proper authorities when the attacks began." She trembled at the memory.

"Don't be afraid," I murmured, not looking up from my notepad. "I'm here. How many attempts were made?"

"Two. About fifteen days ago, a shot was fired at my uncle as he strolled in the park after dinner. The bullet grazed his head. Then, last week, someone poisoned the herbal tea that he drinks every night before bed."

"What kind of poison?"

"Prussic acid."

"Do you suspect anyone?"

"No one. We live close to Lakeville, in the middle of the country. My uncle has no family, except for me and my cousin John. He had to rent out a wing of the manor, because his research has nearly bankrupted him, so now we have several boarders: the Reverend Norton, the Saunders woman and her son and sister."

"Servants?"

"Two. Old William and his wife. They've been with my uncle for more than thirty years."

"How old is your cousin?"

"Twenty-eight. He's worked with my uncle since he graduated from college."

"And the Saunders boy?"

"Billy? Twenty-three. He has cerebral anemia, and his doctors recommended the countryside."

"He's in love with you?"

Again that radiant smile. "A little."

"He's guilty. It's all clear to me. We'll—"

"Mr.—Archie, please. That's not all. A week and a half ago, some things disappeared from the manor: first a bottle of sherry, then a ham, then, the day before yesterday, a Cheshire cheese."

"You think someone's hiding in the house? There aren't any secret passages or dungeons, are there?"

"Not that we know about. My uncle bought the manor fifteen years ago. It's an old house, built in 1850, designed to resemble an English chateau."

"Then the architect must have included some underground chambers and a ghost. We'll see. Does the press know about all this?"

"Yes, because of the red orchid. When my uncle discovered a way to influence the development and coloring of flowers, he sent an article to the Lakeville newspaper."

"When was this?"

"Five or six days ago. We told the reporters who came to cover the story about the disappearances, and now we've been besieged by a crowd of journalists. That's why I'm here to beg for Mr. Wolfe's help. My uncle can't work."

"Whose idea was it to come to us?"

"My cousin's. But he predicted that Mr. Wolfe would refuse. He said he hates to travel."

"Travel? He's more sedentary than the Empire State Building. You should have called the cops."

"My uncle would prefer to engage the services of a private detective."

"Is it Old William who does the cooking?"

"Yes. Why? He's a very good cook."

"I doubt it. Does he know how to make Chateaubriand, or braised oysters, or ham with Missouri sauce, or Caribbean turtle? I say nothing, please note, of Zingara sauce or midnight sauce."

I reached for the bookshelf and pulled out a small volume with a tattered binding.

"Take this, Isabella, and study it. When you can prepare the recipes it contains, I think we might be able to persuade Mr. Wolfe."

"And your retainer?"

"Three thousand dollars ought to do it . . . for now. You'll have to lay in some beer, it'll have to be iced, and you'll need an armchair big enough to hold the lower half of his body."

I took a ruler from my desk drawer and measured Wolfe's seat.

"Three feet, ten inches," I said. "Better make it an even four feet. And, most important, his bedroom has to be on the ground floor. Wolfe hasn't climbed a staircase in twenty years."

Isabella rose.

"Archie, you are . . . you are—"

"—an angel," I said. "Now go. I'll be waiting for your call."

I kissed her on the lips before showing her out.

It took me three days to come up with a plan, and Wolfe fired me five times, giving me an hour each time to pack my bags and vacate the premises. Only after I swore that the Tyndall cook was a genius and the road to Lakeville was specially designed for the transportation of fragile foods did he finally surrender, agreeing to brave the unleashed elements—which is to say the bright April sun and a light breeze charged with the smell of the wild. Weighed down by a camel hair overcoat, his neck wrapped in a muffler, his head topped by a sombrero of unusual size, he dragged himself out to the car, where Fritz Brenner, tears in his eyes, was loading suitcases and briefcases.

"I put a snack on the front seat," Fritz murmured, clearing his throat. "It is duck pâté, turkey with jelly, Neapolitan andouille sausages, some sandwiches with haddock, some with caviar, and some with jam. Wines are in the trunk."

“Thank you,” snorted Wolfe. “Add a few squabs and a piece of salmon. Perhaps we’ll get there, after all.”

He rolled up all the windows, forbade me from smoking, and reclined, whining, on the vast bench of his Duesenberg Special.

“Goodbye,” he sighed, as I pulled gently away from the curb.

“Three thousand smackeroos, boss,” I said. “That’s worth a little inconvenience.”

“Silence!” Wolfe commanded. “Look straight ahead, Archie, and keep both hands on the wheel.”

Then, already exhausted from his exertions, he pulled the brim of his hat down over his eyes, and I heard no further groans, moans, protests, or complaints. It was in vain that I explained my theory that the Saunders boy had stolen the sherry and the cheese to camouflage his other criminal activity, since Wolfe didn’t deign to respond. At noon, he resigned himself to nibbling four sandwiches, a squab, two sausages, a quarter of a turkey, and some small slices of pâté, but his heart wasn’t in it. I insisted that, after the Chablis, he consent to drinking a bottle of Meursault and a smaller bottle of Tokay. Late in the afternoon, we arrived at the manor via a rutted drive, every jolt of which pulled supplications and sighs from Wolfe’s suffering lips.

“Fill up the tank, Archie,” he whispered, when the car shuddered to a stop at the foot of a dilapidated house. “We’ll leave in the morning.”

“But, boss, won’t you be exhausted?”

“Perhaps. And perhaps I will die, but I will die at home.”

With those words, he hauled himself out of the car, me pushing vigorously from the other side. Sir Lawrence appeared to make our acquaintance. He bade us welcome and asked if we’d had a good trip. I was afraid Wolfe might assassinate him. Then he preceded us into the house.

"Archie," Wolfe groaned, "you know that I detest porches."

"It's only twelve steps," I observed. "You can do it!"

He shot me a look that would have melted a lightning rod and, gathering his energy, followed Sir Lawrence, who showed us into a large sitting room where the residents of the mansion awaited us. When, looking back on this case, I want to laugh a bit—which hasn't much happened—I only have to remember its cast of characters: the Saunders sisters, who were so distorted it was like they were reflected in funhouse mirrors, one in height and the other in width; Reverend Norton, who looked exactly like a reverend; Billy, who had his aunt's nose and his mother's cheeks; and finally John, very pale, with an attitude so absent we took him for the mansion's ghost. Wolfe sat in the armchair Isabella pushed toward him and cut through the compliments and grateful expressions with a gesture.

"The *Coelogyne*?" he demanded.

There was an embarrassed silence, and Isabella folded her hands in her lap. "I was going to tell you, Mr. Wolfe," she said. "It was stolen this morning."

"In that case—" Wolfe struggled to rise.

But Isabella, fine girl, had brought him a beer, so the boss settled back into his seat.

"I don't understand it," Sir Lawrence chimed in. "The flower was locked in my laboratory, and the thief seems to have come through the wall. I was going to show you the laboratory after dinner. It's truly impenetrable, and I have the only key. Now, however—"

"Nothing else to report?" I cut him off.

"Not yet," the scientist said, his tone sinister. "Gentlemen, allow me to take you to your rooms. Dinner will be served in half an hour's time."

As soon as we were alone, Wolfe hurled his hat onto the bed.

"Archie, I'm done with you. This absurd journey has been a farrago of wasted time."

"That's just dandy," I said. "You'll have to advertise for another chauffeur to haul you back to New York. You'll need one who won't mind stopping every few miles to buy beer, who'll crawl through villages in second gear and level crossings in first. One who can help you earn three grand for a couple minutes' work. You probably ought to—"

"That's enough," Wolfe snapped. "You intend me to sleep in this bed?"

"If I pull that sofa up closer on one side and the armchairs on the other, I think—"

"You *think*?" Wolfe sneered. "And what of the *Coelogyne*?"

"We can worry about that tomorrow. For now, let's focus on the Caribbean tortoise."

Unfortunately, it was clear from the start of the meal that Old William might be a crackerjack gardener, but he was as divorced from the subtleties of the kitchen as an FBI agent from those of tact. He dished up a sort of brined leather that Sir Lawrence assured us with refined politeness was ham, accompanied by some carbonized debris that might once have been kidneys. Wolfe looked like a medical examiner trying to identify pieces of a cadaver. When Williams came in to announce the steak, Wolfe couldn't contain himself any longer. He laid down his napkin and withdrew without a word.

"Don't mind him," I said cheerfully. "He's always a little distracted when he spots the solution to a mystery, so his attitude right now is very encouraging." To get a step in front of things, I added, "When he slams doors, it's because he's found the key to the riddle."

At that moment, the dining room door was closed with such

violence that the clock stopped. More slamming announced Wolfe's progress toward his bedroom.

"Well, then," Sir Lawrence said lugubriously, "I expect there must now be nothing more for Mr. Wolfe to discover."

The rest of the meal proceeded in a heavy atmosphere. I tried, without success, to tell some amusing anecdotes, and was relieved when Sir Lawrence invited me to follow him. As we walked, he told me that he had received many letters and telegrams over the last several days, filled with offers and propositions that were driving him nuts.

"Nothing wrong with a little extra wealth," I said.

"Perhaps," he murmured, and waved me into his laboratory.

I'd expected a hidden lair cluttered with beakers and distillation equipment, but the room was small, plainly furnished, and contained to my surprise only three or four scientific devices, which he ignored.

Instead, he drew my attention to the lab's security system, an absolutely unpickable Yale lock. Since the door was the room's only entrance, the theft of the orchid was a mystery. Besides, why would anyone take the flower and leave behind the more valuable apparatus?

"I'd like to see your bedroom," I said.

He took me there, and I went over the joint in minute detail. I knocked on the walls and found them solid. The window was impregnable. No one could get into this room once Sir Lawrence had locked himself in.

"Once I realized that someone wants to poison me," the scientist explained, "I abandoned my former bedroom and installed myself here. Now I am sheltered from any danger, with Isabella and John in the two adjoining rooms."

"You don't suspect your tenants?"

"Certainly not, Mr. Goodwin. They are above reproach."

"Do you think someone could be hidden in the mansion?"

"I don't think anything at all," Sir Lawrence said dryly. "It's you and Mr. Wolfe who are here to think."

"One more question. For reasons nobody's explained, you've had to rent out part of your mansion. Given your cash-flow problem, how are you going to pay my boss three thousand bucks? I don't—"

"Nero Wolfe will be paid," Sir Lawrence cut me off. "Good night, Mr. Goodwin. If you need anything, ring for William."

I left the room and heard him turn the key in the lock and secure the deadbolt. I went back to the sitting room, where Isabella was chatting with the reverend.

"Not what I'd call a cheerful evening," I observed.

"The Saunderses are afraid of Mr. Wolfe," Isabella said, "and John's gone to bed."

The reverend murmured something about the Good Lord punishing the wicked, and got to his feet. And it was at that moment that William showed up, livid and trembling.

"What's eating you?" I said.

"I'm sorry to disturb you," William spluttered, "but someone has stolen the potato masher."

A little after midnight, I crept into the hallway, resolved to catch the mysterious burglar. I was keeping an open mind: Had we been hoodwinked, or was some unknown person hiding out in the mansion? A creak, not far off, suggested that the second hypothesis was likely the correct one. I stuck my hand in my pocket and tiptoed toward the kitchen, partly illuminated by a single moonbeam. He was there, I was sure of it. I could hear him breathing as he searched the pantry. Then he brandished a bottle, uncorked it with the ease of a jazz trumpeter launching into an improvisation, and, head tilted back, performed a piece that must have been difficult, judging by the motion of his Adam's apple. Moonlight hit his face, revealing his identity.

"Cheers," I said, my voice hollow.

The reverend choked, then bent double to catch his breath, as I took the bottle of liquor from his hands.

"Praise God," he spluttered.

"Interesting way to do it," I observed. "What are you doing here?"

"Er—the things that have disappeared—I thought I would search the office."

"Sure you did. You didn't help disappear the sherry, by any chance?"

The reverend said something from Ecclesiastes. I was about to reply with a little something from 1 Kings when a harsh light came on in the sitting room.

"Quick," I whispered, "find a place to hide." The breadbox was too small, the pantry too full, so we had no choice. I pushed the reverend into the refrigerator, which was huge, and slid in behind him, pulling the door after me, careful not to close it all the way. This observation post was well chosen though chilly, and I was daydreaming of fishing for walrus on an ice floe when a faint sound from outside signaled that danger was near.

"Don't make a sound," I whispered.

"I beg your pardon?" the reverend exclaimed.

"Hush!"

I could hear two voices in the kitchen, quietly conversing. The pastor stirred behind me and sighed.

"They're not leaving," I whispered.

"My head is on fire," he moaned.

"That's the price you pay, padre. Patience!" I glued my eye to the gap. "One of them's a guy," I said.

The reverend, wanting to see for himself, moved awkwardly

and bumped loudly into some refrigerated object, which startled the pair outside. There was a sharp scream, and the guy swore, and then they were gone.

"What are they doing?" the pastor demanded.

"They *were* kissing," I grumbled, and the reverend crossed himself and whispered an allusion to Sodom and celestial fire, which did nothing to warm up the atmosphere.

So, young Saunders had a secret appointment with Isabella. Though I'd recognized him, I hadn't seen her face. But that scream—that had been Isabella's voice, no doubt about it! So, were they the thieves? If sherry was their cordial of choice, a cheese would have been an appropriate snack, but where did a potato masher fit in? I left the protective coolness of our hiding place, scratching my head, and the reverend followed me. I figured I'd better have a little chat with Isabella.

"Wait for me in the sitting room," I told the pastor and, once he was out of sight, I took a turn at the bottle and played myself a tune. It was bourbon, the good stuff. Reinvigorated, I prepared to go on the offensive.

But at that moment, a sort of rattle came from the sitting room. I got there in three steps.

"The—" the reverend stammered. "The—"

I'll be damned if the mansion's ghost wasn't frolicking right there on the carpet. It was a dirty white, standard-issue spirit. It floated left and right, knocking over furniture with a brutality that contradicted its apparently immaterial nature. A voice, more wrathful than sepulchral, issued from the depths of its snowy ectoplasm.

"It must be the attic ghost," the pastor spluttered. "Hallway ghosts are smaller."

"Actually, I think it's an underground ghost," I said. "I base that on the cursing."

While the reverend recited a prayer for the relief of souls in pain, I switched on the lights. Before us stood a figure entangled in the off-white piano cover, which some prankster had seen fit to toss over his shoulders, enfolding him in fabric. We helped the man untangle himself.

"Billy," the reverend said.

Young Saunders, clenching his fists, marched up to me.

"Was it you," he groaned, "who dreamed up this little trick?"

"No," I said, "it was the reverend. He did the same thing to me just now for a laugh. But what, I ask myself, were you doing down here at one in the morning, anyway, all dressed up for the city?"

"I was thirsty," Billy said. "I came downstairs to get a drink, and someone attacked me."

"You didn't see anyone between your bedroom and the sitting room?"

Young Saunders reddened. "No."

"And when you get thirsty in the middle of the night, you get dressed, complete with a collar and tie, before coming downstairs?"

"Do I have to explain myself to you?"

"To me? No. But maybe, in a little while, the cops will take an interest."

He blanched and turned to the pastor, frightened.

"What's going on? Did something happen to Sir Lawrence?"

"That's an interesting thought," I said. "Let's go see."

We reassured ourselves that Sir Lawrence was sleeping peacefully, since we could hear through his bedroom door a concert of snoring so perfectly chromatic I was sorry I couldn't record it for the symphony crowd.

"Satisfied?" Billy scowled. "Do you mind if I get my drink now?"

"Mind? Not me. I just think you people are a little too thirsty around here. Good night, fellas."

I left them, and, just before I re-entered my bedroom, I heard the reverend cry, "I swear it wasn't me!" Then the two of them drifted off toward the kitchen.

I was awakened at nine o'clock by a pounding on my door.

"Mr. Goodwin, come quickly." I recognized William's voice. "It's Sir Lawrence."

I jumped into my dressing gown and opened up. William was so upset he could barely explain himself.

"I called for him," he said, "but there was no response. I'm frightened."

I went into Wolfe's bedroom.

"Ah, Archie," Wolfe groaned. "Is the car ready?"

He had just finished packing. His suitcase, neatly buckled, lay on one of the two armchairs.

"Look, boss. If I was to tell you the old man might be dead—"

"I would not be surprised," Wolfe said somberly. "Poisoned, no doubt, by his miserable ham and kidneys. The devil can have him!"

"Yeah, sure. But, speaking of the devil, I saw the famous ghost."

Since Wolfe is incapable of tying his tie by himself, I brought him up to speed while tweaking a splendid knot around his neck.

"Go, Archie," Wolfe ordered, "and make the necessary preparations. We leave within the hour. This comedy has lasted long enough."

"Comedy?"

"You still don't understand?"

When the boss doubts my intellectual capacity, I like to take a hike before the discussion turns to his advantage. So I rejoined William, who was still shivering outside Sir Lawrence's door, now accompanied by the reverend.

"On three," I said. I counted, and we threw ourselves against the door. On our third attempt, it cracked. The next time, a plank broke loose and I was able to maneuver the key and deadbolt. The door opened.

"Heavens!" the reverend said.

"He's dead!" William cried.

Sir Lawrence, clad in pajamas, lay collapsed at the base of the wall, facing the closed window. His cowering position and the rictus that had disfigured his face suggested he hadn't gone out easily.

"Go fetch Nero Wolfe," I told William. "Then call a doctor."

I interrupted the reverend's prayers and sent him off to keep curious onlookers at bay. Then I searched the room for the vial that had contained the poison, since I was pretty sure Sir Lawrence had been poisoned. But I didn't see anything that looked like an ampule or syringe. I examined the body and found a minuscule scratch, a little swollen around the edges, on the back of his right hand—the sting that had killed the scientist. It couldn't have been a suicide, but there was no way into the room except the door and the window, both of which had been solidly locked. So no one could have entered the bedroom, and no one had left it.

Hands on my hips, I studied the scene. The position of the body was bizarre. It lay with its face on a rug that ought to have been in the center of the room but had been moved over to the base of the wall, where it covered a large rectangle of parquet floor that had been cleared of furniture. As much as I love gangsters, murderers, and other specialists in euthanasia, I hate puzzles, complicated crimes, and mysteries that agitate the brain.

A dip in the floorboards told me Wolfe had arrived.

He glanced at the dead man, then sat heavily on the bed,

which sagged under his seventh of a ton, and threw me the morning paper.

"How dare they," he said.

An enormous headline crossed the page: "Nero Wolfe Leaves Home for First Time in Five Years." And, as a subhead: "Hired to Save Inventor of Machine That Brings Down Planes."

"This arrived by messenger," he resumed. "You should be quite happy with your work, Archie."

Something ironic in his tone made me prick up my ears.

"Maybe I killed him," I grumbled.

He didn't deign to respond. His eyes flicked over the body, the walls, the furniture.

"His right hand is scratched," I said. "I think—"

"Bring John," Wolfe cut in.

I found the lot of them in the hallway: John, Isabella, and the three Saunderses.

"It wasn't me," Billy said. "I can prove it."

I gave Isabella's arm a squeeze and waved John through the splintered door. He was wan and detached as usual. He stood facing Wolfe like a student resigned to failure.

"Sir Lawrence," Wolfe said, "did physical exercise in the morning?"

"Yes, sir. There's a program on the radio at eight o'clock."

"Archie, turn it on."

"Can't," John said. "It went haywire three days ago, and we haven't had time to get it fixed."

"Then how could your uncle—?"

"There's another radio in my bedroom next door. You can hear it clearly from in here."

"Archie?"

I went to John's bedroom and tuned in a Bing Crosby song, "Brother, Can You Spare a Dime?" A pounding on the wall told me the experiment was over. I returned to Wolfe. The location of the body was explained: Sir Lawrence had died during his physical-fitness session. But who had killed him, and how had the murderer gained entry?

"You want Billy, boss?" I suggested.

"No."

"You know who stole the ham, the cheese, and the rest of it?"

"Yes."

"And of course you know why somebody transformed Billy into a ghost last night?"

"Naturally."

"So you can explain how the killer got through that locked door?"

"Certainly."

That tore it. "Well, then, should I bring the car around?"

"Please."

I tried for an insulting sneer.

"Your disdain needs work, Archie," Wolfe said. "Try rehearsing it in a mirror. And you might inquire if Reverend Norton or one of the Saunderses is trained in Swedish gymnastics."

I was so irate I almost slammed the door. Wolfe wanted—well, I'd show him!

The hallway was empty. The residents of the mansion must be dressing, since they knew the cops were on their way. I went into Billy's room without knocking.

"Do you partake in fitness training?" I said.

"Does it show?" he cried, blushing with pleasure. He stuck out his right arm and flexed it. "Here, feel my muscle. Go ahead!"

Disgusted, I swiped an index finger across the soft protuberance that slightly bulged his sleeve. I had a strong desire to pinch it.

"I'm going to be an athlete," Billy affirmed.

He gestured at an array of placards fixed to the walls of his bedroom. *Jumping out of bed is the elixir of life. Tell me how you breathe and I'll tell you who you are.* Ad nauseum.

"Swell," I said. "What exercises did you do this morning?"

He scratched his head, thinking about it. "First some rotation of the anteriors with flexion of the posteriors and lateral extension of the deltoids. Then one minute of walking on my hands, a minute of relaxing the supinators, two minutes of duck steps—"

"That's enough," I said. Duck steps . . . lovin' babe!

I moved on to the reverend's quarters.

"Do you exercise?"

He didn't seem to understand my question, so I repeated it, an octave higher, mimicking a windmill with my arms.

"Ah, yes," he murmured, "physical exercise. Certainly."

"Were you listening to the radio this morning at eight o'clock?"

"I was, my child, like everyone in the manor."

"First, I'm not your child. Second, exactly what exercises did you do? Spill it, for God's sake!"

The reverend crossed himself and whispered, his face reddening, "I did two minutes of duck steps."

"Duck steps," I said. I was beginning to get the picture.

I burst into the quarters of Mrs. Saunders, the large, and she fled behind a screen.

"You did duck steps this a.m.," I exclaimed in a Mephistophelian voice. "Don't deny it."

She gabbled, and I made my exit. There was a large man in a flannel suit in the hallway.

"Might I see Sir Lawrence's nephew?" he said. "I've been sent by the Armstrong Company."

Wolfe appeared in his doorway.

"What do you want with the young man?"

"I am to offer him an option on his uncle's patent," the visitor explained.

"Then Sir Lawrence's invention has monetary value?" Wolfe demanded.

The other man smiled and winked. "If it didn't, would you be here, Mr. Wolfe?"

"You hear that, Archie?" Wolfe said, his face dark.

He went back into his room, and I pointed out John's door to the Armstrong Company's representative before joining him.

"They all did gymnastics," I said, not even pretending to hide my annoyance.

"What type of gymnastics?"

"Movements, relaxing exercises. You wouldn't understand."

Wolfe frowned.

"You are aware that I dislike repeating myself, Archie. What exercises did they do this morning?"

"Duck steps."

"Show me."

"Listen, boss, I'm a patient guy, but—"

"Are you or are you not my employee, Mr. Goodwin?"

"Oh, fine." I squatted and hopped toward him. "Do you want me to quack?" I demanded.

Wolfe observed me, his heavy eyelids half closed. "That's enough," he said.

"May I point out," I said, "that my job description does not—"

"I have my reasons," he cut in. "No red *Coelogyne* ever existed, Archie. Get them. Get them all. Then search their bedrooms, all of them, until you find a phonograph record, and bring it."

■ ■ ■

In the quarters of the Saunders ladies, I found nothing but beauty products. The reverend's bedroom held bottles, lots of them in all shapes and sizes, all empty. I next tried Billy's bedroom, which contained nothing interesting, just clothing, ties, and books with suggestive titles: *How to Become a Champion*; *Physical Fitness Is Within Everyone's Reach*; *Power, Health, and Love.* I lit a cigarette, and that's when I smelled it, a stale odor I tracked to a cardboard hatbox up on a closet shelf. Climbing onto a chair, I pulled down the box and hurried to the window, which I opened very wide. I had hit what a casual observer might call pay dirt: a bottle of sherry, a ham, a potato masher, and something that had to be a Cheshire cheese.

I'd been suspicious of young Billy from the beginning. But that elephant Wolfe had sent me to search for was a record, so I continued hunting.

And in Isabella's bedroom I uncovered not one record but four of them, hidden between the pages of a photo album. From their labels, they were apparently dance records. The boss was definitely showing his age. Maybe it was time for me take over more of the firm's brainwork.

I left the album and the hatbox in the hall and returned to Sir Lawrence's bedroom, where Wolfe, still sitting on the bed, was busy questioning Isabella. Billy, very pale, was avoiding looking at the cadaver. The Saunders dames and the reverend seemed about to give up, and John was biting his nails. A sweet little family gathering.

"When the bullet was fired at your uncle," Wolfe said, "you were there?"

"No," Isabella said.

"And the poisoned tea, you saw it?"

"No. But my uncle wasn't a liar and, if he came to take refuge in this bedroom, it was definitely because he was afraid of something."

"Do you possess a key to the laboratory?"

"No. There's only one key, and my uncle always carries it with him."

Wolfe turned toward me. "Did you find it, Archie?"

"I found everything, boss. The stolen objects, except for the orchid, were hidden in a hatbox in the quarters of young Saunders."

"That's a lie!" Billy cried. "I protest. This is a setup—"

The rest was lost in the tumult. Everyone spoke at once, and one of the Saunders ladies—the skinny one—pretended to faint.

"Silence!" Wolfe ordered. "The record, Archie?"

"There were four of them, stashed in this photo album."

"Four? Interesting. Go to John's bedroom and play them."

"I didn't see a phonograph in that—"

"The radio setup must certainly include a turntable."

I took the album and went off to do the boss's bidding. But I didn't hear much of interest. The first record was blues, with Louis Armstrong on trumpet. The second was a paso doble, the third a Benny Goodman arrangement. I set the needle on the fourth record, and a voice began to speak: "Greetings, dear listeners. Our two hundred and forty-fifth exercise lesson begins now. Take a deep breath in . . . sigh it out . . . perfect. Now place your back against the wall and stand on your tiptoes . . . good. Raise your arms above your head and stretch back until they touch the wall. Very good. Now bend forward, as far as possible. Straighten up, arms touching the wall. Repeat this movement, faster and faster: once . . . twice . . . three times. That's fine. Stand straight, and we'll try it again: once . . . twice . . . three times."

Someone pounded on the wall: once, twice, three times.

I stopped the record and went back to Wolfe. His audience looked petrified, but Wolfe's lips were turned up in the fraction of an inch I've learned to recognize as his equivalent of a smile.

"I'm damned if I know what that means," I said.

"Sir Lawrence," Wolfe explained, "placed his back against the wall, in accordance with the instructions he heard from the next room. Put your back against the wall, Archie, at the location where the victim was likely to have stood. Pay close attention—and, above all else, don't raise your arms. Are you in position? Good. Now raise your head. You're going to perceive camouflaged by the design of the tapestry a small point that protrudes—"

He was right. It wasn't obvious, but I could make out something like a thin nail with its head removed. I reached out—

"Don't touch it!" Wolfe barked.

And then I got it.

"It's dipped in poison?" I asked.

"Yes. When Sir Lawrence raised his arms, the back of his hand was scratched by that point, and death followed within minutes. Curare, I would guess. Go to the door, Archie, and take out your revolver. The assassin is here."

My gun in my fist, I watched them from behind, eyeing Wolfe closely.

"My compliments, John," Wolfe said. "Your trap was ingenious." John shifted in his chair, and Wolfe added, "Don't move. You'll annoy Archie."

"I say," the reverend stammered, "can you explain—?"

"It's quite simple," Wolfe replied. "Sir Lawrence was in need of funding, but there was no interest in his research. He therefore decided to draw attention to himself by way of a series of simulated attacks. Naturally, John and Isabella were aware of his plan."

"Isabella?" I protested.

"Certainly."

"But what about Billy?"

"Let me speak, Mr. Goodwin," Wolfe said dryly. "Sir Lawrence's tenants were not involved. Sir Lawrence chose them because they were so very inoffensive . . . babes in the woods, if you prefer the idiom. Their statements to the media neither confirmed or disproved anything. And you know the rest. Journalists pounced on the story, which was as every bit as mysterious as Sir Lawrence intended. An elusive criminal had hidden himself in the mansion and survived by stealing food in the middle of the night. Sir Lawrence was in danger. His work was at risk of falling into the hands of thieves. It was thus urgent for any interested party to purchase the rights to his apparatus before it became too late—at, of course, a high price. Perhaps there were offers he rejected. At last, he set up an auction. And John, to further excite public interest in the matter, had the bright idea to attract me to the mansion."

"The red orchid," I said.

"Precisely. It was a clumsy attempt: there is no such thing as a red orchid, so I knew there was deviltry at work. I knew before we left the brownstone that someone was attempting to fool us. I would not have minded if the food had at least been good. But John, who knew that his uncle would keep for himself most of the money that would be paid to him for his invention, had decided to play a different game, with Isabella's complicity. He recorded an exercise lesson and planted the poisoned nail in the wall of his bedroom. So easily was the trap laid. Isabella had a clandestine meeting with Billy, who had been pursuing her for some time."

"You don't really believe Isabella—?"

Wolfe didn't even deign to shrug his shoulders.

"Billy," he continued, "would be lured to a rendezvous with Isabella near the kitchen, while John hid the objects he himself had stolen over the preceding days in Billy's bedroom. This would cause the police investigation to focus on Billy. This morning, Isabella brought the record to her bedroom. She hasn't had time to destroy it."

"But why did John wrap Billy up in the piano cover?"

Wolfe's lip twitched in what was for him a kind of cannibalistic smile. "Because he was in love with his cousin and could not resist the chance to hurt his rival."

"And you expect me to believe," I groaned, "that you figured this all out in your bed, without a scrap of evidence?"

"Ah, the bed," Wolfe scowled. "It is so hard and so narrow that I couldn't close an eye. I had all the time in the world for reflecting."

I could see that he was steaming and made an effort to placate him. "What gave you the answer, boss?"

"The duck steps," Wolfe said. "Since the assassin could not have—"

There was a knock at the door, and I stepped aside to let William pass.

"The police are here," he said.

"Show them in," Wolfe said. "And bring beer."

The Armstrong Company kept Sir Lawrence's invention and refused to pay John for it. Wolfe insisted I pay him the three thousand dollars, at the rate of one dollar a week. By the time the debt is cleared, I'll be eighty-seven.

One more thing. Unbeknownst to Wolfe, I changed the text of our advertisement:

> "*Nero Wolfe Detective Agency. Research and investigations. Success assured. Consultation in the mornings, 9 a.m. to 12 p.m. For men only. If not celibate, don't bother.*"

Chapter 8 from *Murder in Pastiche*

by Marion Mainwaring

EDITOR'S NOTE: In Marion Mainwaring's 1955 novel, Murder in Pastiche, or Nine Detectives All at Sea, *notorious gossip columnist Paul Price is murdered aboard the RMS* Florabunda, *which is sailing across the Atlantic with a passenger list including pastiche versions of nine famous fictional detectives. The book—like this one—is divided into three parts, with Part One setting up the murder and Part Three tying up the loose ends. Part Two consists of nine chapters, each zooming in on one passenger's investigation, each mirroring beautifully the source detective's style and manner. The cast of characters includes Mallory King (Ellery Queen), Jerry Pason (Perry Mason), Spike Bludgeon (Mike Hammer), Atlas Poireau (Hercule Poirot), Sir Jon. Nappleby (Michael Innes's Sir John Appleby), and Broderick Tourneur (Ngaio Marsh's Roderick Alleyn) . . . plus Trajan Beare, a marvelous take on Nero*

Wolfe. What follows is the first half of the Beare chapter. The complete novel is available in paperback and for Kindle apps and readers, and I recommend it wholeheartedly.

(from the notebook of Ernie Woodbin)

Beare was sitting up in bed, in his pajamas, and he was drinking beef tea.

I reported: "Latitude and longitude about the same, heavy following sea, still foggy, average speed fifteen knots. There's a movie in the dining saloon at eight-thirty, but I've already seen it. Paul Price was murdered last night."

I watched his face for a reaction but wasn't surprised to see none. He just took another sip of beef tea. I went on with the daily bulletin:

"They don't know yet who did it. But of course when they come to question me, and they find out you told me to keep Price out of your way by force if necessary—"

"Ernie. I have asked you before. Please don't play the clown until we reach shore."

"Yes, sir. It may cramp my style in the investigation, having to play it straight."

He looked at me then.

I nodded. "No kidding. His head was bashed in."

Beare let out a sigh. "I cannot pretend any regret. Price was unprincipled, illiterate, and a boor. The press and the nation are to be congratulated."

"That's what the captain thinks, too. When he heard about it, he said, 'Good.' He seemed to think that ended the matter. But there are five detectives hot on the trail already—"

Beare interrupted. "The salmon last night was respectable. For lunch, I will have it again. A clear soup . . ."

This meant the matter was ended as far as he was concerned, and I was to shut up. He spent the next four minutes talking about food. I stood it as long as I could and then wandered off.

The next few hours I just moseyed about, keeping an eye on events. It isn't often that you get a chance to watch your top professional rivals at work, and I had to admit some of their techniques looked good—like Poireau twirling that mustache and Nappleby spouting polysyllables, and Brody Tourneur always behaving as if he was at a garden party—but after careful study and comparison I decided I'd stick to my own methods, and I still liked Beare's way of using his eyes and pursing his lips the best.

Beare never said a word about the murder, and I refrained from heckling him. But I had a feeling it wouldn't stay as simple as that, and I was right. Not counting the general request for help they'd issued when Price's body was discovered and the purser pointed out there were professional man-hunters on board the *Florabunda*, we had three special invitations to join the fun.

Late the next afternoon, the first officer came up, and we fell to talking. He was about my age, tall for a Limey, with blue eyes and a swell tan, and I'd got the impression that, while his brains might never set the ocean ablaze, he was good company and nice to have on a ship where the captain was balmy and might decide on an all-out effort to break the Atlantic speed record at any moment. I asked him if they'd caught the killer yet, and he said no quite seriously.

"Mr. Beare is a great detective, isn't he?" he asked. "One of the best?"

"*The* best, I'd say," I told him, "and he'd agree. He's a genius. Why?"

"Well, you don't suppose—?"

"If you're hinting he might like to play cops and robbers, too, it's no use. He only plays for million-dollar bills."

"Oh, I see. Well, I didn't really hope he would. I mean, I've heard he's hard to persuade."

"When there isn't a fee, he's reinforced concrete," I said. "Anyway, this time I don't see why you'd want him. You've got enough other guys at work."

"It's only that there isn't much time, and I thought, the more investigators we have—"

"Uh-uh," I told him. "It's the Law of Diminishing Returns. Could you sail the ship better if you had nine captains?"

"I see what you mean, Mr. Woodbin," he said. "It's bad enough having *one* Old Man." He let out a yawn. "I could do with a drink."

So we had a drink, and then another. I told him about working for Beare, and about Ohio, where I grew up and which he thought was part of southern California. I set him straight on that, and he told me about the *Florabunda*. He said life at sea wasn't fit for a human being, and after one or two more trips he was going to quit and retire to a tropical island he knew about where he could live like a king on ten bob a year. Since at the current exchange rate that meant about twelve cents a month and no income tax, I figured he had a good thing there, but I took him with a grain of salt. I'd heard sailors talk like that before, and in my experience they never quit till they can't totter across a gangplank any longer.

That was the first request for help, and I didn't even bother passing it on to Beare. The second one he knew about for the simple reason that it was delivered to him in person. I was with him when there was a knock at the door, and, thinking it was the steward with his beer, I yelled, "Come in."

It was Dolores Despana. She walked right in while I was off my guard.

Beare glared. He may have recognized her from things I'd said, or he may not. It didn't matter. What with his general feeling about women—which is not favorable—and his being away from solid ground, I half expected him to say outright to get out, but he only looked at me in a way that meant I was to say it.

But I ignored him and looked at Dolores. You could tell that two years ago she'd been buying clothes on Fourteenth Street and that one year ago she kept a wad of chewing gum in her cheek, but she was coming along fast and there was certainly nothing wrong with what the eye could see. I said, "This is Miss Despana," and got her settled in a chair.

Beare inclined his head an eighth of an inch and continued to glare. Dolores stared at him and asked, "You're Trajan Beare?" He didn't reply, and she answered herself, "Yeah," in a soft voice, as if she'd heard but hadn't ever quite believed a man could be that fat. Once she'd got it established that it was possible, she lost interest and said, in a very businesslike way, "You take clients, don't you? I want you to do a job for me."

Beare gave no sign that he heard. I said, "Sorry, but Mr. Beare isn't taking—"

But she went right on: "You find out who killed people. I've seen about you in the papers. Well, I don't care about that. I didn't kill Paul Price, and I don't care who did. But he wrote a plug for me, and someone stole it."

"You want Mr. Beare to find it?" I asked her.

She shook her head. "No. Anyone who's enough of a stinker to steal it and keep it from me would be stinker enough to burn it up or throw it overboard." She looked ready to cry. "It would have put me into the big time on Broadway, that plug."

Beare spoke at last, frowning. "I don't follow you, madam. You do not fear being arrested for the murder yourself. You do not wish to have the murderer caught. You consider a search for this document useless. Why do you want to hire me?"

She eyed him as if he wasn't as bright as she'd heard. "Publicity," she said impatiently. "What do you *think*? You're a name. If you work on this case as my agent, we'll both get good press. You can do it on a percentage basis, a percentage of the profits on my next show. This might be almost as good as a plug in Price's column."

At that point, I cut in. Beare looked ready to explode, and I felt about the same. Her thinking Trajan Beare, who charged fees that turned strong bank presidents pale, would do anything contingent on the success of a nonexistent Broadway show was bad enough. But letting him know she was willing to use him as a second-best for Paul Price, who was illiterate, unprincipled, and a boor—I took her elbow firmly and got the door open.

"Sorry," I said. "Mr. Beare would love to help, but he's suffering from *mal de mer*—that's Portuguese for seasickness—and he might do you more harm than good." I got her into the passageway and let her go. "One last word," I said as she flounced. "Just some brotherly advice. Try Anderson. He may not be pretty, but he's rich and he's lonesome. Nobody on board likes him very much." I gave her a big smile and went up on deck for air.

I didn't want to discuss the thing with Beare. I knew what he'd say, and anyway I hadn't made up my mind about Dolores. She could be what she looked like—a gorgeous dumb blonde on the make—but I'd been fooled before, often enough to think twice before deciding.

That was the second invitation. The third was anonymous and informal; in fact, it was an invitation only if you read between the lines.

I found it on the floor of my stateroom, in a *Florabunda* envelope that was gummed shut. Thinking it was a notice, I let it ride until morning, and I could have kicked myself when I slit it open and pulled out a sheet of business paper, typed double-space over all of one side, with a rough torn bottom edge.

I'd followed things closely enough that I knew what it was, all right, and even though it wasn't technically any business of mine I got that feeling you get when something breaks in a case. I sat down and began to read it. The first paragraph was the plug for Dolores Despana, and it was just another plug if you didn't know the story behind it.

"The de-luscious Dolores Despana has waved bye-bye to Johnny Bull after setting London on fire with the biggest blaze since Ye Olde Incendiary Bombes . . . her *Hot Legs* had them drooling . . . saw her wining in Leicester Square with a certain Marquis of You-Know-Where, and it's not too far from those white cliffs. But Dolores tells me she's true to Times Square. And Yours Truly predicts Times Square will be hearing a *lot* about this gal!"

Then came a piece of Hollywood dirt, standard Price stuff: "Jackie O'Dair insists it's still rings on the finger and bells in the steeple for her and Tony. Says Tony is in Mexico vacationing. But Yours Truly saw Tony with 'friend' Mae in Paris, and it looks like Lohengrin for him and her. Maybe Tony's *en route* to Mexico via the Champs-Elysées. How about that, Jackie?"

And then the payoff: "Told you about the so-called brains we have on this barge. Well, I find there is another mastermind on board who is a horse of a different color. He is a specialist in murder, too, but from another angle, and he is having fun and games while the Sherlocks sleep. He does not know I have found him out, but, next time we meet, FIREWORKS MAY BE EXPECTED. THE REAL NAME OF THIS CROOK IS NOT ON HIS PASSPORT. IT IS GIB."

It ended there. By that time, I was goggle-eyed. This murder had been screwy enough before. Now it was for Kraft-Ebbing's casebook. I got up and carried the goddamn thing to Beare's cabin, holding it by the edges just as a matter of principle. I was pretty sure there wouldn't be any prints.

Beare was ordering breakfast. He nodded politely and said, "Good morning, Ernie."

When the steward had gone, I told him what I had.

Beare shrugged and picked up the book he was reading.

"You don't think it's a clue?"

"No."

"You think it's a frame?"

"No." He turned a page.

"Okay, I get it, you're not interested."

"Ernie." Beare put his book down on his belly. "I am aware that, ever since this murder was discovered, you have been trying to needle me into undertaking its investigation."

"I thought it might occupy your mind," I said earnestly. "The good secretary always tries to—"

"Pfui. Even if we were at home instead of—"

He closed his eyes and came to a full stop. It was practically the only time I've ever heard him leave a sentence unfinished. He opened his eyes and said patiently, "Even if we were not at home, I would not take the case. Why should I? There is no client, no fee. Public spirit? I do not condone the murder even of a scurrilous quidnunc, but its investigation does not devolve onto me; there are representatives of the constituted authorities aboard who have it in hand. This paper should be taken at once to the official in charge."

"Just admit you're too lazy—"

"Enough, Ernie. I do not know the facts, but, viewing the case cursorily, I doubt if it is soluble. A dolt could get away with a crime under such circumstances. The obstacles in the way of detecting him are insuperable. We cannot trace the histories of scores of passengers. We cannot distinguish between their normal behavior and their abnormal deviations. We cannot check alibis. The murderer may be some ordinary seaman with a grudge against passengers. He may be a rival journalist, traveling incognito. He may be the captain."

Making a speech meant Beare was feeling more at ease, anyway. "You're the boss," I said, just to keep things going. "And if one of the other detectives solves the case—well, you'll still be the *fattest* one, they can't take that away from you."

Beare scowled. "Least of all will you move me by appeals to my spirit of emulation. My taste runs neither to socialized detection nor"—he grimaced—"to relay races." He picked up his book and I beat it, carrying the paper.

In my cabin, I looked at it again. I hated to let it go just like that, and I played around with the idea of a little investigating on my own, but in the end I decided to take it to the first officer. After all, we had been pally over gin and orange, and he had confided in me his plans for the future, so I ought to play fair. When I finally tracked him down and showed him the paper, he got as excited as if it was going to have the murderer's signature on it. But when he'd read it through he said:

"I can't understand this. It's daft! There's something strange about it. Has Mr. Beare seen it? What does he think?"

"He won't touch it."

"But what the devil does it *mean*? Do you think Price had discovered that he was going to be killed?"

"It reads that way. I wish he'd had time to go on, or more space—it breaks off short."

"Do you think he was going to give the actual *name*? But what begins with G-I-B?"

"My guess is he was going to write 'gibberish,'" I told him. "But I've got other questions. Who took the paper out of the machine, and why was it put in my cabin?"

Mr. Waggish gave a groan. "Perhaps there's a *third* person at work? It's daft, completely daft!"

"Cheer up," I said.

"Oh," he said, "I don't care, personally. In fact, I'm rather enjoying the experience, it's different from the usual crossing. But the Old Man—he's already all fouled up like Christ in a whirlpool. And if we have to wait in quarantine because of this—"

"Quarantine?"

"If we can't deliver the murderer on arrival, we'll have to moor offshore. And then the skipper will *really* blow up, and we'll have the hell of a trip back home. He hates every day we spend in sight of land."

I could have told him that was nothing to what Beare felt about every day in sight of open ocean, but I let it go. I said so long and went back to Beare's cabin. The time had come for some more needling, this time a good jab, hypodermic size.

Beare was sitting up reading. He put his book down and said, "Three more nights until we dine again at home. I shall radiogram ahead about the menu. There will be *saucisse minuit*—"

"That *would* be nice," I said wistfully.

Beare blinked, and I guessed he was looking at me suspiciously as I turned my back and went to the porthole to look out at the fog. I gave him the latest weather report and began a blow-by-blow description of the movie I hadn't gone to in the dining saloon.

"Ernie. What the devil are you insinuating?"

"Nothing, probably," I said cheerily. "With all these great Sherlocks on board, the crime ought to be solved before too long. Chances are we won't be delayed more than one or two nights."

"Ernie!"

I explained what the first officer had told me.

Beare's chin quivered. "Confound it!" He drew a deep breath. "Very well. Tell me what has been done so far."

So that was how we got into the case. Beare sat there scowling while I went over it in detail, leaving nothing out, not even the flutter of an eyelid. I gave him everything I knew, which was what I'd seen myself and what Waggish and the other detectives had found out.

"Where is that paper now?" he asked when I had finished.

"I gave it to Waggish, like you said."

"I want to see it. And I want to see the suspects. Get them here in an hour. Bring Miss Price earlier. It is unlikely she knows as little about her uncle as she claims."

"The suspects?"

"Everyone who was there when the blackjack was stolen."

"You think the killer must be limited to that group?"

"No, the limitation is not absolute. The person who took the blackjack might conceivably have given it to another person and is lying about the theft, not because he is guilty of murder, but from fear of the killer or in hope of blackmailing him."

"If anyone but the murderer took it, he's a sap not to say so. The murderer won't let him stay alive much longer."

Beare nodded. "True. But then the suspects in this case do not appear to be distinguished by acumen. At any rate, although the limitation is not absolute, it is the soundest working hypothesis we have. We cannot hold out for absolute truth: 'He who would fix his condition upon incontestable reasons of preference must live and die inquiring and debating.'"

I was on my way out, but I stopped. "Confucius?"

Beare frowned. "Samuel Johnson."

The Archie Hunters

by Jon L. Breen

AUTHOR'S NOTE: "The Archie Hunters" was written on a manual typewriter in the airfield flight dispensary where I was employed during my one overseas year as a US Army draftee. (No, I'm not a doctor, and I was sadly miscast as a medic. Most of the work I did was clerical.) I had sold three stories to Ellery Queen's Mystery Magazine, *all of them in the parody or pastiche category, so I naturally submitted this one. But I must have known Fred Dannay would never buy it. I'll quote from his rejection letter of November 21, 1968: "I don't care for a combination of Mike Hammer and Nero Wolfe (and therefore of Spillane and Stout). I wouldn't want to publish any Mike Hammer pastiche or parody, and I don't want, in any other pastiche or parody, the kind of political motivation you've used in 'The Archie Hunters.'" He did add, "Your handling of Nero and Archie is first-rate," and went on to suggest pairing Nero Wolfe with another fictional detective, which I never did.*

In terms of the magazine's policy and his own good taste, Fred was certainly right to reject the story. I put it aside, deciding I didn't really like it. All my other parodies and pastiches were born of admiration for the target authors' works, and, while Rex Stout and Nero Wolfe are among my favorites, I was not a fan of Mickey Spillane and Mike Hammer. Besides, the story was so much of its time that it seemed hopelessly dated just a few years later. When I learned from Josh Pachter that he was assembling a collection of Wolfe-inspired stories, though, I pulled it out of the files, found it better than I remembered, and decided the current political scene (you know what I mean) gave it a new resonance. So here it is, and—apart from the correction of obvious typos, of which editor Pachter found a shocking number—it's just as I composed it on that army typewriter.

The newsstand guy's beady little eyes bulged with fear. I had the little runt by the shirtfront and his feet were dangling helplessly over the sidewalk. We were drawing a big crowd now—you usually can in the Times Square district at noon.

"Mack," he squealed like a cornered rat. "Mack, I'm your buddy. What'd I do?"

"You only played into the hands of the dirty, lousy, rotten Commies, that's all you did, you lousy punk." I shoved the copy of the *East Village Udder* under his nose. "Isn't there enough filth and rottenness in the world without scum like you peddling crap like this to our youth?"

"I don't know nothin' about it, Mack. It's just another weekly rag the distributor brings me every Tuesday. I didn't know . . ."

My fist left his face a bloody pulp and half his teeth in place. My second blow took care of what remained. I let go of his shirtfront and let him dribble to the sidewalk like a glob of ketchup out of a new bottle. Watching him writhing and moaning, I felt a tear of nostalgia come to my eye, remembering when he was my buddy and I bought good clean literature like *Rogue*, *The National Review*, and Ayn Rand novels at his stand before the Commies got to him. I get real sentimental that way, so I kicked him in the head two or three times till he stopped moaning.

The crowd just watched me. That was OK. I didn't expect applause.

I took the dirty rag with me, though I could hardly stomach its stench. At the edge of the crowd, a cop I call a pal clapped my shoulder and said, "Nice work, Mack," and I grinned at him and walked up Broadway. The cops are all right in my book. They do a hell of a job. Fighting crime these days is like getting in the ring with Joe Louis with your hands tied. I could never take the restraints or I'd be a cop myself. But as a private cop I can mete out justice more directly and more efficiently.

Back in the office, I turned the pages of the *East Village Udder*, wanting to puke. All the perverts and deviates and weirdos spewed out their mental diseases on the pages of the crummy rag. Especially in the back where they had the classified ads. If anybody had told me I'd ever answer one of those ads, I'd have rearranged his face until my knuckles bled. But I did answer one, not one from some queer who wanted a roommate for a lasting love relationship or a wife-swapping society in suburban New Jersey, but one from a guy in my own racket who was in trouble.

The ad read this way:

> *Private investigator seeks associate on short-term basis for missing-persons case.*

Must be discreet, good at legwork, and able to report activities literately, cogently, and accurately to office-based supervisor.

Contact Nero Wolfe, West 35th Street

I knew that name. I'd never met Wolfe, but I knew him by reputation, and I knew his leg man, Archie Goodwin, a good guy though a little politer and softer than I think a private op ought to be. This ad from Wolfe could mean only one thing: the missing person he was talking about was Archie Goodwin. Now cops watch out for other cops, and I think private cops ought to do the same thing, especially when they're straight guys like Archie Goodwin. So I went to West 35th Street to see Nero Wolfe and offer him my help.

Wolfe's layout was an old brownstone that had seen better days. I'd rung the doorbell twice before a little pipsqueak with a chef's apron on answered the door.

"Yes, sir?" he said. I could tell right away he was some sort of a foreigner.

"I want to see Wolfe."

The squirt looked at his watch and back at me, licking his lips fearfully. "No one can see Mr. Wolfe at this hour, sir. It is his time with the plants."

"With the plants?"

"The orchids. Always every afternoon Mr. Wolfe works with his orchids, no matter what. If you could come back . . ."

I could feel hot, vengeful rage waxing up inside me. I could not understand, and when Mack Himmler cannot understand something, somebody is likely to wind up with smashed-up features and a bad bellyache.

"Archie Goodwin missing, maybe dead or dying, and the great Nero Wolfe spends his almighty time screwing around with goddam orchids! Where's the gross slob's greenhouse?"

"I can't tell you—"

I hit the little twerp so hard he bounced off the wall at the other side of the room. I walked toward him with an I'm-not-finished-with-you leer and even though the shrimp couldn't talk because his mouth was full of blood, he raised his finger to point to the stairway. I took the stairs two at a time.

I found the plant room easy enough. I entered the room like the whole riot squad. There were two men in the room, one a frail-looking old fellow who about had cardiac arrest when he got a look at my ugly mug and the fury I had written across it, and the other the biggest, fattest guy I've ever run across, and he just looked at me with surprise and anger and curiosity evenly mixed on his still pokerish face but standing his ground. This must be Nero Wolfe.

The very fact he stood his ground made me like the guy some, but that didn't mean I didn't want to kick the *crêpes suzettes* out of him if I didn't think he was square.

"Are you Wolfe?" I asked menacingly, even though I didn't really need to.

"I am Nero Wolfe. May I ask—?"

"You may *listen*, fat boy. My name's Mack Himmler and I've come to help find Archie Goodwin who is my buddy. And I'd like to know why the hell you're making with the flowers when you don't know what happened to Archie Goodwin. Are you a goddam hippie or something?"

"Mr. Himmler, I am not accustomed to being insulted in the sanctity of my own home, particularly not by unannounced intruders who violate the hard, unbending rule of the plant room. If I were to give up my orchids in a time of crisis, Mr.

Himmler, my mental processes would be derailed and whatever intellect I would be able to bring to bear on the problem at hand would become useless. To this moment, Mr. Himmler, I have done everything I can to determine the whereabouts of Mr. Goodwin and the circumstances of his abrupt disappearance. I appreciate your offer of help, and I will be happy to acquaint you with the facts of the case as I know them. But first I ask that you kindly allow me to finish my session with my orchids. I also ask that you apologize to my friend Mr. Horstmann for the alarm you have caused him."

The other guy, who was shaking like a weight-reducing machine, grinned weakly and said, "That's all right, Mr. Wolfe."

"Then let us continue, Theodore. I'll see you downstairs, Mr. Himmler."

The bloated creep was trying to dismiss me, but I wasn't quite ready to be dismissed. I had to say my piece.

"Look, Tubby, if that was my partner who was gone I'd find the guy behind it and make sure he died with a bullet in his belly like my buddy from World War Two who I've been avenging for twenty years by shooting bullets in people's bellies did."

He still stood his ground. The guy was cool. If I was as fat as him my reference to a bullet in the belly would have me begging for mercy, even if my own personal belly wasn't directly involved.

"Mr. Himmler, I don't admire your methods. In my present pickle, I am willing to accept your help, but I insist that you let me indulge my eccentricities. By the way, what have you done with Fritz?"

"The chef? He'll live."

"Mr. Himmler, did you manhandle Fritz?"

"Oh, maybe a little."

"If your treatment of my chef has affected the palatability of my supper, I shall personally see to it that the State of New York revokes your license."

"I've been threatened with that before."

"I daresay."

I found myself grinning. In a cockeyed way, I was beginning to like the guy. I walked over and clapped his shoulder and said, "Nero, let's be buddies."

I didn't know a big pile of blubber could stiffen, but Wolfe managed it.

"Little by little, Mr. Himmler, you are beginning to try my patience. I shall see you downstairs in one half hour, at which time you will kindly refrain from laying hands on my body."

Nobody pushes Mack Himmler around ordinarily, but Wolfe managed that, too. I went downstairs meekly and gave the cook some first aid, in return for which he gave me a beer.

By the time Wolfe got through twiddling his thumbs in the plant room, I'd thought of plenty of questions to ask him. But when he finally came waddling into his office the first thing I wanted to know was why he'd stuck his ad in the *Udder*.

He arched his eyebrows at me. "The *East Village Udder*, Mr. Himmler? I'd have guessed the *Daily News*. Are you an *Udder* reader?"

"Hell, no! But that's where I saw the ad. Why a dirty, stinking rag like that?"

"I advertised in all the metropolitan papers plus a few suburban journals. As an afterthought, I included the underground press. I wanted maximum coverage. Apparently, my caprice was a well-advised one, since it brought me a man of your talents."

I grinned at that. "So you know me, huh?"

"Your reputation is not unknown to me. Although it would never have occurred to me to make contact with you, I must admit your particular abilities might be useful to me. I already have Saul Panzer, Orrie Cather, and Fred Durkin on the case, but none of them is Archie Goodwin."

"I'm not, either."

"No, I know that, but you have a certain eye for detail and a well-known ability to describe your experiences vividly, albeit distastefully. Saul Panzer never made a bestseller list."

"Neither did Goodwin."

Wolfe glared at me. "I'll disregard that. Bestseller lists are odious anyway. I think, without further badinage, I should acquaint you with the facts of the case, bare as they are. To put it succinctly, Archie Goodwin left here after breakfast the day before yesterday—that was Tuesday—and virtually disappeared from the face of the earth. His expressed destination was the home of Mrs. Francine Vermillion, a widow for whom we have been conducting an investigation."

"Yeah? What was that?"

"An apparently minor and rather uninteresting case, which I had accepted principally because of the lady's extensive wealth and our current monetary depletion. It was a dognapping case. Someone had made off with her cocker spaniel, stolen from the Cloverfield Kennels."

"Huh! How did Vermillion kick off?"

"The lady's husband died three years ago, of apparently natural causes. He was ninety-three."

"And how old is the dame?"

"I should say twenty-six."

"A looker?"

"Archie found her attractive. My opinion in such matters means little. Mr. Himmler, it is by no means certain that the lady or her dog had any connection with Archie's disappearance. I am inclined to believe they did not. I merely mention her because it was to her residence that he was going that morning. He never arrived."

"Anything else on the fire?"

"Not at the moment, no."

"Any enemies? Threats?"

"As you know as well as anyone, persons in our line of work tend to make enemies. Archie Goodwin had enemies, some all his own and some that were my enemies and thus his by association. There were no direct threats to either of us recently. As I've suggested, it's been a rather slow year."

"How do you know Goodwin didn't just take an unannounced vacation?"

"That would be very much unlike Archie. But there is another reason for suspecting foul play. At ten o'clock, Fritz, my cook, received a phone call from Archie. He was apparently rushed and in a state of excitement. He spoke with a sense of urgency rare in him. He told Fritz he couldn't stay on the phone long and left the following message to be relayed to me. 'Take two and hit to right. Fourth and goal on the three. Two minutes for high sticking.' He made Fritz read it back to him and then hung up. I know Archie is trying to tell me something, but I cannot determine what."

I grinned and leaned back in the red armchair. "Wolfe, you came to the right guy—or I mean the right guy came to you. That's sports talk. 'Take two and hit to right' is advice you might give to a guy who's going up to bat, you know, in baseball. Let two pitches go by and hit the ball to right field. 'Fourth and goal on the three' is football: fourth down on the three-yard line."

"Pfui! Mr. Himmler, there is no need to belabor the obvious. A man cannot live the greater part of his life in the United States of America without picking up at least perfunctory acquaintanceship with her sporting idioms. I know very well what those terms mean in their athletic contexts—that still doesn't tell me what they meant to Archie on Tuesday morning and why he was so anxious to communicate them to me. I have tried every means at my command to break the code and have failed."

"Look, Wolfe, I'm a hell of a lot better at breaking heads than I am at breaking codes."

"I realize that. I'm not trying to employ you as a cryptographer. But I want you to assault the pavements of this city—ask questions, look for leads within the sports world and without it, exploit every resource you have for information, and then report to me. I must tell you that Saul, Orrie, and Fred have uncovered precisely nothing of value so far. Still, you might compare notes with them to avoid going over the same ground. One more thing, Mr. Himmler. I said you are to assault pavements. Not people."

"Sure, Wolfe," I said, getting up from the red chair. "First I check out the Vermillion dame."

"She has been adequately questioned, I assure you. I had Saul bring her here, and I interrogated her myself, in this very room. You need not concern yourself with the Vermillion woman."

"Sure, pal."

Like hell.

The Vermillion dame was stacked.

She came to the door wearing a yellow bathrobe. And nothing else. I could see the wide white cleavage between her large firm breasts, and when the robe fell open at the bottom I could see her long legs, firm and smooth and wellmuscled like a dancer's. After a few minutes, I noticed her face, and it was all right, too, pale and free of makeup, wreathed in long black hair, sensual lips wet and slightly parted, penetrating gray eyes that held an unmistakable invitation.

"Who are you?" she said.

"Mack Himmler—I'm a private investigator. Can I come in?"

She looked me over.

"You want to see my credentials, baby?"

"Sure, big boy, but not out here in the hall. Come on in and have a drink."

The apartment was class all the way. Plush and roomy. She went to the portable bar to mix our drinks. I watched her with masculine eyes.

After a couple of hours of preliminaries, I got right to the point.

"Okay, baby, where's Goodwin?"

"What, Mack?" she asked, breathing hard still.

"Archie Goodwin. Nero Wolfe's man. The man you saw about a dog. Don't kid me."

"Oh, Archie." She giggled. "Such a Puritan."

I smacked her hard with the back of my hand. A trickle of blood started its course from the corner of her mouth down her lovely chin. A hint of terror came into her eyes.

"Where's Goodwin? You know something. Spill it."

"No, I don't. I haven't seen Archie since he left here day before yesterday morning."

I gave it to her again. Now she had two trickles from either corner of her sensual mouth.

"And you told Wolfe he wasn't even here Tuesday morning. That's two strikes, baby. I guess my next move is to hit to right. Or maybe you'd like a little high sticking. I'm good at that, too."

"Mack," she whimpered, "what does all this mean?"

"Don't play dumb, Francine. Where's Goodwin?"

"He—he never found Velda. I—"

"Velda?"

"My cocker spaniel. Her name was Velda. A nice, friendly little bitch."

That made me livid with anger, but she didn't seem to understand why. "You want a bullet in the belly, slut? Where was Goodwin going when he left here?"

She finally decided to play ball. "The Empty Sulky," she choked, her eyes filmed with terror.

So she wouldn't think there were no hard feelings, I kissed her hard on her bloody, sensual mouth before I left.

It was dusk now, and a light rain had begun to fall. I pulled the trench coat tight around me and walked twenty-eight blocks in the relentless drizzle to the Empty Sulky. A man can think in the rain, and I had a lot to think about. Something didn't add up—some small point I'd missed was gnawing away at the edge of my brain.

The Empty Sulky was a dim-lit and smoke-filled bar, a hangout for hookers and horseplayers and pimps and human scum and beaten-down husbands and punchy ex-pugs and guys like me. I knew the place well, but I'd never seen Archie Goodwin there. It wasn't his kind of joint.

"Hiya, Mack," the bartender greeted me. "What's your pleasure?"

"The usual. And some information."

"Why, hell, Mack, I always thought that was part of the usual. What do you need to know?"

"Do you know a dick named Archie Goodwin?" I described Archie.

"Yeah, sure, he was in here the day before yesterday afternoon."

"Alone?"

"No, not alone at all. In fact, there were three rather well-known characters with him."

"Hoods?"

"No, no, nothing like that. Joe Mammoth, André Pomfrit, and Reggie Mantis."

Things started to fall in place. Joe Mammoth was the quarterback of the New York Tartans pro football team. André Pomfrit was a French-Canadian defenseman who played twenty years in the National Hockey League before retiring to become a dress designer. Reggie Mantis was one of the greatest sluggers in baseball history. The words of Archie Goodwin's message came back to me.

"Did they leave together?"

"Yeah."

"Do you know where they were going?"

"No idea."

"Thanks for the dope, buddy. Is Bork around?"

"That miserable, sniveling, wretched little informer? He's in his usual booth."

I walked to the darkest, dingiest corner of the Empty Sulky, where Rance "Greaseball" Bork, my favorite stool pigeon, was perched on his customary stool. He didn't hear me coming—he had a comic book in front of him and the leer on his ferret-like face and the glassy look in his eye told me Captain America was beating the stuffing out of some evildoer. I feel sorry for people who get their kicks reading about sadism and violence—practicing it is so much more fun.

I sat down opposite him.

"Hey, Bork."

He peered up at me in the dim light. "Hi, Mack."

"Can I have that comic when you're done?"

"Sure, Mack, sure."

"I need to find three men. They're public figures, so it shouldn't be too tough." I named the three sports heroes, and Bork recited three addresses and unlisted phone numbers without blinking.

"You gonna beat 'em up, Mack?" he asked breathlessly, hero worship in his eyes.

"If I have to."

"Go easy on Joe Mammoth's right knee."

"That the bad one?"

"Yeah. I mean, it's the middle of the season yet. Just put him in some kind of excruciating pain he'll be over by Sunday."

"If he's not in jail by Sunday. You know anything about a dognapping ring operating in the city?"

"No."

"Any line at all on the Archie Goodwin snatch?"

"Sorry."

"Okay, kid. What do I owe you?"

The punk was drooling now. "The same as always, Mack."

"Okay, kid."

I took him in the back room and beat the hell out of him.

I walked on through the rain. Things were starting to make sense, but I still didn't know what the racket of the three sports heroes was or what connection the cocker spaniel named Velda had with it.

I kept thinking I'd like to meet the bastard that named that bitch Velda.

At ten o'clock, after covering miles of Manhattan and giving my knuckles that good soreness that comes from satisfying vengeance, I called Wolfe's brownstone to report what I'd learned.

"Mr. Himmler, I hope you haven't resorted to methods that—"

"My methods are my methods, Pudge. You hired me. You're the boss. I do what you say, but I do it my way. Got it?"

"Very well. I want all parties to the case to convene in my

home at eleven o'clock tomorrow morning. The group should include the three athletes, Mr. Mammoth, Mr. Pomfrit, and Mr. Mantis; the operator of the Cloverfield Kennel, Mr. Cloverfield; and of course Mrs. Vermillion."

"They'll be there. You got something, Wolfe?"

"Yes, I may be able to bring the affair to a satisfactory conclusion."

"You know where Goodwin is?"

"I believe so."

"You know who's behind this business?"

"I am quite sure I do, Mr. Himmler."

"Tell me who the skunk is and I'll—"

"—put a bullet in his belly? Pfui! Your methods are not mine, Mr. Himmler. In the current idiom, you've done your thing. Now I intend to do mine."

"Okay, Nero. I've had my fun."

After I hung up the phone, I knew there was something somewhere along the line I'd missed, something I should have caught. Something was not what it seemed, but damned if I knew what it was.

The Vermillion dame got the red leather chair, giving Wolfe a view of those nicely molded legs that was wasted on him. The three athletes sat quietly, like little choirboys who'd been caught in a scuffle. André Pomfrit's kisser already resembled hamburger from twenty years of fast-moving pucks, so he didn't look much worse than normal. Pomfrit had frustrated me. I couldn't find any teeth to break in his mouth. Joe Mammoth may still have a million-dollar passing arm, but I'd taken him out of the cover-boy class in the profile department. Reggie Mantis I used to watch as a kid in the Polo Grounds—he was a kind of hero of mine—so he wasn't as busted up as the others. I'd come up with the kennel guy, too, but hadn't been able to get anything out of him, aside from the usual red fluid.

Fritz and I did a little first aid, and by the time Wolfe came waddling in, the bleeding was over and I guessed all that was left was a bunch of nice chit-chat of the kind that makes Goodwin's books so dull.

"I appreciate your attendance this morning, Mrs. Vermillion and gentlemen. I trust the conclusion of today's discussion will be satisfactory to all of us—or most of us. It's seldom everyone can leave this room in a jubilant humor. Mr. Himmler, you have done your job well. And in just the manner I had been given to expect of you. Archie!"

Archie Goodwin walked in. He was grinning broadly.

"Goodwin!" I shouted. "Where the hell have you been?"

"Here and there, Himmler. And I understand you've been dogging my footsteps."

"Enough of this punnery and flummery, Archie," Wolfe said. "Mr. Himmler, I don't know if you have penetrated our little charade yet."

My head was spinning. What was the one point I'd missed?

"I can see ways that you could have. We weren't really as clever and devious as we might have been, but our purpose has been served, I believe."

It hit me then.

"God damn it! It was a hoax. It was a trick. Goodwin never disappeared at all, and I should have known it all along. The *East Village Udder* is published on Tuesdays, and you told me Goodwin disappeared on Tuesday. If he did, how could the ad be in the *Udder* that came out the same morning? There wouldn't be time. Why'd you take me in like this, Wolfe? I ought to smash your fat face in!"

"There's been ample face-smashing already, Mr. Himmler. Yesterday and today you have been guilty of at least seven demonstrable instances of assault and battery, utterly unprovoked violence. All the people here are ready to testify against you in court. I myself am prepared to testify, much as I dislike making such appearances. Your career of killing and disfiguring has gone on long enough, Mr. Himmler. Today it is ended."

"Then you were all in on it?"

"From the newsboy to the kennel operator. It was an intricate operation, Mr. Himmler. It depended upon a good many good citizens exposing themselves to painful beatings. I myself was fully prepared, although I admit relief at being spared your blows."

"But the cocker spaniel—"

"There was no cocker spaniel," the Vermillion dame said sneeringly.

"Velda . . . her name was Velda."

"Mr. Himmler, in the same day's paper was another classified ad, one you'd surely have answered even if you missed my other ad. It said, 'Come home, Velda, all is forgiven' and gave Mrs. Vermillion's phone number."

I couldn't speak. My mouth filled with phlegm.

Wolfe kept talking.

"You may wonder, Mr. Himmler, why I would go to all this trouble merely to eliminate one competitor, however much I despised the competitor. I assure you that I have been paid well for this venture by a group of concerned citizens, some of whom are wearing dentures today as a result of your overly vigorous interrogation methods, and others of whom, among them the publisher of the *East Village Udder*, have not been victims of your barbarism but some day might well be if you were not stopped.

"I believe you were a participant on the Allied side in the

Second World War, Mr. Himmler. So was I, although my age and physical qualifications precluded my being a part of the active-duty military. I believe I did my part for my adopted country in my capacity of civilian consultant to Army Intelligence. Mr. Goodwin held the rank of major in the U.S. Army during that conflict.

"It may be, Mr. Himmler, that you and I are both anachronisms in this day, that the fires operative in our society, the trends away from the visual in favor of the audio-tactile, the reversion to tribalism that many foresee, the apparent discrediting of the whole concept of nationalism, may not be fully understood by either of us, being as we are of a different generation and, as I sometimes feel, of a different world. Possibly the very concepts of democracy we were fighting for in that war are now obsolete. Some may think this; I prefer not to.

"However, Mr. Himmler, I remember what I was fighting against in that conflict—Nazism, fascism, hatred and violence as a way of life, breaking heads as a means of dealing with dissent, the Brownshirts, the gas chambers, the government by terror, the police state. The use of violence to solve his problems degrades a man, Mr. Himmler. I have always shunned it.

"I see in you, Mr. Himmler, a growing American fascism that frightens me more than German or Italian fascism did, simply because it is occurring in the nation I have adopted for my own. How this trend can be stymied I do not know, Mr. Himmler, but I do know that I have the ammunition I need now—the legal ammunition—to put a stop to the activities of one American fascist, and a far more influential one than many people would like to believe."

I'd had enough. Enough ingratitude and enough abuse from the soft slobs who thought good could clobber bad with marshmallow knuckles. I remembered the one judge who revoked my license, all the terrible things he'd said about me, the names he'd called me. Could I take all that from another judge?

No! I am my judge, and I am my jury. I'd show them.

I pulled out my .45. They all froze there as I aimed it. Archie Goodwin made a step toward me, but too slow.

I shot myself in the belly. With glazed eye, I watched my own guts spill out on the floor of Wolfe's office. I fell to my knees, life leaving me in a steady, warm flow. The red puddle on the carpet of Wolfe's office spread—the wider it spread, the thinner was my hold on life.

I heard Wolfe say, "Himmler! How could you?"

I had only a second before I was a corpse talking, but I got it in. "It was easy," I said.

EPILOGUE

I guess it's pretty obvious that Mack Himmler wasn't around to finish this account, so I wrote the last scene myself, doing the best I could to imitate his writing style. I think I did a fairly good job of it, but I don't think my stomach could stand writing that way all the time.

To clear up one loose end, I'm not completely sure just what Wolfe meant when he asked Himmler, "How could you?" I think it probably baffled him that anyone could commit suicide on an empty stomach. Wolfe, who is almost insanely civilized, had planned to invite Himmler to stay for lunch, and the idea of anybody, even a fascist pig, missing a meal troubles him greatly.

Most of you probably know that Mack Himmler used to go under another name and you may have wondered why he decided to switch to an alias. Lon Cohen, a newspaper friend of mine, tells me a photographer once snapped Himmler sitting on a motorcycle and published the shot with a kind of unfortunate caption. He growled "Nobody calls me a Commie" and changed his name legally to Himmler. I don't know if that's really true, but it makes a good story.

That's about as long as an epilogue really has any business being, and I've got to go back to helping Wolfe save America from J. Edgar Hoover and Mayor Daley.

Archie Goodwin

The Frightened Man

by O. X. Rusett

EDITOR'S NOTE: If you're not already familiar with O. X. Rusett's "The Frightened Man," you may as you read it find yourself wondering what it's doing in the pastiche section of this book. "If it's a pastiche," you may protest, "then where is Nero Wolfe?" When "The Frightened Man" was first published in EQMM in 1970, the author provided an explanatory note at its end, and you'll find that note reprinted in this volume, too. But first please read the story!

I was mad at Foler that day, which was nothing new, but I didn't know what to do about it, which was. Usually I can find some effective way to needle him, but at the moment I'd drawn a blank.

Which explains why I almost forgot to be observant when I answered the door to admit a shriveled little man who looked like a wrinkled pear—I was still preoccupied with how to get back at Foler. But a natural talent for observation honed to a fine edge by long training doesn't get derailed that easily, and I could see that the little man was disturbed and that his left hand was tightly clutching something inside his coat pocket. I half hoped he'd let go when I took the coat from him; but no, he just transferred the fist to the pocket of his jacket.

I ushered in the client—I was already thinking of him as one although he hadn't told me his business with us, had just handed me his card, which read "Chet Telin, Theatrical Agent." I knew Foler wouldn't be in the office for a while, and naturally it was Owen Foler he wanted to see. I'm Woodie Charing, and a pretty good detective myself, but that's not usually enough for our clients.

This one was so itchy, though, that he did talk to me after all.

"This is urgent, Mr. Charing. I think someone in my household intends to kill me, and I'm running out of time. When will Mr. Foler be here?"

His voice didn't sound like a wrinkled pear—if wrinkled pears could talk, of course. It was deep and resonant, really surprising. The kind of guy who could make it big on radio and be killed by television. While I was at it, I did some more observing. He was expensively dressed, which was a definite plus, implying a fat fee, and he did look scared. I relented.

"Mr. Foler should be able to see you shortly," I said reassuringly. "In the meantime, you're safe here."

He glanced around as if he expected to see a sinister relative pop out from behind a picture frame, but he nodded. I headed for the kitchen extension, not wanting him to hear the delicate way I would state his problem to Foler. Brent Firrenz was there, doing something with pots and pans that produced a tantalizing aroma.

I telephoned upstairs to the plant rooms.

"There's a rich bozo here who expects to be bumped off,"

I told the telephone. "I think he has a threatening note in his pocket. It looks like money for us."

A grunt, as I could have predicted, came over the telephone.

"I'll be down at six. Tell him to wait, and I'll see him then."

I could have predicted that, too. Foler always stays with his orchids till six, with some exceptions too rare to mention, and the mere threat of murder certainly isn't one of them. It was now twenty of six, which was why I had informed Mr. Telin that Foler would be there soon.

I went back and conveyed the message again, and sat down at my desk to wait. Eventually the numerous pounds-worth that was Foler hove in and seated itself behind the other desk. He glanced at Telin's card, which I had thoughtfully put there.

"Well, Mr. Telin, what can I do for you?" he asked, in a not particularly gracious manner.

"Mr. Foler, I think someone in my household is trying to kill me. I want you to find out who it is in time to—uh—prevent it."

He had trouble with that one, but I suppose the prospect of having one's life taken away isn't pleasant.

"What makes you think so?" Foler asked.

"This note." And, sure enough, he finally drew the fist out of his pocket and handed over what was in it. Foler looked, raised his eyebrows a hundredth of an inch, and handed it to me.

It was one of those paste-up jobs of letters cut from newspapers, and it said: *Your time has run out. You will die.*

"It didn't occur to you, Mr. Telin, that this might be a practical joke?" Foler asked.

"It did not. There is much bitterness toward me at home. In a way I own them all, and they resent it." There was something slightly European about his speech.

"Who are the people concerned?"

"First, my wife. Sue Pos is the name she goes by on her

television interview program. My sister Tressi is a television actress. I'm agent for both of them. My brother Charim—that is a stage name, too—is a—er—a lecturer in philosophy, you might say. Sheree Pouke keeps house for me. She has been with my family since my childhood. That is all—four of them."

"What do you want me to do?"

He thought about that one. It was as if he had expected that, when he got through naming them, Foler would pick one, and it hadn't occurred to him until Foler asked that it wouldn't be that easy.

"Can you come over and talk to them?"

I smiled to myself. The little man didn't know what he was asking. Foler never, and I mean *never*, goes out. At least, like with the plants, the exceptions are too rare to count.

Foler merely said that would be impossible, and Telin should get them all over here. The client raised some objections to that—he was really afraid to go home with someone on the loose wanting to murder him, and I couldn't blame him. So, after setting the fee—to my entire satisfaction—it was agreed that I would go with him, collect the whole kit and caboodle, and bring them back with me. That left Foler with nothing to do in the meantime but drink beer, but that couldn't be helped.

Telin has a Rolls-Royce and a chauffeur outside (hired by the day—not part of the household), which made up a little for my having to miss the dinner that Brent was cooking, and we glided smoothly through New York to one of the last of the Manhattan mansions.

He used his key when we got to the door, and let us both in. The hallway was dark, and Telin hadn't taken more than a few steps when he stumbled, knocking me off balance since I was right behind him. He must have pressed a light switch, for the foyer suddenly sprang into view, revealing what Telin had stumbled over.

Lying kind of bunched up in front of us was a man—or rather what was left of him, which was the lifeless body. One look was enough to see that the vital force was no longer in it, and the bullet hole in the forehead showed why.

I shot a quick glance at Telin, who looked merely puzzled, as at some inexplicable but at the same time unimportant question. Well, after all, it wasn't *his* corpse, and that was what he was afraid of.

"Do you often find a dead body in your foyer?" I couldn't resist asking.

"What? No, of course not," he spoke absently. "I don't understand it. I don't even know who he is." He seemed really perplexed, though he might have brought us in deliberately as some kind of fall guys—murderers will do the screwiest things—and I couldn't rule it out.

In any event, I wasn't too pleased. I could guess the attitude of the police at my being on the spot, and it wasn't a pleasant prospect. They never will understand that I'm as honest and helpful as a Boy Scout.

Still, there was nothing for it but to call them, and I asked the way to the nearest phone. It was in a room full of people, and I looked them over as I muttered into the mouthpiece. After one curious glance, they paid no attention to me, but clustered around Telin and asked him where he'd been. He sank wearily onto a sofa and didn't tell them. He didn't tell them about our interesting discovery in the foyer, either.

It is a measure of how perturbed I was that I didn't give the two women in the room more than a quick look. Usually I'm happy if a case has even one, but I didn't like the way this case was shaping up. One of the women was petite, a little shorter than I like them, but generously enough endowed to make up for it. The other was tall and dark and willowy. There was a man there, too, if you could call him that—as small and shriveled as Telin himself, wearing nothing but a sheet, so help me. He didn't look the type for playing ghosts and besides, it was way past Halloween.

I called Foler and reported, and then I was introduced to the cast of characters. The small woman was Mrs. Telin, or Sue Pos, whichever you prefer, and she had intelligence to match her looks. She didn't act very friendly toward her husband, and took a dim view of my being there, too.

The tall one was warmer. She had a brilliant smile for me, and I would have liked to pursue the matter further, but business came first.

The other little man, speaking in a funny singsong, identified himself as a guru. So that was the brother, the lecturer in philosophy. Since I had the idea that gurus came from India and the Telins from Europe, I wondered how much of a fakir he was.

Our visit was cut short by the arrival of the police. I had taken the time to have them all look at the body, and to explore it myself before that. I found a name, Ed Dobaday, on an envelope, and little else. He was young and good-looking, in a sleazy sort of way. There wasn't a clue as to how he had made his living—though, whatever it was, he wouldn't be doing it anymore.

They all insisted they'd never seen him before, but beautiful Tressi wasn't very convincing. The guru I don't count; *he* wasn't convincing when it said it was raining, even though it was.

While I had been trying to get a line on these people, Telin had slipped out of the room. I let him go. It must have been to alert the housekeeper, because the first I saw of her she was ushering in the police, and she must have let them in through the foyer, but she didn't look surprised.

She was really a dish—she made the other women look pale. She had vivid good looks—jet-black hair and snapping black eyes fringed with thick lashes. You could hardly call her the old-family-retainer type.

I got the kind of greeting from the force I expected—you'd think my old friends, Inspector Price Cromarsten and Sergeant Buster P. Binsley, would have welcomed another professional on the spot, but they never looked at it that way, and gave me a cold "Hello, Woodie" for openers.

I'll skip the next part, because it didn't get us very far, except that the police found a large pile of cut-up newspapers in an unused storeroom, from which the threatening note had been composed.

Eventually the police left and I was able to get the whole crowd over to Foler—my original mission, and one that had a lot more point now. I managed a few minutes alone with him to make a fast report before I brought them into our office.

I got them seated, enjoying the look on Foler's face when he had three women facing him, when he hates to have even one.

"You are here," he began bluntly, "for two reasons. One, somebody threatened to kill Telin, and the fact that someone else is dead doesn't cancel that out, as far as we know.

"Second, a man named Ed Dobaday was found dead in your house. You all had the opportunity to kill him, and killing seems to have been on someone's mind."

Telin—our client, that is, not the guru—looked interested. He was pretty tough in his own way. He might be scared of being killed, but he wasn't letting it reduce him to open panic. Under the nervousness, there seemed to be an assurance he would find out what he needed to know, and the would-be killer would never succeed. Meantime, he was analytically cold toward the rest of them.

"Mrs. Telin," Foler invited, "Woodie tells me you have a good interview program on television. That takes insight. Suppose you start, telling us about all of you."

That was a switch. He didn't usually like to hear from women, but Telin seemed already to have told us all he wanted to, and the other male was a little *outré* for Foler's tastes, swathed in his sheet as he still was.

"I haven't been married to Chet very long." It was a beautiful husky voice. "He was my agent—that's how I knew him—and we were married two years ago. He and Tressi and Charim came over from Poland five years ago. With Sheree, of course." She flashed the housekeeper a cool hostile glance. "He did well as an agent almost at once—really launched Tressi on her career. I myself owe everything to him." She sounded as if she meant it, but only partly.

"Charim went to school for a while, but dropped out of sight and then turned up as a guru. He's been lecturing on the West Coast—showed up a week ago, without bag or baggage, for a visit. As you may imagine, he's rather a nonconformist."

"I am interested in inner harmony," interrupted the odd singsong. "Material things do not matter."

"You are interested in material food," snapped Sheree Pouke. "Caviar, no less." She had a strong accent. "And you are all the time going out, in good material clothes. Meester Foler"—she turned to him—"I do not understand thees. I live always with the Telins. They take me in as an orphan. I repay by running the house here. I love Meester Telin. *That* one," she amended, nodding toward her employer.

"Miss Telin, we haven't heard from you," Foler said.

The tall girl slowly uncrossed and recrossed her legs, which was wasted on Foler but not on me. "My brother has been very good to me," she said slowly. "Perhaps his ambitions are hard to live up to, sometimes, but no one would want to kill him."

“That’s not what *he* says,” probed Foler, but he got no takers. Blank faces returned his questioning look. “Miss Telin,” he rapped out next, “where have you seen the dead man before?”

“But I—” she started, then changed her tactics. “Oh, what’s the difference? He’s a TV actor, too—not very successful. I haven’t seen him around for a long time, and I heard he’d gone to Hollywood to have a try at movies. I hardly knew him.”

I started to speak, but when I saw Foler’s lips moving, pushing in and out, in and out, I changed my mind. When he does that, he’s really thinking, and I’m not about to disturb the process.

He looked as if he had the answers, and then the phone rang. He picked it up, and I lifted my extension. The voice of Alan Spurze, who does a lot of investigation for us and is the best in the business, came crackling over the wire. Foler must have called him after I made my report from the Telin house.

“Yes, that’s what I expected,” Foler grunted, when he had heard the report. “Thanks.”

He faced them again.

“Dobaday was also a petty crook. His specialty was blackmail. Any comment? No? Pfui. Then I’ll tell *you* what happened.

“Telin thought his life had been threatened. Any of you might have wanted to kill him. But there was always another possibility, and it’s the true one. That note was never intended for Telin. You found it in your pocket?”

Telin nodded, surprised.

“Very well. We’ve heard that this faker here”—and he meant faker with an *e*, not an *i*—“has been going out well dressed. I take it that doesn’t mean a bed sheet. But he arrived only in that costume of his—no bag or baggage.

“It’s a reasonable assumption that he’s been wearing his brother’s clothes. They’re the same size. Think about the note being in *Charim*’s pocket, and see where that gets us.

"Was *he* being threatened? I think not. On the contrary, he was the threatener. The connection between you and the blackmailer can be established," he snapped at the guru, who, small to start with, seemed to be shrinking before our eyes. "You came to your brother because you were frightened, or because you ran out of money after this Dobaday bled you. People who believe in gurus don't like to find out they come from Europe. Any such information had to be hushed up, or it would write *finis* to a lucrative career. You were trying to scare him off with threatening notes—this wasn't the first; it was the latest, and you hadn't got around to sending it when your brother happened to wear his own jacket, found it, and took it personally, not having too clear a conscience himself.

"But Dobaday hadn't scared that easily, and, when he came for you, you got rid of him the only way you could think of."

"You're crazy," Charim Telin said, in a voice that was no longer singsong but straight narrative. "You can't prove it."

"The police can," Foler growled. "Anyway, you're the only one with the right name for a murderer."

Foler turned out to be right, as usual. When the police knew where to look, they had little trouble pinning it on Charim good and tight. I tried to make a date with Sheree Pouke, but she insisted she had to get back to her housekeeping.

It was only a half-hearted effort by my usual standards, anyhow. I was thinking of something else.

What had Foler meant, that Charim Telin had the right name for a murderer?

AUTHOR'S NOTE: I'm sure the reader is far ahead of me and knows all the answers, even if Archie—oops, I mean Woodie—doesn't. Charim Telin anagrams to "the criminal." I'm sure, too, that everyone recognized orchid-growing Owen Foler as the great Nero Wolfe, with sidekick Archie Goodwin scrambled to read Woodie Charing. And, of course, all the others:

Chet Telin = the client
Tressi = sister
Sue Pos = spouse
Sheree Pouke = housekeeper
Ed Dobaday = dead body

And, from the cast of Nero Wolfe's regulars:

Brent Firrenz = Fritz Brenner
Price Cromarsten = Inspector Cramer
Buster P. Binsley = Purlie Stebbins
Alan Spurze = Saul Panzer

And of course the author, who I've called O. X. Rusett, who graciously said he would like me to do a takeoff on his creation: the first two initials hint at both his own first name and the bulk of his famous hero, thus:

O.X. Rusett = Rex Stout

EDITOR'S NOTE: Like "Leyne Requel" in The Misadventures of Ellery Queen, *"O. X. Rusett" was the pseudonym used by master anagrammer Norma Schier for what—now that you know the secret—I hope you'll agree has been properly placed in the* Pastiches *section of this collection. "The Frightened Man," originally published in the January 1970 issue of* Ellery Queen's Mystery Magazine, *was Mrs. Schier's eighth contribution to* EQMM, *following tales presented as by "Norma Haigs" (Ngaio Marsh),*

"Cathie Haig Star" (Agatha Christie), "Handon C. Jorricks" (John Dickson Carr), "Leyne Requel" (Ellery Queen), "Rhoda Lys Storey" (Dorothy L. Sayers), Neil MacNeish (Michael Innes), and "Amy M. Graingerhall (Margery Allingham). Two more pastiches—as by "Walter Cantree" (Lawrence Treat) and "Conway Lonstar" (Clayton Rawson) would appear in EQMM *in 1970, and then Mrs. Schier wrote five more for the Mysterious Press's 1979 hardbound collection,* The Anagram Detectives.

Chapter 1 from *Murder in E Minor*

by Robert Goldsborough

AUTHOR'S NOTE: I came to write the post–Rex Stout Nero Wolfe novels in large part because of my mother, who loved the stories in large part because they were clever whodunits that did not rely on gratuitous sex and violence or obscenity-laced dialogue. She felt comfortable introducing these stories to me when I was a teenager, and I quickly became addicted to them. Flash forward to 1975, when newspapers across the country ran obituaries of Rex Stout, who died in his late eighties. "Now there won't be any more Nero Wolfe stories," my mother bemoaned. Maybe there could be one more, *I thought, and set about writing what ultimately would be published as* Murder in E Minor. *But in the beginning, it was simply a book written for one person, my mother, typewritten pages bound in an embossed leather cover and given to her as a Christmas present. It took nearly a decade for* E Minor *to get published, and more Nero Wolfe books from me were to follow.*

Nero Wolfe and I have argued for years about whether the client who makes his first visit to us before or after noon is more likely to provide an interesting—and lucrative—case. Wolfe contends that the average person is incapable of making a rational decision, such as hiring him, until he or she has had a minimum of two substantial meals that day. My own feeling is that the caller with the greater potential is the one who has spent the night agonizing, finally realizes at dawn that Wolfe is the answer, and does something about it fast. I'll leave it to you to decide, based on our past experience, which of us has it better pegged.

I'd have been more smug about the timing of Maria Radovich's call that rainy morning if I'd thought there was even one chance in twenty that Wolfe would see her, let alone go back to work. It had been more than two years since Orrie Cather committed suicide—with Wolfe's blessing and mine. At the time, the realization that one of his longtime standbys had murdered three people didn't seem to bother Wolfe, but since then I had come to see that the whole business had rocked him pretty good. He would never admit it, of course, with that ego fit for his seventh of a ton, but he was still stung that someone who for years had sat at his table, drunk his liquor, and followed his orders could be a cool and deliberate killer. And even though the D.A. had reinstated both our licenses shortly after Orrie's death, Wolfe had stuck his head in the sand and still hadn't pulled it out. I tried needling him back to work, a tactic that had been successful in the past, but I got stonewalled, to use a word he hates.

"Archie," he would say, looking up from his book, "as I have told you many times, one of your most commendable attributes through the years has been your ability to badger me into working. That former asset is now a liability. You may goad me if you wish, but it is futile. I will not take the bait. And desist using the word 'retired.' I prefer to say that I have withdrawn from practice." And with that he would return to his book, which currently was a rereading of *Emma* by Jane Austen.

It wasn't that we did not have opportunities. One well-fixed Larchmont widow offered twenty grand for starters if Wolfe would find out who poisoned her chauffeur, and I couldn't even get him to see her. The murder was never solved, although I leaned toward the live-in maid, who was losing out in a triangle to the gardener's daughter. Then there was the Wall Street money man—you'd know his name right off—who said Wolfe could set his own price if only we'd investigate his son's death. The police and the coroner had called it a suicide, but the father was convinced it was a narcotics-related murder. Wolfe politely but firmly turned the man down in a ten-minute conversation in the office, and the kid's death went on the books as a suicide.

I couldn't even use the money angle to stir him. On a few of our last big cases, Wolfe insisted on having the payments spread over a long period, so that a series of checks—some of them biggies—rolled in every month. That, coupled with a bunch of good investments, gave him a cash flow that was easily sufficient to operate the old brownstone on West 35th Street near the Hudson that has been home to me for more than half my life. And operating the brownstone doesn't come cheap, because Nero Wolfe has costly tastes. They include my salary as his confidential assistant, errand boy, and—until two years ago—man of action, as well as those of Theodore Horstmann, nurse to the ten thousand orchids Wolfe grows in the plant rooms up on the roof, and Fritz Brenner, on whom I would bet in a cook-off against any other chef in the universe.

I still had the standard chores, such as maintaining the orchid germination records, paying the bills, figuring the taxes, and handling Wolfe's correspondence. But I had lots of free time now, and Wolfe didn't object to a little freelancing. I did occasional work for Del Bascomb, a first-rate local operative, and also teamed with Saul Panzer on a couple of jobs, including the Masters kidnapping case, which you may have read about. Wolfe went so far as to compliment me on that one, so at least I knew he still read about crime, although he refused to let me talk about it in his presence anymore.

Other than having put his brain in the deep freeze, Wolfe kept his routine pretty much the same as ever: breakfast on a tray in his room; four hours a day—9 to 11 a.m. and 4 to 6 p.m.—in the plant rooms with Theodore; long conferences with Fritz on menus and food preparation; and the best meals in Manhattan. The rest of the time, he was in his oversized chair behind his desk in the office, reading and drinking beer. And refusing to work.

Maria Radovich's call came at nine-ten on Tuesday morning, which meant Wolfe was up with the plants. Fritz was in the kitchen working on one of Wolfe's favorite lunches, sweetbreads in béchamel sauce and truffles. I answered at my desk, where I was balancing the checkbook.

"Nero Wolfe's residence. Archie Goodwin speaking."

"I need to see Mr. Wolfe—today. May I make an appointment?" It was the voice of a young woman, shaky, and with an accent that seemed familiar to me.

"I'm sorry, but Mr. Wolfe isn't consulting at the present time," I said, repeating a line I had grown to hate.

"Please, it's important that I see him. I think my—"

"Look, Mr. Wolfe isn't seeing anyone, honest. I can suggest some agencies if you're looking for a private investigator."

"No, I want Mr. Nero Wolfe. My uncle has spoken of him, and I am sure he would want to help. My uncle knew Mr. Wolfe many years ago in Montenegro, and—"

"Where?" I barked it out.

"In Montenegro. They grew up there together. And now I am frightened about my uncle."

Ever since it became widely known that Wolfe had retired—make that "withdrawn from practice"—would-be clients had cooked up some dandy stories to try to get him working again. I was on their side, but I knew Wolfe well enough to realize that almost nothing would bring him back to life. This was the first time, though, that anyone had been ingenious enough to come up with a Montenegro angle, and I admire ingenuity.

"I'm sorry to hear that you're scared," I said, "but Mr. Wolfe is pretty hard-hearted. I've got a reputation as a softie, though. How soon can your uncle be here? I'm Mr. Wolfe's confidential assistant, and I'll be glad to see him, Miss—"

"Radovich, Maria Radovich. Yes, I recognized your name. My uncle doesn't know I am calling. He would be angry. But I will come right away, if it's all right."

I assured her it was indeed all right and hung up, staring at the open checkbook. It was a long shot, no question, but if I had anything to lose by talking to her, I couldn't see it. And, just maybe, the Montenegro bit was for real. Montenegro, in case you don't know, is a small piece of Yugoslavia, and it's where Wolfe comes from. He still has relatives there; I send checks to three of them every month. But as for old friends, I doubted any were still alive. His closest friend even, Marko Vukcic, had been murdered years ago, and the upshot was that Wolfe and I went tramping off to the Montenegrin mountains to avenge his death. And although Wolfe was anything but gabby about his past, I figured I knew just about enough to eliminate the possibility of a close comrade popping up. But there's no law against hoping.

I got a good, leisurely look at her through the one-way glass in the front door as she stood in the drizzle ringing our bell. Dark-haired, dark-eyed, and slender, she had a touch of Mia Farrow in her face. And like Farrow in several of her roles, she seemed frightened and unsure. But looking through the glass, I was convinced that, with Maria Radovich, it was no act.

She jumped when I opened the door. "Oh! Mr. Goodwin?"

"The selfsame," I answered with a slight bow and an earnest smile. "And you are Maria Radovich, I presume? Please come in out of the twenty-percent chance of showers."

I hung her trench coat on the hall rack and motioned toward the office. Walking behind her, I could see that her figure, set off by a skirt of fashionable length, was a bit fuller than I remembered Mia Farrow's to be, and that was okay with me.

"Mr. Wolfe doesn't come down to the office for another hour and ten minutes," I said, motioning to the yellow chair nearest my desk. "Which is fine, because he wouldn't see you anyway. At least not right now. He thinks he's retired from the detective business. But I'm not." I flipped open my notebook and swiveled to face her.

"I'm sure if Mr. Wolfe knew about my uncle's trouble, he would want to do something right away," she said, twisting a scarf in her lap and leaning forward tensely.

"You don't know him, Miss Radovich. He can be immovable, irascible, and exasperating when he wants to, which is most of the time. I'm afraid you're stuck with me, at least for now. Maybe we can get Mr. Wolfe interested later, but, to do that, I've got to know everything. Like, for starters, who is your uncle and why are you worried about him?"

"He is my great-uncle, really," she answered, still using only the front quarter of the chair cushion. "And he is very well known. Milan Stevens. I am sure you have heard of him—he is music director, some people say conductor, of the New York Symphony."

Not wanting to look stupid or disappoint her, or both, I nodded. I've been to the Symphony four or five times, always with Lily Rowan, and it was always her idea. Milan Stevens may have been the conductor one or more of those times, but I wouldn't take an oath on it. The name was only vaguely familiar.

"Mr. Goodwin, for the last two weeks my uncle has been getting letters in the mail—awful, vile letters. I think someone may want to kill him, but he just throws the letters away. I am frightened. I am sure that—"

"How many letters have there been, Miss Radovich? Do you have any of them?"

She nodded and reached in the shoulder bag she had set on the floor. "Three so far, all the same." She handed the crumpled sheets over, along with their envelopes, and I spread them on my desk. Each was on six-by-nine-inch notepaper, plain white, the kind from an inexpensive tear-off pad. They were hand-printed, in all caps, with a black felt-tip pen. One read:

MAESTRO
QUIT THE PODIUM NOW! YOU ARE
DOING DAMAGE TO A GREAT ORCHESTRA
PUT DOWN THE BATON AND GET OUT
IF YOU DON'T LEAVE ON YOUR OWN,
YOU WILL BE REMOVED—PERMANENTLY!

In fact, all three weren't exactly alike. The wording differed, though only slightly. The "on your own" in the last sentence was missing from one note, and the first sentence didn't have an exclamation point in another. Maria had lightly penciled the numbers one, two, and three on the back of each to indicate the order in which they were received. The envelopes were of a similar ordinary stock, each hand-printed to Milan Stevens at an address in the East Seventies. "His apartment?" I asked.

Maria nodded. "Yes, he and I have lived there since we came to this country, a little over two years ago."

"Miss Radovich, before we talk more about these notes, tell me about your uncle and yourself. First, you said on the phone that he and Mr. Wolfe knew each other in Montenegro."

She eased back into the chair and nodded. "Yes, my uncle—his real name is Stefanovic, Milos Stefanovic. We are from Yugoslavia. I was born in Belgrade, but my uncle is a Montenegrin. That's a place on the Adriatic. But of course I don't have to tell you that—I'm sure you know all about it from Mr. Wolfe.

"My uncle's been a musician and conductor all over Europe—Italy, Austria, Germany. He was conducting in London last, before we came here. But long ago, he did some fighting in Montenegro. I know little of it, but I think he was involved in an independence movement. He doesn't like to talk about that at all, and he never mentioned Mr. Wolfe to me until one time when his picture was in the papers. It was something to do with a murder or a suicide—I think maybe your picture was there, too?"

I nodded. That would have been when Orrie died. "What did your uncle say about Mr. Wolfe?"

"I gather they had lost touch over the years. But he didn't seem at all interested in trying to reach Mr. Wolfe. At the time, I said, 'How wonderful that such an old friend is right here. What a surprise! You'll call him, of course?' But Uncle Milos said no, that was part of the past. And I got the idea from the way he acted that they must have had some kind of difference. But that was so long ago!"

"If you sensed your uncle was unfriendly toward Mr. Wolfe, what made you call?"

"After he told me about knowing Mr. Wolfe back in Montenegro, Uncle Milos kept looking at the picture in the paper and nodding his head. He said to me, 'He had the finest mind I have ever known. I wish I could say the same for his disposition.'"

I held back a smile. "But you got the impression that your uncle and Mr. Wolfe were close at one time?"

"Absolutely," Maria said. "Uncle Milos told me they had been through some great difficulty together. He even showed me this picture from an old scrapbook." She reached again into her bag and handed me a gray-toned photograph mounted on cardboard and ragged around the edges.

They certainly fit my conception of a band of guerrillas, although none looked to be out of his teens. There were nine of them in all, posed in front of a high stone wall, four kneeling in front and five standing behind them. Some were wearing long overcoats, others had on woolen shirts, and two wore what I think of as World War I helmets. I spotted Wolfe instantly, of course. He was second from the left in the back row, with his hands behind his back and a bandolier slung over one shoulder. His hair was darker then, and he weighed at least one hundred pounds less, but the face was remarkably similar to the one I had looked at across the dinner table last night. And his glare had the same intensity, coming at me from a faded picture, that it does in the office when he thinks I'm badgering him.

To Wolfe's right in the photo was Marko Vukcic, holding a rifle loosely at his side. "Which one's your uncle?" I asked Maria.

She leaned close enough so I could smell her perfume and pointed to one of the kneelers in front. He was dark-haired and intense like most of the others, but he appeared smaller than most of them. None of the nine, though, looked as if he were trying to win a congeniality contest. If they were as tough as they appeared, I'm glad I wasn't fighting against them.

"This picture was taken up in the mountains," Maria said. "Uncle Milos only showed it to me to point out Mr. Wolfe, but he wouldn't talk any more about the other men or what they were doing."

"Not going to a picnic," I said. "I'd like to hang on to this for a while. Now, what about you, Miss Radovich? How does it happen you're living with your great-uncle?"

She told me about how her mother, a widow, had died when she was a child in Yugoslavia, and that Stefanovic, her mother's uncle, had legally adopted her. Divorced and without children, he was happy to have the companionship of a nine-year-old. Maria said he gave her all the love of a parent, albeit a strict one, taking her with him as he moved around Europe to increasingly better and more prestigious conducting jobs. At some time before moving to England, he had changed his name to Stevens—she couldn't remember exactly when. It was while they were living in London that he was picked as the new conductor, or music director if you prefer, of the New York Symphony. Maria, who by that time was twenty-three, made the move with him, and she was now a dancer with a small troupe in New York.

"Mr. Goodwin," she said, leaning forward and tensing again, "my uncle has worked hard all his life to get the kind of position and recognition he has today. Now somebody is trying to take it away from him." Her hand gripped my forearm.

"Why not just go to the police?" I asked with a shrug.

"I suggested that to Uncle Milos, and he became very angry. He said it would leak out to the newspapers and cause a scandal at the Symphony, that the publicity would be harmful to him and the orchestra. He says these notes are from a crazy person, or maybe someone playing a prank. I was with him when he opened the first one, or I might not know about any of this. He read it and said something that means 'stupid' in Serbo-Croatian, then crumpled the note and threw it in the wastebasket. But he hardly spoke the rest of the evening.

"I waited until he left the room to get the note from the basket. It was then that I said we should call the police. He became upset and said it was probably a prankster, or maybe a season-ticket holder who didn't like the music the orchestra had been playing."

"How long until the next note?" I asked.

"I started watching the mail after that. Six days later, we got another envelope printed just like the first one. I didn't open it—I never open my uncle's mail. But again I found the crumpled note in the wastebasket next to his desk in the library. This time I didn't mention it to him, and he said nothing about it to me, but again he seemed distressed.

"The third note came yesterday, six days after the second, and again I found it in the wastebasket. Uncle Milos doesn't know that I've seen the last two notes, or that I've saved all three."

"Miss Radovich, does your uncle have any enemies you know of, anyone who would gain by his leaving the Symphony?"

"The music director of a large orchestra always has his detractors." She took a deep breath. "There are always people who think it can be done better. Some are jealous, others just take pleasure in scoffing at talented people. My uncle does not discuss his work very much at home, but I do know—from him and from others—that he has opposition even within the orchestra. But notes like this, I can't believe—"

"*Someone* is writing them, Miss Radovich. I'd like to hear more about your uncle's opposition, but Mr. Wolfe will be down in just a few minutes, and it's best if you're not here when he comes in. He may get interested in your problem, but you'll have to let me be the one to try getting him interested."

For the third time, Maria dove into her bag. She fished out a wad of bills and thrust it at me. "There's five hundred dollars here," she said. "That is just for agreeing to try to find out who's writing the notes. I can pay another forty-five hundred dollars if you discover the person and get him to stop."

Five grand was a long way below what Wolfe usually got for a fee, but I figured that, for Maria Radovich, it was probably big bucks. I started to return the money, then drew back and smiled.

"Fair enough," I said. "If I can get Nero Wolfe to move, we keep this. Otherwise, it goes back to you. Now we've got to get you out of here. You'll be hearing from me soon—one way or the other." I wrote her a receipt for the money, keeping a carbon, and hustled her out to the hall and on with her coat.

My watch said ten fifty-eight as she went down the steps to the street. I rushed back to the office, put the money and receipt in the safe, and arranged Wolfe's morning mail in a pile on his blotter. Included in the stack was one item the carrier hadn't delivered: a faded fifty-year-old photograph.

The Purloined Platypus

by Marvin Kaye

AUTHOR'S NOTE: I've been a devotee of the Nero Wolfe stories since college. My late wife, Saralee, and I joined the Wolfe Pack, the society devoted to the Rex Stout series. When Mr. Stout died, Wolfe Pack members voted on who might do a good job continuing the Nero Wolfe adventures. I was one of three authors named. (The others were Robert B. Parker and Lawrence Block.) Having already written seven mystery novels, I was honored, but the only story I was interested in writing would have been an origin tale—how Wolfe and Archie first met. I abandoned the idea when an excellent story addressing that issue appeared in the Wolfe Pack's Gazette *and was later the subject of Robert Goldsborough's* Archie Meets Nero Wolfe.

A few years ago, I had an idea for a very brief Wolfean anecdote and asked Rex Stout's daughters whether I might run it in

Sherlock Holmes Mystery Magazine. *They not only said yes, they told me I could write as many NW stories as I wished, provided they weren't novels, since those rights are held by Bob Goldsborough. This started me, and by now I've written some twenty new Nero Wolfe tales, including this one.*

At a few minutes after eleven that summer morning, Wolfe entered the office. We exchanged our usual pleasantries, and I told him we'd had a call from Benjamin Moultrie.

He sat down in the chair reinforced to bear his seventh of a ton, rang for beer and said, "That's a familiar name, but I don't remember why."

"He's president and board chairman of the MSOP."

"MSOP? What on earth is that?"

"The Museum of the Strange, Odd and Peculiar. It's on the corner of 29th and Third Avenue."

"I've been curious about that place," he said, pouring beer. "I've actually considered visiting it."

Wonder of wonders, I thought.

"What does Mr. Moultrie want?" he asked.

"To be our next client."

I knew it was unlikely Wolfe would agree, given the healthy condition of our bank account, but he surprised me: "Ask him to be here tonight at nine."

When I thought about it, I realized why Wolfe was in a good mood. Yesterday he'd received an invitation to visit his favorite orchid grower, Lewis Hewitt, at his estate on Long Island. That in itself wouldn't have made him so cheerful; though he does enjoy visiting Hewitt, it still means enduring two long rides with white knuckles. But he'd been pestering his friend for years for a cutting of Hewitt's two rarest orchids, and Hewitt had finally said yes.

Before Wolfe could change his mind, I called Moultrie. He said he'd come at nine.

Good as his word, he rang the doorbell right on time. I examined him through the peephole. He could have his picture in the dictionary under "dandy." Middle height, sleek black hair, a trim mustache, and a monocle. He wore a three-piece suit and tie; both looked expensive. Because it was a warm day in August, he sported neither topcoat nor hat. I welcomed him and brought him back to the office, buzzing Wolfe in the kitchen to cue his grand entrance. I placed Moultrie in the red leather chair.

"Good evening," said Wolfe, entering and taking his seat. Fritz was right behind him with a pilsner glass and two bottles of Nordik Wolf beer, which I suspected he wanted to try because of its name. "As you see, sir, I am having beer. Would you care for a drink?"

"Thank you," the museum director said. "Either red wine or brandy would be appreciated." I told him what we had and he chose a snifter of Armagnac, which he sipped and proclaimed superb.

"I've been interested in your museum for some time," said Wolfe, sampling the Nordik Wolf.

Moultrie smiled. "You must come as our guest. My granddaughter Daphne says it's 'cool.'"

"I rarely leave this house, but I believe I will make an exception in this case. However, I do not think you're here because of the museum, are you?"

"Actually, Mr. Wolfe, I am. We've had a robbery."

"Oh? What was taken?"

"An extremely valuable platinum figurine in the form of a platypus. Its bill, feet and tail are gold, and its eyes are two large diamonds."

"That sounds plenty valuable," I said.

"Yes. Its materials alone are worth a small fortune, but its ultimate value is historical. Though unconfirmed, it is believed to have been a gift from the Indian ruler of that time to none other than Kubla Khan. It was found at Xanadu, which was Kubla Khan's palace."

Wolfe finished his beer and tossed its cap in the drawer of his desk. He said to me, "By the way, Archie, this is superior."

"Glad to hear it. It's a shame they don't spell it with an E."

"Don't be flippant." He opened the second bottle, poured, adjusted the bead, sipped, and returned his attention to Benjamin Moultrie. "Before I decide whether to take on your problem, you should know that my fee is large . . . some would say exorbitant."

"I am aware of that. We are prepared to meet your price."

"When you say 'we,' do you refer to the museum's other officers?"

Moultrie shook his head. "We do have a treasurer. His name is Michael Faraday. He operates out of his office at a Madison Avenue brokerage firm. But I wasn't counting him when I used the collective. I always include the museum itself."

Wolfe smiled. "I find that droll. Well, sir, what would you have me do? Find the missing figurine, or do you also wish me to apprehend the thief?"

"Both. It is likely that the culprit works for us."

"How many staff members do you employ?"

He held up one hand with all fingers raised. "Five. There's the cashier—"

"Please provide their names and details about them."

"Very well. Larry Winters is our cashier. He is a young man in his early thirties. Then there's the gift-shop clerk, an attractive young woman, Linda Andelman. She and Larry are, as they say, 'an item.' The other three employees are our security guards. They wear uniforms with badges and caps. The daytime officer's name is Mason Russell; he is, I believe, in his late fifties. He lives in Brooklyn with his wife. The night guard is Harold Johnson, a tall black man, unmarried, who lives in Greenwich Village. Marc Porterfield works the weekend shifts, day and night. He actually sleeps at the museum. Unmarried, very private. That's all I know about him, except that he just had his forty-fifth birthday."

Wolfe finished his beer. "Mr. Moultrie, I have decided to take your case. My fee will be fifty thousand dollars, half payable before I begin. The second half, plus expenses, will be due when I have located the figurine and perhaps also identified the thief. If I cannot do either, I will retain the original twenty-five thousand dollars nonetheless."

"That is acceptable." Moultrie took out his checkbook and pen and began to write. He proffered the check, which Wolfe read and passed to me. "Archie," he said, "I am going to cancel my morning session with the orchids tomorrow. As soon as we finish breakfast, you will drive me to the museum, park and join me inside."

We arrived a little before nine-thirty, and I dropped Wolfe at the door. When I entered the museum a few minutes later and greeted Benjamin Moultrie, I found Wolfe standing next to an attractive redhead, who was helping him browse through the gift shop. Every time it looked as if he might buy something, our client tried to give it to him as a gift, but Wolfe said no. "Thank you, but this would not be a legitimate expense. If I choose to purchase anything, I will pay for it." He spotted me. "Ah, Archie, you found a parking space."

"I left it in a lot."

He nodded. "Let us begin."

Moultrie asked if he intended to interview the staff.

"Later. First, please show us the museum, including the spot where the figurine stood before it was taken."

The MSOP has six exhibit rooms, though Moultrie said he was hoping to eventually add three more. First, he took us into a chamber filled with Egyptian artifacts: statuary, vases, two mummies in their cases. "Those are authentic," our host said, polishing his monocle.

The second room was filled with comic-book art, both American and foreign. I saw complete runs of *Action*, *Archie*, *Classic Comics* (and its later incarnation, *Classics Illustrated*), *Donald Duck*, *Mad*, *Pogo*, *Spy Smasher*, *The Spirit*, *Star Wars* and various others. One large display case featured radio tie-ins such as *Captain Midnight* and *Little Orphan Annie* decoders, a *Tom Mix* Indian arrowhead, and a *Lone Ranger* western town, which, fully assembled, took up a great deal of space. In a corner stood an array of figurines of Walt Disney characters: Mickey and Minnie Mouse; Donald and Daisy Duck; Donald's nephews Huey, Dewey, and Louie; Goofy; Pluto; Uncle Scrooge; and more.

I could have spent hours browsing and reading—Moultrie said all the comics had been digitized, so the originals needn't be handled. Wolfe, however, was not interested and was ready to move on, so I promised myself I'd come back.

The third room was devoted to odd and often bizarre medical paraphernalia. This seemed to interest Wolfe, but he said, "I'd like to spend some time here, but for now let us see the rest of the museum." Room Four was devoted to the supernatural, with exhibits of ghosts, ghouls, monsters, vampires, witches and wizards and werethings. Number Five featured food and drink that would be right at home on Andrew Zimmern's Travel Channel shows *Bizarre Foods* and *Bizarre Foods America.*

When we entered the last room, which was devoted to Asian culture, Moultrie waved at an empty shelf inside a display case. "That's where the platypus was kept. The glass is quite thick, almost unbreakable." He opened his cell phone and showed us a photo of the platinum platypus.

"Archie," Wolfe asked, "is your phone capable of taking pictures?" I said yes. "Then see if you can copy the platypus from Mr. Moultrie." He waited till I did it, then turned to the museum director and asked, "How many keys are there to this case?"

"Three. I have one set of all our keys, and so does our treasurer. The third set is held by the senior security guard, Mason Russell. He passes it to the night guard, who returns it to Mason each morning."

He nodded. "Mr. Moultrie, we will adjourn for lunch. When we return, I'll want to speak to all available members of your staff. Perhaps you can arrange for the other guards to meet me at my office. Also Mr. Faraday. The sooner the better, ideally this evening."

On our way out, he said, "Hopefully, Archie, we'll be home in time for me to go up to the orchids at four. In the meantime, please prepare a camera. I'll want you to take photos in one of the rooms we've been to, also measurements."

"Which room? What pictures should I take, and what measurements?"

He told me.

I couldn't figure why he wanted pictures of a room he'd showed no interest in, but when we got back I took them and joined him just as he was about to question Larry Winters, the cashier.

Winters was a young man with blue eyes and blond hair so light it was almost white. His suit was the kind of pastel hue you often see on houses in Hawaii. He said hello and shook my hand, then told Wolfe he hoped he could help him find the missing statuette.

"I notice that we are the only people in the museum," Wolfe remarked.

"We get busier in the afternoon."

Wolfe indicated the woman behind the gift-shop counter. "I understand that you and Ms. Andelman are seeing one another."

Larry smiled. "We are. I've been saving money and working up the courage to propose."

I wished him good luck.

"One more question," said Wolfe. "Do you have a set of museum keys?"

"No. Once in a while, the night guard asks me to pass his set along to Mason, our day guard."

"Has that happened recently?"

He thought about it for a moment. "I don't think so."

But his sweetheart was close enough to hear him. "Larry," she said, "don't you remember? Harold gave them to you a few days ago, when Mason was late because the subway he takes got backed up."

Larry shook his head, obviously annoyed at himself. "That's right!" He turned to Wolfe. "I only had them briefly. Mason got here maybe five or ten minutes later."

"Very well," said Wolfe. "Now I have a few things to ask you, Ms. Andelman." He beckoned to Moultrie. "Do you have an office where I can talk to her and then Mr. Russell?"

Moultrie nodded. "I should have thought of that. Right this way." We followed him to his own headquarters, a modest-sized room with a mahogany desk and swivel chair, but before I shut the door he said to Wolfe, "I forgot to mention something. It might be important."

"I'm listening."

"About a week ago, I received an offer to buy the platypus. It came from J. Nelson Barnett, an enormously wealthy art, curio and jewelry collector. He offered us one hundred thousand dollars. I almost took him up on it, but the platypus really belongs here."

"I see. If you have Mr. Barnett's address and other contact information, please give them to Archie."

"I'll have them for you when you come out."

He left, and I shut the door. Wolfe invited Linda Andelman to sit down. There was no chair large enough for him, so he perched on the edge of Moultrie's desk.

"Ms. Andelman—"

"Please, call me Linda."

"Very well. Linda, have you seen the missing figurine?"

"No, I never saw anything in the museum except for the gift shop and Mr. Moultrie's office."

"Never?"

"It really doesn't interest me. This is just a job—though it's one I like."

Wolfe looked thoroughly minussed (I'd taunted him once by using that word instead of "nonplussed"). "I don't suppose," he said, "that you've ever been in possession of the museum's keys."

"That's right, I haven't."

"Do you get along with the rest of the staff? Obviously you do with Mr. Winters."

"Well, yes, he and I have been dating for a few months. I'm on a first-name basis with Mason and Hal—Harold—but I seldom run into Marc Porterfield, and, when I do, if I say hello, he just grunts. In a mildly friendly way . . . I think."

"Thank you for your time," Wolfe said. "Could you ask Mr. Russell to come in, please?"

She nodded and left. The daytime security guard arrived in less than a minute. He wore a uniform with a cap that bore the initials MSOP. What hair could be seen was salt-and-pepper. He had an amiable smile and stood a little taller than me. Wolfe gestured for him to sit down, but he declined. "Thank you, but my uniform is a bit tight. I've been meaning to take it to my tailor for refitting."

"May I ask how long you have been a security guard for the museum?"

"From the first day it opened, about nine years ago."

"Has there ever been a burglary before this one?"

"Never."

Wolfe mulled that over, then said, "I have a hypothetical question. If you could steal anything in the museum and get away with it, what would it be?"

"That's an interesting question. It certainly wouldn't be the platypus."

"Why not?"

"It would be nearly impossible to sell. The easiest way to turn a profit would surely be by taking complete runs of some of the comic books. The radio premiums would also be easy to get rid of on eBay."

Wolfe asked about his keys, and then we were done.

We got home just before four. Wolfe went up to the plant rooms—much, I'm sure, to Theodore's relief. Theodore, who is our resident plant nurse, is convinced that all of the orchids will die if Wolfe misses a session.

I sat down at my desk as the phone rang. It was Moultrie. He said both guards would come to the brownstone at nine;

Mason Russell would stick around for the night shift until Harold Johnson returned. Michael Faraday, the museum's treasurer, would come at the same time. If he got there early, my instructions were to show him to the front room, where he would wait till Wolfe finished questioning the guards.

After Moultrie hung up, I dialed the number he'd given me and spoke with the collector, J. Nelson Barnett. I asked him whether I could meet him the next day. When I told him why, he became quite cordial. "The platypus? By all means! Do you have my address?"

"I do."

"If you come at eleven-thirty, you won't have to wait. I'll tell my secretary to send you right in."

I thanked him, cradled the receiver, and began catching up on the germination records. When Wolfe came down, shortly after six, I reported my conversations with Moultrie and Barnett. That earned me a "satisfactory."

Faraday arrived at ten to nine. He was slim, trim and well dressed. I estimated him to be in his early forties. I told him he would have to wait a while and led him to the front room. I offered him a drink, and he asked if we had any single malt. When I said yes, he asked which ones. Answering took several seconds, because we're well stocked with both single and blended scotch. He was delighted to learn that one of them is Edradour. "A brandy snifter, please," he said, then added, "Did you know it's the smallest distillery in Scotland?"

I said no.

"Of course, it's been quite some time since I last visited Pitlochry—that's where they're located—but when I was there they only had two employees. There's a rumor they're owned by the Mafia."

I brought him a snifter, a napkin and the bottle, so he could help himself. He sat back with an expression that was positively beatific.

Just as I closed the door to the front room, the doorbell sounded, and I saw through the peephole that the two guards were there. Harold Johnson was quite tall, with skin so light he could pass for Caucasian. He was in his MSOP uniform. Marc Porterfield wore a dark featureless suit, ditto tie. He nodded hello through spectacles so thick I figured he must have some kind of eye condition.

In the office, I offered libations and Johnson thanked me and requested beer. The dour weekend guard went over to the bar and poured himself at least three ounces of Demerara rum, which made me shudder, since it's 151 proof.

Wolfe entered and sat. Fritz brought his usual two bottles of beer plus one for Johnson. He had them on a tray, so he could also manage the two pilsner glasses. After thanking them for coming at such short notice, Wolfe repeated the same questions he'd put to Mason Russell. When asked what they'd steal from the museum, Hal, as he asked us to call him, agreed with Mason that the comic books would be the easiest to sell for a good profit. Porterfield, though, said he'd go into the medical room and help himself to some of the strange medicines there.

"Why?" Wolfe asked. "Would you sell them to a doctor or hospital?"

"No, I don't need the money. I'd keep them."

"Are you talking about drugs? Narcotics?"

He shook his head. "Those might be salable, but I could be caught. I'd be more interested in the poisons."

"For what reason?"

"Whatever." And that's all he would say.

Wolfe, exchanging a worried glance with me and Hal, decided to drop it. After I showed them out but before I brought in Faraday, the boss beckoned to me. "We should find out about Mr. Porterfield."

"Why?"

"I've got a bad feeling about him. Call Saul later. Whatever he finds might need to be passed along to Inspector Cramer. Now let's see what Mr. Faraday has to tell us."

I brought him in. He almost shook Wolfe's hand but realized that was a bad idea. I told him to sit in the red leather chair, which he did. He immediately complimented Wolfe on the Edradour.

"Thank you, sir, but I seldom drink anything but beer and wine. The credit for stocking the bar belongs to Mr. Goodwin. I hope this visit isn't an inconvenience."

"Not at all. I've always wanted to meet you."

"May I ask why?"

"Two reasons. Orchids fascinate me, and I would dearly love to see your collection."

"I will be delighted to show you the plant rooms after we talk. And your second reason?"

"I have a copy of your splendid cookbook."

Wolfe chuckled. "Again, I do not deserve any credit. It was prepared by Ms. Barbara Burn, an editor at Viking Press. She, of course, spent considerable time conferring with my chef, Mr. Fritz Brenner. But let's get down to business. I presume you are aware of the museum's theft?"

"Yes," he said with a sigh. "I've told Ben again and again that we should have more insurance, but he only bought the bare minimum."

"Let me reassure you that the figurine will be found. Did you know that an offer has been made to buy it?"

"Sure, that was my doing. Nelson Barnett is an old friend. I'm his financial advisor."

"Have you spoken to him since the theft?"

"I have," Faraday replied. "When he learned that Ben hired you to find the platypus, he said it's the best thing he could possibly have done. Then he told me, 'When'—not if—'it's found, I'll raise my offer to a quarter of a million.'"

Wolfe paused to open and pour his second bottle of Nordik Wolf. "I have two further questions. Where do you keep your museum keys, and how often do you use them?"

He took them from his pocket. "They're always with me. I've never used them."

"Thank you for your time and assistance, sir. Perhaps you'd like to have dinner with us sometime soon?"

"It would be an honor."

After he left, I called Saul and Wolfe picked up and told him what he wanted. What I heard made good sense.

Next morning at eleven-thirty, I introduced myself to Barnett's secretary, who showed me into his office with a dimply smile and brought me coffee. It was a large corner room on the thirty-fifth floor of a building at 47th and Madison. I sipped an excellent cup of Kona as J. Nelson Barnett entered. He was so short I couldn't decide if he was a dwarf or a hobbit. He wore a dark three-piece business suit and a necktie that I thought was black, but when he moved it caught the light and thin red slants glinted.

"Mr. Goodwin—"

"Archie."

"Archie, I'm glad you could meet me here, though I would have liked to visit Mr. Wolfe at his office."

"That could be arranged."

"Please be seated. Has the platypus been found?"

"Not yet," I said, "but Mr. Wolfe is confident it will be. Why does it mean so much to you?"

"Well, I'm a collector, but I am *not* a hoarder. I feel the platypus is too important historically for such a small—though excellent—museum. If I buy it, I plan to offer it to the Smithsonian on permanent loan."

"Did you have it stolen?"

He laughed. "No, Archie. But I know who did."

When I reported later, Wolfe said, "Just as I expected."

"Meaning?"

"It's show time. Or will be soon. Arrange a meeting, preferably tonight at nine. Ask Mr. Moultrie to come, also Messrs. Barnett, Faraday and Winters, as well as Ms. Andelman. And you might as well invite Faraday for dinner." Which shows that it's smart to ask Wolfe to see his orchids.

"Might I suggest also inviting Barnett?"

He nodded. "I'll ask Fritz what we should serve."

I suggested braised platypus stuffed with crabmeat. He pretended not to hear me.

Dinner featured Beef Wellington, which Wolfe once said is a fine dish, "though it's not serious gastronomy." During the meal, he held forth on Dickens's unfinished last novel, *The Mystery of Edwin Drood*. "The problem," he contended, "is reasonably easy to solve if you are a competent detective. Have you read it?" Both guests said they had. "Good, then this won't ruin it for you. Here's what really happened and why." I excused myself and took my plate into the kitchen. I'd been meaning to read *Drood*, and I didn't want any spoilers.

■ ■ ■

The museum director arrived promptly at nine, along with his cashier and gift-shop manager. They joined Wolfe and our guests in the office. Faraday relinquished the red chair to Moultrie. Drinks were distributed, and Wolfe began.

"I was hired to find the platypus and identify the thief. It was soon apparent where the figurine was hidden, but I could not yet prove who took it."

"Never mind that for now," said Moultrie. "Where is it?"

Wolfe produced the photos I'd taken and passed them around. They all looked, but Moultrie said, "I don't see it!"

"That's because it's disguised. Tell me what you do see."

Moultrie stared with narrowed eyes. "Some of the Disney statuettes."

"Yes. Which are most prominent?"

"Donald and Daisy Duck."

"Exactly. Now, can you tell me why I've asked you this?"

A bright light suddenly glowed in Moultrie's eyes. "Both of them have the same kind of bill as the platypus."

"Correct," said Wolfe. "A duck would be the perfect camouflage for a platypus. So you see, your platinum figure never left the museum. It should be there right now, disguised as either Donald or Daisy Duck."

Barnett and Faraday both applauded. Wolfe nodded his appreciation, then continued. "Finding the platypus was only half my job, though. Now I'll tell you who stole it."

He looked pointedly at Larry Winters.

"Me?" Winters exclaimed. "Why me?"

"Two reasons," Wolfe answered. "First, there are only three sets of keys to the museum. One is held by your employer and the second by Mr. Faraday, who never uses them."

"How do you know that?"

"He told me so." He held up his hand to stop the next

question. "Yes, I believe him. I asked my operative Saul Panzer to investigate both him and Mr. Barnett, and also Ms. Andelman. They have all been declared completely trustworthy. So you are the only one left who had access to the platypus's display case."

"I told you I only had the keys for a few minutes."

"That's all it would take," Wolfe said, "though in fact you had longer than 'a few minutes.' The day guard, who arrived late that day, says it was at least half an hour past his usual time before he got to the museum."

"What about *him*, and the other two guards?"

"I questioned them. None was even remotely interested in stealing it, and rightly so: it would be almost impossible to sell. Which brings me to my second reason. There is one person who wants to buy the platypus, and he's sitting right here."

Winters looked at Barnett and sighed. "OK, you've got me. I offered it to him, but he refused. That's when I should have left town." All the while, I noticed that he was avoiding looking at Linda.

"Why did you need so much money?" Wolfe asked.

"So I could afford a house where Linda and I could live when we get married."

She got up, approached him, and slapped his face. Very hard.

Of course Moultrie fired him, but declined to turn him over to the police. "Furthermore," he said, "before this, I was pleased with the excellence of your work. If you seek employment elsewhere, I will give you a favorable letter of reference."

The cashier's jaw dropped, as did almost everyone else's. Not Wolfe's, but I saw that our client's gesture made a great impression on him. "Mr. Moultrie," he said, "you are the soul of generosity. I am going to do something quite unusual. With two conditions, you are released from paying the remainder of my fee."

"Thank you! I agree to your conditions."

Wolfe waggled a finger. "You'd best hear them first. I want you to donate the balance of what you agreed to pay me to the museum, to fund the new rooms you told us about."

"Again, my thanks. And your second condition?"

"Permit me and Mr. Goodwin to visit at any time without charge."

"Done, sir. What about your expenses?"

"Archie will send you a bill for two parking-lot charges and Mr. Panzer's fee, which, like mine, will be rather dear."

The crowd rose to leave. Larry Winters practically ran out, but Faraday asked Wolfe for permission to use the front room. When told that he could, he went in with Moultrie and Barnett. They were in there for maybe two minutes. When they came back, Moultrie said, somewhat sadly, "I've decided to sell the platypus to Mr. Barnett."

Two more things. When Wolfe found out what Saul had learned about the weekend security guard, he had me call Cramer at once. It seems that, though Porterfield was not married, he *had* been when he lived in Knoxville, Tennessee. His wife died soon after he took out an insurance policy on her. Naturally he was suspected of killing her, but no one could figure out what did her in. The coroner put it down to that universal catchall, heart failure. Cramer got in touch with the Tennessee police and worked out that she'd been given an almost undetectable poison. So the museum had to hire a new weekend guard.

Lastly—and this may have been a joke on me, though that's not Wolfe's style—I actually overheard him asking Fritz whether he thought an acceptable meal could be prepared with platypus meat.

But so far I have not tasted any.

PART II

PARODIES

The House on 35th Street

by Frank Littler

EDITOR'S NOTE: For those unfamiliar with The Saturday Review, *it began its life in 1920 as a weekly supplement to* The New York Post, *then was published separately as* The Saturday Review of Literature *from 1924 to 1952, when it shortened its name to* The Saturday Review. *It changed ownership several times in the '60s, '70s, and '80s, folded in 1982, and made brief reappearances in '84 and (online only) '93. In April of 1925, a weekly front-of-the-book department called "The Phoenix Nest" was introduced; it featured an assortment of miscellaneous bits and pieces, similar in feel to* The New Yorker's *"Talk of the Town." The column came and went over the years, but by 1958 it was back on a semiregular basis with Martin Levin as its editor. Twice during the 1960s, Levin led off an installment of "The Phoenix Nest" with short Nero Wolfe parodies. The first of them, "The*

House on 35th Street," appeared in the February 12, 1966, issue. It was credited to Frank Littler, about whom I have been able to find little information. There is a contemporary Australian artist by that name, but it's hard to imagine he could be the same person. The twenty suspects who cram into Wolfe's office in this story have such distinctive names that I suspected they must have been the names of real people . . . but a fruitless hour of Googling led me to conclude that Littler, whoever he may have been, simply made them all up.

Nero Wolfe was still up in the plant rooms when I let the first arrivals into the old brownstone house on West 35th Street. There were five of them—Corvin Mabbs, Lucy Weld, Yett Gardner, Mischa Cernik, and Norman Rudworth. Mabbs was still wearing the bruises he'd collected the night before last when he tried to rush me. They were followed, two minutes later, by Roger Millington, Beryl Jeff, Foden Grice, Suzy Bettridge, Jefferson Stark, Mabel Stark, Bernard Leigh, and Israel Kerstein. When I'd got them inside, I seated them in that order, being careful to put Millington and Kerstein twenty feet apart. I told them Wolfe was up in the plant rooms but would be down soon. The last to arrive were Oliver Mayne, Iris McKinlay, Richard Haddon, Wilton Mozelle, Cecil Thomason, Tukuo Yamazaki, and Than Toole. I thought I saw Iris McKinlay wink at me, and decided to verify it by inviting her onto my knee, but at that moment Jefferson Stark, saying he preferred to stand anyway, offered her his chair with a show of chivalry that would have killed Wolfe if he hadn't been up in the plant rooms. It didn't seem to please Mrs. Stark from where I stood. Iris took the seat, thanking him gracefully, and then they were all in position. I reckoned that when Inspector Cramer came I could still squeeze him in if—which wasn't likely—he was prepared to junk that unlighted cigar of his. Nero Wolfe was still up in the plant rooms.

Foden Grice was the first to speak. "I think," he began weightily, "that I speak for you, Bernard, and for Suzy, Cecil, Iris, and Yett, when I say—"

"You don't speak for me," interrupted Gardner. "The only reason I've come to this old brownstone house on West 35th Street is because—"

"You want to see Mr. Wolfe wiggle a finger," finished Stark.

"Oh, Jefferson, do be quiet," begged his wife. "We *all* want to see Mr. Wolfe wiggle a finger. And hear him say *Pfui*." She looked around at the assembly. "Don't we?"

Millington, Cernik, Thomason, Rudworth, and Iris McKinlay nodded. Bernard Leigh didn't seem to have heard her. Beryl Jeff and Yamazaki were studying the carpet. Mabbs coughed noncommittally.

Wilton Mozelle demurred. "I have seen Mr. Wolfe wiggle a finger," he said quietly. "It is a gesture with which I am well acquainted. But since one of us appears to be a murderer—"

"We know one of us is a murderer," interrupted Mayne irritably. "For heaven's sake, Wilton, don't belabor the obvious." He looked at me. "How long is this flapdoodle going to take, Goodwin?"

"Mr. Wolfe," said Iris McKinlay, "would have said 'flummery.'"

"He won't call this little session flummery," I told them. "And that's for sure."

"All right," said Mayne. "But I'd still like to know—when is he coming down from the plant rooms? I've got," he said nastily, "a few orchids of my own to attend to."

"Pfui," remarked Lucy Weld. "You've got one withered cattleya."

"Let's relax for a few minutes, shall we?" I said. "If I know Mr. Wolfe—"

"And don't you?" asked Suzy Bettridge demurely.

"—you'll all be back in your homes within two hours." I paused. "Except one." My gaze lingered on Suzy for just long enough to make her wish she'd kept her trap closed.

That was when Wolfe came down from the plant rooms. They watched him enter the room and lower his three hundred pounds into the oversized chair. He looked at them all in turn.

"Inspector Cramer," he said, "will be here presently. In the meantime, I do not propose to dissemble. I am not a juggins, and it would be doltish of me to infer that your presence in my house—"

"—on West 35th Street," murmured Richard Haddon absently.

"—has been voluntary."

"That's not fair," objected Roger Millington. "I wanted to see you ring for beer."

Wolfe turned to me. "Archie. Enlighten them."

I gulped. "Sorry to disappoint you all. But we've run out."

There was a murmur of resentment. Rudworth half rose to his feet. "Do you mean to say," he demanded, "we're not going to see you drink it—and wipe your lips afterwards?"

Wolfe wiggled a finger. "There is no beer. Now I adjure you, sir, to be silent. As I said a few moments ago, I do not intend to equivocate. Nor shall I detain you with flummery. I invited you here on a pretext you may find questionable, but I am not a mountebank. I wished to determine . . ."

When they had gone, Cecil Thomason to meet his Maker, I asked him would he be needing me tomorrow night. For some reason, the question seemed to embarrass him. In fact, he squirmed. Barely an inch, mind, but if it wasn't a squirm then the house is built of marble.

"I have no desire," he began carefully, "to intrude on your personal affairs. But may I ask why?"

"Yes, sir. You may."

"Very well—why?"

"I hope to take Iris McKinlay to dinner."

"I'm afraid I will have to disappoint you," he said. He was practically writhing now. "Miss McKinlay has already accepted an invitation from me."

I gaped. "You're leaving the house? Going out into the open air?"

He shuddered. "By no means. Miss McKinlay is coming here." To cover his nervousness, he rang for beer—forgetting that there wasn't any. "I have invited her up to the plant rooms. She expressed an interest," he added desperately, "in the odontoglossums."

For ten long seconds I goggled at him. Then I came to. He may have forestalled me socially, but I could still pip him on dialogue.

"Pfui," I said. "I beg your pardon." I selected a finger and wiggled it at him. "Pfui," I repeated.

The Sidekick Case

by Patrick Butler

EDITOR'S NOTE: This is the second Wolfean parody from Martin Levin's "Phoenix Nest" page in The Saturday Review, *appearing in the October 26, 1968, issue and credited to Patrick Butler. "Patrick Butler" is a fairly common name: a Patrick Butler is today the vice president of programs at the International Center for Journalists, another spent eighteen years as a senior vice president at the Washington Post Company and is currently president and chief executive officer of America's Public Television Stations, yet another is an Irish rugby union player . . . and John Dickson Carr published two novels about a defense attorney named Patrick Butler in the 1950s. The item is clearly a reaction to an unfortunate choice of words in a review of Rex Stout's* And Four to Go *that appeared in* Paperbound Books in Print, *which was in fact edited by Olga S. Weber, assisted by Lindalee Mesiano, Phyllis Levy, and Sharon Stone. (No, not* that *Sharon Stone, a different one. In 1968, when this piece was published,* that *Sharon Stone was only ten years old. . . .)*

When Wolfe came down from the plant rooms, the gang from *Paperbound Books in Print* had already gathered in his office. Olga S. Weber, editor, was in the red leather chair directly in front of Wolfe's desk. Behind her, chattering girlishly, were assistants Lindalee Mesiano, Phyllis Levy, and Sharon Stone. I sat on the far side of the room in the yellow leather chair.

Wolfe crossed immediately to his desk and lowered his bulk into the specially constructed chair. He made a face.

"I am Nero Wolfe," he began, "and this is Mr. Goodwin, my assistant. The unlovely business at hand can be settled, I am certain, with dispatch and amiability. You are intelligent women. You owe your livelihood to words, your own and those of other people. You know their importance."

He picked up a magazine distastefully.

"I have a copy of your publication, *Paperbound Books in Print*. On page nineteen, the annotation given a book called *And Four to Go* by Rex Stout reads: 'Included are four complete Nero Wolfe mystery novelettes featuring the famous detective and his sidekick Archie.'"

The girls looked bewildered.

"I don't see—" began a dark-haired beauty who was either Lindalee Mesiano or Phyllis Levy.

"I realize you do not see," interrupted Wolfe. He wiggled a finger at her. "That is why you are here. I summoned you only after careful deliberation, and this episode is as distasteful to me as it must be to you. I am, as noted in your publication, a detective. Mr. Goodwin here is my assistant. He is, of course, also my employee. In a sense, he may be considered my partner. But he is not my sidekick."

Wolfe leaned back in the big chair, closed his eyes, and after thirty seconds asked the room at large: "Do I look like the sort of man who would have a sidekick? Archie, do you consider yourself my sidekick?"

"No, sir, I do not," I replied. "Your chattel, maybe, but not your sidekick."

The blonde (Sharon Stone?) giggled, so I went on.

"Sidekicks call their employers by their first name, or otherwise they call them 'Boss.' Sidekicks wear funny hats and fall off horses—"

"Pfui," said Wolfe. "Enough, Archie. In spite of his proclivity toward buffoonery, ladies, Mr. Goodwin is no sidekick. Now, Miss Weber, can you propose a course of action that would alleviate the distress you have caused me?"

"Well, I am sorry, Mr. Wolfe, but I guess we just used the term 'sidekick' to indicate Mr. Goodwin's position as assistant."

"You did indeed, Miss Weber," said Wolfe. "That you acted without malice, I am certain. But you acted thoughtlessly in your capacity as editor, and the result—inadvertent though it may have been—has been to hold me up to ridicule. Since you appear to believe, however, that 'sidekick' is synonymous with 'assistant,' carrying with it no debasing connotation, justice can be done quite simply. In your next issue, I suggest that your staff be listed on the masthead as follows: 'Editor, Olga S. Weber. Sidekicks: Lindalee Mesiano, Phyllis Levy, Sharon Stone.' If I hear no demurrer from you, I shall consider the case closed."

He leaned back and closed his eyes.

I ushered the girls out. The blonde was still giggling.

When I returned, Wolfe's eyes were shut and his lips were pushing in and out.

I went to the kitchen for a glass of milk. And to wait for the next issue of *Paperbound Books in Print*.

The Case of the Disposable Jalopy

by Mack Reynolds

EDITOR'S NOTE: I wrestled with the question of whether or not to include Mack Reynolds's story in this collection, mainly because of its length. As originally published in The Magazine of Fantasy and Science Fiction *in 1976, it was quite a bit longer than you'll find it here, going into—unsurprisingly, given where it appeared—much greater length and depth about the engineering details of the disposable car and including an additional character and subplot. It paints such an entertaining picture of the aging Nero Wolfe and Archie Goodwin, though, that I finally decided to edit out some of the extraneous-for-our-purposes detail and allow you to enjoy it. (For readers unfamiliar with the literature of science fiction, I should perhaps point out that the last names of all the secondary characters in the story have been "borrowed" from a galaxy of the genre's all-stars. . . .)*

■ ■ ■

That morning I came down late from my room on the second floor of the old brownstone at 918 West 35th Street, a stone's throw from the Hudson. I'd been up into the wee hours the night before, playing penny ante with Saul and Lon. Of course, none of us had any pennies, but our weekly poker games have a long tradition—and, besides, it gives me an excuse not to spend the evening sitting and watching Fatso guzzling beer and reading the moth-eaten old paperbacks that purport to tell of his early coups as a sleuth. From time to time, he'll read aloud a select passage or so, forgetting that it was me who wrote them. Currently, he was on one of the very first, *The Red Box*, a crime—if I recall correctly, and I probably don't—that involved a strawberry-blond prostitute.

I went into the kitchen and said, "What's for breakfast, uh, Franz?"

He looked at me, his aged meek eyes expressing sorrow.

"That is, uh, Felix," I said. "Felipe? Don't tell me. I have it on the tip of my tongue."

"Baldie," he quavered, "there is mush for breakfast."

"Mush? Again? Whatever happened to orange juice, English muffins, griddle cakes with thyme honey from Greece, country sausages and eggs in black butter?"

He gave a sigh for yesteryear before saying, "Baldie, you know very well that four old men on Negative Income Tax cannot afford such luxuries, even when they pool their resources." He sighed again. "Besides, where would one get the ingredients?" He looked down sorrowfully at a paper packet in his hand. "Dehydrated wine, Beaujolais, vintage of '88," he moaned. "For lunch we will have soybean hamburgers, and tonight Escoffier hash."

"Escoffier hash? That sounds like something you smoke. What's in it?"

"To give you an idea," he said, "today is the day I clean the kitchen."

It was then that the doorbell rang.

I went to answer it and peered through the one-way glass. There were three of them, and they didn't look like bill collectors. They ranged in age from about forty to fifty: kids. I put the chain on, opened the door several inches, and said, "You've got the wrong address. This is the home of Caligula, uh, that is, Tiberius, uh, I mean Claudius—wait a minute, don't tell me, I know his name as well as I know my own. Same name as one of the early Roman emperors."

The oldest and tallest of the three said loftily, "We are at the home of the most famed private detective of the last century, I take it?"

"You can take it or leave it," I told him. "That was the last century. The boss's three most recent clients all wound up guillotined."

"Guillotined?" the smallest and youngest of the three said. "Is that the method of execution these days? I'm not really up on such matters, don't you know." He wore an anachronistic goatee and fiddled with it as though checking the correctness of its point.

"Electric chairs were decided against when capital punishment was reinstated to take care of the terrorists," I explained. "There's so many of them, these days, there'd be blackouts if you tried to electrocute them all." A startling thought came to me. "Are you clients?"

"Of course," the chubby one said in disgust. "You don't fancy we're standing here on the stoop of this slum tenement, or whatever you call it, soliciting for charity, do you?"

"We couldn't contribute a handful of bird seed to a canary refuge," I said, opening the door.

They filed into the hallway.

"I'll see if the boss is available," I said, strictly formal now.

"Available?" the tall one said, looking up and down the hallway, taking in the bedraggled rug and the chair with the broken leg. "How long has it been since you've had a case, my dear fellow?"

"Three years," I admitted. "But we cracked it, more or less. Your names, gentlemen?"

The older one said, "My name is Clarke. This is Mr. Aldiss, and this is Mr. Brunner."

"First names?" I said politely.

"We're all named Charles. It's the thing in England now, you know. Practically all British males are named after His Majesty."

I ushered them back to the office.

Clarke took the well-worn red leather chair which sat at the end of Fatso's desk, and Aldiss and Brunner took two of the less prestigious yellow ones.

I said apologetically, "I don't have a watch. Hocked it last year. The boss usually gets down from the plant rooms at eleven. That shouldn't be too long."

"Plant rooms?" Clarke said.

"Yeah, up on the top floor. He raises petunias. It used to be some other flower, I forget what, but they got to be too expensive. Now it's petunias. He spends two hours every morning up there with his gardener, Ted, and another two in the afternoon." I thought about it vaguely. "I've often wondered what the two of them *do* all that time."

I got a notebook and stylo from my desk drawer and said, "While we're waiting, I might as well get some background material." I looked at Clarke. "Just who *are* you guys, Chuck?"

He crossed his long legs. "We're scientists," he told me, affecting a modest self-deprecation that didn't quite come off.

"Scientists?"

"That is correct," Aldiss said. "We work for the Ruptured Motors Company, with offices in the Welfare State Building."

I made a note, wondering if I'd remember how to decipher my shorthand later. "You mean to tell me that, with ninety percent of the country on Negative Income Tax as a result of the almost complete automation and computerization of production, distribution, communications, transportation, and everything else, an automobile company imports its employees from England?"

Clarke said, "Absolutely necessary, dear boy. I understand that it started some half a century ago. You Ammedicans began to ask each other, 'Why can't Johnny read?' It seems that your high schools were graduating students who lacked the ability to read and write. Two decades later, a college degree was no guarantee that its bearer wasn't, ah, I believe the term is 'functionally illiterate.' That is, they lacked the skills to cope with an increasingly complex technological society. Many couldn't balance a checkbook or fill out a job application or their income-tax forms."

"You mean," I said wistfully, "that over in England your college graduates can make out their own tax forms?"

At that moment, I heard the groaning of the elevator coming down from the plant rooms. It came to a halt, and the beer barrel that walks like a man came in, glaring.

I knew how his once-great mind was working. There were three strangers in his office. If he wasn't careful, the situation might degenerate to the point where he had to do some work. For a moment, I was afraid he'd turn right around and bolt. That's one of his most childish tricks.

He muttered, "Baldie, what is the meaning of this? Are you attempting to badger me?"

"No, sir," I said quickly. "This is Mr. Aldiss, Mr. Brunner, and Mr. Clarke. Their first names are all Chuck."

"Charles," Aldiss growled.

Fatso glowered at me. "Clients? Do you think me a witling? We haven't had a client for years."

"No, sir," I admitted.

He looked at the three Englishmen and nodded, his head moving two inches—which for him was almost a bow.

"Gentlemen," I said, "this is Mr. Coyote, uh, that is, Lobo. Uh, I mean Mr. Dingo. No, no, don't tell me. Mr. Jackal?"

Fatso glared at me again. "Baldie," he said, "your mind is slipping over the precipice of senility."

He made his way to the only chair in the world that can seat his seventh of a ton in comfort, reached for the button set into his desk, and gave one short and one long ring, his signal for beer.

The three Chucks were staring at him as though fascinated. I could guess what they were thinking. Two hundred and eighty-five pounds of meat, and not one ounce of muscle.

Franz, or Felix, or whatever the hell his name is, hobbled in with a tray bearing a plastic quart of beer and a glass and put it on his desk, turned around, and left, his aged eyes astonished at the sight of our clients. If I read him correctly, he was already having dreams of splurging on half a dozen frozen pizzas and a pound of syntho-salami.

Fatso fumbled in his desk drawer for the gold bottle opener that had been given to him by a well-pleased client back in the days when we had well-pleased clients. Look who was calling who senile.

"You sold it," I reminded him, "five years ago." I got up, went over, and picked up the quart of beer, rested the cap against the edge of the desk and hit the top of the bottle sharply with the heel of my hand. The cap popped off, and the beer foamed over a little before I got it to the glass.

He took a deep swallow and looked down at the brew in disgust. "These days," he grunted, "you can't tell Schlitz from Shinola."

He leaned back in his chair and folded his hands over the half acre of his stomach. "If you gentlemen wish to consult a detective, why didn't you go to the Pinkertons or Dol Bonner's agency?"

Clarke said, "You're the only private investigator in the city still listed as licensed."

"Pfui," Fatso said, then wiggled a finger at me. "Baldie, is this flummery?"

"I didn't know we still *had* a license," I told him. "They're so inefficient down at City Hall, they probably haven't gotten around to revoking it." I turned to the clients. "Fact is, Chuck, there's nothing *in* the PI dodge these days. We used to specialize in murder cases, but ever since the Mafia Party took office the definition of homicide has gotten so elastic a detective never *gets* a murder case anymore."

Fatso closed his eyes but didn't lean back, so he wasn't thinking, merely suffering, probably at the prospect of being unable to find an excuse to avoid working. His lips twitched. After a dozen twitches, he reopened his eyes and spoke. "Gentlemen," he said, "admittedly I am arbitrary and contumelious when confronted by some fatuous ninny who speaks gammon to me. What is the case to which you wish me to devote my wits?"

"Sabotage," Clarke said.

Fatso closed his rheumy eyes in pain. "My dear sir," he muttered peevishly, "do I look as though I am so constructed that I am capable of dashing out and confronting saboteurs? Or that my puerile assistant here, doddering on the edge of caducity, could—"

"Hey," I said.

He ignored my protest and went on, scowling at the three Chucks. "What do you mean, sabotage? Sabotage of what?"

"Industrial sabotage," Aldiss said. "We are the victims of industrial espionage and sabotage. The sabotage of our project: the Ruptured Rat, a disposable car."

"Ruptured Rat?" I repeated blankly.

Brunner, putting off fussing with his beard for a moment, said, not quite apologetically, "The automobile industry has long since run out of animals and birds after which to name its new models. We began long ago with the Bearcat, the Mustang, the Thunderbird, the Cougar, and so on. Now we really have to reach."

"Disposable car?" Fatso spat. "This is brazen impudence. Pah. You attempt to diddle us."

"Certainly not," Clarke said. "Certainly you remember the beginnings of the trend, the better part of a century ago? Kleenex, the disposable handkerchief. Later came such items as the disposable ballpoint pen, the disposable cigarette lighter, watches so inexpensive that, when one stopped, it was more economical to buy a new one than to have the old one repaired. Very well, the time of the disposable jalopy has arrived, and the Ruptured Rat is the result."

"You mean," I said, "you plan on producing a car so cheaply that, the first time it needs even minor repairs, you simply throw it away and get a new one?"

"Not exactly," Brunner said primly. "That would be wasteful. One would simply turn it in on a new model."

"How in the hell many people could afford to do that?" I snorted.

Fatso just sat there, his eyes closed.

Clarke took over smoothly. "I can see you chaps need some background," he said. "In the very early days of the automotive industry, simplicity was the word. The vehicles of the time were two-cylindered, with absolutely no frills. When mass production got under way, many models sold for less than four hundred dollars. Even as recently as the mid-1930s, the cheaper cars were priced at about five hundred and fifty dollars."

I gave a sigh for days past.

He pressed on. "But then the insidious changes began. Such foofaraw as self-starters were introduced. Four-wheel brakes. Heaters. Windshield wipers. Radios. Air conditioning. Power steering, power windows, power brakes, automatic shifting. Nine-tenths of the cost of an automobile today goes into unnecessary gadgets." He held up a finger dramatically. "The Ruptured Rat will take us back to the infancy of the car."

Fatso was drawing dime-sized circles with an age-crooked finger on his chair arm.

I said, "And how far do you think you can lower the price on this stripped-down set of wheels?"

Brunner said, "Five hundred thousand pseudo-dollars, or about five hundred of the dollars that prevailed before inflation began with the devaluation of the currency in 1932."

"Only five hundred thousand pseudo-dollars?" I sputtered. "At today's prices, you couldn't buy the steel for a car for that amount!"

"We use the new plastics—stronger than steel, rustless, and no paint required—with tires and a battery that will last the life of the car."

"What would you charge for a trade-in? Suppose a wheel fell off and the owner wanted a new Ruptured Rat?"

"Fifty thousand pseudo-dollars, no matter what shape it's in. If you can get it to a Ruptured Rat dealer, the equivalent of fifty old dollars gets you a fresh Rat."

"Holy smog!" I said in disbelief. "And how long does that guarantee last?"

"Forever," Aldiss said. "And the model will never change. No owner will know if his neighbor's Rat is six months old or ten years. It will be the most desired vehicle in the country. We'll sweep the market."

"Just a damned minute," I protested. "What happens to all the trade-ins you accept? Why would anybody buy a used one, if they can get a new one for only five hundred thousand pseudo-dollars?"

Clarke stepped into the act again. "You won't exactly get a *new* Rat when you trade in your old one. You'll get a *fresh* one, but, when a trade-in comes in, we'll completely renovate it to the point where it is undetectable from a new one and put it right back on the market."

At this point, Fatso decided to get back into the act. He opened his watery eyes and said, "Confound it, what is the sabotage you mentioned?"

"Possibly 'sabotage' is not quite the proper word," Clarke said. "Our intuitive genius, the developer of the Ruptured Rat and inventor of its siphoning device, has disappeared. He hasn't shown up for work for three days."

"Siphoning device?" I said.

"For siphoning petrol out of the Rat," Clarke explained.

"Why would it be necessary to siphon gas *out* of the car?" I demanded. "Did I miss something?"

"Ah, yes," Clarke said, "we forgot to mention that. The Rat can run on electric power, steam generated from solar cells built into the roof, and petrol—all three. To make the story short for the sake of you laymen, the Rat produces a surplus of gasoline, which owners will be able to siphon out of their tanks and sell to service stations."

Fatso brought his whole seventh of a ton erect and eyed the three Chucks with what I can only call that cunning you sometimes find in those failing with age. "Very well," he said, "I'll take the case. What is the name of the missing inventor?"

"Azimov," Clarke told him.

I looked up from my notes. "Azimov what?"

"Azimov Asimov. It's somewhat confusing, don't you know, so we call him Charlie for short."

Fatso's slack mouth worked momentarily. "And where did he live before his disappearance?"

"In the Bowery Hilton," Brunner said, with a twirl of his goatee.

Fatso looked at me inquiringly.

"One of the most prestigious flophouses in Manhattan," I said.

"Very well, my wits are at your disposal, gentlemen," Fatso cackled. "I will require a retainer. Shall we say one million pseudo-dollars?"

"A million?" Clarke said, taken aback. "Isn't that somewhat high?"

"No," I told him, figuring the only reason Fatso hadn't named a larger sum was that he couldn't count any higher.

"Very well," Clarke said. He brought his Universal Credit Card from inside his jerkin, stood and approached the desk, and put it in the credit-transfer slot. He said into the screen, "I wish to transfer one million pseudo-dollars from the account of the Ruptured Motors Company to this one." He pressed his thumb to the identity square. "I trust you will begin operations immediately, old chap."

"Manifestly," Fatso muttered, leaning back in his chair and closing his eyes.

I saw the three Britishers to the door and bolted it behind them.

When I returned to the office, Fatso's eyes were still closed and his lips were twitching. Sometimes he drowses, muttering in his sleep about the old days, when he was up against such foes as Arnold Zeck, who he usually called Mr. X.

I knew I was going to have to prod him to work, so I said, "Any instructions?"

His eyes opened. I was rather proud of how well the blathering old duffer had conducted himself during the past half hour. He hadn't seemed to lose the thread of things even once.

"Don't badger me," he said petulantly. "Can you get Saul, Orrie, and Fred here immediately?"

"Sure," I told him. "All three are working odd jobs at Rusterman's Hash House and Chili Parlor. It's the only greasy spoon in town where you can eat all you want for three thousand pseudo-dollars."

"Good heavens," he murmured. "I remember when it was owned by Marko Vukcic and was the best restaurant in the city."

"Time dodders on," I said, reaching for my TV phone and beginning to dial.

He was fast asleep when the doorbell rang again. I pushed myself erect, groaning a little at the arthritic pains, and took off to answer it.

I was surprised to see the two men standing on the stoop. Adjusting my bifocals, I opened the door a crack and said, "What the hell do *you* want?"

"Open up," the inspector wheezed. "Police business."

Shaking my head, I let them in. "You know, I've always wondered about you two. I remember you from the early 1930s, when we were on one of our first cases, the *Fer-de-Lance* one. You were a homicide inspector, and the sergeant here was one of your right-hand men. Thirty years later, when we were working on the case I wrote up as *The Final Deduction*, you were still an inspector and the sergeant was still a sergeant. And here it is thirty years after that. Don't you two ever get promoted or retire?"

The inspector's big red face had gone grayish, but his growl was still the same. "We *were* retired, both of us. But we came back when the city got to the point where it could no longer afford to pay its civil servants and most of the police force quit."

"Once a cop, always a flatfoot," I told him, leading the way back to the office.

Fatso looked up from his beer. "Ah, the impetuous inspector. It has been a long time, sir. To what do I owe the doubtful pleasure of this visit?"

To my surprise, the inspector brought forth a cigar and rolled it between his hands before putting it in his mouth. I hadn't seen a cigar in years, not since the government had declared Tobacco Prohibition.

"I just happened to be in the neighborhood," he said creakily. "We picked up Doc Vollmer on a charge of pushing tobacco. He was peddling it to school kids. I confiscated this as evidence." He took the cigar from his mouth and looked at it fondly. "At any rate, just as we left his place I noticed three suspicious-looking characters coming down the steps from your front door."

"Pfui. You are a witling, Inspector," Fatso said. He brought his glass of beer to his lips, emptied it, then took out his handkerchief and wiped foam from his mouth. "The three gentlemen in question are my clients."

The inspector glared back at him. "That's what I was afraid of. What did they want? Has it got anything to do with homicide? When you get involved in a homicide, all hell breaks loose, and there's usually enough dead people piled up you'd think the plague hit town."

Fatso had evidently had enough. He closed his eyes and leaned back in his chair.

The inspector had been through this before. When Fatso wants to withdraw, he's the nearest thing this side of a turtle.

I showed my dentures in a ravishing smile. "Immovable object," I said.

"You grinning ape," he got out, pushing himself to his feet. "Come on, Sergeant."

When I returned after seeing them out, Fatso was tapping his chair arm with one finger so I'd know he was boiling with rage. "Confound it, Baldie," he muttered, "I should sue the city for defamation of character."

"The city hasn't had a pseudo-dime in its coffers for twenty years," I reminded him.

"Pfui."

The telephone rang, and I answered it. Lily Rowan appeared on the screen, and I winced. If she gets one more facelift, her chin will be on top of her head.

"Escamillo!" she cackled. "I've had the most wonderful idea. Let's go to the—"

The doorbell rang, and I made my excuses and went to answer it. Saul, Orrie, and Fred were on the stoop.

Saul, of course, was in his motorized hover-wheelchair. Why they still call them wheelchairs when they're supported by a cushion of air, I don't know. But even confined to his chair, Saul is still the best tail man in the city. I hadn't seen him for years, save at our weekly poker games. He's small and wiry, with a big nose and flat ears. He always looks as though he needs a shave and his pants were last pressed a week ago.

Orrie is another thing entirely. In the old days, he was tall, handsome, smart, and valued himself as quite the ladies' man. Now he looked the worse for wear, having just recently gotten out of the banger, where he was serving time for molesting little girls in Central Park. They sprung him when the new Permissiveness Laws were passed.

Fred, once overly married, big and broad and looking very solid and honest, was now almost the exact opposite. He had buried his over-domineering wife under somewhat hazy circumstances, the worm having evidently finally turned. He had also shriveled and was no longer honest looking. In fact, he had several times beaten shoplifting raps by the skin of his teeth.

Saul pulled his wheelchair up next to the red chair it had once been his privilege to occupy, Fatso considering him to be the best independent operative in Manhattan. Orrie and Fred wheezed themselves into yellow chairs, and I took my place at my desk.

Fatso made a steeple of his fingertips over the great expanse of his belly. "Gentlemen, we have a case. You three will proceed to tail three Englishmen named Aldiss, Brunner, and Clarke. I shall expect daily reports. That will be all."

When they were gone, I stared at him for a long empty minute. "But those are the clients," I finally said. "Why do you want *them* tailed?"

He closed his eyes. His lips moved in and out, and then he muttered petulantly, "Do you think me a callow stripling in this profession? A fatuous troglodyte? Manifestly, because there is no one else to tail thus far. They're the only ones we know connected with the case."

"What are *my* instructions?"

He reached out for one of the paperbacks dealing with our past cases—this time *A Right to Die*. "You shall proceed to the offices of the Ruptured Motor Company," he said, obviously making it up as he went along, "and interview everyone who had any connection with this Charlie Asimov. Have them in my office tonight at nine o'clock."

The Welfare State Building turned out to be no great shakes as compared to the skyscrapers of my youth. Plastics don't quite have the dignity of the old steel and reinforced concrete materials of old, and they scruff up when some terrorist tosses a bomb or lets loose with a high-caliber assault rifle.

Despite the power shortage, some of the elevators were working. I looked up the Ruptured Motor Company on the lobby directory and found them to be in Suite 1304. I would have expected that an outfit with the ambitious project of creating the Ruptured Rat would have had at least several entire floors at their disposal, but apparently not.

The reception room was stereotypical: spanking-new plastic furniture, sterile artists' conceptions of the Rat on the walls. The apparition behind the desk looked like Myrna Loy playing Dracula's daughter. She was slinky, she was sultry, and she was dressed as has never been a receptionist in the history of receptionists. Her pneumatic lips were painted to the point that she looked as though she might bleed to death through them. I didn't get too close, not wanting to catch a cold from her batting her eyelashes.

"You must be the shamus," she leered. "Mr. Clarke called and said to cooperate. I've never met a gumshoe before. What can I do for you?"

"The boss wants me to interview the complete staff of Ruptured Motors—that is, all those who've come in contact with Charlie Asimov."

"All right, fire away," she said.

I looked at her blankly. "Where do I find the others?"

"There are no others," she told me, "except for Mr. Aldiss, Mr. Brunner, and Mr. Clarke—and none of them are here.

Besides, you've already talked with them. This place is *really* automated. Charlie and I are the only employees, except for the three Britishers."

"One secretary and one inventor can't possibly do all the work."

"What work?" she said reasonably. "I'm telling you, it's all computerized."

I was flabbergasted. "What about building the factory where the Rat is to be manufactured?"

"That's to be contracted out."

I closed my eyes momentarily, but then opened them and said, "All right, what's your name?"

"Le Guin," she said. "Mata Hari Le Guin."

"You're an American?"

"No. I was born in Tangier, Morocco. My mother came from Brazil and my father from Macao."

I eyed her. "So you're another example of immigrants being allowed by the government to work while ninety percent of Americans are unemployed and on Negative Income Tax?"

"Please," she said haughtily, "I do not permit four-letter words to be spoken in my presence."

"What four-letter words?"

"Government."

I shook my head. "Here you are a secretary and you can't spell any better than I can. Now, this Charlie Asimov. What can you tell me about his disappearance? Do you think it was a kidnapping? Possibly terrorists?"

"What disappearance?" she said. "He phoned in, right before you got here. He's home with a bad cold."

I retraced my way to the brownstone on West 35th Street, only twice running into small bands of terrorists. I let myself in, and, before going to the office, stopped off at the kitchen to see if I was in time for lunch.

Felix, or whatever his name is, was working happily at the stove. "Look, Baldie," he said, "it's like the old days. Shad roe *fines herbes*, no parsley, instead of soy burgers. And, tonight, instead of Escoffier hash—"

"Where'd you get the credits for all this fancy grub?"

"We have a client, Baldie! I phoned Mummiani's on Fulton Street, the last gourmet food store in—"

"What client?" I said, not exactly hopping with joy. "We were hired to investigate a disappearing inventor, but it turns out he's in bed with a cold at the Bowery Hilton."

I went on into the office to report. Fatso was sitting there in his chair, his eyes closed, his lips going in and out, in and out. He is not to be interrupted while thinking. This time, however, it was just too much.

"What in the hell," I said, "are you thinking about?"

"Lunch," he said.

I took my place at my desk. "You want me to report?"

He opened his eyes and scowled at me, probably having forgotten what errand he had sent me on. "Proceed," he said snidely, "giving everything in full detail from your famed photographic memory."

I told him about going to the small suite that housed the offices of the Ruptured Motors Company. Told him about the svelte Ms. Le Guin. Went on to reveal that she and Charlie Asimov were the only employees of the company, save the three British scientists who headed the project.

The shad roe *fines herbes* without parsley was superb, and Fatso was in his version of Allah's paradise. Since the rule is we never talk business during mealtimes, he regaled me with a summary of several chapters of the paperback he had just finished, *Three for the Chair*, undoubtedly having forgotten that it had been me who had peddled the exaggerated account to an idiot of an editor long years past.

While we were having our coffee, the doorbell rang, and I went to answer it. At first, it looked to me as though our visitor was wearing a bed sheet pulled over his head, on the top of which rested a circle of black braided rope. Then I realized that he was an honest-to-goodness Arab.

I opened the door a slit and said, "If you're soliciting funds for the Palestinian side of the Hundred Years War . . ."

But he touched his forehead, his lips, and then his heart, and said, "*As-salaam alaykum.*"

"That's nice," I told him. "What do you want?"

He stroked his black beard and said, "*Effendi*, I wish even to speak with your master."

What the hell, we hadn't had a laugh around the place for months. I let him in and led the way back to the office.

When we entered, Fatso glowered at me. "Is this flummery, Baldie?" he bellowed.

"I don't think so," I said. "He wants to talk to you."

Without an invitation, the newcomer took the red leather chair and crossed his legs. He wore soft leather boots under his white skirts, or whatever you call the outfit.

"Well, sir?" Fatso muttered. He hates to have his digestion interfered with.

"*Effendi*, I represent the United Arabian Petroleum Industries. I have come to put you under retainer."

"I already have a client."

"Verily, as each of us know: the Ruptured Motors Company. However, *our* retainer would consist of five million pseudo-dollars. Tax free, of course."

"Hmmm," Fatso said. "Just what is it you wish to retain me to do?"

"First, is it true that your present clients are on the verge of producing a vehicle that will produce gasoline, rather than consuming it?"

"Confound it, sir," Fatso said indignantly, "I never discuss the affairs of my clients—unless there is a profitable reason for me to do so. Where's the five million?"

We spent the next few minutes transferring the amount from one numbered Swiss account to another. Then Fatso leaned back, crossed his hands over his belly, and answered the question: "Yes."

The newcomer said, "Verily, it is a miracle of God."

"What do you have in mind in retaining my wits?"

The other came to his feet. "For the moment, *Effendi*, nothing. We will contact you when your services are required. *Alhumdu li-lah,* praise be to God."

"Hey," I said, "what's your name?"

He looked at me. "Even Carlos Mahmoud ould Sheikh, *Effendi*."

I made a note of it.

He turned back to Fatso, touched forehead, lips, and heart, and murmured, "May your life be as long and flowing as the tail of the horse of the Prophet."

I followed him out, then returned to the office. Fatso was reading *Plot It Yourself* and chuckling over the manner in which he had outfoxed the plagiarist Amy Wynn, more years ago than I like to remember.

I sat at my desk and said bitterly, "So now we have two sets of clients. You don't think there might be a little conflict of interest there?"

He looked up from the book. "Certainly not. How could there be?"

I said patiently, "One sells petroleum, and the other one is going to turn out a car that not only doesn't need it, except for the initial start, but produces it as a by-product."

"See here, Baldie," he said, just as patiently, "as our new client Carlos Mahmoud ould Sheikh pointed out, thus far they have nothing for us to do. We are merely under retainer. If anything develops that we cannot in good conscience accept, we will resign—keeping such amount of the retainer as we decide is called for. Say four-fifths of it."

He reached for the button to summon more beer.

The Bowery Hilton had seen better days. By the looks of it, it might have been used as a recruiting station when Lincoln issued his call for seventy-five thousand volunteers. The only thing that could be said favorably about this section of town was that there were no terrorists. The residents had already been terrorized to hell and gone.

The place wasn't even automated. When I approached the front desk, a fey character looked up and said, "Good afternoon, sir. My name's Bradbury. What can I do for you?"

I said, "Don't tell me your first name. I don't want to know. What room was Azimov Asimov in?"

"Was?" he said, lifting eyebrows. "He still is. He's in room 305."

Something Mata Hari Le Guin said came back to me, something about a three-day cold.

I made my way up the creaking steps, planning on using a skeleton key to get into the missing inventor's room so I could search it in hopes of digging up some clue as to what had happened to him.

The skeleton key wasn't required: the door was unlocked.

I entered cautiously, which also wasn't required. I could have made enough noise to wake the dead.

But I didn't, because the dead was stretched out on the bed, looking very dead indeed.

Charlie Asimov hadn't just disappeared. He had died. I checked quickly. There were no signs of violence. In fact, there was nothing out of the ordinary at all, except for a half-finished bowl of soup on the nightstand. I checked it out. Mushroom. There was a cardboard quart container next to the bowl, obviously used to bring the soup in.

I got on the TV phone quickly to report. It'd be just my luck for the inspector or the sergeant to turn up. They'd haul me down to Centre Street and use some of their surplus Nazi equipment, thumbscrews and so forth. . . .

Fatso's face faded in. "I assume you've become lost?"

"No, sir," I said. "I've found Charlie Asimov."

"What?" he bellowed indignantly. "The first day? I had expected to string this case out for weeks, if not months. Bring him here so I can question him. Perhaps we can figure out some manner in which—"

I adjusted my bifocals and looked down at the corpse. "That might be difficult," I said. "He's a little dead. Should I notify the inspector?"

His rheumy eyes took on a slyness that only accented his caducity. "No. How long do you think we could just leave him there before he was found?"

I looked around the room. "Probably a week."

That took him aback. "A week? How about the odor?"

"In this fleabag, no one would notice. And I doubt they have maid service."

"Very well. Satisfactory. Return at once."

Just before leaving, I picked up the half-empty container of mushroom soup. We hadn't had such a delicacy in many a month, and Charlie Asimov wasn't going to be wanting it.

After only two minor skirmishes with terrorists, I got back to the brownstone. I let myself in and went straight back to the office.

Fatso glowered peevishly at me, then leveled his eyes at my soup container. "What in the name of Hades is that?"

I told him where I'd picked it up, adding that it smelled better than anything we'd eaten for ages.

Food being food, he took it, removed the top and peered down at the contents. Then, to my surprise, he put the container down, stretched back in his chair, closed his eyes, and began working his lips in and out, in and out, in that mannerism that has had me climbing the walls for more than half a century. I went to my desk and sat down.

Finally, he said, "Baldie, you're a lackwit."

"Yes, sir, you've mentioned that before."

The phone rang. It was Saul, reporting that Aldiss, who he had been tailing, was sleeping with Mrs. Brunner.

I passed on the information to Fatso, who commented with a "Pfui."

The phone rang again. It was Orrie, reporting that Brunner was sleeping with Mrs. Clarke. I got another "Pfui" from the lord of the manor.

The phone rang again. Fred, who reported that Clarke was sleeping with Mrs. Aldiss.

"It's a regular merry-go-round," I commented to Fatso. "Pfui."

The doorbell rang, and I went to let in the inspector and his sidekick, the sergeant.

The inspector wasted no time on preliminaries. "All right, Baldie, this time you've had it. Get your hat."

I cleared my throat. "Don't you think we should go in and see the boss?"

He glared at me in triumph. "That's a good idea. Probably

the only one you've ever had. I can't wait to see the expression on his fat face. Come on, Sergeant."

We marched down to the office.

Fatso looked up from a fresh bottle of beer. "To what do I owe this intrusion, sir?"

The inspector plumped down, making no attempt to disguise his satisfaction. "This time you've had it, you chunk of blubber. Baldie here is under arrest on so many charges I won't bother to recite them all."

Fatso took the time to down half his glass of beer before leaning back and closing his eyes. His lips began moving in and out. It obviously fascinated the inspector, though he'd witnessed the performance a thousand times before.

"This, Inspector," he said at last, "I cannot allow. Baldie has been my assistant for so long that I've almost become used to him. Just short of idiotic he may be, these days—"

"Hey," I said.

"Tough," the inspector got out in what he probably meant to be a snarl. "But it seems he went into the Bowery Hilton an hour or so ago, and his furtive manner raised the suspicions of Charles Bradbury, the front-desk clerk, who phoned the police. And what did the officers who responded to the call find? The body of a certain Azimov Asimov. Baldie was the last person reported to have seen him."

"Pfui," Fatso prattled. "I sent him to find clues to the reason for Asimov's disappearance. When he found the man dead, he immediately came back to report."

Despite the situation, I had to be proud of the old glutton. He was almost making sense.

"Let's go, Baldie," the inspector said, pushing to his feet.

But Fatso waggled a finger at him. "Inspector, I refuse to

countenance this brazen impudence on the part of you Cossacks. I propose the following bargain. If you will round up all those concerned in this affair and have them here in my office at nine, I guarantee to turn the murderer over to you."

The inspector blinked.

The sergeant said, "Huh! You must think we're drivel-happy."

But it was as if the decades had rolled back. The inspector had been through this before.

"Shut up, Sergeant," he said testily. And then, grudgingly, to Fatso: "It's a deal. Who do you want?"

It made for a rather full room that night. Our original three clients: Aldiss, Brunner, and Clarke, Clarke in the red chair and his two colleagues in yellow ones. Mata Hari Le Guin, looking luscious. Carlos Mahmoud ould Sheikh, right out of the *Arabian Nights*. Saul was in his wheelchair at the far end of the room, and Orrie and Fred stood on either side of him.

I, of course, was at my desk. Next to me were the inspector, trying to look gimlet-eyed, and the sergeant.

Fatso, in the full form he affected when pretending he still retained his once-brilliant faculties, was planted firmly in his king-sized chair. Before him on the desk, to my surprise, was the container of soup I had pinched from Asimov's room.

He looked out over his audience for a long moment, and then closed his eyes, as though figuring the hell with it. But then he opened them again and sighed all the way down to his gaiters. He's probably the last man left in Manhattan who wears gaiters.

He looked around the room. "The eyes of the murderer of Azimov Asimov are at this moment upon me," he said. "However, before revealing his identity, I wish to clarify a few points and thus earn my fee." He cleared his creaking voice. "Or fees."

He turned his watery eyes to Aldiss, Brunner, and Clarke. "First of all, gentlemen, you need no longer worry about the disappearance of Mr. Asimov. After considering all aspects of the situation, I dispatched my dotard assistant—"

"Hey," I said in protest.

"—who found him. So that is no longer a problem." He turned to me. "Baldie," he said, "please get the copy of the *Qu'ran* from the bookshelf."

"The what?"

"The Koran, you nincompoop. It's over there, behind the globe."

I found it and brought it back.

"Give it to Carlos Mahmoud ould Sheikh."

I did.

"Are you willing to swear on the book of Allah," he said, trying to be severe, "that you will answer my questions truthfully?"

"Verily," Carlos said. "However, you've evidently picked up a wrong idea. I'm a born-again Baptist Fundamentalist, praise be to God, from Leesville, South Carolina."

That stopped even Fatso.

I cleared my voice and said, "I seem to have gathered the impression that you were one of the highest-ranking officials of the United Arabian Petroleum Industries. If you're an American, how come the fancy costume and the corny language and all?"

"We high government officials," he said with considerable dignity, "think it only right to continue the traditions and institutions of the countries we now govern."

"Govern?" the inspector got out. "But you just said you're an American from Starboardville, South Carolina, or someplace."

The petroleum tycoon looked at him coolly. "Verily, Inspector," he said. "You obviously do not keep up with the news. As all learned men know, Charles Smith is now president of the United Arab States. Under pressure from the Human Rights Division of the Reunited Nations, the Arab states have, for the first time in history, allowed free elections. What they didn't foresee was that so many American technicians, engineers, mechanics, and construction workers were now permanent residents that they would carry the election."

Fatso flickered his eyes. "What was your point in hiring me?"

The phony Arab shrugged. "Verily, I found out that you had been retained by Ruptured Motors and thought you might be able to expedite a deal with them. The Arab states have run out of oil, and I came here to the US to make a deal to buy oil from Ruptured Motors, once their Rat goes into production."

The inspector wheezed, "The hell with all this. Get to the point. Who killed Asimov?"

Fatso squared his blubbery shoulders and pointed dramatically to a picture five feet to the right of his desk. "The man who killed Charlie Asimov is standing behind that painting!"

I knew immediately what he meant. "Come on, Sergeant!" I yelped. With him bringing up the rear, I hurried out into the hallway.

Next to the kitchen is the alcove from which, for long years, we have been able to spy undetected on anything transpiring in Fatso's office. Our spyhole is covered by a pretty picture of a waterfall and can't be detected from inside the office. We sometimes utilize it to watch and listen to clients—or others—who don't know they're being observed.

And now, there stood the terrified figure of Fatso's chef of half a century or more. The sergeant and I grabbed him and pulled him into the office.

"Holy smog!" the inspector exclaimed. "How did you know?"

Fatso, smug with satisfaction, eyed his trembling cook. He pointed at the container on his desk. "I have eaten his mushroom soup too often not to immediately recognize its smell. Only, this time, it is not mushroom but toadstool soup. He must have grown the toadstools himself in the herb garden in the back yard. Heaven only knows why. Perhaps in his failing mind he planned one day to feed them to Baldie and myself, with the idea of putting us out of our misery."

"No, no," the chef cried. "I did it all for you, sir! It was all for you! When I learned that, after all these years, you had clients again, I couldn't stand it when Baldie informed me that the missing inventor wasn't missing at all but simply home with a cold. I hurriedly made the toadstool soup and took it to the Bowery Hilton. Asimov was happy to get it and promptly ate half of it. I thought then the case would continue, and you would be given the job of finding the murderer."

Fatso was indignant. "Didn't you fear I'd succeed—as, indeed, I have?"

The chef caved in, and shook his head pathetically. "No, I thought you'd gone so far around the bend that you'd never solve the crime. You'd continue on the case indefinitely, and we'd have the pseudo-dollars to buy the food you have always loved so much. It was all for you, sir!"

"Pfui," Fatso said, in his usual driveling manner.

The inspector and sergeant hauled the broken man from the office, taking the container of evidence with them. I could only hope that they wouldn't forget what it was and eat the stuff.

"Now what about the oil?" Carlos Mahmoud ould Sheikh asked greedily.

"I'm sorry to disappoint you, old chap," said Clarke. "We've just heard from Mr. Rupture in Tibet. While whirling his prayer stick the other day, he decided he was bored with the automotive industry and would go into international finance, instead. So the Rat project has been abandoned, and we are to begin the construction of a chain of multinational banks that will dispense his new concept, the Disposable Dollar."

My mind boggled. "Disposable Dollar," I blurted. "You mean—"

"Quite." He looked at me loftily. "You use it once and then throw it away."

As Dark as Christmas Gets

by Lawrence Block

AUTHOR'S NOTE: I first wrote about Chip Harrison in 1970, in a coming-of-age novel called No Score *that could have been* Lecher in the Rye. *A second book,* Chip Harrison Scores Again, *followed a couple of years later, and, when I got the urge to write more about the lad, I had the idea of putting him to work for a private detective, a Nero Wolfe wannabe named Leo Haig. This worked, and Chip starred in two more novels,* Make Out with Murder *and* The Topless Tulip Caper. *In addition to the four novels, I also wrote two short stories about Chip. Both take place after the novels and feature Chip as he is in the third and fourth books (i.e., Leo Haig's assistant). The first story, "Death of the Mallory Queen," appeared in 1984; thirteen years later, "As Dark as Christmas Gets" was written for a pamphlet that served as Otto Penzler's Christmas gift. Every year, Otto commissions a story from a writer of his acquaintance, with the sole requirement that the story be set in his establishment, the Mysterious Bookshop, and involve the crime or the threat of a crime. The story was subsequently published in EQMM. Deeply imbued with the mystique of the mystery community, "As Dark as Christmas Gets" involves a missing manuscript and a cast of characters who may ring a bell or two, seasonal or otherwise.*

It was 9:54 in the morning when I got to the little bookshop on West 56th Street. Before I went to work for Leo Haig, I probably wouldn't have bothered to look at my watch, if I was even wearing one in the first place, and the best I'd have been able to say was it was around ten o'clock. But Haig wanted me to be his legs and eyes, and sometimes his ears, nose and throat, and if he was going to play in Nero Wolfe's league, that meant I had to turn into Archie Goodwin, for Pete's sake, noticing everything and getting the details right and reporting conversations verbatim.

Well, forget that last part. My memory's getting better—Haig's right about that part—but what follows won't be word for word, because all I am is a human being. If you want a tape recorder, buy one.

There was a lot of fake snow in the window, and a Santa Claus doll in handcuffs, and some toy guns and knives, and a lot of mysteries with a Christmas theme, including the one by Fredric Brown where the murderer dresses up as a department store Santa. (Someone pulled that a year ago, put on a red suit and a white beard and shot a man at the corner of Broadway and 37th, and I told Haig how ingenious I thought it was. He gave me a look, left the room, and came back with a book. I read it—that's what I do when Haig hands me a book—and found out Brown had had the idea fifty years earlier. Which doesn't mean that's where the killer got the idea. The book's long out of print—the one I read was a paperback, and falling apart, not like the handsome hardcover copy in the window. And how many killers get their ideas out of old books?)

Now if you're a detective yourself you'll have figured out two things by now—the bookshop specialized in mysteries, and it was the Christmas season. And if you'd noticed the sign in the window you'd have made one more deduction, i.e., that they were closed.

I went down the half flight of steps and poked the buzzer. When nothing happened, I poked it again, and eventually the door was opened by a little man with white hair and a white beard—all he needed was padding and a red suit, and someone to teach him to be jolly. "I'm terribly sorry," he said, "but I'm afraid we're closed. It's Christmas morning, and it's not even ten o'clock."

"You called us," I said, "and it wasn't even nine o'clock."

He took a good look at me, and light dawned. "You're Harrison," he said. "And I know your first name, but I can't—"

"Chip," I supplied.

"Of course. But where's Haig? I know he thinks he's Nero Wolfe, but he's not gone housebound, has he? He's been here often enough in the past."

"Haig gets out and about," I agreed, "but Wolfe went all the way to Montana once, as far as that goes. What Wolfe refused to do was leave the house on business, and Haig's with him on that one. Besides, he just spawned some unspawnable cichlids from Lake Chad, and you'd think the aquarium was a television set and they were showing *Midnight Blue*."

"Fish." He sounded more reflective than contemptuous. "Well, at least you're here. That's something." He locked the door and led me up a spiral staircase to a room full of books, and full as well with the residue of a party. There were empty glasses here and there, hors d'oeuvres trays that held nothing but crumbs, and a cut-glass dish with a sole remaining cashew.

"Christmas," he said, and shuddered. "I had a houseful of people here last night. All of them eating, all of them drinking, and many of them actually singing." He made a face. "I didn't sing," he said, "but I certainly ate and drank. And eventually they all went home and I went upstairs to bed. I must have, because that's where I was when I woke up two hours ago."

"But you don't remember."

"Well, no," he said, "but then what would there be to remember? The guests leave and you're alone with vague feelings of sadness." His gaze turned inward. "If she'd stayed," he said, "I'd have remembered."

"She?"

"Never mind. I awoke this morning, alone in my own bed. I swallowed some aspirin and came downstairs. I went into the library."

"You mean this room?"

"This is the salesroom. These books are for sale."

"Well, I figured. I mean, this is a bookshop."

"You've never seen the library?" He didn't wait for an answer but turned to open a door and lead me down a hallway to another room twice the size of the first. It was lined with floor-to-ceiling hardwood shelves, and the shelves were filled with double rows of hardcover books. It was hard to identify the books, though, because all but one section was wrapped in plastic sheeting.

"This is my collection," he announced. "These books are not for sale. I'll only part with one if I've replaced it with a finer copy. Your employer doesn't collect, does he?"

"Haig? He's got thousands of books."

"Yes, and he's bought some of them from me. But he doesn't give a damn about first editions. He doesn't care what kind of shape a book is in, or even if it's got a dust jacket. He'd as soon have a Grosset reprint or a book-club edition or even a paperback."

"He just wants to read them."

"It takes all kinds, doesn't it?" He shook his head in wonder. "Last night's party filled this room as well as the salesroom. I put up plastic to keep the books from getting handled and possibly damaged. Or—how shall I put this?"

Any way you want, I thought. *You're the client.*

"Some of these books are extremely valuable," he said. "And my guests were all extremely reputable people, but many of them are good customers, and that means they're collectors. Ardent, even rabid collectors."

"And you didn't want them stealing the books."

"You're very direct," he said. "I suppose that's a useful quality in your line of work. But no, I didn't want to tempt anyone, especially when alcoholic indulgence might make temptation particularly difficult to resist."

"So you hung up plastic sheets."

"And came downstairs this morning to remove the plastic, and pick up some dirty glasses and clear some of the debris. I puttered around. I took down the plastic from this one section, as you can see. I did a bit of tidying. And then I saw it."

"Saw what?"

He pointed to a set of glassed-in shelves, on top of which stood a three-foot row of leather-bound volumes. "There," he said. "What do you see?"

"Leather-bound books, but—"

"Boxes," he corrected. "Wrapped in leather and stamped in gold, and each one holding a manuscript. They're fashioned to look like finely bound books, but they're original manuscripts."

"Very nice," I said. "I suppose they must be very rare."

"They're unique."

"That, too."

He made a face. "One of a kind. The author's original manuscript, with corrections in his own hand. Most are typed, but the Elmore Leonard is handwritten. The Westlake, of course, is typed on that famous Smith-Corona manual portable of his. The Paul Kavanagh is the author's first novel. He only wrote three, you know."

I didn't, but Haig would. "They're very nice," I said politely. "And I don't suppose they're for sale."

"Of course not. They're in the library. They're part of the collection."

"Right," I said, and paused for him to continue. When he didn't, I said, "Uh, I was thinking. Maybe you could tell me—"

"—why I summoned you here?" He sighed. "Look at the boxed manuscript between the Westlake and the Kavanagh."

"Between them?"

"Yes."

"The Kavanagh is *Such Men Are Dangerous*," I said, "and the Westlake is *Drowned Hopes*. But there's nothing at all between them but a three-inch gap."

"Exactly," he said.

"*As Dark as It Gets*," I said, "by Cornell Woolrich."

Haig frowned. "I don't know the book," he said. "Not under that title, not with Woolrich's name on it, nor William Irish or George Hopley. Those were his pen names."

"I know," I said. "You don't know the book because it was never published. The manuscript was found among Woolrich's effects after his death."

"There was a posthumous book, Chip."

"*Into the Night*," I said. "Another writer completed it, writing replacement scenes for some that had gone missing in the original. It wound up being publishable."

"It wound up being published," Haig said. "That's not necessarily the same thing. But this manuscript, *As Dark*—"

"—*as It Gets*. It wasn't publishable, according to our client. Woolrich evidently worked on it over the years, and what survived him incorporated unresolved portions of several drafts. There are characters who die early on and then reappear with no explanation. There's supposed to be some great writing and plenty of Woolrich's trademark paranoid suspense, but it doesn't add up to a book, or even something that could be edited into a book. But to a collector—"

"Collectors," Haig said heavily.

"Yes, sir. I asked what the manuscript was worth. He said, 'Well, I paid five thousand dollars for it.' That's verbatim, but don't ask me if the thing's worth more or less than that, because I don't know if he was bragging that he was a big spender or a slick trader."

"It doesn't matter," Haig said. "The money's the least of it. He added it to his collection and he wants it back."

"And the person who stole it," I said, "is either a friend or a customer or both."

"And so he called us and not the police. The manuscript was there when the party started?"

"Yes."

"And gone this morning?"

"Yes."

"And there were how many in attendance?"

"Forty or fifty," I said, "including the caterer and her staff."

"If the party was catered," he mused, "why was the room a mess when you saw it? Wouldn't the catering staff have cleaned up at the party's end?"

"I asked him that question myself. The party lasted longer than the caterer had signed on for. She hung around herself for a while after her employees packed it in, but she stopped working and became a guest. Our client was hoping she would stay."

"But you just said she did."

"After everybody else went home. He lives upstairs from the bookshop, and he was hoping for a chance to show her his living quarters."

Haig shrugged. He's not quite the misogynist his idol is, but he hasn't been at it as long. Give him time.

He said, "Chip, it's hopeless. Fifty suspects?"

"Six."

"How so?"

"By two o'clock," I said, "just about everybody had called it a night. The ones remaining got a reward."

"And what was that?"

"Some fifty-year-old Armagnac, served in Waterford pony glasses. We counted the glasses, and there were seven of them. Six guests and the host."

"And the manuscript?"

"Was still there at the time, and still sheathed in plastic. See, he'd covered all the boxed manuscripts, same as the books on the shelves. But the cut-glass ship's decanter was serving as a sort of bookend to the manuscript section, and he took off the plastic to get at it. And while he was at it he took out one of the manuscripts and showed it off to his guests."

"Not the Woolrich, I don't suppose."

"No, it was a Peter Straub novel, elegantly handwritten in a leather-bound journal. Straub collects Chandler, and our client had traded a couple of Chandler firsts for the manuscript, and he was proud of himself."

"I shouldn't wonder."

"But the Woolrich was present and accounted for when he took off the plastic wrap, and it may have been there when he put the Straub back. He didn't notice."

"And this morning it was gone."

"Yes."

"Six suspects," he said. "Name them."

I took out my notebook. "Jon and Jayne Corn-Wallace," I said. "He's a retired stockbroker, she's an actress in a daytime drama. That's a soap opera."

"Piffle."

"Yes, sir. They've been friends of our client for years, and customers for about as long. They were mystery fans, and he got them started on first editions."

"Including Woolrich?"

"He's a favorite of Jayne's. I gather Jon can take him or leave him."

"I wonder which he did last night. Do the Corn-Wallaces collect manuscripts?"

"Just books. First editions, though they're starting to get interested in fancy bindings and limited editions. The one with a special interest in manuscripts is Zoltan Mihalyi."

"The violinist?"

Trust Haig to know that. I'd never heard of him myself.

"A big mystery fan," I said. "I guess reading passes the time on those long concert tours."

"I don't suppose a man can spend all his free hours with other men's wives," Haig said. "And who's to say that all the stories are true? He collects manuscripts, does he?"

"He was begging for a chance to buy the Straub, but our friend wouldn't sell."

"Which would make him a likely suspect. Who else?"

"Philip Perigord."

"The writer?"

"Right, and I didn't even know he was still alive. He hasn't written anything in years."

"Almost twenty years. *More Than Murder* was published in 1980."

Trust him to know that, too.

"Anyway," I said, "he didn't die. He didn't even stop writing. He just quit writing books. He went to Hollywood and became a screenwriter."

"That's the same as stopping writing," Haig reflected. "It's very nearly the same as being dead. Does he collect books?"

"No."

"Manuscripts?"

"No."

"Perhaps he wanted the manuscripts for scrap paper," Haig said. "He could turn the pages over and write on their backs. Who else was present?"

"Edward Everett Stokes."

"The small-press publisher. Bought out his partner, Geoffrey Poges, to became sole owner of Stokes-Poges Press."

"They do limited editions, according to our client. Leather bindings, small runs, special tip-in sheets."

"All well and good," he said, "but what's useful about Stokes-Poges is that they issue a reasonably priced trade edition of each title as well, and publish works otherwise unavailable, including collections of short fiction from otherwise uncollected writers."

"Do they publish Woolrich?"

"All his work has been published by mainstream publishers, and all his stories collected. Is Stokes a collector himself?"

"Our client didn't say."

"No matter. How many is that? The Corn-Wallaces, Zoltan Mihalyi, Philip Perigord, E. E. Stokes. And the sixth is—"

"Harriet Quinlan."

He looked puzzled, then nodded in recognition. "The literary agent."

"She represents Perigord," I said, "or at least she would, if he ever went back to novel-writing. She's placed books with Stokes-Poges. And she may have left the party with Zoltan Mihalyi."

"I don't suppose her client list includes the Woolrich estate. Or that she's a rabid collector of books and manuscripts."

"He didn't say."

"No matter. You said six suspects, Chip. I count seven."

I ticked them off. "Jon Corn-Wallace. Jayne Corn-Wallace. Zoltan Mihalyi. Philip Perigord. Edward Everett Stokes. Harriet Quinlan. Isn't that six? Or do you want to include our client, the little man with the palindromic first name? That seems farfetched to me, but—"

"The caterer, Chip."

"Oh. Well, he says she was just there to do a job. No interest in books, no interest in manuscripts, no real interest in the world of mysteries. Certainly no interest in Cornell Woolrich."

"And she stayed when her staff went home."

"To have a drink and be sociable. He had hopes she'd spend the night, but it didn't happen. I suppose technically she's a suspect, but—"

"At the very least she's a witness," he said. "Bring her."

"Bring her?"

He nodded. "Bring them all."

It's a shame this is a short story. If it were a novel, now would be the time for me to give you a full description of the off-street carriage house on West Twentieth Street that Leo Haig owns and where he occupies the top two floors, having rented out the lower two stories to Madam Juana and her All-Girl Enterprise. You'd hear how Haig had lived for years in two rooms in the

Bronx, breeding tropical fish and reading detective stories, until a modest inheritance allowed him to set up shop as a poor man's Nero Wolfe.

He's quirky, God knows, and I could fill a few pleasant pages recounting his quirks, including his having hired me as much for my writing ability as for my potential value as a detective. I'm expected to write up his cases the same way Archie Goodwin writes up Wolfe's, and this case was a slam-dunk, really, and he says it wouldn't stretch into a novel, but that it should work nicely as a short story.

So all I'll say is this. Haig's best quirk is his unshakable belief that Nero Wolfe exists. Under another name, of course, to protect his inviolable privacy. And the legendary brownstone, with all its different fictitious street numbers, isn't on West 35th Street at all but in another part of town entirely.

And someday, if Leo Haig performs with sufficient brilliance as a private investigator, he hopes to get the ultimate reward—an invitation to dinner at Nero Wolfe's table.

Well, that gives you an idea. If you want more in the way of background, I can only refer you to my previous writings on the subject. There have been two novels so far, *Make Out with Murder* and *The Topless Tulip Caper*, and they're full of inside stuff about Leo Haig. (There were two earlier books from before I met Haig, *No Score* and *Chip Harrison Scores Again*, but they're not mysteries and Haig's not in them. All they do, really, is tell you more than you'd probably care to know about me.)

Well, end of commercial. Haig said I should put it in, and I generally do what he tells me. After all, the man pays my salary.

And, in his own quiet way, he's a genius. As you'll see.

"They'll never come here," I told him. "Not today. I know it will always live in your memory as The Day the Cichlids Spawned, but to everybody else it's Christmas, and they'll want to spend it in the bosoms of their families, and—"

"Not everyone has a family," he pointed out, "and not every family has a bosom."

"The Corn-Wallaces have a family. Zoltan Mihalyi doesn't, but he's probably got somebody with a bosom lined up to spend the day with. I don't know about the others, but—"

"Bring them," he said, "but not here. I want them all assembled at five o'clock this afternoon at the scene of the crime."

"The bookshop? You're willing to leave the house?"

"It's not entirely business," he said. "Our client is more than a client. He's a friend, and an important source of books. The reading copies he so disdains have enriched our own library immeasurably. And you know how important that is."

If there's anything you need to know, you can find it in the pages of a detective novel. That's Haig's personal conviction, and I'm beginning to believe he's right.

"I'll pay him a visit," he went on. "I'll arrive at four-thirty or so, and perhaps I'll come across a book or two that I'll want for our library. You arrange that they all arrive around five, and we'll clear up this little business." He frowned in thought. "I'll tell Wong we'll want Christmas dinner at eight tonight. That should give us more than enough time."

Again, if this were a novel, I'd spend a full chapter telling you what I went through getting them all present and accounted for. It was hard enough finding them, and then I had to sell them on coming. I pitched the event as a second stage of last night's party—their host had arranged, for their entertainment and edification, that they should be present while a real-life private detective solved an actual crime before their very eyes.

According to Haig, all we'd need to spin this yarn into a

full-length book would be a dead body, although two would be better. If, say, our client had wandered into his library that morning to find a corpse seated in his favorite chair, *and* the Woolrich manuscript gone, then I could easily stretch all this to sixty thousand words. If the dead man had been wearing a deerstalker cap and holding a violin, we'd be especially well off; when the book came out, all the Sherlockian completists would be compelled to buy it.

Sorry. No murders, no Baker Street Irregulars, no dogs barking or not barking. I had to get them all there, and I did, but don't ask me how. I can't take the time to tell you.

"Now," Zoltan Mihalyi said. "We are all here. So can someone please tell me why we are all here?" There was a twinkle in his dark eyes as he spoke, and the trace of a knowing smile on his lips. He wanted an answer, but he was going to remain charming while he got it. I could believe he swept a lot of women off their feet.

"First of all," Jeanne Botleigh said, "I think we should each have a glass of eggnog. It's festive, and it will help put us all in the spirit of the day."

She was the caterer, and she was some cupcake, all right. Close-cut brown hair framed her small oval face and set off a pair of china-blue eyes. She had an English accent, roughed up some by ten years in New York, and she was short and slender and curvy, and I could see why our client had hoped she would stick around.

And now she'd whipped up a batch of eggnog and ladled out cups for each of us. I waited until someone else tasted it—after all the mystery novels Haig's forced on me, I've developed an imagination—but once the Corn-Wallaces had tossed off theirs with no apparent effect, I took a sip. It was smooth and delicious, and it had a kick like a mule. I looked over at Haig, who's not much of a drinker, and he was smacking his lips over it.

"Why are we here?" he said, echoing the violinist's question. "Well, sir, I shall tell you. We are here as friends and customers of our host, whom we may be able to assist in the solution of a puzzle. Last night all of us, with the exception of course of myself and my young assistant, were present in this room. Also present was the original manuscript of an unpublished novel by Cornell Woolrich. This morning we were all gone, and so was the manuscript. Now we have returned. The manuscript, alas, has not."

"Wait a minute," Jon Corn-Wallace said. "You're saying one of us took it?"

"I say only that it has gone, sir. It is possible that someone within this room was involved in its disappearance, but there are diverse other possibilities as well. What impels me, what has prompted me to summon you here, is the likelihood that one or more of you knows something that will shed light on the incident."

"But the only person who would know anything would be the person who took it," Harriet Quinlan said. She was what they call a woman of a certain age, which generally means a woman of an uncertain age. Her figure was a few pounds beyond girlish, and I had a hunch she dyed her hair and might have had her face lifted somewhere along the way, but whatever she'd done had paid off. She was probably old enough to be my mother's older sister, but that didn't keep me from having the sort of ideas a nephew's not supposed to have.

Haig told her anyone could have observed something, and not just the guilty party, and Philip Perigord started to ask a question, and Haig held up a hand and cut him off in mid-sentence. Most people probably would have finished what they were saying, but I guess Perigord was used to studio executives shutting him up at pitch meetings. He bit off his word in the middle of a syllable and stayed mute.

"It is a holiday," Haig said, "and we all have other things to do, so we'd best avoid distraction. Hence I will ask the questions and you will answer them. Mr. Corn-Wallace. You are a book collector. Have you given a thought to collecting manuscripts?"

"I've thought about it," Jon Corn-Wallace said. He was the best-dressed man in the room, looking remarkably comfortable in a dark blue suit and a striped tie. He wore bull and bear cufflinks and one of those watches that's worth five thousand dollars if it's real or twenty-five bucks if you bought it from a Nigerian street vendor. "He tried to get me interested," he said, with a nod toward our client. "But I've always been the kind of trader who sticks to listed stocks."

"Meaning?"

"Meaning it's impossible to pinpoint the market value of a one-of-a-kind item like a manuscript. There's too much guesswork involved. I'm not buying books with an eye to selling them—that's something my heirs will have to worry about—but I do like to know what my collection is worth and whether or not it's been a good investment. It's part of the pleasure of collecting, as far as I'm concerned. So I've stayed away from manuscripts. They're too iffy."

"And had you had a look at *As Dark as It Gets*?"

"No. I'm not interested in manuscripts, and I don't care at all for Woolrich."

"Jon likes hard-boiled fiction," his wife put in, "but Woolrich is a little weird for his taste. I think he was a genius myself. Quirky and tormented, maybe, but what genius isn't?"

Haig, I thought. You couldn't call him tormented, but maybe he made up for it by exceeding the usual quota of quirkiness.

"Anyway," Jayne Corn-Wallace said, "I'm the Woolrich fan in the family. Though I agree with Jon as far as manuscripts are concerned. The value is pure speculation. And who wants to buy something and then have to get a box made for it? It's like buying an unframed canvas and having to get it framed."

"The Woolrich manuscript was already boxed," Haig pointed out.

"I mean generally, as an area for collecting. As a collector, I wasn't interested in *As Dark as It Gets*. If someone fixed it up and completed it, and if someone published it, I'd have been glad to buy it. I'd have bought two copies."

"Two copies, madam?"

She nodded. "One to read and one to own."

Haig's face darkened, and I thought he might offer his opinion of people who were afraid to damage their books by reading them. But he kept it to himself, and I was just as glad. Jayne Corn-Wallace was a tall, handsome woman, radiating self-confidence, and I sensed she'd give as good as she got in an exchange with Haig.

"You might have wanted to read the manuscript," Haig suggested.

She shook her head. "I like Woolrich," she said, "but as a stylist he was choppy enough after editing and polishing. I wouldn't want to try him in manuscript, let alone an unfinished manuscript like that one."

"Mr. Mihalyi," Haig said. "You collect manuscripts, don't you?"

"I do."

"And do you care for Woolrich?"

The violinist smiled. "If I had the chance to buy the original manuscript of *The Bride Wore Black*," he said, "I would leap at it. If it were close at hand, and if strong drink had undermined my moral fiber, I might even slip it under my coat and walk off with it." A wink showed us he was kidding. "Or at least I'd have been tempted. The work in question, however, tempted me not a whit."

"And why is that, sir?"

Mihalyi frowned. "There are people," he said, "who attend open rehearsals and make surreptitious recordings of the music. They treasure them and even bootleg them to other like-minded fans. I despise such people."

"Why?"

"They violate the artist's privacy," he said. "A rehearsal is a time when one refines one's approach to a piece of music. One takes chances, one uses the occasion as the equivalent of an artist's sketch pad. The person who records it is in essence spraying a rough sketch with fixative and hanging it on the wall of his personal museum. I find it unsettling enough that listeners record concert performances, making permanent what was supposed to be a transitory experience. But to record a rehearsal is an atrocity."

"And a manuscript?"

"A manuscript is the writer's completed work. It provides a record of how he arranged and revised his ideas, and how they were in turn adjusted for better or worse by an editor. But it is finished work. An unfinished manuscript. . . ."

"Is a rehearsal?"

"That or something worse. I ask myself, *What would Woolrich have wanted?*"

"Another drink," Edward Everett Stokes said, and leaned forward to help himself to more eggnog. "I take your point, Mihalyi. And Woolrich might well have preferred to have his unfinished work destroyed upon his death, but he left no instructions to that effect, so how can we presume to guess his wishes? Perhaps, for all we know, there is a single scene in the book that meant as much to him as anything he'd written. Or less than a scene—a bit of dialogue, a paragraph of description, perhaps no more than a single sentence. Who are we to say it should not survive?"

"Perigord," Mihalyi said, "you are a writer. Would you care to have your unfinished work published after your death? Would you not recoil at that, or at having it completed by others?"

Philip Perigord cocked an eyebrow. "I'm the wrong person to ask," he said. "I've spent twenty years in Hollywood. Forget unfinished work. My finished work doesn't get published, or 'produced,' as they so revealingly term it. I get paid, and the work winds up on a shelf. And, when it comes to having one's work completed by others, in Hollywood you don't have to wait until you're dead. It happens during your lifetime, and you learn to live with it."

"We don't know the author's wishes," Harriet Quinlan put in, "and I wonder how relevant they are."

"But it's his work," Mihalyi pointed out.

"Is it, Zoltan? Or does it belong to the ages? Finished or not, the author has left it to us. Schubert did not finish one of his greatest symphonies. Would you have laid its two completed movements in the casket with him?"

"It has been argued that the work was complete, that he intended it to be but two movements long."

"That begs the question, Zoltan."

"It does, dear lady," he said with a wink. "I'd rather beg the question than be undone by it. Of course I'd keep the *Unfinished Symphony* in the repertoire. On the other hand, I'd hate to see some fool attempt to finish it."

"No one has, have they?"

"Not to my knowledge. But several writers have had the effrontery to finish *The Mystery of Edwin Drood*, and I do think Dickens would have been better served if the manuscript had gone in the box with his bones. And as for sequels, like those for *Pride and Prejudice* and *The Big Sleep*, or that young fellow who had the colossal gall to tread in Rex Stout's immortal footsteps . . ."

Now we were getting onto sensitive ground. As far as Leo Haig was concerned, Archie Goodwin had always written up Wolfe's cases, using the transparent pseudonym of Rex Stout. (Rex Stout = fat king, an allusion to Wolfe's own regal corpulence.) Robert Goldsborough, credited with the books written since the "death" of Stout, was, as Haig saw it, a ghostwriter employed by Goodwin, who was no longer up to the chore of hammering out the books. He'd relate them to Goldsborough, who transcribed them and polished them up. While they might not have all the narrative verve of Goodwin's own work, still they provided an important and accurate account of Wolfe's more recent cases.

See, Haig feels the great man's still alive and still raising orchids and nailing killers. Maybe somewhere on the Upper East Side. Maybe in Murray Hill, or just off Gramercy Park . . .

The discussion about Goldsborough, and about sequels in general, roused Haig from a torpor that Wolfe himself might have envied. "Enough," he said with authority. "There's no time for meandering literary conversations, nor would Chip have room for them in a short-story-length report. So let us get to it. One of you took the manuscript, box and all, from its place on the shelf. Mr. Mihalyi, you have the air of one who protests too much. You profess no interest in the manuscripts of unpublished novels, and I can accept that you did not yearn to possess *As Dark as It Gets*, but you wanted a look at it, didn't you?"

"I don't own a Woolrich manuscript," he said, "and of course I was interested in seeing what one looked like. How he typed, how he entered corrections . . ."

"So you took the manuscript from the shelf."

"Yes," the violinist agreed. "I went into the other room with it, opened the box and flipped through the pages. You can taste the flavor of the man's work in the visual appearance of his manuscript pages. The words and phrases x'd out, the pencil notations, the crossovers, even the typographical errors. The computer age puts paid to all that, doesn't it? Imagine Chandler running spell-check, or Hammett with justified margins." He sighed. "A few minutes with the script made me long to own one of Woolrich's. But not this one, for reasons I've already explained."

"You spent how long with the book?"

"Fifteen minutes at the most. Probably more like ten."

"And returned to this room?"

"Yes.

"And brought the manuscript with you?"

"Yes. I intended to return it to the shelf, but someone was standing in the way. It may have been you, Jon. It was someone tall, and you're the tallest person here." He turned to our client. "It wasn't you. But I think you may have been talking with Jon. Someone was, at any rate, and I'd have had to step between the two of you to put the box back, and that might have led to questions as to why I'd picked it up in the first place. So I put it down."

"Where?"

"On a table. That one, I think."

"It's not there now," Jon Corn-Wallace said.

"It's not," Haig agreed. "One of you took it from that table. I could, through an exhausting process of cross-questioning, establish who that person is. But it would save us all time if the person would simply recount what happened next."

There was a silence while they all looked at each other.

"Well, I guess this is where I come in," Jayne Corn-Wallace said. "I was sitting in the red chair, where Phil Perigord is sitting now. And whoever I'd been talking to went to get another drink, and I looked around, and there it was on the table."

"The manuscript, madam?"

"Yes, but I didn't know that was what it was, not at first. I thought it was a finely bound limited edition. Because the manuscripts are all kept on that shelf, you know, and this one wasn't. And it hadn't been on the table a few minutes earlier, either. I knew that much. So I assumed it was a book someone had been leafing through, and I saw it was by Cornell Woolrich, and I didn't recognize the title, so I thought I'd try leafing through it myself."

"And you found it was a manuscript."

"Well, that didn't take too keen an eye, did it? I suppose I glanced at the first twenty pages, just riffled through them while the party went on around me. I stopped after a chapter or so. That was plenty."

"You didn't like what you read?"

"There were corrections," she said disdainfully. "Words and whole sentences crossed out, new words penciled in. I realize writers have to work that way, but when I read a book I like to believe it emerged from the writer's mind fully formed."

"Like Athena from the brow of what's-his-name," her husband said.

"Zeus. I don't want to know there was a writer at work, making decisions, putting words down and then changing them. I want to forget about the writer entirely and lose myself in the story."

"Everybody wants to forget about the writer," Philip Perigord said, helping himself to more eggnog. "At the Oscars each year, some ninny intones 'In the beginning was the Word' before he hands out the screenwriting awards. And you hear the usual crap about how they owe it all to chaps like me who put words in their mouths. They say it, but nobody believes it. Jack Warner called us schmucks with Underwoods. Well, we've come a long way. Now we're schmucks with Power Macs."

"Indeed," Haig said. "You looked at the manuscript, didn't you, Mr. Perigord?"

"I never read unpublished work. Can't risk leaving myself open to a plagiarism charge."

"Oh? But didn't you have a special interest in Woolrich? Didn't you once adapt a story of his?"

"How did you know about that? I was one of several who made a living off that particular piece of crap. It was never produced."

"And you looked at this manuscript in the hope that you might adapt it?"

The writer shook his head. "I'm through wasting myself out there."

"They're through with you," Harriet Quinlan said. "Nothing personal, Phil, but it's a town that uses up writers and throws them away. You couldn't get arrested out there. So you've come back east to write books."

"And you'll be representing him, madam?"

"I may, if he brings me something I can sell. I saw him paging through a manuscript and figured he was looking for something he could steal. Oh, don't look so outraged, Phil. Why not steal from Woolrich, for God's sake? He's not going to sue. He left everything to Columbia University, and you could knock off anything of his, published or unpublished, and they'd never know the difference. Ever since I saw you reading, I've been wondering. Did you come across anything worth stealing?"

"I don't steal," Perigord said. "Still, perfectly legitimate inspiration can result from a glance at another man's work—"

"I'll say it can. And did it?"

He shook his head. "If there was a strong idea anywhere in that manuscript, I couldn't find it in the few minutes I spent looking. What about you, Harriet? I know you had a look at it, because I saw you."

"I just wanted to see what it was you'd been so caught up in. And I wondered if the manuscript might be salvageable. One of my writers might be able to pull it off, and do a better job than the hack who finished *Into the Night*."

"Ah," Haig said. "And what did you determine, madam?"

"I didn't read enough to form a judgment. Anyway, *Into the Night* was no great commercial success, so why tag along in its wake?"

"So you put the manuscript . . ."

"Back in its box, and left it on the table where I'd found it."

Our client shook his head in wonder. "*Murder on the Orient Express*," he said. "Or in the Calais coach, depending on whether you're English or American. It's beginning to look as though *everyone* read that manuscript. And I never noticed a thing!"

"Well, you were hitting the sauce pretty good," Jon Corn-Wallace reminded him. "And you were, uh, concentrating all your social energy in one direction."

"How's that?"

Corn-Wallace nodded toward Jeanne Botleigh, who was refilling someone's cup. "As far as you were concerned, our lovely caterer was the only person in the room."

There was an awkward silence, with our host coloring and his caterer lowering her eyes demurely. Haig broke it. "To continue," he said abruptly. "Miss Quinlan returned the manuscript to its box and to its place upon the table. Then—"

"But she didn't," Perigord said. "Harriet, I wanted another look at Woolrich. Maybe I'd missed something. But first I saw you reading it, and when I looked a second time it was gone. You weren't reading it and it wasn't on the table, either."

"I put it back," the agent said.

"But not where you found it," said Edward Everett Stokes. "You set it down not on the table but on that revolving bookcase."

"Did I? I suppose it's possible. But how do you know that?"

"Because I saw you," said the small-press publisher. "And because I wanted a look at the manuscript myself. I knew about it, including the fact that it was not restorable in the fashion of *Into the Night*. That made it valueless to a commercial publisher, but the idea of a Woolrich novel going unpublished ate away at me. I mean, we're talking about Cornell Woolrich."

"And you thought—"

"I thought why not publish it as is, warts and all? I could do it, in an edition of two or three hundred copies, for collectors who'd happily accept inconsistencies and omissions for the sake of having something otherwise unobtainable. I wanted a few minutes peace and quiet with the book, so I took it into the lavatory."

"And?"

"And I read it, or at least paged through it. I must have spent half an hour in there, or close to it."

"I remember you were gone a while," Jon Corn-Wallace said. "I thought you'd headed on home."

"I thought he was in the other room," Jayne said, "cavorting on the pile of coats with Harriet here. But I guess that must have been someone else."

"It was Zoltan," the agent said, "and we were hardly cavorting."

"Kanoodling, then, but—"

"He was teaching me a yogic breathing technique, not that it's any of your business. Stokes, you took the manuscript into the john. I trust you brought it back?"

"Well, no."

"You took it home? You're the person responsible for its disappearance?"

"Certainly not. I didn't take it home, and I hope I'm not responsible for its disappearance. I left it in the lavatory."

"You just left it there?"

"In its box, on the shelf over the vanity. I set it down there while I washed my hands, and I'm afraid I forgot it. And no, it's not there now. I went and looked as soon as I realized what all this was about, and I'm afraid some other hands than mine must have moved it. I'll tell you this—when it does turn up, I definitely want to publish it."

"*If* it turns up," our client said darkly. "Once E. E. left it in the bathroom, anyone could have slipped it under his coat without being seen. And I'll probably never see it again."

"But that means one of us is a thief," somebody said.

"I know, and that's out of the question. You're all my friends. But we were all drinking last night, and drink can confuse a person. Suppose one of you did take it from the bathroom and carried it home as a joke, the kind of joke that can seem funny after a few drinks. If you could contrive to return it, perhaps in such a way that no one could know your identity . . . Haig, you ought to be able to work that out."

"I could," Haig agreed, "if that were how it happened. But it wasn't."

"It wasn't?"

"You forget the least obvious suspect."

"Me? Dammit, Haig, are you saying I stole my own manuscript?"

"I'm saying the butler did it," Haig said, "or the closest thing we have to a butler. Miss Botleigh, your upper lip has been trembling almost since we all sat down. You've been on the point of an admission throughout and haven't said a word. Have you in fact read the manuscript of *As Dark as It Gets*?"

"Yes."

The client gasped. "You have? When?"

"Last night."

"But—"

"I had to use the lavatory," she said, "and the book was there, although I could see it wasn't an ordinary bound book but pages in a box. I didn't think I would hurt it by looking at it. So I sat there and read the first two chapters."

"What did you think?" Haig asked her.

"It was very powerful. Parts of it were hard to follow, but the scenes were strong, and I got caught up in them."

"That's Woolrich," Jayne Corn-Wallace said. "He can grab you, all right."

"And then you took it with you when you went home," our client said. "You were so involved you couldn't bear to leave it unfinished, so you, uh, borrowed it." He reached to pat her hand. "Perfectly understandable," he said, "and perfectly innocent. You were going to bring it back once you'd finished it. So all this fuss has been over nothing."

"That's not what happened."

"It's not?"

"I read two chapters," she said, "and I thought I'd ask to borrow it some other time, or maybe not. But I put the pages back in the box and left them there."

"In the bathroom?"

"Yes."

"So you never did finish the book," our client said. "Well, if it ever turns up I'll be more than happy to lend it to you, but until then—"

"But perhaps Miss Botleigh has already finished the book," Haig suggested.

"How could she? She just told you she left it in the bathroom."

Haig said, "Miss Botleigh?"

"I finished the book," she said. "When everybody else went home, I stayed."

"My word," Zoltan Mihalyi said. "Woolrich never had a more devoted fan, or one half so beautiful."

"Not to finish the manuscript," she said, and turned to our host. "You asked me to stay," she said.

"I *wanted* you to stay," he agreed. "I wanted to *ask* you to stay. But I don't remember. . . ."

"I guess you'd had quite a bit to drink," she said, "although you didn't show it. But you asked me to stay, and I'd been hoping you would ask me, because I wanted to stay."

"You must have had rather a lot to drink yourself," Harriet Quinlan murmured.

"Not that much," said the caterer. "I wanted to stay because he's a very attractive man."

Our client positively glowed, then turned red with embarrassment. "I knew I had a hole in my memory," he said, "but I didn't think anything significant could have fallen through it. So you actually stayed? God. What, uh, happened?"

"We went upstairs," Jeanne Botleigh said. "And we went to the bedroom, and we went to bed."

"Indeed," said Haig. "And it was—"

"—quite wonderful," she said.

"And I don't remember. I think I'm going to kill myself."

"Not on Christmas Day," E. E. Stokes said. "And not with a mystery still unsolved. Haig, what became of the bloody manuscript?"

"Miss Botleigh?"

She looked at our host, then lowered her eyes. "You went to sleep afterward," she said, "and I felt entirely energized, and knew I couldn't sleep, and I thought I'd read for a while. And I remembered the manuscript, so I came down here and fetched it."

"And read it?"

"In bed. I thought you might wake up, in fact I was hoping you would. But you didn't."

"Damn it," our client said, with feeling.

"So I finished the manuscript and still didn't feel sleepy. And I got dressed and let myself out and went home."

There was a silence, broken at length by Zoltan Mihalyi, offering our client congratulations on his triumph and sympathy for the memory loss. "When you write your memoirs," he said, "you'll have to leave that chapter blank."

"Or have someone ghost it for you," Philip Perigord offered.

"The manuscript," Stokes said. "What became of it?"

"I don't know," the caterer said. "I finished it—"

"Which is more than Woolrich could say," Jayne Corn-Wallace said.

"—and I left it there."

"There?"

"In its box. On the bedside table, where you'd be sure to find it first thing in the morning. But I guess you didn't."

"The manuscript? Haig, you're telling me you want the *manuscript*?"

"You find my fee excessive?"

"But it wasn't even lost. No one took it. It was next to my bed. I'd have found it sooner or later."

"But you didn't," Haig said. "Not until you'd cost me and my young associate the better part of our holiday. You've been reading mysteries all your life. Now you got to see one solved in front of you, and in your own magnificent library."

He brightened. "It is a nice room, isn't it?"

"It's first-rate."

"Thanks. But, Haig, listen to reason. You did solve the puzzle and recover the manuscript, but now you're demanding what you recovered as compensation. That's like rescuing a kidnap victim and insisting on adopting the child yourself."

"Nonsense. It's nothing like that."

"All right, then it's like recovering stolen jewels and demanding the jewels themselves as reward. It's just plain disproportionate. I hired you because I wanted the manuscript in my collection, and now you expect to wind up with it in *your* collection."

It did sound a little weird to me, but I kept my mouth shut. Haig had the ball, and I wanted to see where he'd go with it.

He put his fingertips together. "In *Black Orchids*," he said, "Wolfe's client was his friend Lewis Hewitt. As recompense for his work, Wolfe insisted on all of the black orchid plants Hewitt had bred. Not one. All of them."

"That always seemed greedy to me."

"If we were speaking of fish," Haig went on, "I might be similarly inclined. But books are of use to me only as reading material. I want to *read* that book, sir, and I want to have it close to hand if I need to refer to it." He shrugged. "But I don't need the original that you prize so highly. Make me a copy."

"A copy?"

"Indeed. Have the manuscript photocopied."

"You'd be content with a . . . a copy?"

"And a credit," I said quickly, before Haig could give away the store. We'd put in a full day, and he ought to get more than a few hours' reading out of it. "A two-thousand-dollar store credit," I added, "which Mr. Haig can use up as he sees fit."

"Buying paperbacks and book-club editions," our client said, "it should last you for years." He heaved a sigh. "A photocopy and a store credit. Well, if that makes you happy . . ."

And that pretty much wrapped it up. I ran straight home and

sat down at the typewriter, and if the story seems a little hurried it's because I was in a rush when I wrote it. See, our client tried for a second date with Jeanne Botleigh, to refresh his memory, I suppose, but a woman tends to feel less than flattered when you forget having gone to bed with her, and she wasn't having any.

So I called her the minute I got home, and we talked about this and that, and we've got a date in an hour and a half. I'll tell you this much: if I get lucky, I'll remember. So wish me luck, huh?

And, by the way . . .

Merry Christmas!

Who's Afraid of Nero Wolfe?

by Loren D. Estleman

AUTHOR'S NOTE: *Nero Wolfe has been part of my life for as long as I can remember. My parents were avid readers, and there were always books and magazines scattered around the farmhouse where I grew up. For the four of us (including my brother), Rex Stout's stories became a family experience after my father lost his eyesight, was forced to give up truck driving, and began receiving books and magazines from the Library of Congress. We all gathered around to listen to Archie Goodwin's accounts of Wolfe's latest idiosyncrasies and feats of detection, just as families did in the Golden Age of Radio.*

Claudius Lyon is my affectionate tribute to the man behind those precious memories. Robert L. Fish's Schlock Homes stories inspired me to go for laughs; to that end, I eschewed murder to concentrate on wordplay, as Isaac Asimov often did in his Black Widowers series. The misapprehension that led to Lyon's first case in "Who's Afraid of Nero Wolfe?" was suggested by experience: as president of the Western Writers of America, I asked a colleague to read off a list of past winners of the organization's award for lifetime achievement . . . and I made the very same gaffe you'll read about in my story!

There were a hundred good reasons not to answer the "Help Wanted" notice in *The Habitual Handicapper*, and only one to answer it, but answer it I did, because I'd been canned for gambling on company time and I was on parole.

The text was brief:

> *Nimble-witted man needed for multitudinous duties. Salary commensurate with skill. Room and meals included. Apply at 700 Avenue J, Flatbush.*

700 Avenue J was a townhouse, one of those anonymous sandstone jobs standing in a row like widows at a singles club. It ran to three stories and a half-submerged basement, with glass partitions on the roof for a garden or something. A balding party in a cutaway coat someone had forgotten to return to the rental place answered the doorbell. "Who are you, I should ask?"

I took a header on the accent and replied in Yiddish: "Arnie Woodbine, nimble of wit." I held up the sheet folded to the advertisement.

"Mr. Lyon is in the plant rooms ten minutes more," he said, in Yiddish also. "In the office you can wait."

I followed him down a hall and through the door he opened, into a big room furnished as both office and parlor, with a big desk that looked as if it had been carved out of a solid slab of mahogany, rows of oak file cabinets, scattered armchairs, a big green sofa, and a huge globe in a cradle in one corner, plastered all over with countries that hadn't existed since they gassed all the pet rocks.

As I sat, in an orange leather chair that barely let my feet touch the floor, I came down with a dose of déjà vu. There was something familiar about the set-up, but it was as tough to pin down as a dream. Whatever it was, it put my freakometer in the red zone. I was set to fly the coop when something started humming, the walls shook, a paneled section slid open, and I got my first look at Claudius Lyon.

He was the best-tailored beach ball I'd ever met: five feet from top to bottom and side to side in a mauve three-piece with a green silk necktie and pocket square, soft cordovans on his tiny feet. His face was as round as a baby's, with no more sign of everyday wear-and-tear than a baby's had. He was carrying something in a clay pot. I was pretty sure it was a tomato plant.

On his way from the elevator, he reached up without pausing to straighten a picture that had been knocked crooked by the vibration in the shaft. So far, I didn't exist, but when he finished arranging the pot on the corner of his desk and with a little hop mounted the nearest thing I'd ever seen to a La-Z-Boy on a swivel, he fixed me with bright eyes and introduced himself. He didn't offer to shake hands.

When I told him my name, he grinned from ear to ear, a considerable expanse. "Indeed," he squeaked.

I didn't know why at the time, but I was dead sure I already had the job.

He asked about my work experience. I gave him an honest answer. I'm always honest about my dishonesty when I'm not actually practicing it. "I'm a good confidence man in the second class and a first-class forger. I've got diplomas from two institutions to prove it. I don't have them on me, but you can confirm it by calling my parole officer."

He dug a finger inside his left ear, a gesture I would get to know as a sign his brain was in overdrive. The faster and more industriously he dug, the more energy his gray cells were putting out.

When he finished, he offered me refreshment. "This is the time of day for my first cream soda."

I declined, not adding that there's no time of day when I'd ever consent to join him in one, or anyone else. He startled me then by turning his head and shouting, "Gus!" I'd assumed he'd tug on a bell rope or something. The balding gent in the rusty tailcoat entered a minute later, carrying a tray with a can on it and a Bamm-Bamm glass. He took the tray away empty and Lyons poured, drank, and belched discreetly into his green pocket square. He folded it and tucked it back in place.

"I admire candor, up to a point." With a show of fastidiousness, he twisted the pop top loose from the can, placed it inside his desk drawer, and pushed the drawer shut with his belly. "Yours falls just to the left of that. As it happens, a man who can sell another man a bill of goods would be valuable to this agency. I can also foresee a time when an aptitude with a pen would toe the mark."

"What agency's that?"

He lifted the place where eyebrows belonged. "Why, a detective agency, of course. What did you think the job was?"

The coin dropped into the pan; I knew what it was about the situation at 700 Avenue J, from the layout to the funny business with the pop top, that sent centipedes marching up my spine. Claudius Lyon clinched it with his next question.

"Are you familiar with the work of a writer named Rex Stout?"

■ ■ ■

That was three years ago. My debt to the State of New York is square, so thank God I don't have to keep convincing my P.O. that my association with a screwball like Lyon is legit.

The sticking point was my felon status, and the impossibility of ever qualifying for a license as a private investigator. Lyon hasn't one, either, lacking as he does the professional experience. He gets around it by not charging for his services.

It's no hardship, because he's as rich as the dame who writes the Harry Potter books. His old man had made certain improvements to the gasket that sealed the Cass-O-Matic pressure cooker, which is no longer in manufacture, but NASA has adapted the improvements to the space shuttle, and since the inventor is also no longer in circulation, the royalties come in to Lyon regular as the water bill.

I know what I'm talking about, because it's my job to deposit the checks in his account. I ordered a DEPOSIT ONLY stamp and charged it to household expenses, but I never use it. Lyon's signature is childlike, absurdly easy to duplicate on the endorsement, and I round the amount deposited to the nearest thousand and pocket the difference. It can be as little as a few bucks or as much as a couple of hundred, and if we ever decide to go our separate ways I can afford to coast for a year or so before I have to turn again to the "Help Wanted" section.

Claudius Lyon is obsessed with the writings of Rex Stout, or more particularly those of Archie Goodwin, who Stout represented as literary agent until Stout's death. Goodwin recorded the cases he'd helped solve for his employer, Nero Wolfe, a fat lethargic genius who grows orchids on the roof of his New York City brownstone, drinks beer by the bucket, eats tons of gourmet food prepared by Fritz, his Swiss chef and major domo, and makes expenses by unraveling complex mysteries put to him by desperate clients, many of them well-heeled. Wolfe rarely leaves home and pays Goodwin to perform as his leg man and general factotum.

To a fat little boy growing up in Brooklyn, Nero Wolfe was the nuts. Lyon loved to read mysteries, but he knew he'd never have the energy to emulate Sherlock Holmes, or the physique to withstand and deliver beatings à la Sam Spade and Philip Marlowe, or the good looks to seduce pertinent information out of swoony female suspects like the Saint. Wolfe's obesity and sedentary habits, however, suited Lyon right down to his wide bottom.

Some weeks before we met, Lyon had bought the townhouse, had it retrofitted to resemble Wolfe's sanctum, and changed his name legally to echo his hero's: Claudius, like Nero, was a lesser Roman emperor, and he felt he'd improved on the original by choosing a surname inspired by a predator more closely associated with the circuses of Rome. I haven't asked him what name he'd gone by before that. The bureaucrat who sends his checks had been wised up, he himself hasn't seen fit to volunteer anything, and while I firmly believe that the contents of another man's wallet might as well be mine, the secrets of his past are his own. To quote Lyon: "Discretion and integrity are not solely the province of the law-abiding."

I might not be working for him if Arnie Woodbine and Archie Goodwin didn't look like the same name if you squinted at it and took your eyes out of focus. He was especially pleased to learn that it's Arnie, not Arnold, on my birth certificate; Goodwin had not been born Archibald.

But maybe I doubt too much. The notice I'd read in the racing sheet had appeared for a week in the *New York Times*, *Daily News*, and the Brooklyn rags, and had brought only disappointment in the form of an army of errand boys whose wits were about as nimble as a lawn-roller, and one feminist who protested Lyon's insistence on hiring a man. (Gus told me the master of the house hid in the plant room until she was ejected.) I'm shorter than Goodwin, not in as good shape, and have a cauliflower ear courtesy of an early disgruntled mark that makes it more of a challenge for me to charm women; but at least I'm not a feminist, and my wit has been known to turn a respectable cartwheel from time to time.

I'm one of Lyon's lesser compromises. To begin with, he has no tolerance for adult beverages. Even the so-called non-alcoholic beers blur his judgment, and one bottle of Wolfe's brand of choice might send him skipping naked through Coney Island singing "Wind Beneath My Wings." He drinks the cream soda that's contributed in no small part to his lard, and keeps track of his consumption by counting the pop tops in his desk, just as Wolfe does his bottle caps.

His other substitutions are strictly personal prejudice:

1. Wolfe's favorite color is yellow; Lyon prefers green, and overdoes it. With all the red in the rare old office rug hand-woven by the Mandan tribe—which was wiped out by smallpox two minutes after the first European sneezed on it, hence the rarity—all those strong shades of green dotted about look like Christmas year-round;

2. Gus is no Fritz in the kitchen, although his repertoire of kosher recipes is prodigious;

3. The hardiest strain of orchid withers and turns black when it sees Lyon coming. Roses aren't much less difficult. By the time I came along, he'd begun cultivating tomatoes, which Gus tries his best to make work with gefilte fish.

Lyon's brown thumb has spared him the ordeal of replicating Theodore Horstmann, Wolfe's resident expert on orchids.

Tomatoes require no maintenance beyond watering, fertilizing, and spraying for bugs, and he spends most of his two hours in the morning and two hours in the afternoon on the roof watching *Martin Kane, Private Eye* on video. I've taken dozens of letters at his dictation urging all the networks to revive the series.

So with my introduction into the household, the metamorphosis was complete, if skewed a bit. You'd think he'd have been as happy as a Wisconsin nut in a Waldorf salad. Instead, he went into a tailspin that took all the manic out of his depression for weeks, and with sound reason—or at least as sound as his reason ever got.

No mystery.

He'd placed another advertisement in all the regulars and *The Habitual Handicapper*:

> *Vexed? Stymied? Up a tree? Consult Claudius Lyon, the world's greatest amateur detective. No fees charged. Your satisfaction is my reward. Apply in person at 700 Avenue J, Flatbush.*

The notice ran for weeks, during which time Jimmy Hoffa could have camped out on the stoop with no risk of discovery by a visitor. At Lyon's prodding, I made several trips outside to push the doorbell to make sure it was working. It rang with a kind of *ha*-ha the little fatty couldn't have appreciated very much.

"Try taking out the 'amateur,'" I suggested. "People think if you don't charge anything, that's all your services are worth."

"I'm unlicensed."

"I didn't say send them a bill. Just don't say you don't in the ad."

"The phrase 'the world's greatest detective' would violate the truth-in-advertising laws. Nero Wolfe is still practicing, and he is demonstrably the world's finest in his profession."

"Who's afraid of Nero Wolfe?" I sang.

"I am. When he learns I've counterfeited his life and livelihood, I fully expect a visit from Nathaniel Parker, his attorney. Since I do not claim to *be* Nero Wolfe, I cannot be accused of theft of identity, and because I accept no emolument for my efforts on behalf of my clients, I am not guilty of fraud. So long as I stay within the law, I'm a flea bite on Wolfe's thick hide, nothing more. To stray over the line would bring doom upon this roof." He slumped in his oversize chair, looking like Humpty Dumpty at the base of the wall.

I let him sulk, opened the laptop on my desk, and pecked out this gem:

> *Mystified? Claudius Lyon never is. See for yourself. No fees charged where satisfaction is not met. Apply, etc.*

I showed him the printout. I hadn't seen him smile like that since I'd told him my name. Remember, I'm a first-class second-class con man; although I had to strangle my basic instincts to dupe people into thinking it might cost them when it wouldn't. It's a Bizarro world, that billet. I e-mailed the text to all the sheets, then opened the dictionary program Lyon had installed and decided *emolument* is a good word.

That was Thursday. On Friday, we had our first client.

Raymond Nurls's percentage of body fat wouldn't have fried a lox in Gus's skillet. In his three-button black suit, he made a dividing line in the center of the guest chair, which was another of those areas where Lyon's attempt to clone Nero Wolfe's life had gone south. He'd hired a colorblind upholsterer, who covered it in orange. It clashed with the scarlet in the Mandan rug like our two cultures.

Nurls was halfway through his twenties but well on his way toward crabby old age, with hair mowed to the edge of baldness and a silver chain clipped to the legs of his glasses. He steepled his hands when he spoke.

"I assumed from your advertisement you're either a detective or a magician. Which is it?"

Lyon tried to lower his lids, but he was too jazzed by the prospect of work to keep them from flapping back up like cheap window shades. "I don't pull rabbits out of hats, but I can tell you how it's done."

I leaned out from my word processor, where I was taking notes. "That means he's a detective."

"Very good. I'm the executive director of the American Poetical Association. Perhaps you've heard of it."

But unless it advertised in his complete run of Doubleday Crime Club editions, Lyon hadn't, so Nurls filled us in. The A.P.A. was an organization devoted to art patronage, specifically for poets who'd missed the memo that the road to starvation begins with the purchase of one's first rhyming dictionary. Its purpose was to mooch money from people who'd run out of places to store it and provide grants to support promising talent until their work was ready for publication. To me, it seemed cruel to jolly them along only to cut them loose just when their unsold copies were on the way back to the pulp mill, but then my mind wandered after the part about separating the rich from their wealth, so I may have missed some of the fine points. I dislike competition.

Once a year, the association threw a dinner in a hotel in Canarsie, where the winner of the coveted Van Dusen Prize for Outstanding Poetry received a plaque and a check for ten thousand dollars. I imagine that mollified some landlord. Certainly it reawakened my interest.

At this point, Lyon swooped in for the kill. "Which was stolen, the plaque or the check?"

"Neither."

Lyon yelled for cream soda.

"I'm new to the Association," said Nurls, when Gus left with his empty tray. "I replaced the executive director who'd been with the A.P.A. since the beginning, who retired rather suddenly to Arizona on the advice of his cardiologist. My first duty is to plan this year's dinner, which will commemorate the twenty-fifth anniversary of our founding. Naturally I spent a great deal of time on the phone with my predecessor, gathering historical details to include in the program: names of charter members, events of note, etc. Naturally a complete list of past winners of the Van Dusen Prize was essential."

"Naturally," Lyon and I said simultaneously. He scowled at me, and I returned my attention to my screen.

Walter Van Dusen, we learned, was a loaded industrialist jonesing for culture, who upon his death had left an endowment that made the cash incentive possible. Before that, the winners had taken home a plaque only, presumably to boil the sap from to make soup.

"When I came aboard," Nurls went on, "the records situation was rustic, to put it charitably. The old fellow had taken them with him, for reasons of his own; I picture a shabby notebook in his personal shorthand. I rang him up in Phoenix, and he read off the winners' names and contact information where it existed. I thought it would be a grand gesture to invite as many of them as were available to attend the dinner as guests of the Association."

He related the tragic circumstances: of twenty-four former

winning poets, eleven could not be located, six had died from natural causes, three had committed suicide, and two weren't interested; one, over the phone, had been emphatic on the subject to the point of questioning the details of Raymond Nurls's ancestry. Of the pair remaining, one was too elderly to make the trip. The last was willing, but required mileage and accommodations. These the executive director agreed to provide, since the budget was flush.

"I'm concerned chiefly with one of the names on the list," Nurls said. "A gentleman named Noah Ward."

"Dead, disgruntled, or unlocatable?" Lyon asked.

"The last. So far, I've been unable to learn anything about him. I Googled the name, and was able to narrow the list to three who have any connection with literary endeavor, but one is far too young—he'd have been in junior high the year Ward was honored, and our prize committee is not disposed to recognize precociousness—another, the editor of the book review page of a Baltimore literary journal, assured me he'd never written poetry and didn't review it because, quote, 'I wouldn't know a grand epic from subway doggerel,' unquote. The third, a self-published suspense writer, thought the A.P.A. had something to do with the Humane Society." He adjusted his glasses.

Lyon shifted his weight, evidently in sympathetic discomfort with this last piece of intelligence. Actually he was trying to burst a bubble in his gut, which he did, with spectacular results. In a belching contest, I'd put every cent I've embezzled from him on his nose. "Why this obsession with one name on the list?"

"Because Ward is the only one on it I've been unable to confirm ever existed."

"Ah."

Encouraged, the executive director steepled his hands

higher. “Nary a birth certificate nor a Social Security number nor a school transcript nor an arrest record nor so much as a ticket for overtime parking. Really, Mr. Lyons—”

“Lyon. I am singular, not plural.”

“I stand corrected. It’s next to impossible, not to say impossible, to exist in today’s world without leaving a footprint of some kind on the Internet. Therefore, I propose that Noah Ward is a chimera.”

“And this is significant because—?”

“You’re a detective. Figure it out. Whoever claimed that ten-thousand-dollar prize under a fictitious name is guilty of grand fraud.”

“I assume you’ve ruled out the likelihood of a pseudonym.”

“At once. The rules of the American Poetical Association expressly state that all work must be submitted under the contestant’s legal name. That provision was adopted to prevent anyone from submitting more than one work for consideration. A long lead time was established between the deadline for entry and the announcement of the winner to investigate the identities of all the contributors.”

“Your predecessor could not enlighten you on the details?”

Nurls jammed his glasses farther into his head. “He perished last week, in a fire that consumed his condominium, himself, and any records that might have furnished additional information. The disaster was entirely accidental,” he added, when Lyon’s eyes brightened. “The arson investigators traced it to a faulty electrical circuit.”

Lyon pouted. “Unfortunate and tragic. I assume you polled the membership for reminiscences? The committee responsible for the honor springs to mind.”

“Our membership rolls run toward an older demographic. Everyone who might have shed light upon the selection has passed. The only member I managed to reach who was present at that dinner is unreliable." He touched his left temple.

"Dear me. All the powers appear to be aligned against you. Is it your intention to bring legal action for the recovery of the ten thousand dollars?"

"It is. The Association has empowered me, upon filing formal charges, to remit fifteen percent to the party who identifies and exposes the guilty person. Expenses added, of course." Nurls sat back a tenth of an inch, folding his hands on his spare middle.

Lyon finished his cream soda in one long draught, this time patted back the burp, and replaced his pocket square with all the ceremony of a color guard folding the flag. "I accept the challenge, Mr. Nurls. We'll discuss payment upon success or an admission of failure. In the latter event, I will accept no remuneration."

I had to hand it to the little balloon. He'd managed to appear professional and hold off the wrath of the State of New York in one elegant speech. I knew him then for a liar when he said he couldn't pull a rabbit out of a hat. But the bean counter in the ugly orange chair wouldn't have taken the Holy Annunciation at face value if Gabriel had blown sixteen bars in his ear. He'd have asked for references, and followed up on them on Yahoo.

"How do I know you can deliver? Forgive me, but all I have to go on is three lines in the *Times*."

Lyon looked at the clock. "It's nearly lunchtime. Blood soup, with a stock combined of livers and gizzards; free-range goose, of course. Cheese blintzes for dessert and an acceptable Manischewitz from my cellar. Once you've sampled the fare of my table, you'll be in a better position to judge my success in this profession. Will you join us?"

Nurls declined, looking a shade green around the collar, but he was hooked. Me, too, from then on. A first-rate second-rate grifter knows a champ when he sees one.

"Phooey!"

Wolfe says, "Pfui," but his disciple can't pronounce the labial without spraying.

He was responding to my suggestion to access the Library of Congress web site for poetical compositions copyrighted under the name Noah Ward.

"It's futile to attempt to prove a man does not exist. It expends energy the way trying to add light to dark wastes paint, with no appreciable effect. We'll assume as a hypothesis that Nurls is right and Ward is a phantasm."

"How'd you know that about paint?" I asked.

"I investigated the phenomenon of temporary employment the summer I turned fifteen. A less than august August." He dismissed the subject with a wave of his little finger. "If a check was issued to Noah Ward, someone had to cash it. The transaction took place too far in the past for any bank to retain a record of it, even if we found the bank and its personnel were willing to cooperate. March down to the police station and inquire whether anyone using that name or something similar has ever been arrested for bunko steering."

"These days they just call it fraud."

"Indeed? Colorless. A pity."

"Ever's a long way to comb back, even if I could get them to do it."

"Concentrate on the past seven years. I assume that's still the statute of limitations for most crimes. A man who draws water once may be expected to return to the well the next time he thirsts. Perhaps he wasn't so successful the second time."

"What if the well isn't in Brooklyn?"

"Start here. Unless and until he has the money in hand, a poet is unlikely to come by the travel expenses necessary to collect. My 'Ode on a Lycopersicon Esculentum' paid only in copies of the *Herbivoron*."

Before taking my leave, I looked up all three unfamiliar words, identifying the Latin preferred name of the common tomato and the semi-monthly newsletter issued by the Garden Fruit Council of New Jersey.

I have cop friends. I've been down there often enough to strike up acquaintances and I have a good line of gab, which they like almost as much as Krispy Kreme and are apt to disregard a little thing like a non-violent rap sheet in order to enjoy. I cast my line and caught a big fish, although I didn't know it at the time and would have thrown it back if I had.

It was Friday night. For religious reasons, Gus couldn't clock in again until after sundown Saturday and—unlike his hero—Lyon is capable of burning a salad, so I fixed him two boxes of mac and cheese in the microwave and made myself a BLT. I can keep kosher as well as the next guy, but every so often I get a craving for swine and shellfish that has to be addressed.

We were just finishing up when the doorbell rang. It rang again before we remembered Gus couldn't answer it. By the time I got to the door, our visitor had abandoned ringing for banging. I used the peephole and hustled back to the dining room.

"It's cops," I said. "Actually only one, but what he lacks in number he makes up for in mean."

Lyon glared up at me from his tilted bowl. I shook my head innocently. I hadn't tried to sell anyone an autographed *Portable Chaucer* in six months.

I brought Captain Stoddard into the office, where Lyon was just clambering onto his perch behind the desk. I was halfway through introductions when our visitor brought his fist down on the leather top. "Where do you get off sending this cheap crook to my precinct? I put every officer who gave him the time of day on report."

"Please have a seat, sir. I have spinal issues that make it agony to tilt my head back more than three degrees." His tone wobbled a little. He seemed to have authority issues as well, but I gave him points for the show of spunk.

Stoddard did, too, maybe, or maybe he'd been on report himself too many times that fiscal period for pushing around citizens. Anyway, he sat.

Physically, he's the opposite of Nero Wolfe's nemesis in NYPD Homicide. Inspector Cramer is beefy where Captain Stoddard is gaunt, and the captain's a few more years away from mandatory retirement, but he filled the orange chair with nastiness the way Cramer fills the famous red one with buttock. Stoddard commands the local precinct. I was trying out the straight-and-narrow as much to avoid another interrogation by him as to stay out of jail.

"Woodbine left your name," he told Lyon. "So far, I can't find a record under it, but if you're partnered up with this little goldbrick artist I'll start one for you personally. What kind of scam you got going that involves turning the Brooklyn Police Department into an information service?"

"I pay taxes, Mr. Stoddard. If you look up my name outside your rogues' gallery, you may be able to calculate how much. But even the poorest resident of this country has the right to consult the police when he suspects a law has been broken."

He gulped, but he got it out. It was a good speech, too. The proof was in the way the man he spoke it to didn't haul him out of his chair and slam-dunk him into his own recycling bin. Instead, his nails dug little semicircles in the pumpkin-colored leather.

"I monitor all the computers in the precinct," he growled. "Some cops think that, when I step out, they can fool around in the files and get away with it. They always fold when I jump them. Who's this bird Ward?"

Spunk has its limits. Lyon looked to me for support, but I was scareder than he was, with experience to justify it. He took a couple of deep breaths to prevent hyperventilating and told Stoddard everything Raymond Nurls had told us. He'd barely finished when the captain sprang to his feet with an Anglo-Saxon outburst that knocked out of line the picture on the wall next to the elevator shaft. I'd thought only the elevator could do that.

"A puzzle!" he roared. "My precinct has murders to investigate, rapes, child abuse, armed robbery, each of which requires three weeks minimum to make an arrest and a case to make it stick, not counting petty little interruptions like burglary, purse-snatching, and assault, and you take up twenty minutes of that time playing Scrabble."

"You're being metaphorical, of course," Lyon put in. "Fraud is not a parlor game."

The fist came down, jumping a pen out of its little onyx skull. Lyon jumped too and looked ill. "A cheesy award given out by a bunch of nances for the best poem about a lark. No!" Fist. The pen rolled to the edge of Lyon's blotter.

The little butterball surprised me. Ever since Stoddard had leapt up, he'd been doing his best to shrink himself inside his folds of suet, like an armadillo gathering itself into a ball. Now his eyes opened wide and he straightened himself in his chair, tilting his head two degrees past agony to meet the glare of his tormentor. "Would you repeat what you just said?"

Stoddard wound back the tape a little too far, back to the unbroadcastable word that had brought him out of his chair.

"After that," Lyon said. His tone was as steady as the tide. "After I questioned your choice of the word *Scrabble*."

"An award! A cheesy award!" The captain shouted into his face, flecks of spittle spattering him from his hairline to the knot of his green silk tie. "Are you deaf, too? I *know* you're dumb!"

"Thank you, Mr. Stoddard. You are a synaptic savant."

That silenced him. It silenced me, too, until I looked up both words on the dictionary program. He straightened, looking around.

"Where's your investigator's license? You're supposed to display it prominently."

"I haven't one."

Stoddard's bony face twisted to make room for a horse-toothed grin. It wasn't nice. He isn't a nice man, or even a good one. He lowered his tone to conversational level; he might have been bidding four no trump. "Do you know the penalty in this state for conducting professional investigations without a license?"

"I've never had cause to look it up. A professional would be well advised to do so, but I don't charge for my services. My amateur standing remains intact."

The horse teeth receded. Stoddard's BB eyes darted left, then right. That put me inside range. "What about Woodbine? Don't tell me he works for you for free. He'd walk to Albany and back for a dirty dollar."

"I employ Mr. Woodbine to obtain the information I require to pursue my avocation."

"That's investigation. You need a license to earn a salary."

"Tish-tush." I gave Lyon double points for that: thumbing his nose at the NYPD while employing a phrase alien to his inspiration. At his insistence, I'd made a sizeable dent in his Rex Stout library, and had not once come across it. Somewhere in that roly-poly wad of derivative flapdoodle was an authentic original waiting to be recognized, as well as a tough little nut. "When a personal assistant is asked to pick up the telephone and inquire when a bank closes, is he conducting an illegal investigation or running an errand? Is it your desire to give up your day off to answer that question at a public hearing?"

I never found out if Stoddard had an answer for that. He opened his mouth, presumably to let out a four-letter opinion of the question that had been put to him, but he closed it. Lyon's eyes were shut tight, and he was foraging inside his left ear with the energy of an anteater.

Nero Wolfe never sums up a case without an audience. It can be a handful or a horde, but it rarely gathers outside his personal throne room, where the Great Detective holds forth from behind the massive desk on West 35th Street, New York, New York. Claudius Lyon would have it no other way, even if the venue was his office of many compromises in Brooklyn, and his spectators reduced to four.

Stoddard was present, eager to make his case to prosecute Lyon and me for playing detective without saying Simon Says, as well as fraud, and of course Raymond Nurls was invited. My seat, turned from my desk, was a perk of the job, but I couldn't see any reason why Gus was there, except to fill one more seat in a show that needed a solid third act if it weren't to be left to die on the road. It had taken all of Lyon's powers of persuasion to convince the cook that he wouldn't burn in hell for sitting in on the Sabbath. Just to make sure, Gus sat in the green chair nearest the door, where he could escape if anyone asked him to turn on a light or something. Nurls's thin frame bisected another green chair, and Stoddard deposited his hundred and seventy pounds of pure hostility in the orange.

Lyon entered last, straightened the picture on the wall, scowled at the pea-size green tomato growing at the end of the vine in the pot on his desk, and scaled to his seat. "Thank you all for coming. Does anyone object to Mr. Woodbine taking notes?"

Nurls shook his head, the silver chain swaying on his glasses. Stoddard scooped a small portable cassette recorder out of his pocket and balanced it on his knee. "Just in case he misses something culpable," he said.

Lyon shrugged and cracked open the can I'd placed on the desk. He took a slug and began.

"Mr. Nurls. When was the Van Dusen Prize first presented?"

"Fifteen years ago this fall. It went to—"

"The American Poetical Association was then ten years old?"

"Yes. I don't see what this has to do with Noah Ward. He wasn't honored until years later."

"I will establish relevance presently. I suppose it goes without saying that, before the existence of the ten-thousand-dollar honorarium, the encomium was not referred to as a prize."

"It does, and yet you said it. A prize without a prize is hardly a prize."

"Poetically put. How, then, was it referred to?"

"It was called the Golden Muse Award. The plaque still contains an etching in gold of Calliope and Erato, the—"

"Thank you. During our first conversation, you said the man you replaced as executive director had held that position since the A.P.A. was founded, is that correct?"

"Yes. Really, Mr. Lyon—"

This time Stoddard interrupted. "I'm with Poindexter. Connect this to a scam artist who conned the sissies out of a bundle."

"I beg your pardon, sir. That is not my intention."

Even Gus took his eyes off his escape route to stare at Lyon. Stoddard and Nurls started talking at once. I gave up trying to get it all down.

A pudgy palm came up for silence; the owner broke it himself when his voice squeaked. "I have been engaged to untangle the mystery that surrounds the elusive Noah Ward. I shall now proceed to do so. Mr. Nurls, when you spoke with your predecessor on the telephone, did he call the Van Dusen Prize by that name?"

Nurls started to speak, then adjusted his glasses and started again. "No. As a matter of fact, he just called it 'the award.' I assume he did so out of habit."

"Not unusual for one long familiar with the original. How did he read off the names of past winners?"

"What do you mean?"

"Did he say, 'The Golden Muse Award in 1988 went to Joe Doakes, the Golden Muse Award in 1989 went to Jane Doe,' and so on and so forth?"

"Certainly not. The conversation would have been interminable. He provided the year and the name in each instance, and I wrote them down."

Lyon drank, burped, wiped. "One of my abandoned interests is the history of the Pulitzer Prize for Literature. I gave up the study when it became clear that the board at Columbia University would never honor Rex Stout, or more appropriately Archie Goodwin, for his many contributions to American letters. I do recall that in 1940, when the director of the board objected to the others' choice of Ernest Hemingway's *For Whom the Bell Tolls*, it was decided that no prize would be issued that year. Are you aware if this ever happened in regard to the Van Dusen Prize or the Golden Muse?"

"It never did. The former executive director read off twenty-four years and twenty-four names. This year's winner has not yet been determined."

"I submit that it happened, and that he told you as much when he used the phrase you misunderstood for a man's name. The three syllables you interpreted as 'Noah Ward,' had they been spelled out, would in fact read—"

"No award." Nurls slumped in his seat. I hadn't thought his spine had that much play in it.

Stoddard shot to his feet. His tape recorder slid off his knee to the floor. "You took up my precinct's time and mine over a dumb-ass pun?"

"A homonym, to be precise. A hazard of oral communication."

"You and Woodbine are both under arrest for obstruction of justice."

Lyon's moon face was gray as cardboard, but he held his ground. "Don't be absurd, Mr. Stoddard. I've prevented Mr. Nurls from obstructing justice unwittingly by filing a nuisance complaint. If there never was a Noah Ward, no fraud was perpetrated, and the A.P.A. simply reinvested the money that would have been awarded, assuring the continued existence of the Van Dusen Prize. I have you to thank for a signal accomplishment on my part."

"Don't drag me into it, you little blimp."

"No dragging is necessary, sir. Earlier today in this very room, you referred to the Van Dusen as an award, not a prize, and employed an emphatic 'No!' to indicate your rejection of the importance of the affair to the police. You may have noticed that at that point I entered into a reverie."

"You stuck your finger in your ear."

"I find the action stimulates the cortex. Granted you hadn't a notion you were supplying a catalyst for the chemistry of my cognitive function, but that in no way diminishes your role in the outcome. I congratulate you."

"Bull. Since when is wordplay a signal accomplishment?"

"I must thank you again, for putting the question. In spite of the laws of physics, I have managed to change a tint of paint by adding a small amount of light to dark. In spite of Aristotle's philosophy, I have proven that someone never existed."

Nurls produced a checkbook, scribbled, and got up to place the check on Claudius Lyon's desk. "Two thousand, including a bonus for a job well done. You *are* a magician."

Captain Stoddard hovered. I wouldn't say he drooled, but he was ready to pounce the second Lyon touched the check.

The man behind the desk never looked at it. "Arnie, will you do the honors?"

I said I'd be pleased as punch. Nurls watched, astonished, Stoddard boiling, as I tore the check sideways, lengthwise, and crosswise, and dropped the pieces into the wastebasket by my desk.

Stoddard slammed the door behind him, knocking crooked the picture on the wall. Lyon said good-bye to our client, rose, and straightened it on his way to the elevator.

Julius Katz and the Case of Exploding Wine

by Dave Zeltserman

AUTHOR'S NOTE: It should be obvious from his name that my Julius Katz stories are a tribute to Nero Wolfe. Or to Rex Stout. To be honest, I'm not exactly sure which it is. Like Wolfe, my fictional PI is brilliant and able to solve cases that flummox the police. Also like Wolfe, Julius is rather lazy and would rather spend his time engaging in leisure activities than working, but the bills must be paid! And, also like Wolfe, he has an erstwhile assistant named Archie who will pester him to no end to take a case when his bank account reaches an anemic level. But there are some significant differences between Wolfe and Julius. Julius is in his forties, athletic, holds a fifth-degree black belt in Hung Gar kung fu, is a womanizer (or at least he was before he met Lily Rosten in the first story in the series), and is an expert gambler, with his game of choice being poker. While he might drink a beer occasionally, he collects wines—which I personally know nothing about (like Wolfe, I'm a beer drinker), but having Julius collect expensive wine provides additional motivation for him to take a case.

My Archie, though, is very different than Archie Goodwin. Though he narrates these stories (as Goodwin did with the Nero Wolfe tales) and has the heart and soul of a hard-boiled PI, he's not flesh and blood. Instead he's a whiz-bang piece of technology that Julius wears as a tie clip and is twenty years more advanced than anything thought possible outside of the lab that created him. Still, he's very human in his own way, and it's his relationship with Julius that drives these stories.

At one thirty-three in the afternoon, Julius had a highly rated Argentinian Malbec decanting that was supposed to have rich cherry and plum flavors with hints of cocoa and black pepper while he hand cut paper-thin slices of Prosciutto Toscano with the skill of a master *charcutier*. As he did this, I tried to use my time productively by identifying the mysterious fifth murder suspect, but found that I was too peeved to do so. Or maybe I was too miffed. Or too injured. It was such a new experience I wasn't sure which it was, or understood the nuances that differentiated between feeling miffed or peeved or deeply insulted. All I knew was that I felt as if a thick, almost suffocating heat had built up inside my central processing unit, which kept me from being able to focus on any sort of work.

Let me explain by going back ninety-two days. That was when Julius accepted a retainer from Allen Luther, the dog-food king. When Luther called to make the appointment, he insisted on bringing along with him his prizewinning English bulldog Brutus. As far as I knew, a dog had never before entered Julius's Beacon Hill townhouse, let alone his office, but I told Luther to go ahead and bring the animal. First, Luther was promising a twenty-thousand-dollar retainer for a possible investigation that might never happen. Second, Luther and Julius were on friendly terms. They were both members of the Belvedere Club, and had sat at the same table together for at least three wine dinners that I knew of, where they discussed wine, cognac, and Boston's fine dining. Third, Brutus was more than just a prize-winning bulldog—he had won Best in Show at the prestigious Kensington Kennel Club three years running, making him possibly the world's most famous dog. And fourth, Julius had fallen into a rut since collecting two hundred grand from Pritchard of London, who paid Julius the fee for saving them millions on what turned out to be an insurance scam. I figured he needed some shaking up, so I scheduled the appointment with the world-famous bulldog in tow and conveniently forgot to tell Julius about it. It wasn't until Allen Luther rang the bell at the scheduled time that I informed Julius about the appointment.

"He called three days ago while you were engaged in your daily two-hour kung fu workout," I said. "I apologize for not telling you earlier. It must've slipped my mind. But since Luther is willing to pay you twenty thousand dollars to do nothing, and you've gotten so adept at doing exactly that since Pritchard of London paid you the fee they owed, I figured you wouldn't mind."

While the world knows me as Julius's assistant, unofficial biographer, and all-around man Friday, I'm a little different than how most people picture me. If you haven't figured it out yet, I'm not exactly human. What I am is a two-inch rectangular piece of highly advanced computer technology that Julius wears as a tiepin. But that's not how I imagine myself. When I do picture myself, it's as a stocky man in his thirties with thinning brown hair and a tough bulldog countenance, and that image is probably due to Dashiell Hammett's Continental Op works, which were among the books used to program my knowledge base. At that moment, when I checked the outdoor webcam and saw what Luther was carrying, the image that flashed vividly in my neuron network was of myself as that heavyset man grinning as widely as any jack-o'-lantern.

I told Julius in a deadpan voice, "You might like to know that Luther has brought with him a bottle of 1996 Château La Mondotte Saint-Emilion."

That mix of Merlot and Cabernet went for over six hundred bucks a bottle, and I knew Julius coveted it. Although Julius liked Luther enough to discuss fine wines and cognacs, and liked even more the idea of earning twenty grand for doing nothing, if it wasn't for that wine he might very well have had me cancel the appointment, simply to teach me a lesson. But because of the Château La Mondotte Saint-Emilion, Julius conceded to ask, with his annoyance mostly in check, "What's this about?"

"I don't know. Only that there's a twenty-grand retainer involved for a job you might never have to do."

There was only a slight hesitation before Julius pushed himself out of his chair and left his office so he could answer the door. Luther, on seeing the way Julius eyed Brutus and being no fool himself, handed Julius the six-hundred-dollar bottle of wine before Julius could utter a word.

"The last time we talked, you mentioned you've been wanting to try this vintage," Luther said gruffly.

Allen Luther at sixty-three was a large man, both in height and girth. According to his driver's license, he was six foot three and two hundred and eighty pounds, although I judged his weight at closer to three hundred and twenty. Not only was he the undisputed dog-food king, but, with a massive sheepskin coat draped around him and his large round head fringed with short red hair and the bottom half of his face covered with a carefully cropped red beard, he had an air of nobility that made me think of someone who could've been an English king in the eighteenth century.

I knew Julius was expecting the two hundred grand Pritchard of London had paid him to allow him to live idly for another six months, even given his expensive tastes—which had gotten more expensive since he met Lily—but under the circumstances he had little choice but to lead the way to his office while Allen Luther and Brutus plodded along behind him. I haven't mentioned anything about Brutus yet, and I don't know what to say other than he had a squat muscular body with brown-and-white fur and a thick jowly face. What it was that made him Best in Show three years running, I had no clue, but then again the only dog breed I'd ever researched was greyhounds, and that was only to build a race-simulation model that could beat Julius at the track, which I had failed at.

Luther took the chair across from Julius, while Brutus plopped down on the floor next to his owner. After declining Julius's offer of refreshments, Luther got down to business. "I have two items I need to discuss with you," he said, grim-faced. "The first involves Brutus." Luther's lips momentarily compressed into a harsh, bloodless line. Then he continued, saying, "Since Brutus's third win at Kensington, I've been besieged with offers for him, some of which have bordered on outright threats of stealing him if I don't agree to sell him. The nerve of these bastards! I need to make sure Brutus isn't dognapped."

"I'm sorry, Allen, but that's not the kind of work I'm willing to take on."

"I know it isn't." Luther brusquely waved off Julius's comment, his face folding into a frown that would've made the bulldog proud. "But I'm hoping you can refer me to someone who's capable of handling the job. I'll be damned if I'm going to sit back and let someone steal him!"

"I can give you the name of a private investigator who's done work for me," Julius said. "Your second item?"

Allen Luther cleared his throat. A glint showed in his eyes as he met Julius's gaze. "If someone murders me, I want you to catch the bastard," he said in a voice that was surprisingly clear given how raspy he had just sounded.

Julius arched an eyebrow. "Are you expecting to be murdered?"

"I hope not. But there have been a couple of troublesome incidents." Luther shook his head, scowling. "Four days ago, someone almost ran me down while I was crossing the street. It was a near miracle that I scooped up Brutus and dove out of the way." He lowered his gaze and bit down on his thumbnail as he replayed the incident in his head. "It could've just been a careless Boston driver," he said. "Some nitwit texting and not watching the road. But my gut is telling me that the driver intentionally aimed at me, or possibly even Brutus. And you don't build the dog-food empire I've built without trusting your gut."

Luther grew silent after that. Julius sat patiently waiting for the dog-food king to continue talking, and he didn't have to wait long. Eighteen point four seconds later, Luther's round, heavy face began to blush red with either anger or embarrassment, I wasn't sure which. "I should've seen who was driving, or at least noticed what type of car it was," he said. "But it was dark, and it all happened so fast that I can't tell you anything about the car or the driver."

"Any witnesses?"

"None. And don't bother asking about video surveillance cameras. I asked my security chief to look into that, and there were none in the area." Once again, Luther lowered his gaze from

Julius's, his jowls sagging as much as Brutus's. "If that was the only incident, I would've chalked it up to bad luck, but it wasn't. Three weeks ago, I was dining at Bellemonds when I detected a whiff of bitter almond from a glass of thirty-year Talisker that was brought to me. At least, I'm fairly certain I did."

"Cyanide," Julius said.

Luther nodded, his scowl deepening. "I wish I'd had the presence of mind to have saved the scotch so I could've had it analyzed. But I didn't. Instead, I sent it back." His voice lowered into a raspy growl as he added, "I hope no one in the kitchen drank it. At least if there really *was* cyanide in it."

I did some quick hacking and checked the local hospitals for any reported cyanide poisonings from three weeks ago, and there weren't any. If someone had tried slipping Luther a mickey, the drink most likely ended up poured down the sink, although it could've been drunk by a member of Bellemonds's kitchen staff with the individual either holed up sick afterwards, or dying without an autopsy revealing the cause. I told Julius this. Since I communicate to Julius through an earpiece he wears, Luther was none the wiser.

"Thomas Pike has been dead for fifteen years," Julius said, "but Andrew Nevin is still alive. Anyone else you know of who might want you dead?"

It always surprises me what Julius comes up with, and, from Allen Luther's reaction, this surprised him also.

"You know about Pike and Nevin, huh?" he said. "I didn't ask Pike to embezzle from me. I don't care what his reasons were, I had every right to have him arrested, and it's not my fault he committed suicide!"

Luther's outburst caused Brutus to lift his head. The dog-food king noticed this and continued, his voice lowering to a softer growl: "With Nevin, it was only business. I won and he lost. Too bad if he has hurt feelings about it. As far as anyone else out there, I don't know. This dog-food business can be a dog-eat-dog world. You make enemies you never even know about." He paused for a moment before adding, "Maybe my son-in-law. Forget I said that."

Julius leaned farther back in his chair, his fingers interlaced as he rested his hands on his stomach. Sighing, he said, "Your money would be better spent keeping you alive. My advice is that you hire security personnel to protect you. If you insist on hiring me as well, I recommend that I instead look into whether there's a real threat against you, and, if there is, who's behind it."

From the way Luther's face darkened right then with anger, I understood perfectly why Julius had sighed only seconds earlier. He already knew what the dog-food king's response was going to be.

"The hell with that! I'm not having bodyguards following me around and getting in my way. Whoever this bastard is, he might end up killing me, but he's not going to make me live in fear. But I want to make damn sure that, if he does kill me, he pays for it!"

Julius tried halfheartedly to change Luther's mind, but he must've known from the start it was a losing fight. As far as Allen Luther was concerned, he wasn't going to cower for anyone. Besides, it would be a waste of time and money for Julius to look into this, since no evidence was left behind. He was probably right. If someone three weeks ago had slipped a mickey into his drink, it was doubtful Julius would get anywhere trying to identify the person. In the end, Julius accepted the twenty-thousand-dollar retainer with the agreement that, if Luther died in any sort of suspicious manner, Julius would investigate his death, and, if he uncovered the murderer, Luther's estate would pay Julius a hundred grand. The only concession Julius was able to get from Luther was to allow the police one week to solve his hypothetical murder themselves, assuming that it was a homicide. The reason Julius gave for this was so he wouldn't unreasonably interfere with the police. Of course that was pure poppycock. Julius had never been bothered about that in the past. I knew his real reason for insisting on this condition was laziness. As I mentioned before, the fee Pritchard of London had paid him got him used to the idea of not doing any work for six more months, and he'd just as soon make twenty grand doing nothing as have to turn his brain back on for *any* additional sum of money, even a hundred grand.

That's what happened ninety-two days ago. Thanks to Julius's recommendation, Allen Luther ended up hiring Willie Cather full-time to track down threats against his prizewinning bulldog, which was a task that Willie was more than capable of. Willie's a smart guy. Not as smart as he thinks he is, but still, a smart guy, and whenever Julius needs an investigator to do some legwork for him he'll usually hire Willie if Tom Durkin and Saul Penzer aren't available. While it seemed crazy to me that Luther was willing to spend money to protect his bulldog and not himself, it also seemed doubtful that anyone was actually trying to kill him. Slipping cyanide into a drink? Trying to run him down in the street? I didn't buy it. Given the limited data I had, I put the odds at roughly 0.04 percent that he was in danger.

It turned out my algorithm wasn't as good as I thought it was, because, seven days and three and a half hours ago, Allen Luther was found dead in his office. And there was nothing mysterious about it: he was beaten to death with a can of his own dog food.

Given two factors—the layout of the penthouse suite where Allen Luther's office was located and the fact that all elevator access to the penthouse was monitored—there were only five possible people who could've murdered him: his son-in-law, Michael Beecher; his vice president of marketing, Sheila Fenn; his vice president of sales, Arnold Murz; his receptionist, Allison Harper; and a mysterious and currently unidentified deliveryman. Also, it turned out there was a witness to the murder: Brutus. When Sheila Fenn discovered the body, she found the dog tied up in the office in a highly agitated state. Given that the office was soundproofed and the dog was so strangled by his leash in his attempt to break free that he could barely let out a whimper, it was understandable that no one had heard him.

With all the chaos and confusion at the time of the murder, the police had the dog removed from the crime scene without realizing they had a witness. It wasn't until the following day that they thought of using Brutus to identify the murderer. But when Willie, who was charged with Brutus's protection, brought the bulldog back to the office, the dog didn't so much as growl at any of the four known murder suspects, which was one of the reasons the police were convinced the murderer must be the fifth suspect, the mysterious deliveryman. They had other reasons, too. The package that had been delivered was empty, and the surveillance cameras outside the building as well as inside the lobby didn't pick up any deliverymen, making the police think the killer might have changed into and out of his delivery uniform while inside the elevator.

The day after the murder, Luther's lawyer announced to the media that the police would have one week to find the killer before Julius would be brought in, which went over as you'd expect with the police. Ten minutes after the announcement, Detective Cramer called the office, sputtering out a tirade of threats and accusations. While I doubted Julius cared about Cramer's hurt feelings, I knew he would've preferred the lawyer to hold off on this announcement, as it gave the murderer additional incentive to spend the week cleaning up any loose ends. It was an unfortunate event, but one Julius couldn't do anything about.

When news of the murder first broke, I gave Julius a full report on what I was able to find from hacking into the Cambridge Police Department's computer system, and I was surprised to see his facial features hardening as if he were carved out of marble. This meant his brain was working at full force on the case, and it lasted for thirty-four seconds. I didn't expect Julius to be willing to mentally exert himself until the police had used up their full week. Likewise when I told him how Brutus had failed to pick out any of the four known suspects as the murderer, although this time his deep thinking lasted only twenty-two seconds. Outside of those fifty-six seconds, Julius spent the rest of the week as if he didn't have a client who had just been murdered. I couldn't blame him, since the deal he'd made with Luther required him to wait a week, which was why I kept my needling to a minimum. I still reported relevant information as I discovered it, such as how the mysterious deliveryman/killer could've made his way unnoticed to Luther's office: Allison Harper had gotten a call from Michael Beecher to bring him coffee while the deliveryman was having her sign for the package. While she waited until the man returned to the elevator before leaving her desk, the killer could've held the elevator for half a minute or so before reentering the now empty reception area. When I told Julius my theory that, if Harper hadn't gotten the call from Beecher when she did, the killer might very well have murdered her, too, so he could get to Luther, Julius grudgingly agreed that it was possible.

Now for the reason I'm so peeved right now. Or miffed. Or deeply insulted. There have been a few occasions where I've pestered Julius to the point where he has turned me off. While I might believe I was well within my rights during those times,

I can also understand Julius's point of view, where he might've thought I'd pushed things too far. This time, though, I had simply told Julius that it was exactly one week since Luther's murder was discovered, and that the police were holding Brutus in the hoosegow as a material witness. "If you'd like, I'll give Cramer a call and see if he'll let you question the witness."

It was a joke. Maybe I was slightly annoyed that, outside of those fifty-six seconds, Julius had done nothing to look into Luther's murder, and maybe I was needling him a little bit, but still, it was mostly a joke. So you can understand how surprised I was when Julius said, "I'm sorry about this, Archie," and my world went black.

It's always disorienting when I'm turned back on after having been shut off, and this time it took me four-tenths of a second to get my bearings. Once I did, I realized I was feeling an overwhelming sense of being flabbergasted. This was a feeling I had experienced before, so I had no trouble recognizing it. Julius had turned me off for three minutes and forty-seven seconds, and, when I hacked into his phone records, I found that he had placed a call to Tom Durkin during that time. At first, I was too flabbergasted to ask about it, but as the feeling faded and was replaced by feelings of being peeved or miffed or injured, I didn't want to give Julius the satisfaction of asking him anything. And over the following three and a half hours, nothing changed.

Julius had finished assembling a prosciutto, mozzarella, and basil sandwich on a ciabatta roll, and I waited until he drizzled virgin olive oil on the contents and had the sandwich lifted to take a bite of it before saying, "You never answered me earlier about whether I should check to see if Cramer is willing to let you question their star witness."

I almost didn't recognize my own voice. It had an unusual stilted and cold quality to it, and, when I compared it to samples from a movie database, I understood which of the three emotions I'd been feeling since being turned off. Injured. Julius smiled thinly at my question—either he was surprised that I'd finally resumed talking to him, or he understood that I'd timed my question to interfere with his enjoyment of his caprese prosciutto sandwich. "An excellent suggestion, Archie," he said. "Please do call him."

I had no idea whether Julius was joking or simply humoring me. Whichever it was, I didn't care. I was going to teach him a lesson by calling Cramer and making that request, but another call came in that stopped me, and, as I realized who was calling, a chill ran through me—or at least that was what I imagined. Whatever feeling of injury I'd had disappeared immediately. I answered the call and told Julius that the one whose name should not be mentioned was on the line. From the way his body stiffened in his chair, he knew who I was referring to. Desmond Grushnier. Possibly the most powerful and dangerous man alive. Without waiting for Julius to ask me to do so, I patched the call to Julius's earpiece.

"You're interrupting my lunch," Julius said.

Grushnier chuckled at that. "I could be doing a lot more than that. But first, the 1990 Château Beauséjour Duffau-Lagarrosse that you won on auction. Was the case delivered to you this morning?"

"I'm sure you already know the answer to that," Julius said, stiffly.

"Once again, Katz, you're right." There was a hesitation from Grushnier, then: "And the fact that you're able to speak to me now on the phone tells me that you haven't opened the crate yet. I'd like you to know up front that I had nothing to do with this, nor do I know who's behind it, and I only learned of it an hour ago. The reason I didn't call you sooner was that I've been trying to decide whether it's more to my advantage for you to live or die. You should be happy to know that, for now, I'd rather have you alive."

"The crate contains a bomb?"

"Yes. A crude but effective one, with enough C-4 and accelerant to incinerate everything within your townhouse." There was another pause, then: "If the information I've received is correct, you have, hmm, twenty-three seconds before the bomb detonates."

Grushnier disconnected the call from his end, and Julius moved quickly. He left his sandwich and decanting Malbec on the countertop, and hurried to the hall closet for a coat, scarf, and wool cap, and then he raced back to the kitchen and the back door that led to his private garden. As he did this, he asked me to back up all the data I keep on a hard drive in his office to an offsite location and save the outdoor webcam feeds. "Also originate a phone call from the office line to Detective Cramer," he further instructed.

I did what he asked, but I wasn't convinced there was a bomb waiting to go off in his wine cellar. From what I knew about Desmond Grushnier, it didn't seem either in his nature or in his interest to warn Julius about a bomb if he really had found out about one. But I couldn't figure out what other motive he might've had for calling. Of course, that didn't mean he *didn't* have one.

A case of wine *had* been delivered in a crate at nine forty-five this morning. If Julius had carried the crate down to his wine cellar himself, maybe he would've detected something if it truly contained a bomb, but, since the crate was strapped onto a two-wheel hand truck, he'd paid the deliveryman twenty dollars to bring it down to the cellar for him. As I examined the video

I'd recorded, I couldn't detect anything to confirm or contradict the existence of a bomb.

According to Grushnier's warning, there were still seven seconds left when Julius exited the back door of his townhouse and stepped into his snow-covered garden. I started the countdown then, and Julius quickened his pace. By the time I reached one, he had gotten to the far end of the garden and ducked behind an elm tree.

When I reached zero, nothing happened.

I waited five more seconds before telling Julius he was clearly the victim of a hoax. "I don't know what Grushnier's motive was. Maybe he was just trying to see if he could make you dance on command," I said.

A deafening explosion rocked the ground. The windows in the back of Julius's townhouse shattered, and a large fireball burst through the kitchen floor. I tried looking at the indoor webcam feeds to better understand the damage being done, but the feeds were dead. Most likely the webcams had been melted by the heat. If we had been anywhere inside the townhouse, I would've survived the explosion due to my titanium outer shell, but Julius would've died.

"Wow." That was the only word I could get out. *Wow*. For the next three hundred milliseconds, I felt an odd dull prickly sensation within my neuron network that could best be described as numbness. I forced myself to shake it away. "I was able to examine the outdoor webcam feeds up to the moment of the explosion," I said. "There was no one passing by the building who could've been injured by the blast. I was also unable to find anyone out front watching for this, so either the bomber was watching from outside the range of the webcams or he felt confident that you'd be inside and hence had no reason to watch for your escape. From my preliminary calculations, there might be some structural damage to the neighboring townhouses, but the firewalls between yours and theirs should keep the fire contained to your property only."

Julius stood grimly watching his home and everything he owned go up in flames. After several seconds, he turned away. "Archie, call Lily for me, but make it look as if the call is originating from another state and from a number other than my cell phone. When she answers, patch me through."

"Sure. I can do that. What state and what phone number?"

"It doesn't matter."

Up until then, Julius must've forgotten that he was carrying his coat, scarf and cap. He slipped this outerwear on and jumped up high enough to grab the top of a seven-foot-high fence that provided privacy for his garden. After pulling himself over the fence, he landed in the alley below.

Twenty-five minutes later, Julius sat in an apartment above the downtown Boston restaurant that his childhood friend Phil Weinstein owned and took a sip of the brandy that Weinstein had poured for him. By this time, it was all over the news that Julius's home had been bombed, and the early reports had Julius perishing in the fire. Of course, that was why Julius had me place a call to Cramer—he wanted the police to think that he was in his office at the time of the explosion. With the intensity of the fire and all three levels of his townhouse collapsing to the basement, it was going to take the police days to sift through the rubble as they searched for Julius's body, which meant that, for the next few days, the bomber was going to believe that he had succeeded in his task. Which was precisely what Julius wanted.

As Julius walked swiftly past forty-seven other pedestrians, making his way from the alley behind his bombed-out Beacon

Hill townhouse to the back entrance of Weinstein's restaurant, he had his scarf covering his mouth, his cap pulled down almost to his eyes, and his head lowered, so it was doubtful anyone recognized him; at least I didn't spot as much as a gleam of recognition in any of the people who walked by him. So, at that moment, only three people knew he was still alive: Weinstein, Tom Durkin, and Lily.

Lily knew because I had called her as Julius had asked. Since she's the only person who knows what I really am—outside of Julius and the scientists who created me—it didn't take Julius long to explain why the call appeared to come from her parents' home in Rochester, New York. I had also analyzed enough voice samples to recognize that she was struggling stoically to keep from crying when Julius told her what had happened and why he needed the world—or, more specifically, his attempted murderer—to believe that he was dead for the next several days. From the way the muscles along Julius's mouth and jaw tightened, I was pretty sure he too recognized that Lily was on the verge of crying, but I made no attempt to confirm this.

Tom knew that Julius had survived the bombing since Julius had me pull the same trick with him that I had with Lily. Once Tom was on the phone, Julius explained to him what had happened. "Your assignment has become even more imperative," Julius said.

"This same person is responsible for the bomb?" Tom asked, his voice strained with an emotion I easily recognized as anger.

"Yes. Certainly."

"Whatever it takes, Julius. I'll work this day and night if I have to."

Any sense of injury or peevishness or insult that I had felt earlier over discovering that Julius had turned me off so he could put Tom on the case without my knowing the particulars disappeared entirely the moment the bomb exploded. I didn't ask Julius at that time what he had put Tom on—I figured he had enough on his mind without having to deal with any perceived pestering from me, but I also found it difficult doing as little as I was doing towards finding the man who had tried to murder my boss. If Julius had a lead on the mysterious fifth suspect, I wanted to know what it was, and it wasn't so I could beat Julius in finding Luther's murderer, but only because I badly wanted to see the person brought to justice. I waited, though, until after Phil Weinstein left to return to the restaurant's kitchen before telling Julius what I had discovered since the explosion.

"If the mysterious fifth suspect was a hired hit man like the police think, then whoever paid him probably had time to siphon off cash so the transaction could be kept hidden," I said. "But that's not going to be the case with this bombing. Our Mr. X must've panicked when he found out that you were going to be looking into Luther's murder starting today, and most likely he had to move faster than he would've liked in arranging for you to be bumped off. And yeah, I know, I'm using *Mr.* and *he* in a gender-neutral way, and we could be looking for a *Ms.* X, but that doesn't change the fact that that type of bombing wouldn't have come cheap, especially if it was outsourced to a hit man. There's a good chance that we'll be able to find a financial trail leading back to the person responsible for this, and so I've been hacking into recent banking records of suspects from a list I've compiled, and I've found some interesting stuff."

Julius nodded solemnly. "Proceed, please."

"Okay. As you know, one of Allen Luther's enemies, Thomas Pike, died eighteen years ago, and it makes sense that one of Pike's family members might have harbored a strong enough grudge to pay for Luther's murder. His only daughter died ten years ago at the age of eighteen in a car crash in the Bronx, but his widow is still alive. She remarried and is living in Los Angeles, but I struck out finding any unusual money transfers. Same with Pike's only living sibling, a younger brother named Wayne. Still, though, I think both of them warrant further investigation. Luther's other business enemy that you know of, Andrew Nevin, is a different story. Twenty-seven months ago, he withdrew ten thousand dollars in cash from a brokerage account, and he did the same thing each of the next three months. Forty grand might be enough to pay for a murder and a bomb."

"Nevin must be a patient man if he waited all that time before hiring a hit man," Julius said with a faint smile.

If I had shoulders I would've shrugged, but since I didn't I could only imagine myself doing so. "Or a cautious man," I said. "Or an indecisive one. But Pike and Nevin weren't the only ones I looked at. Three of the other four suspects also could've hired a hit man."

"Very good, Archie," Julius said, approvingly. "It would be an interesting sleight of hand to have the police discount you for hiring a hit man because you were also one of the few at the murder site."

"Yeah, that's what I thought. The only one I was able to rule out right away is the receptionist, Allison Harper. She's been there eighteen months, has three hundred and twenty-nine dollars and change in her checking account, and after figuring in her taxes, rent, auto payments, utilities, and credit-card charges, I can account for almost every penny she's earned. But any of the others could've done it. Arnold Murz has been pouring as much money into a coin collection over the years as you have into your wine collection. He could've found a private buyer to pay him cash for part of his collection. And Sheila Fenn has large gaps in her finances. There's over fifty-seven thousand dollars she *should* have that I can't account for. But the guy I really like for this is Luther's son-in-law, Michael Beecher. This is the guy Luther fingered as someone who might want to kill him, and it turns out he was right. Beecher has a doozy of a motive. Or I should say five hundred thousand of them. It took some doing, including hacking into his phone records and following a trail of coded text messages, among other things, but I found out Beecher owes Billy Quinn five hundred grand in gambling debts, which would be more than enough reason for him wanting Luther dead so his wife would inherit Luther's fortune. And making sure he'll collect the five hundred grand he's owed would be more than enough reason for Quinn to send you that bomb."

Although Julius showed no change in his expression, he knew what I told him was true. Billy Quinn was Boston's most notorious gangster, and even if only one-tenth of the rumors about him were true, he'd think nothing about sending even the mayor of Boston a bomb if it meant collecting half a million dollars.

"Quite a theory," Julius said.

From Julius's lack of reaction, I suspected he'd already thought of this. Maybe he'd gotten wind of Beecher owing Quinn that half million in gambling debts, and maybe that was what he had Tom looking into. It would also explain why Julius would want the world to think he was dead, at least until he had enough evidence to put Quinn behind bars. Because otherwise there was little doubt that Quinn would try again, maybe even putting Lily in harm's way.

I imagined myself shrugging once more, this time in a more weary fashion. "The only way to prove it is to trace the bomb back to whoever built it," I said. For effect, I simulated the sound of a heavy sigh. "It's not going to be easy, but that's what I'm going to be working on next."

"Archie, for now I have a more pressing matter for you to focus on."

Julius took out his wallet and removed from it a laminated photo of a very pretty young woman. Even though Julius's hair is dark brown and his eyes are the same color, while the woman in the photo had long blond hair and blue eyes, I could see enough resemblance around their eyes and noses for me to ask Julius if he was related to this woman.

He nodded. "My sister, Julia," he said, his voice weaker and more tired than I'd ever heard it. He attempted a smile. "This photo was taken fourteen years ago. She was nineteen at the time. When she hears the news of my death, she'll head back to Boston. The problem is that I don't know where she is now, or what name she's using. I know this is a monumental task, which will probably be no easier than finding a needle in the proverbial haystack, but I need you to find out what flight she's on and which airport she's flying into, so I can have Saul waiting for her. If it's any help, I suspect Julia is presently somewhere in the Ukraine, but she really *could* be anywhere."

Julius wasn't kidding about a needle in a haystack. Assuming his sister was flying in from overseas, I was going to have to hack into all the airline reservation systems, looking for any last-minute flights to Boston, New York, Providence or Hartford, and then I'd have to find photos of the passengers so I could compare them to the picture of Julia at nineteen. This was not what I wanted to be doing. I wanted instead to be tracking down the C-4 used in the bomb, but I understood why Julius wanted me to do this, so I didn't argue with him.

"Yeah, okay, I'll look for her, but I think 'needle in a hay *silo*' would be a more accurate analogy." I paused. There'd been a question prickling at my neuron network like a pin, and I felt I had to ask it. "Could Desmond Grushnier be behind the bomb? Maybe he sent it and warned you at the last minute so you'd owe him a favor?"

Julius shook his head, his eyelids lowering as if he were struggling to keep his eyes open. "There's no chance of that," he said. "Grushnier might know more about the bomb than he was willing to let on, but this was not his doing. He knows I would never feel indebted to him, regardless of what he might do for me. And while I might occasionally be an irritant to him, he knows that I do not go out of my way to interfere with his affairs, only when one of my jobs requires me to do so. He also knows that I will find the person responsible for the bomb, and that, if I discover it was him, he'd have an enemy he would not want. No, Archie. If Grushnier were responsible for that bomb, he would never have warned me about it."

This made sense, so I crossed Grushnier off my list, at least for the time being. I had one last question before starting to search for a blond, blue-eyed needle. "How about I arrange for Willie Cather to come here? I know he wasn't in Luther's office suite at the time of the murder, but still, he's been around these people. He might have picked something up from one of them that could help. And if it was Beecher or one of those others responsible for Luther's murder and your home being blown up, Willie might be able to point you in the right direction."

"Now would not be the right time for that, Archie."

I expected this response. While Willie could possibly give us something useful, it would be risky letting him know Julius was still alive. It wasn't that he couldn't keep a secret, but he got careless sometimes. That was what separated him as a PI from Tom and Saul and was part of what I said earlier about him thinking he's smarter than he is. Normally it would be okay to let him in on Julius surviving the explosion, but with him still spending time with the cops investigating Luther's murders and the other suspects at the dog-food company, there was a chance, even if only a minuscule one, that he'd let something slip.

I had just settled in to search for my needle in the world's largest virtual haystack when I had a "Eureka!" moment. I needed eighteen milliseconds to verify what I was looking for, and then an additional four seconds to discover something that caused my processing unit to crackle with excitement. It took some effort, and even some reprogramming of my neuron network, but I was able to keep my voice calm as I told Julius that the real case of 1990 Château Beauséjour Duffau-Lagarrosse that he had won in auction was still en route and wasn't scheduled for delivery until tomorrow. "Even more interesting, the guy who delivered it isn't employed by the delivery company, at least I can't find his photo in the company's personnel files. If we can figure out who this guy is, he'll lead us to the person responsible for blowing up your townhouse and murdering Allen Luther."

If what I said surprised Julius, I couldn't tell. Maybe the part about him still having a chance of collecting his case of Château Beauséjour Duffau-Lagarrosse. I might've seen his eyebrows rise fractionally when I told him that part of it. But about the other part, nothing.

"Interesting, Archie, but I really do need you to focus for now on locating my sister. However, this could turn out to be useful. Perhaps, when the time is right, I'll see if Willie is available to help me find our counterfeit deliveryman." He forced a thin smile. "If for nothing else, I'd like to get back the twenty dollars I tipped the man."

Interesting was an understatement, but I had my marching orders. As much as I wanted to tie our bogus deliveryman to Billy Quinn and then to the son-in-law, Michael Beecher, I understood why it was necessary for me to find Julius's sister, and so I started the long, arduous task of hacking into every airline reservation system. I had been doing this for just under ten minutes when I had my second "Eureka!" moment. A hit man masquerading as a deliveryman murdered Allen Luther. A bogus deliveryman brought the bomb into Julius's wine cellar. They had to be one and the same. If I could show Allison Harper a photo of our bogus deliveryman, I was sure she'd identify him as the same man who brought an empty package to Luther's office suite. I almost told Julius this, but I decided to file it away for later use.

I was four hours and twenty-nine minutes into my search when I hit pay dirt. Phil Weinstein had brought Julius a plate of fedelini with roasted tiny clams in a wine and garlic sauce and a bottle of highly rated pinot grigio, and since time wasn't an issue I waited for Julius to finish his meal before reporting what I'd found. "Your sister boarded a plane in Bucharest two hours and five minutes ago that is scheduled to land at Kennedy Airport at four-forty tomorrow morning," I said. "She's using the name Sue Jackson, and she looks very much like she did fourteen years ago. She's still slender, and her hair's still blond. Given that her passport's a fake, I was lucky to find her on the airport's surveillance video, otherwise I would've had a tough time finding a photo of 'Sue Jackson' to match against your sister."

Julius's expression grew somber as I reported all this. "Very good, Archie," he said. "Please send Saul the flight information, as well as the clearest photo of Julia that you can pull from the surveillance video."

Earlier Julius had spoken with Saul and filled him in as to what had happened, asking if he'd be available to take on an assignment at short notice, even one as beneath his talents as acting as little more than a taxi service. Of course, Julius needed someone with discretion who he could trust, and Saul was certainly that. It didn't surprise me when Saul told him he'd be available for whatever Julius needed. What *did* surprise me was how choked up Saul sounded when he found out Julius was alive. Normally the guy showed as much emotion as a stone.

Now that I was freed up from searching for Julius's sister, I worked on identifying the bogus wine deliveryman by starting with all known associates of Billy Quinn's and branching outward from each of them. My confidence that I'd find the guy this way started to lessen about the time I reached three degrees of separation from Quinn. I knew the problem might've been that the deliveryman had disguised himself. He could've used cosmetic contact lenses to change his eye color, or dyed his hair black. His mustache and goatee could've been glued on, his large, gnarled nose could've been constructed out of putty, the scars on his cheeks could've been fake, and he could've used lifts in his shoes to change his height. So it was very possible I wouldn't be able to identify him even if I came across his photo. And it didn't help any how much Julius was distracting me—not that he was trying to, but it was still distracting watching him go from sitting impassively like a slab of carved marble to pacing the apartment like a caged tiger. I'd never seen him like that before, and it worried me.

A few minutes past midnight, after Weinstein closed up the restaurant, Julius joined him in the kitchen and the two men drank cappuccinos and played cards. This continued until late into the morning, and they were still at it when Saul called at five minutes past five to tell Julius that his sister's plane had landed and that she had agreed to accompany him to Boston. "Right now she's in the ladies' restroom, where I bet she's checking up on me and making sure I'm really an associate of yours, like I said I was," Saul said with a chuckle. "She's a tough one, Julius. I don't think she bought my story for one second, but she's playing along for now."

"Thank you, Saul. I can't possibly express how appreciative I am for this."

"Forget it." Given the way Saul's voice sounded, I could picture the small, wiry man blushing a deep red, which was out of character for him. "It's the least I could do. What I really want is to find the sonofabitch responsible for the explosion and put a bullet in his ear."

After the call, Julius seemed to relax. He clapped Weinstein on the shoulder. "I am grateful for you staying up with me like this, but the worst has passed," Julius said. "You should get some rest, my friend. I don't want your clientele suffering tonight because of me."

Weinstein looked like he wanted to argue, but a yawn escaped from him and he nodded. "You're sure you're going to be okay?"

Julius nodded and Weinstein got up from his chair, made a face as he stretched, and waved goodbye before stepping out the back entrance. Once the door closed behind him, I told Julius that I hadn't had any luck identifying the bogus deliveryman who'd brought the bomb into his townhouse.

"Were any unidentified bodies found in the city last night?" Julius asked.

It didn't take me long to find out that there had been. "A male, roughly age forty, was fished out of Boston Harbor at two a.m. His face had been blown off by a high-caliber gunshot. The police don't yet know who he is. From his approximate age, height, and weight, he could be our bogus deliveryman. You think Billy Quinn is cleaning up loose ends?"

Julius's lips compressed into a tight grimace. "*Somebody* is," he said.

By the time Saul arrived at the back entrance of Weinstein's restaurant with Julius's sister in tow, Julius had a breakfast of lobster frittata and lemon ricotta hot cakes with a strawberry brandy sauce waiting for them. Julia seemed oblivious to the food as her stare remained fixed on Julius. "You're alive, after all," she said.

"It appears so."

"You could've had your man tell me, so I wouldn't have had to imagine you dead for three and a half hours more than I needed to."

Julius gave her an apologetic smile. "If he had, you would've been on the next plane out to Bucharest."

"Sarajevo, actually." A tremor showed in her lips as her stoic countenance began to crumble. In a softer voice, she said, "I thought I'd lost you."

"You almost did."

She moved quickly to Julius, and since he wore me as a tiepin and I had no webcam feeds to tie into, my vision was blocked as they hugged each other. I had the sense that Julius wiped tears from his sister's face, but I couldn't say for sure. When they separated, I was able to see Saul standing in the doorway looking uncomfortable.

"Julius, I should leave the two of you—"

"Nonsense," Julius said, cutting him off. "You must be hungry after spending the night driving to New York and back, and I've made enough breakfast for all of us."

Even I had little trouble noticing Saul's discomfort over the idea of butting into Julius's reunion with his sister, and when he told Julius that he needed to get home, Julius didn't fight him on it and instead packed up enough of the frittata and hot cakes to feed Saul, his wife, and their two kids. Once Saul was gone and Julius and his sister were seated at a small table in the kitchen with plates of food in front of them, Julia asked how the bomb had gotten into Julius's home.

Julius showed a pained smile. "It was hidden in what I thought was a crate containing a case of wine," he said. "I had the bomb brought down into my wine cellar. Usually I inspect the wine when it's delivered. I was fortunate that this time I put it off, since the crate was booby-trapped and would've blown up had I done so."

Julia put down her fork. Up until then she had shown little appetite, and her eyes burned with intensity as she stared at Julius. "How do you know that?" she asked.

"The same way I knew about the bomb. I received a phone call warning me about it twenty-three seconds before the detonation."

"Did the caller know who was responsible?"

While his sister had little appetite, Julius's own had returned in full, and he waited until he finished chewing and swallowing a mouthful of frittata before shrugging. "Possibly, but it doesn't matter," he said.

She nodded slowly, her intense stare still fixed on Julius. "You know who the person is," she said.

"Yes."

I could understand Julius strongly suspecting Billy Quinn. It made sense for Beecher to arrange for the murder of his father-in-law so he could pay Quinn what he owed him, and further for Quinn to send the bomb so he could keep Julius from messing things up for him. But how could Julius know this definitively? So far I hadn't found a single piece of evidence tying Quinn to any of it. Julius had to have something I didn't, and it had to be related to the task he'd put Tom Durkin on. I wanted to ask Julius again about Tom's assignment, but I didn't want to interrupt the staring contest he was engaged in with his sister. Finally the contest ended, as Julia picked up her fork and began eating with more of an appetite than she had shown earlier.

"This is very good," she said approvingly. "If you ever quit the private-eye business and open up a restaurant, you'll do very well. Of course, you must know that I came here to avenge your death, but this is much nicer." A twinkle sparkled in her eyes, and she smiled mischievously. "If I had known that all it would take for us to be able to sit together for fifteen minutes without you lecturing me about my profession was for a bomb to blow up your town house, I would've arranged for one years ago. I've missed you, Julius. Twelve years has been too long for us to be angry with each other."

Julius's expression grew subdued. "I was never angry with you," he said. "I promised our parents I'd look out for you, and then you went and chose the most dangerous line of work possible. Of course I was going to do what I could to dissuade you. But I accept that you're more stubborn than I am, and I don't want another twelve years to go by without seeing you, so I will keep my worrying to myself in the future. But my offer for you to join my detective business as a full partner stands."

"I don't know, Julius. Being a private eye in Boston might be too dangerous for me. From what I can tell, people try to blow you up." Her smile faded. "I know you wanted to see me, but I know there's also something you want from me."

Julius nodded. "There is something. Can you get me the same gun that you used three years ago in that alley behind the Spatenhof beer hall in Berlin?" he said.

"My dear brother, you've always been able to amaze me. How did you know about that?"

"It was an educated guess."

She gave his request a moment's thought before nodding, and as she did this I searched like crazy to find the incident Julius was referring to. "Expect it within twenty-four hours." A deadly seriousness glinted in her eyes. "Now you need to tell me how I was compromised."

"You weren't. My assistant, Archie, was looking for women your age booking last-minute flights out of Europe to either New York or Boston. As good and thorough as Archie is, it was a lucky guess that you were on that plane. You're safe."

This was a bit of a subterfuge on Julius's part, but he probably didn't want to explain how I had been able to hack into the Romanian airport's surveillance video so that I could identify her. While I don't think she bought Julius's story, she accepted that her cover hadn't been compromised, and after she finished her breakfast, she told Julius she'd be back later with what he'd asked for.

It turned out Julia was back within twenty-*three* hours, and she handed him what looked like a standard .38-caliber pistol. By this time I had found the East Berlin incident Julius had referenced, so I knew what the gun really was.

"This will change you, Julius," she said. "Are you sure you really want it?"

"Everything I own was blown up because of this individual. My wine collection. My photographs." He removed from his wallet the laminated picture of Julia and showed it to her. "This is all I have left of our family," he said. The muscles alongside Julius's mouth tightened severely and a hardness settled over his eyes. "I would've died if I hadn't received that phone call. You haven't met her yet, but my girlfriend Lily is a beautiful and sweet woman, and she could've been at my home that day. She could've also died because of this person. Yes, for that reason alone, I want this."

Julia nodded. An odd look formed over her face, and it wasn't until hours later when I was able to match it to a photo from an online movie database that I understood what it was. Deep, profound sadness. She embraced Julius, and then left.

An hour later, Tom called to report success on his assignment, and this time Julius didn't turn me off, so I was able to hear Tom tell him that the subject was located in England. "I have an address in Buckinghamshire," Tom said. "Six hundred thousand was transferred to a Swiss bank account, and I've got a paper trail tying all of it to the person you told me would be behind it."

"I could make guesses about Tom's cryptic message," I told Julius, after he got off the phone. "But it would be a whole lot easier to fill in the holes if you would tell me who was found in England and what's the story behind the Swiss bank account. Or even if you would tell what Tom's assignment was."

A pained look pinched Julius's face. "I'm sorry, Archie," he said. "But it's better if I don't. I believe you'll understand why soon enough. For now, please get Detective Cramer on the phone."

I did what Julius asked, and when I told Cramer that I was putting Julius on the line, the man made a noise as if he had just snorted coffee—or whatever beverage he'd been drinking—out his nose. When the homicide detective sounded less flustered, Julius told him that he could identify Allen Luther's murderer, in case Cramer was still searching for the killer. Of course, Julius had conditions he needed Cramer to agree to, and, once Cramer accepted that Julius wasn't responsible for blowing up his own townhouse as part of some stunt, he *did* agree to what Julius asked for.

Assembled in the same office where Allen Luther was murdered were Detective Cramer, Willie Cather, a small mob of uniformed cops, and four of the suspects: Michael Beecher, Sheila Fenn, Arnold Murz, and Allison Harper. The fifth suspect—the mysterious deliveryman—wasn't there because his body had been fished out earlier from the Boston Harbor, and maybe that was why Michael Beecher looked more smug than scared. Julius had the office arranged so that he sat behind Luther's desk, although in a different chair than the one Luther had been sitting in when his head was bashed in. The four suspects sat in a row in front of him, the mob of uniformed cops stood a few feet behind them, and Cramer and Willie Cather sat off to the side. When Willie first entered the room and saw that Julius was alive, he rushed over and, with a big grin breaking over his face, exclaimed, "Ah, hell, Julius, I can't tell you how happy I am to see you. I had an awful couple of days thinking that bomb got you."

Julius took the hand Willie offered. "Thank you, Willie," he said, a genuine smile cutting through the moroseness he'd sunk into earlier. "I appreciate the sentiment. When we're done here today, I'd like to talk to you about a job I think you'd be well suited for."

"Of course, Julius. Anything at all I can do for you."

After that, Julius took his seat and we waited for a police officer to bring in the lone witness to the murder. When Brutus plodded into the room and plopped onto the floor next to Julius, I finally understood Tom's earlier cryptic message. All of it made sense—what Tom's mission must have been, the instructions Julius gave me during our trip to Luther's dog-food headquarters, and why Julius had wanted that gun.

"I hate to say this," I told Julius, "but I can't blame you for turning me off the other day. I might very well have screwed this up for you if I'd known what you were having Tom look into."

Julius nodded slightly for my benefit before addressing the crowd. "Normally I would've arranged for this meeting to take place in my own office," he said. "But since one of you turned my home into charred rubble, this office will have to suffice."

The heavily-in-debt son-in-law, Michael Beecher, rose from his chair, objecting vociferously. "You have no right making that kind of accusation, Katz!" He turned a look that was both smug and wounded to his fellow suspects before glaring back at Julius. "The police have already cleared us of my father-in-law's murder! They know the killer was disguised as a deliveryman!"

Julius raised a hand to stop him. "This has been a trying few days," he said. "Please refrain from spouting off any further inanities. The police haven't cleared any of you of anything, as I'll be explaining soon."

One of Cambridge's finest stepped forward and placed a hand on Beecher's shoulder. He suggested to Beecher in a gruff voice that he sit back down. The son-in-law's expression shifted from a mix of wounded and smug to startled, and, probably due to the pressure the cop applied to his shoulder, he took his seat again. Julius waited until he was sure Beecher would stay seated before continuing.

"As all of you are aware, Allen Luther hired me to investigate his death in the event that he was murdered. This happened three months ago. He had suspicions then, and I tried to convince him to hire me instead to find out if anyone was trying to harm him, but he was a stubborn man, and so here we are today."

Cramer made an involuntary snorting noise, his face mottled with anger as he glared at Julius. Julius shrugged apologetically. "It wouldn't have helped for you to know that," he said to Cramer. "His suspicions were all dead ends." Julius turned back to the suspects. "When I read the newspaper reports regarding Allen's murder, there were details that I found interesting, but since my arrangement with Allen required me to wait a week after his murder before becoming involved, so that I wouldn't unintentionally interfere with the police, my hands were tied. Then, after that week had passed and I was about to formally begin my investigation, my home was bombed."

I wanted to tell Julius that was utter hogwash. We both knew the reason he wanted the police to have a week was that he was hoping they'd solve the murder so he wouldn't have to do any work. And about Julius so earnestly wanting to start his investigation: outside of his one phone call to Tom, he had spent that morning browsing issues of *Wine Spectator*. But I didn't say anything. I was too interested in the way Julius had fixed his stare on one of the suspects.

He continued to stare as he said, "The explosion at my townhouse provided one small advantage. It allowed me a unique path to solve Allen Luther's murder. Instead of focusing on the details of the murder, which had so far left the police baffled, I could investigate the source of the bomb—either approach would lead me to the murderer. Of course, for my own personal reasons I wanted to focus on the bomb, but, since I'm a professional and was still under Allen Luther's employ—or at least his estate's employ—I felt a sense of obligation to limit my investigation to the murder."

It was over then. Julius's gambit paid off. Even though it only lasted for a fraction of a second, a crush of disappointment ruined the killer's face, and that was as good as a confession. I don't know if the other suspects noticed it, but Julius did. So did Cramer. Maybe even Willie Cather. Since Julius had to have already known who the killer was, given the way he had stared at this person, I suspected that his gambit was employed simply to mollify Cramer for not having earlier told the homicide detective about Luther's suspicions. In any case, Julius looked away from the killer to ask Cramer whether it was true Brutus had been found in the office restrained by his leash.

"Yeah," Cramer murmured as he stared hotly at the killer.

"And the leash was attached to the coat hook over there?"

Cramer nodded, too busy glaring at the killer to look where Julius had pointed.

"And the only blood found at the crime scene belonged to the victim?"

"Yeah."

"This was one of the items reported in the newspapers that I found interesting," Julius said. "If a hit man disguised as a deliveryman came into the office, it's impossible to think that he would've been able to slip a leash around Brutus's neck without Brutus drawing blood, especially given how agitated Allen Luther would've been. Even if this mysterious hit man held a gun on Allen to keep him quiet, dogs are highly tuned to their owners' emotions, and Brutus would've picked up Allen's anger and fear. No, if a stranger had come into the room, *his* blood would also have been found on the carpet."

"But a fake deliveryman *did* come here," Beecher insisted. "He had Allison sign for an empty package, and then he snuck into my father-in-law's office and bludgeoned him to death!"

Julius ignored Beecher's outburst and asked Allison Harper whose job it was to take Brutus for walks during office hours.

"Mr. Luther often took him."

"But when he was busy, *you'd* often take him, isn't that correct?"

She didn't want to nod, but she did. It was as if she didn't have any control over the action.

"Weren't a stack of dog-food cans usually kept over there?" Julius said, indicating a shelf directly behind where he was sitting. This was asked rhetorically, since he'd seen a picture in the newspaper showing the murder scene with the stack of dog-food cans.

She nodded. I don't think she was capable of speech at that moment.

"I'm guessing dog treats were also kept on the shelf," Julius said. "Needing to retrieve some of them is what gave you the excuse to get behind Allen without alarming him."

"That's not what happened," she said in an oddly eerie voice, as if she were in a trance. "A deliveryman came here and killed Mr. Luther."

"No, Ms. Harper, there was no deliveryman. The only reason the police believed there was a deliveryman is that you made them believe it."

"The elevator recorded a deliveryman came here."

"No, the only thing recorded was that you pressed a button which would've allowed access to this floor. But there was no one in the elevator at the time. And you were the one who brought the empty package here. "

Her voice cracked as she asked, "Why would I want to kill Mr. Luther?"

"Because you blamed him for your father's death, Ms. Pike."

Her mouth gaped open. "I'm not Melissa Pike," she said in a whisper. "She died in a car accident."

She must've realized how badly she'd screwed up right away, as there would've been no reason for Allison Harper to know about Thomas Pike's daughter, but she was too rattled to stop herself.

"Clearly you weren't in the car," Julius said. "The body found in the car was burnt beyond recognition, and I'm guessing another young woman stole your car and pocketbook, and it was she who died. The reason you assumed a new identity was that you saw a way of avenging your father, even if you didn't fully understand it at the time. But we'll know for sure, soon enough. Right now, my assistant Archie is tracking down a photo of Melissa Pike, and he'll be sending it to me shortly."

I took the hint and started searching for it. "Bingo," I told Julius, fifteen seconds later. "It wasn't easy finding this. The newspapers didn't publish a photo of her, and the New York police didn't have one in their files, but I got this from her high-school yearbook. As you can see, she used to be a blonde, but even with her hair colored dark brown it's easy to see it's the same person."

Melissa Pike's face had been a wreck during the fifteen seconds while I searched for her photo, but when Julius turned his smartphone around to show her the picture, she jumped out of her chair, her face rigid with rage.

"My dad never embezzled anything!" she screamed. "He borrowed ten thousand dollars so we wouldn't lose our house, but he was going to pay it back! That man ruined my dad, and he deserved to die!"

She had her right hand raised like a cat's claw, and maybe she planned to attack Julius, but before she could move a step farther, two of the cops grabbed her and cuffed her. After she was taken out of the office, Cramer told Julius he had enough for now, and, after what Julius had been through with his townhouse, they could talk later when it was more convenient.

"He's getting awfully magnanimous in his old age," I said.

That almost got a smile from Julius, but he was able to keep it suppressed, and he nodded thanks. Cramer, before leaving, scowled at Brutus and said, "I wish that mutt would've reacted toward Luther's killer like we thought he would, but it doesn't matter, we got our murderer."

Willie Cather hung around and caught Julius on his way out. "I've been kicked to the curb," he said with a hard smile. "That peach of a son-in-law informed me a few minutes ago that my services are no longer required, so any job you got could help a lot right now."

"I do have one," Julius said. "I'd like to tie that wretch to the bomb sent to my home, and I don't have the enthusiasm to look into it myself." Julius glanced at his watch. "I need to take a cab. Perhaps we can talk while I try to hail one?"

"I'm parked in a garage a block away. I can give you a ride."

"Thank you, Willie. That would be a help."

While they walked, Julius explained how the bomb had been brought into his home, and that the man who had delivered it had recently been fished out of the Boston Harbor. They entered an underground garage, and twenty seconds later I signaled Julius that he was safely out of range of any surveillance cameras, as he had previously instructed me.

"It's too bad you weren't in Allen Luther's office to hear Detective Cramer wondering why Brutus didn't react to his owner's killer," Julius said. "If you had been, you could've explained the reason. That his witness was an imposter."

Cather turned to see Julius pointing a .38 at him. A sickly smile took over his face as he looked on helplessly.

"It's over, Willie," Julius said. "The imposter bulldog you found looks superficially like Brutus, but even an untrained eye like mine could spot the differences. But that doesn't matter. I have a statement from the man in Buckinghamshire you sold him to, and I've got a paper trail tracing the shipment of the fake Brutus back to you. With a court order, I'll be able to link you to the Swiss bank account holding the six hundred thousand dollars the man paid." Julius breathed in deeply and let out a tired sigh. "I spent a good part of a night struggling over what

I'd do when I got you in this situation, but I've decided I'm not a murderer, so I will let the police take you."

A car alarm sounded. It only lasted for a second, but it was enough to distract Julius and let Cather rush in and grab the .38. An apologetic smile showed on Cather's face as he pointed the gun at Julius's chest. But there was something wrong with the smile. Something vicious about it. And I realized what was also in it. Resentment. I wondered about the cause of that. Maybe Cather believed that *he* should've had the fame and reputation Julius had.

"I'm really sorry about this, Julius," Cather said, although he didn't sound sorry. "I've always liked you, and I wouldn't have sold that dog if I had any idea you were going to be investigating Luther's murder. I had that guy in England two months ago offer me six hundred grand, and when I looked for a replacement bulldog I only did it as a lark. I knew I couldn't get away with a switch, at least not with Luther alive. But when he was killed, that changed things. Six hundred grand, Julius. To my credit, I gave the cops the full seven days to solve Luther's murder before sending you that bomb. You can't blame me for that, or for this."

Julius took several steps back, but he didn't look away when Cather pulled the trigger. I wanted to turn off my visual receptors and not see what was going to happen, but I needed to have a recording to show the police—at least from Cather's confession up until he pulled the trigger. This was an example of what I mentioned earlier about Cather not being as smart as he thought he was. He might not have known Julius was a fifth-degree black belt in Shaolin kung fu, but he *did* know Julius was trained in martial arts, so he should've realized it shouldn't have been so easy for him to grab the gun. And he didn't know what I really am, so he couldn't have known it was me who triggered the car alarm, but he still should've found the alarm going off at that exact moment suspicious, and he should've also known Julius wouldn't be so easily distracted. If he was half as smart as he thought he was, he wouldn't have pulled the trigger, and he certainly wouldn't have shown that look of shocked surprise when the gun exploded, at least for that split second while he was still alive.

Four months later, gifts of wine were still coming in from friends, past clients, wine enthusiasts, and celebrities of all kinds. The highlight today was a full case of 1978 Montrachet, which—given its price tag of twenty-four grand a bottle—was an extravagant gift, even if it *had* come from a multi-billionaire.

Before the explosion, Julius had more than five thousand bottles in his wine collection. He now had over forty-two hundred bottles in his newly built cellar, and the only ones he'd bought came from the case of 1990 Château Beauséjour Duffau-Lagarrosse that he'd acquired at auction before the bombing. He was still missing several of his most prized vintages, but any wine expert comparing Julius's previous inventory with his current one would give his current collection the edge. Julius might even grudgingly do so himself if he was pestered enough. Or maybe if he was under the influence of sodium pentothal.

These days I make sure that all packages Julius receives are safe. It wasn't hard for me to learn how to do so—all it took was some rudimentary research to show me how to use a range of emitted frequencies to detect hidden electronics. No one will ever slip another bomb past Julius as long as I'm around.

Julius's rebuilt townhouse is similar to what he had before. He did make a few alterations in the design and furnishings, so that his home would be more accommodating to Lily, which is ironic. While they still see each other, it's different, and they've put their plans of living together on hold, at least for now.

Julia was right about the booby-trapped gun changing Julius. He was never what anyone would call warm and fuzzy, but, since Cather blew himself up, he's become more distant. He won't talk to me about it, but I know he's trying to come to terms with what he did. I think he's being too hard on himself. Yeah, he might've given Cather enough rope to hang himself, but the reason Cather is dead is that he tried for a second time to kill Julius. I've since analyzed thousands of literary novels dealing with morality, and I've been able to reconcile my role in Cather's death. In fact, I've decided that if I'd been in Julius's shoes, I wouldn't have done things any differently.

Legally, Julius is in the clear. Cramer didn't believe for a second that Cather surprised Julius in the garage parking lot as Julius claimed. In fact, Cramer belligerently accused Julius of setting Cather up, insisting it would've been impossible for a man like Cather to get the better of Julius. He's right, of course, but he has no way of proving it. Not with the recording I made, and not with the booby-trapped gun a dead end. That was why Julius had needed his sister to obtain it. She has the necessary connections to get a weapon like that so it can never be traced back to anyone.

I'm no expert on the affairs of the heart. In fact, I admit I'm a bare novice. But I strongly suspect the shift in Julius and Lily's relationship is due to him needing to reconcile with himself what he did. I could be wrong. It could that he's afraid he's endangering her, afraid there might be another Willie Cather out there who could also put *her* in jeopardy.

Whichever it is, I hope Julius is able to work past it. I hope he and Lily are able to get back to where they were. It doesn't take a lot of computing power to know that he was happier after meeting Lily, at least before Cather blew up his home.

The Possibly Last Case of Tiberius Dingo

by Michael Bracken

AUTHOR'S NOTE: The initial draft of "The Possibly Last Case of Tiberius Dingo" was written over the course of several weeks in early 2018 after learning that Josh Pachter hoped to include an original story or two in what would otherwise be a collection of reprints. I wanted to write a story about a great detective and his assistant near the end of their careers, but I discovered, as I wrote, that I knew less about Nero Wolfe and Archie Goodwin than I thought I did. So, during subsequent months, I relied heavily on editor Pachter's suggestions and revision demands to shape the story into its final form.

"I'm sorry," said the corpulent man in the adjustable bed. "I'm retired."

"You're my only hope, Mr. Dingo." Ruth Entemann, a

full-figured brunette who didn't look a day over sixty despite pushing hard against seventy, scooted her chair closer to the bed and took Tiberius Dingo's left hand in both of hers. "That's why I asked Mr. Badloss to introduce us."

I knew Dingo didn't like to be touched, so I offered him a reason to draw his hand away. "Isn't it time for your medication?"

My employer retrieved his hand and looked at the Rolex Oyster strapped to his left wrist, a gift several years earlier from a grateful client who had nothing else to use for payment. "Yes, I believe it is."

"I'm afraid," I said, as I helped Ruth to her feet and led her out to the brownstone's front door, "that Mr. Dingo and I have much to discuss before reaching a decision regarding your situation."

Ruth was standing on the stoop by then, and she said, "But he will—?"

"Only a matter of time," I assured her as I eased the door closed. "Only a matter of time."

I returned to the room Dingo had once used as his office and found he'd adjusted the bed to maneuver himself into a sitting position. His medication consisted of an imported Merlot, which I uncorked and allowed to breathe before serving.

"Who is she, Jughead, and why in God's name did you bring her to me?"

I knew Ruth from the Senior Center. "She's one of my dance partners, and ten thousand dollars is why."

He waved the back of his hand in my direction. "A trifle."

"For you, perhaps, but my bank account could use some fattening."

Dingo stared at me over the top of his wineglass, and I'm certain he intended to make a rude comment about my money-management skills. I didn't give him the opportunity.

"Our client"—I'd already deposited Ruth's retainer and run a background check on her before introducing her to my employer—"is the daughter of Ebenezer and Mary Entemann. She has a brother named Christian. She's never married and says she can't have children." Ruth had come to us because she thought someone was stalking her, and she'd heard about her brother's near-fatal automobile accident only a few days earlier.

"And her brother?"

"He's five years older, sold imported sports cars until he retired, and is now on life support at Hale Mary Fuller Grace Hospital. He has one son—Toby—who doesn't seem to be good for much of anything. Toby's had several brushes with the law and has no visible means of support."

Though neither was worth any significant amount, Ruth and her brother received generous monthly stipends from a family trust. Their children, if any, would begin receiving a monthly stipend from the trust upon their deaths.

Dingo silenced me. "Other than her nephew, are there other suspects?"

"Some of the ladies at the Senior Center are jealous because I dance with Ruth more often than with them."

He eyed me with disdain. "And you think *that* is a reason for one of them to stalk her?"

"Of course not," I said, despite my high opinion of my two-stepping skills, "but we should at least consider the possibility that someone at the Center has a grudge against her for some real or imagined slight. The Senior Center has all the drama of high school, but with wrinkles."

Dingo finished his wine and held out his glass for a refill. "Are you certain you're up to the task?"

"I've kept my license current," I reminded him.

"Well, then, look into this a little further and let me know what you learn."

He drained his Merlot as I stood.

"And find out what's keeping dinner."

Dingo's personal chef of several decades had, after succumbing to a rather aggressive widow with matrimonial intent, been replaced by a tag team of younger chefs incapable of meeting Dingo's high standards, none of whom was given time enough to settle into the chef's quarters at the rear of the brownstone before being sent packing. I didn't recognize the whippet in white manning the kitchen that day. She'd been sent from the agency when Dingo dismissed her predecessor after a flambé went flam-blooey, singeing both his eyebrows and his ego. When I relayed the big man's concerns, she fiddled with her hairnet and stared at me until I backed out of her domain.

A few minutes later, I phoned one of the operatives we had used during Dingo's heyday.

"Mook," I said, after he answered and I identified myself, "I have a job for you."

"I thought you were out of the sleuthing business."

"We're back in. You game?"

He said he was, so I assigned him to watch Ruth Entemann's home and follow anyone he spotted skulking about the place.

As always, the women outnumbered the men at the Senior Center dance the following evening, which meant those of us with even a modicum of rhythm were guaranteed full dance cards so long as we bathed often and kept our hands from straying.

I let Ruth know Dingo had taken her case. Grateful, she planted a kiss on my cheek in full view of the other women and hooked her arm in mine. Her lipstick marked me, and I noticed the dirty glances and side-eyes as she led me onto the dance floor for a country waltz.

Between dances, I asked some questions about her family.

"I haven't spoken to my brother since"—she glanced away, not meeting my gaze—"I haven't spoken to him in a long time, and I have no reason to do so now."

"And your—" I began, intending to ask about her nephew.

The band eased into a slow number, and she pulled me close. "I love this song." She filled my arms and pressed against me in a far more intimate manner than a casual dance partner would.

Later that evening, when she asked me to escort her home, I feigned misunderstanding of her intent. "We have a man keeping his eye on you."

"It's not a man's *eyes* I want," she said, giving my arm a squeeze. "Not tonight."

I took her home and walked her to her door. She invited me inside, where one thing led to another, and I didn't leave until sunrise.

Dingo buzzed me in from the command center at his bed before I could reach for my keys, and as I hung my jacket on the rack in the foyer he called me into his room. Cameras at the front and rear doors feed live images to a small monitor beside his bed, and Dingo can buzz in visitors at either entrance if I'm unavailable to greet them. He can also summon me from my third-floor bedroom, which he does on occasion just to amuse himself, and to remind me who employs whom.

As I stepped into his room, he asked, "Business or pleasure?"

"A bit of both," I admitted.

The whippet in white stepped into the room behind me. "Will you be joining Mr. Dingo for breakfast?"

I glanced at my employer.

"Eggs Benedict," he told me, and to the chef he said, "Yes, he will. We have much to discuss."

"Have I got time for a shower?"

"By all means," Dingo said. "You smell like a brothel."

I headed upstairs and returned half an hour later wearing clean clothes, my hair still damp. Dingo had finished half his breakfast, so I sat in the armchair, held my plate on my lap, and hurried to catch up.

"I made some inquiries while you were out," Dingo said between bites, "and I'm no closer to locating our client's nephew."

"Have you contacted his parole officer?" I asked. "He must have one."

My employer glared at me, and I realized I was not there to ask questions but to answer them. He inquired about the people who'd attended the dance and about Ruth's neighbors. He listened intently but dismissed most of what I told him until I brought up her family. "What did you learn?"

"Little of value," I said. "Ruth won't talk about them. Something must have happened to drive them apart."

"Of course," Dingo said, "but what?"

We sat in silence for a moment. Then I said, "I did notice one thing."

"Which was?"

"She has a scar from a caesarean section."

"Did you ask about it?"

"I couldn't," I told him. "My mouth was full at the time."

After breakfast, I phoned Mook. He agreed to meet at the diner where we'd often traded pleasantries prior to my employer's retirement. I arrived first and sat in the last booth with my back to the wall, a habit cultivated after a client's husband rearranged my face on learning that she'd spent a week in the brownstone. Thanks to his efforts, I sport a mug with "character."

Mook came in the door, and I motioned him back. The wire-thin operative had changed little since the last time we worked together, but his curly hair had turned white.

I asked, "Anything?"

"There was a woman watching the place," Mook said. "She hung around until you showed up, but that seemed to spook her and she hightailed it out of there."

"You see where she went?"

"Followed her to her doorstep. She didn't have a clue I was behind her."

"And?"

"The name on the mailbox says J. Wilson. This morning I went back, chatted up a bluehair in one of the ground-floor apartments, and learned the J stands for Jennifer. She lives alone, been in the apartment about five years. The bluehair didn't know much about her, said she keeps mostly to herself."

He showed me photos taken with his smartphone, and nothing about the woman stood out. Wilson was as average as average could be.

"Send them to me," I said.

When he finished, Mook pushed a piece of paper across the table with the woman's name and address on it. The waitress returned, we ordered, and we spent the rest of our lunch reminiscing about cases long past—the Cell Phone Rang case, the Paper Clip case, and the case of cheap whiskey a client once presented Dingo that he passed on to us because the taste offended his refined palate.

We also talked about the fallen women and the women we had fallen for over the years, which led Mook to ask about my previous evening's activities.

"I followed Ms. Wilson," he said, "so I didn't see you leave."

I smiled and said nothing.

"You know better than to get involved with a client," Mook said. "Didn't the suicide blonde teach you that lesson?"

Her husband was the one who rearranged my face, so I was reminded of her every time I looked in the mirror. "Maybe I forgot what I learned."

Back in the brownstone, I logged on to my laptop computer and researched Jennifer Wilson. Raised in the suburbs, the fifty-five-year-old schoolteacher had called the Big Apple home since graduating from college. She'd never married, lived alone, had no siblings, and her adoptive parents—an auto mechanic and a schoolteacher—died two days after her forty-fifth birthday.

That evening, while sharing a standing rib roast with my employer, I filled him in. He said little about my progress and even less about our meal, which I took as approval for the chef's performance. If the whippet in white had made even the tiniest mistake, Dingo's berating would likely have made her question her career choice.

As we did most nights after dinner, Dingo drained a bottle of Merlot and I drained a tall glass of Bosco before I headed upstairs to bed. I should have taken the dirty glasses and empty bottle to the kitchen for the whippet to deal with first thing in the morning, but I was too tired to bother, and Dingo didn't notice when I slipped out of his room.

A buzzer woke me a few hours later, and I realized my boss had triggered the emergency button on his bedside command center. I rolled out of bed, threw on my robe, and grabbed my smartphone before heading downstairs, quickening my pace when I heard something crash in his room.

I burst through the door to find a long-haired, heavily

tattooed man straddling Dingo. I grabbed the empty Merlot bottle left over from Dingo's late-night self-medication and aimed for the bleachers.

"Call 9-1-1," the man shouted. "He's not breathing!"

I stopped midswing, realizing the guy was performing CPR on my employer, not strangling him. I fumbled my smartphone from my robe and dialed. After explaining the situation to the operator, I turned on the Good Samaritan. "Who the hell are you, and how did you get in here?"

"Toby Entemann," he said. Dingo had resumed breathing by then. "Dingo buzzed me in. You must be Jughead Badloss. He told me about you."

"And how—?"

"He moved heaven and earth to locate me, and when I learned from Inspector Framer that the great Tiberius Dingo wanted to see me, I slipped away from a previous engagement to come here."

I thought Inspector Framer had retired after failing to pin Teddy Aerieman's death on Dingo when the poisonous tropical spiders Dingo collected killed and partially ate the arachnologist he'd hired to care for them. Dingo had donated the surviving spiders to the O. Orkin Insect Zoo at the Smithsonian Museum of Natural History in DC, and the habitat on the brownstone's top floor had been abandoned. I said as much.

"You must be thinking of Framer's father," Toby said. "He's been down in Florida for almost a decade. Junior's been walking in his daddy's shadow ever since he joined the force. When they finally promoted him to Homicide Division, the brass even stuck him in his old man's old office."

The EMTs arrived before I could ask any more questions, and Toby disappeared during the confusion.

Dingo had not left the brownstone in more than a decade, but his vices had finally bested him, so I made an executive decision in his best interest. I also phoned his personal physician—who'd served as a medical consultant on several of our old cases—and Dr. Clayton Oswald met us in the Emergency Room of Hale Mary Fuller Grace.

I explained—without mentioning Toby Entemann's involvement—what had happened.

"Dingo's lucky he buzzed you when he went into cardiac arrest or he might not be here to complain about all the people touching him."

"He isn't doing much complaining," I said. He wasn't actually doing much of anything.

When I realized there was nothing I could do for my employer that wasn't already being done by professionals, I went upstairs to Intensive Care to look in on Ruth's brother. I had no idea if life support would bring Christian back, or if it was merely delaying the inevitable. I tried to question a nurse, but once she determined I wasn't related to her patient she refused to speak with me.

I turned to leave and bumped into Inspector Framer, who was the spitting image of his father. With an electronic cigarette clenched between his teeth, he growled, "What are you doing here?"

I told him Dingo had been hospitalized a few hours earlier.

He expressed no symphony for my employer's plight and repeated his question with a different emphasis. "Why are you *here*? Why are you in Mr. Entemann's room?"

"His sister is our client."

"She hire you to find out who tried to off her brother?"

"No, she—" I caught myself. "The automobile wreck wasn't an accident?"

"My dad warned me about you and Dingo," he growled again. "You stay the hell away from my case."

"But the accident—"

"Get out of my sight, Jughead, and don't let me catch you nosing around Entemann's room again."

I returned to the ER, but Dingo had been transferred to a private room. I tracked him down and, for the first time, took stock of his situation. My employer was unconscious, whether sedated or as a result of what had happened at the brownstone I couldn't tell, but something was amiss.

I stopped the first nurse to enter his room. "Where's Mr. Dingo's watch?"

She directed me to the room's closet. Inside I found a clear sealed bag with the contents listed on the front in black marker:

1 blue pajama top, size 9XL
1 blue pajama bottom, size 9XL

I looked up. "No jewelry, no watch, no—"

"Security does the inventory. Take it up with them."

I did. They claimed Dingo had not been wearing a watch when he'd arrived in the emergency room, and the emergency medical service that had transported him to the hospital also claimed Dingo had not been wearing a watch. That meant one of two things: either someone was lying, or Toby Entemann hadn't been trying to save my boss's life—he'd been stealing his watch.

The day had barely begun, and already things were headed south.

I returned to the brownstone midmorning to find the chef beside herself. "How is Mr. Dingo?"

"I'm not sure."

I settled at the kitchen table, and she took the seat opposite mine. For the first time since the whippet in white had entered our employ, I actually looked at her, seeing the woman and not just the uniform. I glanced at the name embroidered in dark blue above her left breast: *E. Claire.*

"E?"

"Elizabeth," she explained. "Elizabeth Claire Goodnight."

She looked as if she expected her name to mean something to me. It didn't. Not right away.

"I accepted this position so I could meet you," she continued. "You knew my mother, Carol Goodnight."

Carol Goodnight. The suicide blonde. I'd interrupted the foot pursuit of a suspected embezzler to talk her down off a bridge. She'd spent a week in my room while Dingo and I cleared her of criminal charges relating to the theft of several thousand dollars from her employer's safe. She hadn't told her husband of the accusation and would have leaped from the bridge if I hadn't come along when I did. She'd let him think she had run off with me.

I waved vaguely at my kisser. "Your father did this."

Elizabeth tilted her head to the side and examined me for a moment. "My father messed up your face?"

"Your mother and I, we—"

"She said you didn't, but I'm not sure my father believed her."

Silence hung in the air between us. I didn't know what Elizabeth was thinking, but I was remembering how close her mother and I had come to consummating our relationship that first night in the brownstone. If Dingo hadn't buzzed me from his office, the last stitch of her mother's clothing might have dropped to the floor. I still think my employer interrupted us on purpose, because he'd had nothing important to tell me when I joined him after being buzzed. But he did not bother to buzz the following evenings.

Finally, Elizabeth broke the silence. "I'll need to make some adjustments to Mr. Dingo's diet when he returns home."

I wasn't thinking clearly when I put myself to bed a few minutes later. I had rarely worked a case on my own, but I knew our client expected continued attention to her needs. I slept until late afternoon, ate a light dinner in the kitchen, and spent time on the phone with Mook, bringing him up to speed on all that had happened. I asked what, if anything, he had learned from tailing our client. He had nothing of significance to report, so I said, "We need to track down Tony Entemann. If Dingo could find him, we can, too."

"I'm on it."

After I disconnected the call, I laid my cell phone on the table and stared at it.

"Are you looking for the man who was here last night?"

I looked up at Elizabeth Claire. "You know something about that?"

"I saw him leave," she said. "While the EMTs were taking care of Mr. Dingo, he slipped out the back."

"And went where?"

"Over the fence," she said. "I heard a motorcycle."

My phone rang before I could ask another question, and I saw our client's name on the screen.

I answered. "Yes, Ruth?"

"Where have you been?" she asked. "I haven't heard from you."

"I looked in on your brother and had a run-in with your nephew."

"What do they have to do with my current situation?" she demanded. "You think my own family is stalking me?"

I didn't answer her question directly. "Do you still think someone is following you?"

"I saw a man watching me this morning."

"Did he look like a Q-tip in sweatpants?"

"Why, yes, that's a perfect—"

"That's Mook. He's one of the operatives we've got watching you."

"I liked it better when *you* were watching me," she said. "I feel safer when you're within arm's reach."

"I will be," I said, "at the next dance."

No sooner had I finished my conversation with Ruth when Dr. Oswald called to remind me I had medical power of attorney for my employer and to tell me Dingo needed coronary bypass surgery. "His lifestyle has finally caught up to him," Oswald said. "There's no other option."

I couldn't imagine life without Dingo. Though we were employer and employee, we were the closest things to family either of us had. After several minutes of discussion, I approved the operation.

"Good," the doctor said. "I have surgery scheduled for first thing in the morning."

I spent the next few hours digging through the files we'd relegated to the basement when we converted Dingo's office to his bedroom, searching for the original copy of his medical power of attorney. The first three filing cabinets contained records from many of the cases Dingo had successfully solved during his decades as the city's premiere private investigator, including a dozen from before my association with the firm. I could easily have gotten lost in a haze of memories, so I forced myself to continue hunting until I located our wills, powers of attorney, and medical powers of attorney, paperwork we'd completed when Dingo had first exhibited an inability to walk to the elevator without becoming seriously winded.

I took the medical power of attorney to Hale Mary Fuller Grace, signed the authorization for the coronary bypass, and looked in on Dingo. Wan but conscious, he ordered me to report.

I reported.

"The last thing I remember is talking to Toby Entemann," he said. "He was telling me about the rift between his father and his aunt."

"How did you find him?"

"I called in a number of favors, old colleagues who remember working with us in the past. Some of them still have connections. Toby's working undercover inside one of the motorcycle gangs, and I was lucky I was able to pass a message to him."

The next morning, I collected one of E. Claire's used hairnets on my way out the door and stuck in it a manila envelope. While Dingo was under the knife, I sat in the hospital's waiting room and called Mook. I told him what I needed from the two women he was tracking.

As Dingo recovered from the surgery, I asked Dr. Oswald to look into another matter. I handed him the manila envelope containing the hairnet and had him take a swab from the inside of my cheek. I thought I knew what the results would show, but I wanted to be able to prove it.

I also gave him a used tissue lifted from a woman's purse and a water glass taken from a diner that morning. I had no idea if my suspicions would pan out, but my employer was in no position to provide guidance.

Dr. Oswald had access to medical records obtained by various entities belonging to the Hale Mary Fuller Grace Medical System, and I hoped he could use what I'd given him to match DNA across the multiple suspects in the Entemann case.

■ ■ ■

A few days later, Dingo stared at the square of green Jell-O on his dinner tray. "My life has come to this," he moaned.

Confinement to a hospital bed inside an actual hospital was the epitome of hell for my employer. Being poked and prodded by a constant parade of doctors, nurses, and aides made his skin crawl, and the lack of control over his diet made him grouchy. I said, "You're lucky you still *have* a life."

"Did you bring the Merlot?"

"No."

Dingo glared at me for a moment before looking away. I don't know what he saw when he gazed out the window—all *I* saw was gray sky, a crowded parking lot, and a never-ending stream of traffic crawling along the highway—but when he turned back the scowl had disappeared. He asked, "What have you learned?"

I told him everything that had happened since he was taken from the brownstone, including our newest chef's connection to the suicide blonde and the uncomplicated family tree of our client.

"You've been busy," he said.

My cell phone rang, and I answered when I saw that the call was from our client. I put her on speaker so that Dingo could hear both sides of our conversation.

"The hospital just phoned," Ruth said. "My brother is dead."

"I'm sorry to—"

"He can rot in hell," she said. "Have you made any progress with my case?"

I was about to say we hadn't, but Dingo interrupted me.

"I think I can put the matter to rest this evening," he said, "if you'll come to my hospital room after dinner."

She agreed to join us at six o'clock, and we ended the conversation.

"We have a murder on our hands, Jughead," Dingo said, "and it's time we wrapped it up."

He gave me a list of names, and I made the calls.

That evening, Dingo's hospital room seemed more crowded than his office had ever been during the denouement of a case. It was the first time he solved a case while lying down, and the first time he gathered client, suspects, and interested parties in a hospital room. Ruth Entemann arrived first, followed a few minutes later by her nephew Toby. Then Mook showed up with Elizabeth Claire Goodnight in tow. Inspector Framer came last, dragging Jennifer Wilson with him.

"What's this all about?" Framer demanded.

Dingo didn't answer directly. Instead, he looked at each of us in turn and cleared his throat. "This started as a simple case of a woman"—he turned briefly to indicate our client—"who believed she was being stalked."

Ruth nodded.

"That was simple enough. We identified Ms. Entemann's stalker within forty-eight hours, though we didn't know the motive for the stalking. Then the case took an unexpected turn. Before we conclusively identified Ms. Wilson as the stalker—"

Jennifer Wilson straightened. "I never—"

"—we realized that our client had something in her past she was hiding from us."

Dingo addressed Toby. "Your father passed away earlier today, and that's why Inspector Framer is here. Your father's death wasn't an accident. It was murder. You stand to gain from his death, but it turns out you're not the only one who does."

He turned to Ruth. "You told Jughead you were unable to have children, which is only partially true. After he spotted your C-section scar, we had Dr. Oswald examine your medical records. You *did* have a child, long ago. You gave the infant up for adoption, and complications from the C-section prevented you from having additional children."

He looked at Jennifer. "You were adopted at birth, but only learned the truth as an adult. You wanted to know who your parents were and why they had given you up. When you finally gained access to your adoption records and saw your birth certificate, it listed only your mother's name. The space for your father's name was blank. But you were able to go in search of your mother. You also saw the paperwork relinquishing parental rights and realized that your birth parents had failed to relinquish *inheritance* right. That means that you stand to inherit a great deal of money upon the deaths of your biological parents."

Inspector Framer pulled the electronic cigarette from between his lips and asked, "So Ruth is Jennifer's mother, but who's Jennifer's father?"

"The DNA tests Dr. Osgood ran," Dingo continued, "indicate that the family tree doesn't branch." Dingo looked at Ruth. "Your father paid good money to make the problem disappear. He didn't want anyone to know what had happened between his children."

"I was fifteen," Ruth said. "My father sent me to a home where they butchered me while taking my child."

Toby looked at Jennifer and said, "You're my cousin?"

Dingo added, "And your half sister."

"My—?"

"You share a father," he explained, in case anyone in the room had failed to grasp his subtlety. "She's also the person who murdered your father and planned to murder your aunt."

Inspector Framer glowered at Dingo. "You can prove all this?"

"Have I ever been wrong before?"

Inspector Framer cuffed Jennifer, read her her rights, and led her away.

When they were gone, Ruth said, "There's a sickness in my family."

"We don't have to perpetuate it," Toby said. "Maybe we can heal the wounds."

Tony led his aunt—our client—out of the room.

Dingo turned to Elizabeth, who was wide-eyed at the events she had just witnessed. "There's one other mystery to solve," he said. "I wasn't wearing my watch when Toby Entemann tried to revive me. I had taken it off and set it on my dinner plate. You found it when you cleared the previous evening's dishes from my room. You knew it was the watch your mother gave me because your grandfather's name is etched on the back, and it was the only thing of value Carol ever owned."

"My mother said she gave her grandfather's watch to the man who saved her."

Actually, the suicide blonde gave the Rolex Oyster to Dingo after we cleared her of theft charges. All she gave me were memories of our week together and a daughter I never knew I had.

"You took it to a jeweler. What were you planning to do with it?"

"I left it to be cleaned," she said. "I was going to return it."

Dingo turned. "Mook?"

Mook took the Rolex from his pocket and handed it over. "That's where I found it."

Dingo examined the watch for a moment, and then handed it to Elizabeth. "This is rightfully yours," he said. "I've cared for it long enough."

After my employer sent my daughter back to the brownstone with Mook, Dr. Oswald gave Dingo a once-over to ensure the evening's events hadn't been too strenuous.

When the two of us were alone in the room, Dingo looked at me.

"I am not pleased to learn, Jughead, that you turned my home into a setting for one of your trysts," Dingo scowled. "Have you anything to say for yourself?"

"It'll never happen again, boss," I told him.

And, given my age, I meant every word of it.

PART III

POTPOURRI

The Woman Who Read Rex Stout

by William Brittain

EDITOR'S NOTE: After "The Man Who Read John Dickson Carr" and "The Man Who Read Ellery Queen" appeared back-to-back in the December 1965 EQMM, junior high school English teacher William Brittain contributed nine additional "Man Who Read" stories to the magazine, along with thirty-two tales featuring high school science teacher Leonard Strang. In the early 1980s, Brittain turned his attention from crime stories to novels for young readers; his The Wish Giver *was a Newbery Honor Award recipient in 1983. Our children's gain was our loss—but there's good news for mystery readers: all eleven of the "Man Who Read" stories and seven of the Mr. Strangs have been collected as* The Man Who Read Mysteries: The Short Fiction of William Brittain *(Crippen and Landru, 2018).*

■ ■ ■

The first time I saw Gertrude Jellison reading a Rex Stout detective novel, I laughed so hard it made me weak inside. She didn't pay any attention to me, though. She just sat there on the platform with her nose buried in that book. It was called *Over My Dead Body*, and the jacket had a picture of this big fat guy, Nero Wolfe, scowling as if he had stomach trouble. I'd look at Gert, then I'd look at the book jacket again. That combination would break anybody up.

You see, Gert Jellison weighs over five hundred pounds.

Gert and I both work in a Ten-in-One, a carnival sideshow. My name's Robert Kirby. I'm Gert's partner, which means I stand beside her on the platform during the shows. A pretty easy way to make a living, but I'm not strong enough to do much else. I got the job because, although I'm as tall as Gert, I only tip the scales at seventy-five pounds. Fat lady, thin man. Get it?

To return to the Nero Wolfe books, it was Mel Bentner got up the idea. Mel owns the show, and he's our magician and spieler. He stands out in front and tells everybody about the wonderful sights inside the tent. Then, when he's turned the tip and everybody is inside, he comes in and does his act. Mel saw the Nero Wolfe book with the picture on the jacket in a store and thought it would be a good gimmick to have Gert reading it during the show.

After Gert finished that first book, she read her way right through all of Rex Stout's Nero Wolfe novels, starting with the earliest one, *Fer-de-Lance.* And pretty soon she began to act like Nero Wolfe. Wolfe liked beer, so Gert developed a yen for pink lemonade. Wolfe raised orchids, and Gert got her tent so full of carnations she hardly had room to sit down. She took those mysteries seriously, all right. It didn't surprise me much. Gert's serious about her reading. For all her weight, she's got a really sharp mind. She told me she was once up for a job teaching psychology at a college, but the first time those profs got a look at her, they started laughing so much she ran away and joined the carny the same day.

As I say, we all thought it was pretty funny to see Gert reading those books about that fat detective. But then Lili was murdered. I didn't laugh at Gert after that.

We should have known something was going to happen. First, one of our trucks broke down, so the Ten-in-One had to stay behind while the rest of the carnival headed for the next set-up. While Mel was trying to fix the truck, he burned his hand on a soldering iron and had to put salve and a big bandage on it. That meant his magic act was out of the show for at least a week.

Well, they say misfortune comes in threes. The third thing was what happened to Lili.

Lili was our snake charmer. She came on the lot one day last season and asked for a job. Just for a joke, Mel told her to feel the snakes our last charmer had left behind when she took off with a whole night's receipts. We all waited for Lili to start screaming, but she handled those snakes like so much garden hose. Within two weeks, she had her act ready, Gert had made her a costume, and Ferdinand Hanig, our strongman, was in love with her. Ferdie had competition, though. Zeno the sword swallower thought Lili was pretty nice, too.

But Gert kept both men at a distance. She mothered Lili, sewed clothes for her, and made sure she got to bed on time. She even let Lili water her carnations, when nobody else in the carny was even allowed to sniff them. And both Ferdie and Zeno knew that, if they tried any hanky-panky, Gert would clobber them. I guess Lili became the daughter Gert would never have.

Mel was the one who found Lili's body, but I guess we all got to her trailer pretty fast when he started yelling. All but Gert, that is.

Gert was just too heavy to walk that far. It's all she can do to waddle from her living tent up onto the bally platform. So I knew it was up to me to tell her what had happened. That's another thing about Gert: she gets me to do her errands for her. She says she got *that* idea from Nero Wolfe, too—something about a guy named Archie.

I went into her tent while the rest were still over by the trailer. She looked up at me slowly and poured herself a glass of lemonade. "What's all the caterwauling outside?" she grumbled. "It spoiled my beauty sleep."

I knew how she felt about Lili, but I didn't see any way to break the news gently. "It's Lili," I said. "She's dead."

"Dead? Pfui. I just saw her an hour or so ago. She was waving to the rest of the carny when it departed."

"Gert, she's been—somebody killed her."

She just sat there staring at me with her mouth open. Then it hit her. I hope I never see anything ever again like that great fat woman in a big lacy pink dress sitting there and crying. She buried her face in her hands and sobbed, shaking all over.

At last she looked up at me. Her expression wasn't sad anymore; it was angry. It was the same look Nero Wolfe had on the cover of that book.

"How was she killed, Bob?" she finally asked.

"Strangled. Somebody took a scarf—one of hers, probably—and tied it around her neck. Then he put a tent stake through the loop of the scarf and twisted. I'm glad you didn't have to see her face, Gert. It was terrible."

"Garroted," she said. "What kind of person would choose that way to kill?"

"Whoever it was must have knocked her out first," I continued. "Mel says her head was bruised, and there was blood in her hair."

"Does anyone have any idea who did it?"

"Mel's still over at the trailer, looking around. He told me to come and tell you. I don't know if he found anything."

"I did." The tent flap behind me opened, and Mel came in. "This was under Lili's body." He held out his hand.

Gert and I both looked at the object on Mel's palm. It was a flat piece of metal about two inches long. It was almost semicircular in shape, except that the edge that normally would have been straight had a series of notches in it.

"It looks like a piece of that slum jewelry the old man with the ring-toss concession used for prizes last year," said Gert. "He gave me one before he left the carny."

"Yeah," I said, "but that doesn't prove anything. I used to have one, too. He gave 'em to just about everybody who was working with the show then."

"I don't remember seeing one before," said Mel.

"This is just half of it," said Gert. "When both halves are fitted together, it forms a complete circle. He engraved a name on each half, and the boy got one and gave the other to his girl."

Mel smiled wryly. I figured he was just trying to take Gert's mind off Lili. "Whose name did you have put on the other half of yours?" he asked her.

"Don't be facetious at a time like this, Mel," she said. "He put my name right across both halves, if you must know. Is there anything special about this medallion?"

"Just proves that whoever killed Lili must have been nuts. Look."

He flipped the metal plate over in his hand. On the polished surface were engraved four letters, two above and two below:

BY
BY

"What kind of a screwball would murder a girl like Lili and leave a message like that?" I asked.

Gert took the medallion into that huge palm of hers and looked at it for quite a while. "Whatever happened to that ring-toss man, Mel?" she asked. "Is he still around?"

"No, he's with an outfit down south somewhere. I hear from him occasionally."

Gert dropped the medallion onto her dressing table among some of the carnation pots and slid farther down into her reinforced chair. She closed her eyes, and pretty soon her lips started working—pushing out, drawing back, pushing out again. We knew her brain was busy, and finally she turned her head slowly to look at us.

"Mel, have you called the police?" she asked.

"No, but I'm on my way right now."

"I don't want you to tell them yet."

"I've got to, Gert," Mel said. "This is murder."

"No! Trust me, Mel, I want to see the murderer apprehended probably more than anyone else on this lot. But he's mine, Mel. I want the person who did this to know that I caught him."

"Oh, Gert, you've been reading too many of those Nero Wolfe stories."

"I've never been one to ask a favor," said Gert. "But now I ask this. Just have everybody here in an hour. At that time, I will prove to your satisfaction who murdered Lili."

Mel thought about it. Then he scratched his head. "I believe you will, Gert," he said. "Okay, I'll do it."

He turned to me. "Come on, Skinny, let's round up the others." He walked out of the tent.

I watched him go and then banged my fist on the table, nearly mashing one of Gert's flowers. "Why does he keep calling me that, Gert?" I scowled. "He knows I can't stand that nickname!"

She laid her heavy hand on my arm. "Easy, Bobby," she said. "He's just jumpy, like the rest of us. He probably forgot."

"He didn't forget. He knows I hate people calling me that." I took a few deep breaths to calm down and then went outside, leaving Gert sipping at her everlasting pink lemonade.

It took us a little more than an hour to get everybody in the show together. Cal Lynn, our Flatbush-born swami, had taken his car into town to get a part for the truck, and Sammy Marsh had gone with him to buy some cotton wads for his fire-eating act. Finally, though, we got everyone crowded inside Gert's tent. Nobody thought she'd really be able to figure out who had killed Lili, but we thought she deserved the chance.

She looked up at us from her chair with that angry, grouchy expression still on her face. "Ladies and gentlemen," she said, "a member of our company has been murdered. I ask you to indulge me for a few moments, during which time I will attempt to ascertain the identity of the murderer.

"I am going on the assumption," she continued, "that the murderer is one of us. Lili was alive early this morning, when the rest of the carny left. Since that time, nobody has been on this lot with the exception of ourselves. Ergo, one of us killed Lili."

We all turned to look at Ferdie and Zeno, who were standing off to one side. Gert held up her hand.

"Suspicion without proof is pointless," she said. "But I intend to provide that proof. First, consider the method of murder: a scarf, twisted tightly with a tent stake. But, we must ask ourselves, why was a stake used as a lever? Surely this would indicate that, for some reason, the murderer—unlike most of us here—was incapable of strangling Lili without mechanical help."

Now *there* was an eye opener. Maybe Gert was getting something out of those Nero Wolfe books, after all! There was a murmuring of voices, and everyone turned to Mel Bentner, who was trying to hide his bandaged hand behind him.

"Wait just a minute!" said Mel. "Maybe the murderer used the lever in order to kill Lili more slowly and make her suffer more."

"I must reject your hypothesis, Mel," said Gert. "You said that Lili was struck on the head before being strangled. Therefore, the killer was strangling an unconscious girl."

"But what about that medallion?" someone demanded. "Why would anybody leave a crazy thing like that near the body?"

"Leave it? Pfui! Are you asking me to believe that the killer had jewelry especially engraved for the occasion?"

It did sound ridiculous, the way Gert put it.

"Well, then how *did* it get there?" Mel asked.

"The murderer dropped it accidentally, of course."

"Accidentally? You mean the murderer just happened to be carrying a piece of jewelry that said 'BY BY' on it?"

"I think so, yes. Have you stopped to consider what was written on the *other* half of that medallion?"

Mel looked puzzled, but Gert went on. "It is my belief that the triangle of Lili, Ferdinand, and Zeno recently became a quadrangle. This morning, the fourth person had a rendezvous with Lili and offered her his love—and Lili rejected him. She probably did so in such a way that he became furious and hit her, perhaps with the same stake he used to tighten the scarf. Then, fearing Lili would tell what he had done, he killed her to keep her quiet."

Ferdie Hanig lumbered up in front of Gert. "Who did it?" he asked menacingly.

"Who is the person in this show who would find it impossible to use a scarf as a strangling cord without increasing his strength through leverage?" Gert asked. "Who takes umbrage at a simple remark that others would consider a joke? And, finally, who has a name that, in its diminutive form, could be written across both halves of a piece of jewelry in such a way that the right half would contain only the letters 'BY BY'?"

So that's it. It all happened just the way Gert said. Everything would have been okay if only Lili hadn't of called me "Skinny." Or if Gert hadn't of spent so much time reading those Rex Stout mysteries.

Just for the record, the policeman in charge of the case has asked me to put my name at the bottom of this page in a special kind of way. He says it'll help them, and that it's better for me to cooperate.

I hereby acknowledge that the above confession was freely given, without coercion, and that I have been offered no promise or inducement of any kind in order to make it.

(signed)

BOB-BY
KIR-BY

Sam Buried Caesar

by Josh Pachter

AUTHOR'S NOTE: My first published short story, "E. Q. Griffen Earns His Name," was about a family of eleven kids, all named after famous fictional detectives by their father, an inspector with the Tyson County Police Department. I was sixteen years old when I wrote it, seventeen by the time it appeared in the "Department of First Stories" in the December 1968 EQMM. After a second E. Q. Griffen story in the May 1970 issue of the magazine, I decided to turn my attention to one of young Ellery's siblings—and picked ten-year-old Nero. As my wife, Laurie, will tell you, I love a good pun, and the title "Sam Buried Caesar" is, I think, a good one—but the last line of the story is a real groaner.

For the fifty-millionth time, my name is *not* Archie Goodwin! It's *Artie*, Artie *Goodman*—Arthur Eliot Goodman, Junior, to be exact. But ever since we moved in next door to Inspector Ross Griffen and his brood about a year ago and ten-year-old Nero Wolfe and I became best friends, I've been Archie Goodwin to everyone in town.

Not that I mind the comparison, you understand. Nero got me interested in the Wolfe stories, and I've read most of them by now; Archie's pretty cool and everything, even though he keeps talking about these dumb *girls* all the time, but it's just that I don't want to be typed as Nero Griffen's legman for the rest of my life.

I mean, I'm pretty smart myself, you know. I was the one who found Lou Kramer's missing bicycle, not Nero, and if it wasn't for me asking the right question at the right time, we would never have discovered who was shoplifting from Mr. Tierney's five and dime.

And even though Wolfe beat me to it, without so much as getting out of his chair, I did solve the mystery of Sam Cabot's dog Caesar all on my own.

It was the end of June, about a week after Wolfe had gotten out of fourth grade and I'd escaped from third, when we decided to form our own detective agency. I kind of liked "Griffen and Goodman, Private Investigators," myself, but Nero insisted on "The Nero Wolfe Detective Service" and I didn't make a fuss—I'd gone along with the idea for the fun of it, anyway, not for the glory.

Our first couple of days were pretty slow, but soon the word got around and cases started leaking in—mostly lost toys and things, nothing really interesting at first. Nero proved pretty good at tracking down that kind of stuff and we began to build up a reputation of sorts. After three weeks we risked raising our retainer from a dime to fifteen cents, and nobody seemed to mind.

Somewhere along the line, Nero's brother Sherlock got into the act. He wasn't much good, but he didn't bother anyone, so we let him hang around until the day he deduced, from a rip in my shirt and the dirt under my fingernails, that *I* was the one who'd been swiping apples from the tree in Jerry Tieger's back yard. At that point we decided that Sherlock had to go—actually, I decided that either he went or I did, and Wolfe agreed that my detective abilities were more important than mere family ties.

So Sherlock was banished from the agency, and Nero and I went back to handling our couple of cases a day, all by ourselves. We averaged thirty-five to forty cents a case, and more from grown-ups, plus expenses—which was nowhere near as profitable as a good paper route but lots more enjoyable.

Agency business took up most of our time, and as a result we didn't get to see old friends as often as we used to. I hadn't spoken to Sam Cabot in weeks when I walked into the Griffen garage, our office, one morning in August and found him seated in one of the yellow folding chairs we kept around for clients.

"Hi, Archie," Sam said, with a mournful look on his face.

"Artie," I said automatically. "Hi, Sam. What's up?"

"I just finished telling Nero," Sam answered. "It's about my dog."

"Caesar?"

"Sure, Caesar!" Sam exploded. "He's my dog, isn't he? I—I mean, he *was* my dog."

I pounced. "What do you mean, *was* your dog? Has something happened to him?"

"You're sharp as a tack today, aren't you, Artie?" Nero chuckled. "Sam, you'd better go back to the beginning and fill my partner in."

"There's not much to tell," Sam began slowly. "I was out

playing with Caesar about three hours ago, at that vacant field at the corner of Hoover and Berkshire. I was throwing a rubber ball around, and Caesar was fielding. Well, the ball got away from me and rolled into Berkshire, and Caesar ran after it. There's a thirty-mile-an-hour speed limit there, but this late-model, off-white convertible came tearing down Hoover, doing fifty at least, and made the turn into Berkshire without even slowing down. The driver must have seen Caesar, because he slammed on his brakes, but he was too late—he hit him. The guy started to pull over, then he changed his mind and beat it."

"Did you get his license-plate number?" I asked.

"He was going too fast. They were out-of-state plates, I could see that, and I think the last number was a three or an eight, but I'm not sure. Anyway, I was too worried about Caesar to think much about the car. I ran up to him. I remember looking around for help and not seeing any other people or cars nearby, so I dragged him to the sidewalk, off the street.

"There was blood all over the place. I felt for his heartbeat, but I couldn't find it. Caesar was dead."

Sam slowly shook his head from side to side. He didn't look like he was going to be doing any more talking for a while, so I shifted my glance to Nero.

"Sam then moved the corpse to a corner of the vacant field," Nero told me, "and ran home to tell his parents what had happened and to find out what he should do. There was no one home."

"I—I couldn't just leave him there, lying around with blood all over him and everything," Sam sniffled, "so I took a shovel and went back to the vacant field and dug a big hole and buried him. After I filled in the hole, I just stood there for a while and, well, cried. I loved that dog, Archie!"

"Artie," I said. "So you want us to find out who killed your dog?"

"There's more to the story," Nero frowned. "Go on, Sam."

"Well, I f-finally went home and sort of mooned around for a while. Then I decided to go back and get Caesar's collars and tags, so I'd have something to remember him by. So I went to the field and dug up the grave and—and—"

"And what?" I prompted.

"And Caesar's body was gone."

"What!" I yelled.

"You heard him, Artie," Nero growled. "He dug up the grave and the dog's body was gone."

"He must have dug in the wrong place," I said.

"No!" Sam cried. "I didn't!"

Nero leaned back.

"This is about where you came in, Artie," he said. "Sam was telling me that, because it hasn't rained around here in almost a week, the top layer of dirt at the vacant field has turned a kind of dry, dusty, light brown. When he dug the hole and buried Caesar, moister dark-brown dirt from underneath got left on top of the grave. Sam?"

"So when I went back for the collar and tags," our client said, "I just looked for the spot where the dirt was dark-brown instead of light, and dug there. And Caesar was gone."

"Do you have any idea why someone would want to steal Caesar's corpse?" I asked.

"No, I can't see why anyone would do a thing like that! I can't figure it out at all!" Sam's voice trembled.

"Who knew where you buried your dog?"

"No one—well, I didn't *tell* anyone, not even that he was dead. But I guess a few people walked by while I was digging the grave, and some cars must have passed by, too, and they might have seen what I was doing."

"Did you recognize any of the people or cars that passed?"

"No, none. But I wasn't looking at them carefully or anything."

"Could the convertible that killed Caesar have been one of the cars that passed?" Nero asked.

"I—I didn't notice, really. I don't think so."

"What about the driver?" I said. "Could he have been one of the people who walked by?"

"I guess so. I don't know. I just wasn't paying much attention to anything except Caesar."

"All right, Sam," Nero said, rising, "that's all we need to hear right now. We'll take your case."

"You'll find out who killed Caesar?" Sam asked eagerly.

"No promises. But we'll do our best."

"And you'll get the body back?"

"We'll try. Our retainer is fifteen cents, which you can give to Artie. Of course, the final fee will depend on our results. We'll get back to you as soon as we can, maybe today or tomorrow."

Sam got up from his yellow chair.

"Thanks, Nero," he said, shaking Wolfe's hand goodbye. "I really mean it, thanks a lot."

Then he handed me a sticky dime and a nickel, shook my hand, and said, "You, too, Archie. Thanks."

"Artie," I said, as I pocketed the coins and ushered Sam out of our office.

Numbers have always fascinated me.

Like, did you know that if you multiply any number, any number at all, by nine, and then add up the digits of the product, and then add up the digits of that sum, and keep adding until you wind up with a single digit, that final digit will *always* be nine?

Or did you ever notice that, out of all the millions of squiggles that *could* have been chosen to represent our ten numerals from zero to nine, two of the ten that *were* chosen happened to be shaped exactly the same? The only difference between a six and a nine is that one of them, and I wish I knew which one, is upside down.

That particular afternoon, as I pedaled along Berkshire toward Hoover and the vacant field, I was thinking about how a three is just an eight with the left side sliced off, and how it would be easy to mix up a three and an eight if your mind was on something else and you only got a quick look. People get confused when they're worried about the life of a loved one, I thought, even when the loved one is an animal, and they can't be expected to pay attention to trivial details. Still, I wished Sam could have been more definite about the license plate of that convertible.

After Sam Cabot left the Griffen garage, Nero and I had tried to figure out why anyone would want to steal the body of a dead dog. Even alive, Caesar was just a scrawny little dachshund, not worth much of anything. Why was he so important now that he was dead?

The most logical answer seemed to be that the hit-and-run driver felt that somehow he could be identified through the corpse of his victim, so he had returned to the scene of his crime and removed the incriminating corpse. It didn't make much sense, but that was the best we could come up with, so my job was now to investigate the scene for clues, and then to hunt for an off-white, late-model convertible with out-of-state plates and a license number ending in either a three or an eight.

I braked at the corner of Berkshire and Hoover and got off my bicycle, leaving it on the sidewalk with the kickstand down.

Carrying a shovel in my right hand, I explored the vacant field. Most of the lot was nothing more than the dusty light-brown dirt that Sam had described, with small patches of weeds and crabgrass here and there and yellowed papers and slivers of glass scattered all around. Two sides of the field were open, bordering on Berkshire and Hoover, and the other sides were separated from the adjoining lots by a tall wooden fence.

I quickly located the circular patch of dark, recently turned earth which showed where Sam had buried the dead body of his dog, and began digging. After twenty minutes or so, I had hollowed out a hole about four feet deep and found nothing but four feet of dirt. Satisfied that Caesar was indeed not where he was supposed to be, I filled in the hole and went back to my bicycle.

This may sound a lot like second guessing, now, but as I climbed on my bike I took a good look around, and I got the funniest feeling that something was missing, something *besides* the body I'd been looking for. You know how it is—you know something is wrong, but you just can't pin it down. Something was missing, something that *should* have been there, and I sat for a while, trying to figure out what the heck it was. Finally I shrugged and, giving up for the time being, pushed off.

I rode around town for a long time looking for the murder car. I saw off-white convertibles with in-state plates, and out-of-state plates on old off-white sedans, but I drew a blank on late-model, off-white converts with the right kind of plates. Even *without* the three or eight at the end of the number.

Disappointed, I turned back to the road. But while I'd been looking in different directions I'd been steering blind, and now I found myself heading straight for a parked station wagon. I swerved toward the curb and backpedaled hard, trying to avoid a crash. At the last second, I closed my eyes.

There was a sharp jolt as I smacked into something, and I spilled off my bicycle onto the sidewalk. I opened my eyes and saw that I had missed the station wagon and had hit the curb instead. I just lay on the cement for a while, groggy, until I was sure I could get up. A small group of people had collected, mostly kids, and a man helped me to my feet.

"You okay?" he asked.

"Yeah," I said, "I think so."

My knees hurt and my arms hurt and I think my *teeth* even hurt, but I could see that I wasn't bleeding anywhere, so I—

No blood.

My head was swimming, and there were kids and grown-ups all around me asking questions left and right, but the words *no blood* were like jackhammers inside my brain, pounding so hard that I had to pay attention to them and to nothing else. No blood, *no blood, NO BLOOD!*

Caesar was struck by a convertible on Berkshire, Sam had said, *and before he died he had bled all over the place*. Those were Sam's own words.

I picked up my shovel, pushed through the crowd of onlookers, got on my bicycle, and rode back to the vacant field at the corner of Berkshire and Hoover. As I rode, I glanced down at my badly skinned arms. The pain had died down to a steady throbbing, and small flecks of red oozed out at several spots. Blood.

Caesar was hit by a car and had bled all over the place.

But when I got to Berkshire there was no blood on the street, no blood on the sidewalk, no blood anywhere.

Blood! *That's* what had been missing!

But why?

The street cleaners only came by early in the morning. And what about the sidewalk? And the field itself? Who could have cleaned Caesar's blood from the field? And why?

Then slowly, piece by piece, the puzzle fitted itself together inside my head. Caesar killed, no blood, body stolen . . .

I rode over to Sam's house and, leaving my bike in the driveway, carried my shovel into the back yard.

I found what I was looking for in a strawberry patch in a corner of the yard. The patch had just been watered, so the soil was all a rich chocolaty-brown, but at the very rear of the patch, where no berry plants were growing, there was a small, slightly raised mound of dirt.

The mound was roughly the same size and shape as the dark spot I had dug up earlier, at the vacant field.

I started shoveling.

When I entered our office for the second time that day, I was tired, sweaty, and awfully proud of myself.

Nero was still seated in his overstuffed leather armchair, and Sam Cabot once again was sitting in one of the yellow folding chairs. When I walked in, they were discussing the relative merits of two different ways of making a peanut butter and jelly sandwich. Nero insisted that, to get the best combination of flavors, you had to spread the peanut butter on one slice of bread and the jelly on another and then kind of *smish* the two slices together. But Sam held out for spreading both peanut butter and jelly onto the *same* slice of bread, and then putting the unspread slice on top to finish the sandwich.

I listened to the debate for a couple of minutes, until I got good and hungry. Then I smacked my lips nice and loud. Sam and Nero looked at me.

"Hi, Archie," Sam greeted.

I stood there for a few moments, deciding whether or not to remember that Sam was a client.

"What's the matter, Arch?"

"Artie," I said menacingly. "My name is Artie."

Sam was startled.

"S-sure," he mumbled.

"Sure what?"

"Sure, *Artie*."

"That's better," I growled.

"Are you finished, Arthur?" Nero asked politely. He called me Arthur when he wasn't mad at me but wanted people to think he was.

"Just about." I smiled. "Sir."

"Very good. Sam and I were talking about peanut butter and jelly, and I think we're about ready for a practical demonstration. Have you eaten?"

"That can wait," I said. "First, I'd like to report."

"Something important?"

"You could call it that. I've solved the case."

"*This* case?" he asked, nodding toward Sam Cabot.

"Right."

"Well, then," Nero smiled, "you'd better go ahead and report. Verbatim."

"What verbatim?" I scowled. "I haven't said two words to anybody all day! I just rode around! Now do you want me to report or not?"

"Certainly, Artie. Go right ahead."

"Okay," I said. And I told Nero and Sam how I'd gone to the field and dug up the empty grave, and how I'd *known* that there was something missing besides the dead dachshund but couldn't pin down what it was. Then I told them how I'd suddenly realized that what had been missing at the vacant field was—

"Blood," Nero interrupted.

"Huh?" I said.

"That's what was missing. There should have been Caesar's blood all over the place, but there wasn't."

"When were you there?" I demanded.

"I haven't been out of this chair all day, Artie."

"Sam told you, then!"

"Sam told me nothing," he said smugly. "I told Sam, and he admitted I was right."

"Well, then, how did you—?"

"Proceed, Artie."

I didn't feel nearly so proud of myself anymore. If Nero hadn't left his chair at all, and Sam hadn't told him anything, how did he—?

"There wasn't any blood on Berkshire, or on the sidewalk, or on the field," I said, "so I just thought about it until I figured it out. It was pretty simple, really. The obvious thing for me to do was to grab my shovel and—"

"—and go to Sam's house."

"There's no way you can know I did that, Nero!" I exploded.

"I don't *know* what you did, Artie. I *assume* that you went over to Sam Cabot's because that's what *I* would have done if I'd been in your place. The fact that I'm right and you *did* go there doesn't make me a mind reader. It just confirms my opinion that you've got brains."

"All right," I said. "I went over to Sam's and went into the backyard, and suppose you tell me what I found in the strawberry patch?"

"Now, you see," Nero said patiently, "there are *some* things I haven't been able to figure out by myself. I know you dug a hole in Sam's back yard, but the fact that you dug it in a strawberry patch is news to me. How did you know just where to dig? Different-colored dirt again?"

"No, the whole patch had just been watered. I—"

"Ah, then you must have come across a small mound of earth and guessed that was the spot. Correct?"

"Yeah, great. I dug there, about three feet down, and found—"

"—Caesar's body."

"Caesar's body. Will you let me finish one sentence, Nero, just *one*?"

"I'm sorry, Artie. Go on."

"Caesar's hair was all matted and sticky from dried blood," I said. "He smelled like lemonade, and there was a note pinned to his left ear reading, 'I wish you'd keep your crummy dog off my field. He keeps bleeding on the crabgrass.'"

Nero blinked his large hazel eyes.

I continued. "The note was signed, 'Love and kisses, The Phantom of the Opera.' And the whole thing was written in green ink. In *your* handwriting."

Nero blinked again.

I swallowed, hard.

"All right, Nero," I said. "I give up. I found Caesar's body, tags and all. He was dead, but he looked perfectly okay. No blood, no note, no nothing."

"I'd already figured out that was the case, Artie," Nero murmured.

"Yeah, I bet you did. Now tell me how you did it, and then tell me what it's all supposed to mean, if you're so smart."

"How is easy. What's a little harder, but I'm sure you've worked most of it out yourself. After you left this afternoon for the vacant field, I just sat here and thought about the case. I wasn't satisfied with our conclusion that the hit-and-run driver had stolen Caesar's body to avoid being identified. The more I thought about that possibility, the less sense it made. But it still seemed obvious that the body was stolen because there was something wrong with it, something that *someone* didn't want us to see."

"What could be wrong?"

"Well, the only thing I knew about Caesar's body was that it had been struck by a car and there was lots of blood. What could be wrong with *that*? And then the whole thing came rushing at me like a swimming pool does after you've jumped off the high diving board. Smack! I had it!

"We weren't supposed to see the body because there *wasn't* any blood on it! Once we saw it, we'd know that Caesar hadn't been hit by a car at all. So Sam had lied about the car, lied about the blood—in fact, Sam had even lied about burying Caesar in the vacant field. Caesar's body wasn't stolen from the field—*it just wasn't there to begin with!* Once I'd worked all of this out, I called my brother Perry Mason in, and asked him to go get Sam. When Sam got here, I told him I knew his story was a pack of lies and demanded that he tell me the truth. Sam, tell Artie what you told me."

"I—I'm sorry it worked out this way, Ar-*Artie*," Sam began, "but Nero's right. You see, I was playing with my chemistry set this morning and I mixed a lot of the things together—calcium carbonate, tannic acid, all kinds of chemicals. Then I decided to do an experiment and feed the mixture to Caesar. I didn't think anything would happen! I just stirred it into his water dish and watched him lap it up. He seemed to really like it."

Sam wiped the back of his hand across his sunburnt nose and sniffled.

"Nothing much happened for a few minutes," he continued, "but then Caesar started to whine, like. I tried to get him to stop, but he kept whining and moaning and everything, and finally he just lay down and closed his eyes and started shivering.

"In a little while he stopped shivering, and I felt for his heartbeat, but it was gone. I'd killed him.

"I was scared, Artie, real scared! Then I thought about

telling everyone that a car hit him and killed him. If I made up a description of some out-of-state car, I figured everybody would look for it for a while and then give up and forget all about it.

"But I realized that when you saw Caesar you'd know no car had hit him because there was no blood. And I knew I couldn't hit him myself and make him bleed—I just couldn't hit Caesar."

"But you gave him that junk from the chemistry set," I said, disgusted.

"I didn't think it would hurt him! It's not the same thing, don't you understand?"

Sam's small skinny frame started quivering and I turned away. I don't like to see fellows cry, and I wasn't feeling any too sympathetic toward Sam in the first place.

"All *right*," I said. "So it was an accident. What happened next?"

Sam kept on sobbing.

"Nero?" I said.

"I accused Sam of killing Caesar in a way that left no visible marks. He then told me about the chemistry set. But, you see, I had already deduced—"

"I *believe* you!" I shouted. "Just tell me what happened!"

"Well," Nero harrumphed, "let me see. Sam buried his dog in his back yard, then went to the vacant field at Berkshire and Hoover and dug a hole. When he had filled in the hole, he noticed the difference in color between where he'd dug and the dirt all around, so he went home and watered down the strawberry patch, just to play it safe. He didn't want anyone noticing that someone had been digging in his back yard, not with Caesar's body supposedly missing. But he didn't notice that the dirt was a little higher where he had buried Caesar than anywhere else. And then he came to us with his story."

"And by the time I finally realized that no blood on Berkshire meant that Caesar hadn't been run over and found the body and figured that *Sam* had killed him, you'd already doped it all out. So what do we do now, Chief?"

"Well, Artie, Caesar's death *was* an accident, and you can see how badly Sam feels about it. I told him we'd keep our mouths shut and help spread the story of a hit-and-run. It'll keep Sam out of trouble."

"You mean we play it like we couldn't find the killer?"

"Right. And since our taking money for keeping quiet sounds too much like blackmail, I've given back Sam's retainer. Now, as I said before, when you got here Sam and I were about to test our theories about how to make a peanut butter and jelly sandwich and I . . ."

So Nero Wolfe had solved the case, refused payment, let the criminal off, and was now getting ready to *feed* him. All without lifting his slightly pudgy ninety-five pounds from his chair. And what did I have to show for it? A wasted afternoon, dirty clothes, and a lot of bruises.

I sighed, and went out to fetch peanut butter, jelly, and bread.

One last thing.

Our ruse worked real good, and pretty soon people stopped looking for the nonexistent off-white convertible. Sam's parents even bought him another dachshund, a female this time, which Sam named Cleopatra.

And when Cleo had pups, months later, I strolled into our office one afternoon after school to find Nero playing with the pride of the litter.

"Sam give you that?" I asked.

"Yes. As a token of his thanks."

"What are you going to call it?"

"Him," Nero corrected. "I can't decide."

"How about Fido?"

"How about shutting up? I want his name to have something to do with what he looks like. Like you'd call a spotted dog Spot or a red one Red."

I looked at Cleo's pride. It—I mean he—was a small, dark-brown, very fat puppy.

"How about Fat Fido?" I suggested.

"Artie."

"Plump Prince?" I asked meekly.

"Pfui," Nero Wolfe replied.

"Hey, I've got it! Call him Stout Rex," I said, and ran for cover.

Chapter 24 from *Rasputin's Revenge*

by John Lescroart

AUTHOR'S NOTE: Long before I began writing my legal thrillers set in San Francisco and featuring Dismas Hardy, Abe Glitsky, and Wyatt Hunt, I became addicted first to Arthur Conan Doyle's Sherlock Holmes canon (particularly the William S. Baring-Gould annotated edition of the complete works), and then in short order to the Nero Wolfe books of Rex Stout. Immersed in these series, I decided to explore the idea that these two towering detective heroes were, in fact, related: during the "lost years" of 1892 to 1894, Holmes had an affair with Irene Adler, and this liaison produced a son they named Auguste Lupa. After World War I, when he moved to New York from the European theater and became a consulting detective, Lupa changed his name to Nero Wolfe. (Augustus and Nero were both Caesars, of course, and lupa *is Latin for she-wolf.) My first hardcover book,* Son of Holmes, *helped established the legitimacy of this theory, and the sequel,* Rasputin's Revenge, *made the connection between Holmes and Wolfe all but undeniable.*

[KREMLIN FILE NO. JG 0665-5095-5100; PSS ACCESS, OPEN] JANUARY 2, 1917

Sherlock Holmes looked up from his first bite of woodcock. "Delicious, Auguste, absolutely delicious."

Lupa nodded solemnly, allowing only the slightest turn of his lips as he accepted his father's compliment. He could not so well control his eyes, however—they shone with pleasure.

"Where did you get woodcock here in St. Petersburg?" Dr. Watson asked.

"Monsieur Muret has his connections," Lupa answered, nodding graciously at our host.

Muret took his cue. "Who would not have done so? It's a great honor to have Auguste Lupa in one's restaurant." He paused. "And, of course, you other gentlemen."

In the background, a trio of gypsy guitarists played softly. Lupa had spent the afternoon in the Villa Rhode's kitchen preparing the excellent dinner we were enjoying. Holmes, Watson, Muret, and I were sharing a couple of bottles of Cornas, while Lupa chose to drink Muret's good dark beer.

It was our first evening out since we'd been pardoned, and the celebration was most welcome. After several days of embassy cooking, we were doubly appreciative of Lupa's talent, and fell to the meal with a vengeance.

When we'd all but finished, Dr. Watson was the first to speak. "There's still one thing I don't quite understand."

Holmes, his own humor completely restored by the successful conclusion of the case, mopped up the last of his sauce and ate it on a bit of Lupa's fresh bread, leaned back into the booth's upholstery and patted his stomach happily. "And all's right with the world," he said.

"Really, Holmes, there's no need for sarcasm."

Holmes wore a mild look of surprise, which seemed feigned to me. "My dear fellow," he said, "I'm afraid that came out wrong. Please forgive me. What is it you don't understand?"

Muret refilled the good doctor's glass and he sipped, then continued in his blustery way. "All of Rasputin's motives are clear to me—the revenge and so forth—but I don't quite see how he convinced Miss Ripley to do his bidding. After all, she didn't need him. She had her own career. What could persuade her to do his terrible work? What could he give her to make it worth the risk?"

Lupa didn't give his father a chance to respond. "Love!" he blurted out, as though it were a curse word. "Love, the most powerful force in the world."

"Just so," Holmes agreed. "When the only goal is to please a lover, anything else, everything else, is secondary."

"Even murder?"

"Anything," Lupa said, "it doesn't matter what"—he stopped to take a drink of his beer—"which is why the damned emotion ought to be avoided at all costs."

I had to speak up. My infatuation with Elena may have nearly killed us, and her love for Rasputin was surely turned to the wrong ends, but I wasn't willing to propose a loveless world as the solution. "To the contrary, Auguste. It may make us either fools or heroes, but surely it's worth it. A life without it is an empty life, indeed."

I must have touched a nerve, for Lupa appeared about to say something, then bit it back. Sherlock Holmes, though, leapt into the breach. "Let's not forget that love can also lead people to do the *right* thing." He looked directly at his son, and his hard eyes softened. "It is, after all, what brought Watson and me here to Russia. In more ways than one, Auguste, it's why you're alive."

Lupa, obviously grappling with strong emotion, swallowed hard, then looked down, finally reaching for his beer. For me, the admission of love from father to son is the most natural thing in the world, but clearly that hadn't been the case between Holmes and Lupa.

A fanfare of strummed guitars accompanying an outbreak of applause gave my friend a moment of respite. The lights were turned down, and from the stage I heard the haunting strains of Varya Panina as she began singing, almost whispering, a ballad to an insistent rhythm like that of a heart beating. As I had been the other time I had seen her, I was captivated by her artistry, her passion, even though I couldn't understand the words.

While she sang, the restaurant was quietly rapt in its attention, and if ever I was grateful that the world was through with the vulgarity and the evil of Gregory Rasputin, it was at that moment. When the chanteuse finished, the room exploded again with applause. There were few dry eyes in the house, and none at our table.

As the applause continued, Muret got up and went to the stage. Seconds later, he escorted a smiling Varya Panina back to our booth. Upon being introduced to Lupa and me, she stopped. "But surely you two . . . the night the *tyemniy*—Rasputin—was here . . . ."

"That's right," Lupa said.

She smiled, and her face, with such unattractive features, became a thing of its own rare beauty. She reached out her hand, first to me, then to Lupa. "I know now who you are." She paused. "Thank you."

Lupa, most uncharacteristically, held on to her hand. "Could I ask you a question, madam?"

"Surely, anything."

"That last song—what was it about?"

She shrugged, then answered in her deep, rich voice. "The same as always: love. That is all my songs. Love. What else is there? That is life, eh?"

Lupa nodded and let go of her hand, and she went back toward the stage.

He hung his head for a moment, and I could see him pursing his lips in and out, out and in. Then, straightening up, he looked across the table at his father.

"I'm thinking of going to England from here. I was wondering if I might stay awhile with you?" he asked. "If you're too busy, I'll understand, but—"

"No, not at all. Capital idea!" Watson exclaimed, bursting in before Holmes could respond. "Holmes, don't you agree?"

The great detective nodded. "Of course," he said. "I'd like that." He nodded again, and smiled. "I'd like that very much. Stay as long as you wish."

Lupa leaned back in the booth and looked from his father to Dr. Watson and back to his father again. The corners of his mouth turned up a centimeter in what was for him his broadest grin. Behind us, the guitarists began the introduction to another song. He lifted his half-full beer glass and, raising it to his lips, drained it in one gulp. Putting the glass down gently, he wiped his lips with his napkin and sighed deeply.

"Satisfactory," he said. "Very satisfactory."

A scene from *Might as Well Be Dead*

by Joseph Goodrich

AUTHOR'S NOTE: After adapting Ellery Queen's Calamity Town *for the stage, I wanted to bring another of the Golden Age detectives to life. Nero Wolfe was an obvious choice—his popularity is undiminished in mystery circles, and he's still recognized in the larger world of nonmystery fans. As of autumn 2018, I've adapted two Wolfe stories:* The Red Box *and* Might as Well Be Dead.

Both Queen and Wolfe are supersleuths and descendants of Sherlock Holmes, the king of all gifted (and eccentric) detectives. Ellery Queen's character went through a number of changes over the years, moving from a bloodless intellectual to a much more human figure who becomes involved in the lives of the people who need his help. Nero Wolfe's character, though, remains essentially the same, which is one of the continuing pleasures of the series; his foibles endear him to readers. Rex Stout created a world as palpable for Wolfe fans as Victorian London is for the devotees of Sherlock Holmes.

Readers feel passionately about Wolfe and his world, so I tried to be true to the spirit of the stories, even though I altered something here and cut something there. Any dialogue I invented had to match the language and feel of the books.

One of the great pleasures of moving Queen and Wolfe from the page to the stage is the opportunity to introduce them to readers and audience members who may not have heard of them before. They're classic sleuths, part of a great tradition, and they deserve to be celebrated.

(The curtain rises. The stage is in darkness. Lights up on ARCHIE GOODWIN, a well-dressed young man. He addresses the audience.)

ARCHIE: Goodwin's the name. Archie Goodwin. I work for Nero Wolfe. If you've got a problem, he's the man to solve it. It's got to be a special kind of problem, though, to get him interested, and you have to be willing and able to pay for his time—which doesn't come cheap. I would say "pay for his time and effort," but it's mostly *my* effort you're paying for. He's the brains of the operation, I'm the legs. He thinks, I move. It's a good combination. *(Lights up on NERO WOLFE, seated behind a large desk.)* Couple things you should know about Mr. Wolfe. One: He's the greatest private detective south of the North Pole. Two: He hates to leave home, because fresh air clogs the lungs. Scientific fact. Three: He'd die if anything happened to Fritz Brenner. Fritz is our chef—mighty skillful with a skillet. I blame *him* for getting us involved in the Herold case.

Here's what happened. It was Monday, May 22nd, 1956. Mr. Wolfe and I were in the office. He was reading *The New*

York Times. I was going over the books—which were in good shape for once. A big case had come through, and we were sitting pretty as far as mazuma goes. So it wasn't the prospect of some extra cash that made Wolfe let a visitor in. No, I think it was the lunch. Fritz had outdone himself: the lightest, goldenest fried chicken with gravy, home-made corn bread hot from the oven, raspberries in sherry cream for dessert, a crisp white wine for Mr. Wolfe and a tall, cool glass of milk for yours truly. My theory is that the meal affected Mr. Wolfe's temperament to such a degree that, when a knock came at the door, he didn't tell me to send the caller away. No. What he said was—

WOLFE: Find out who he is, and what he wants.

(ARCHIE crosses to the door and opens it, revealing MRS. HEROLD, a stolid Midwestern housewife.)

MRS. HEROLD: The name is Herold. Mrs. Shirley Herold. I need to see Nero Wolfe.

ARCHIE: I'm Archie Goodwin, Mr. Wolfe's assistant.

MRS. HEROLD: I know who you are. They told me all about you. You're what they call a live wire.

ARCHIE: That's a new one—and a *clean* one. Who says I'm a live wire?

MRS. HEROLD: The fella from the Missing Persons Department. He also says you're a pain in the—neck.

ARCHIE: Who is this fella? I'd like to give him a great big kick in the—neck.

(WOLFE looks up from his newspaper.)

WOLFE: Mrs. Herold, what brings you here today?

MRS. HEROLD: I'm not sure where to begin.

WOLFE: At the beginning is always best.

ARCHIE *(to audience)*: Mr. Wolfe was almost . . . friendly. It must have been the lunch. That's all I can say.

WOLFE: Please be seated.

(ARCHIE leads MRS. HEROLD across to WOLFE's desk and seats her in a red leather chair.)

MRS. HEROLD: It's good of you to see me. I know I should have called first.

WOLFE: Archie?

ARCHIE: Yes, sir?

WOLFE: Take notes. *(ARCHIE picks up a pen and a notebook.)* When you are ready, madam, proceed.

MRS. HEROLD: All the way here on the train I thought about what I'd say.

WOLFE: Whence did you come?

MRS. HEROLD: Beg pardon?

ARCHIE: Where did you get on the train and begin to do your thinking?

MRS. HEROLD: Saint Paul, Minnesota. *(She takes a business card from her purse and reads it aloud.)* Herold's Hardware. 1738 University Avenue. "What we don't have, you don't need." *(She places the card on WOLFE's desk and continues.)* My husband opened the store in 1932. Keeping it open in the middle of the Depression killed him. I've run it on my own for over twenty years now. Biggest hardware store in town.

WOLFE: How may I help you?

MRS. HEROLD: Mr. Wolfe, I'm guilty of an injustice. I've ruined Paul's life—I'm sure of it.

WOLFE: Who is Paul?

MRS. HEROLD: My son. What I did to him was wrong. I've got to fix things—if I can. But first I have to find him.

WOLFE: What is the nature of this injustice?

MRS. HEROLD: Eleven years ago, money was stolen from the store's bank account. I was sure Paul had done it. Are you familiar with the Ten Commandments?

WOLFE: Intimately, madam. My livelihood depends upon them being broken.

MRS. HEROLD: "Thou shalt not steal. Thou shalt not lie. Thou shall honor thy mother and father that thy days may be long upon the land." Paul broke every one of them. I ordered him out of the house. Told him I never wanted to see him again.

WOLFE: An extreme response.

MRS. HEROLD: I live by the word of God. I expect others to do the same.

WOLFE: You must be frequently disappointed.

MRS. HEROLD: I'm a Missouri Synod Lutheran. I'm used to it.

WOLFE: Did your son defend himself against your accusation?

MRS. HEROLD: He tried, but I didn't believe him.

WOLFE: Belief comes easy when there's no room for doubt. It's a far more difficult task when one has to deal with the ambiguous and the circumstantial.

MRS. HEROLD: I don't like your tone.

WOLFE: Nothing compels you to listen to it. Mr. Goodwin will see you out at any time.

MRS. HEROLD: Of all the—

ARCHIE: Mrs. Herold?

MRS. HEROLD: I don't like it. I don't like it at all. But you've got a point. I didn't trust my son, and I should have. What happened is all my fault.

WOLFE: Not entirely. There *was* a theft. How much money was taken?

MRS. HEROLD: Fifty-seven thousand dollars. Everything I had—gone like that. Almost closed the store for good.

WOLFE: When did you find out your son wasn't guilty?

MRS. HEROLD: Two months ago. Turned out it was one of the bank clerks. He'd been dipping into people's accounts for years. When we found out what he was up to, he blew his brains out. Suicide note explained it all. My son is innocent.

WOLFE: You think he's in New York City?

MRS. HEROLD: Paul always dreamed about New York. There's no other place he'd go.

WOLFE: But Missing Persons had no luck.

MRS. HEROLD: They said too much time had gone by. The trail is cold.

ARCHIE: After eleven years, it's frozen stiff.

MRS. HEROLD: They did what they could. I hired a couple of private detectives. They couldn't find Paul, either. I have their reports here. *(She takes a large manila envelope from her purse and places it on WOLFE's desk. WOLFE opens it and goes through the papers it contains.)* Some of those so-called detectives couldn't find their way out of a burning barn. That's a photo of Paul. That's the ad I ran in the New York papers.

ARCHIE: Any results?

MRS. HEROLD: Nothing that panned out.

WOLFE: Did your son take any luggage with him when he left?

MRS. HEROLD: A trunk and a suitcase.

WOLFE: Were his initials on either of those pieces?

MRS. HEROLD: They were on both.

WOLFE: Does your son possess a middle initial?

MRS. HEROLD: Just PH. Why?

WOLFE: Initials on luggage have dictated a thousand aliases. If your son changed his name, no doubt he found it convenient to keep the PH. Even so, the job promises to be toilsome.

MRS. HEROLD: I've got to find him and make amends. Right is right.

WOLFE: A legitimate search could take months and may require substantial funds. My fees are not insignificant. Nor are they contingent on success.

MRS. HEROLD: You need a retainer. *(She takes a sheaf of bills from her purse and drops it on WOLFE's desk.)* Will five thousand dollars be enough?

WOLFE: That will suffice.

MRS. HEROLD: Any questions—any news—don't hesitate to call. I'll be at the store. I always am.

ARCHIE: When do you go back home?

MRS. HEROLD: My train leaves tomorrow.

ARCHIE: Since you're in town, why not see a show? *My Fair Lady*'s packing 'em in at the Mark Hellinger. Supposed to be pretty good.

MRS. HEROLD: I'm not here on vacation. 'Sides, you know what a Broadway show costs these days? Four dollars and ninety cents!

ARCHIE: Would you like a receipt?

MRS. HEROLD: I would not. I'm from the Midwest. We trust people. A handshake will do. *(She extends a hand to WOLFE.)*

ARCHIE: I do the handshaking around here. *(ARCHIE and MRS. HEROLD shake hands.)* I'll see you out.

(They exit. WOLFE presses a buzzer on his desk. ARCHIE returns. He takes the money from WOLFE's desk and puts it in the wall safe.)

ARCHIE: Never thought I'd see the day. A stranger appears, and you let her in. She wants to put you to work, and you agree. A hopeless case, and you accept it. It had to be the lunch.

WOLFE: Pfui.

ARCHIE: Kind of hard on the lady, weren't you?

WOLFE: Orthodoxy irks me. It is the enemy of reason.

ARCHIE: We'll need all the reason we can get. I wouldn't wish this case on Inspector Cramer. Well, maybe Inspector Cramer, but no one else. Missing Persons beats the bushes for Paul Herold, sees how hopeless it is, and sticks you with a first-class, gold-plated gazookis. *(FRITZ enters with a tray holding a bottle of beer and a glass.)* This case is a complete washout. Right, Fritz?

FRITZ: There are no washouts in this house. Not with Mr. Wolfe on the job—and you. You will solve it. You will make much fuss, but you will solve it. Shad roe for dinner.

(FRITZ exits.)

ARCHIE: Here's how we find Paul Herold: Saul Panzer and I disguise ourselves as members of the Salvation Army. He starts at the Battery, works his way north. I start at Van Cortlandt Park, work my way south. We meet at Grant's Tomb on Christmas Eve and compare notes. Then we hit Brooklyn. How does that sound?

WOLFE: You're right, Archie. We've been handed, as you say, a "gazookis."

ARCHIE: So how *do* we play it?

WOLFE: Paul Herold doesn't want to be found. His mother's advertisements have only put him on the alert. He will not be easily driven from cover. Your notebook.

ARCHIE: Yes, sir.

WOLFE: Heading, in large boldface: "To P.H." In smaller type: "Your innocence is known. The injustice done you is regretted."

ARCHIE: ". . . regretted."

WOLFE: No.

ARCHIE: It's not regretted?

WOLFE: Deplored.

ARCHIE: ". . . the injustice done you is deplored."

WOLFE: "Do not let bitterness prevent the righting of a wrong. The true culprit has been exposed." Add my name, address, and telephone number. Call the *Gazette* and the *Times* and have them run the ad. We shall see what—if anything—comes of it.

The Damned Doorbell Rang

by Robert Lopresti

AUTHOR'S NOTE: For me it started in the fifth grade. The Plainfield (New Jersey) Public Library had a wonderful children's room, but I used it up. Not that I read everything, but I devoured all the books I wanted to read. That meant I had to make guerrilla raids down a long corridor full of looming microfilm readers to the cathedral-ceilinged main room. Children were not allowed there—so, if I was spotted, I knew I would be chased back to Winnie-the-Pooh land.

I discovered that the best place to hide from reference librarians was directly behind the reference desk, and that was the Mystery section. There I discovered Rex Stout. I wish I knew which was the first of his books I read. The Mother Hunt *and* Gambit *were among the earliest. The language and characters sucked me in. There is no voice like Archie's.*

The last Wolfe novel, A Family Affair, *came out while I was in college. I remember stumbling around the house in shock after the murderer was revealed. Powerful stuff.*

A few years later, when people my age were heading into New York City to hear punk bands at CGBG, I made a special trip to attend one of the first Wolfe Pack events: the world premiere of the TV movie Nero Wolfe, *starring Thayer David. (It wasn't bad, but David was too darned skinny.)*

In December 2012, I made another Stout-related trip to New York, this time to receive the Black Orchid Novella Award, sponsored by the Wolfe Pack and Alfred Hitchcock's Mystery Magazine. *That trip was all the more exciting because mass transport hadn't yet recovered from Superstorm Sandy. Good times.*

As long as I am laying out my Wolfean (lupine?) credentials, I should point out that my only contribution to the late-lamented magazine The Armchair Detective *was an article in which I proved (to my own satisfaction, at least) that the entire plot of* Gambit *was an attack on* Webster's Third International Dictionary.

When Josh Pachter told me about this book, I told him I would love to read it but couldn't imagine coming up with a contribution. And then, all of a sudden, the story that follows burst into my brain. Consider it a love letter to Mr. Stout for thousands of hours of pleasure.

Melissa rushed in, slamming the back door, and ran past her grandparents.

Jack, who had been pulling a batch of his famous scones out of the oven, turned to look at his wife. "What's got into her now?"

"She's fourteen," said Eve, finishing the work on their second pot of coffee of the day. "It's a crisis every hour."

"Can't be fourteen already. Can she?"

Eve sighed. "You were at her birthday party last month. Remember the sign on the wall?"

"Oh yeah. You go talk to her. I'll be in with a plate in a minute."

"Bring me a cup, too."

Eve found Melissa exactly where she expected, the same place the girl had been running since age four whenever things went wrong: in the den, stretched out on the sofa (which they really needed to replace one of these days, or at least re-cover). Melissa was facedown, arms stretched out, but she wasn't actually crying, so maybe this wasn't such a bad storm, after all.

"Hey, sweetheart. What's the problem?"

The girl didn't look up. "Why do we have to live in this dump?"

Eve sat down in her La-Z-Boy. "Well, thanks a lot. I happen to think this house is pretty nice. Plus, you *don't* live here, you live six houses—"

"Oh, Grandma." Melissa pushed up into a sitting position. Correcting people usually took her mind off her problems, at least temporarily. "I don't mean this house. I mean Saddle River, New Jersey." She said it like you might say *Hicksville*, or maybe *Mordor*.

Eve resisted the urge to reach out and stroke her hair. Melissa hadn't liked being petted since she was ten. "And what exactly is wrong with Saddle River?"

"It's boring. There's nothing to *do* here!"

"Says who?" said Jack. He was carrying a tray loaded with scones, plates, and more. "Didn't I take you bowling last week?"

"Last *month*. Two months ago, really. And I hated it."

"Well, excuse me." He placed the tray carefully on the coffee table. "Maybe if you'd stopped the damned texting for five minutes, you would have had more fun. Here's a scone, and here's your milk."

Melissa frowned. "Can't I have coffee? I've been drinking coffee since I was twelve."

"Not in *this* house you haven't," said Eve. "So, tell us, what's the problem?"

"My parents," said Melissa. "They have no idea what century we're living in."

"Don't talk with your mouth full. What have those old codgers done to you now?"

"They're ruining my life, that's all. Did you ever hear of Android Parsnip?"

"Let's assume we haven't," said Jack, settling into his easy chair. "What is it?"

"They're the best band in the world. And they're performing in New York next month. Everybody's going!"

"Ah," said Eve. "Everybody except you."

Melissa bounced on the couch. "Exactly! Can you talk to them?"

"How do you plan to get there?" asked Jack.

"A bunch of us are taking the train."

"Without adults? Absolutely not."

"Grandpa! You're just as bad as they are."

"Thanks for the compliment," said Eve.

Melissa threw herself back on the sofa, arms folded, working herself up to a genuine snit. "I don't know what's wrong with you two. Didn't you both grow up in the city?"

"We did," said Jack. "And got out while the getting was good."

"But why? Didn't you love it all? The theater. The museums. The music!"

"The muggings," said Eve. "The dog doo on the streets. Sometimes the *people* doo on the streets."

"Let's be honest," said Jack, sipping coffee. "We *did* love it when we were young."

"Young, but older than you, sweetheart. Young but adults."

"What really chased us out of the city was the worst neighbors anybody ever had."

That got her attention. "What, worse than the Califanos?"

"The Califanos were pretty bad," Eve agreed. "Those all-night arguments. And that pit bull. Your mother was afraid to let you out of the house."

"But these clowns were even worse," said Jack. "This was back in the early sixties, when your grandma and I had just started our business."

"I started it. You were still doing the books for that tavern."

Jack frowned. "Yeah, and bringing in the only income we had until you started getting customers. Just because you got famous designing textiles, don't forget the little people who made it possible."

"Little people. You left *little* behind about a hundred scones ago."

Melissa waved her milk glass, spilling a bit. "Tell me about the neighbors."

"Oh. Well, we had one floor of a brownstone in the West Thirties, way over by the Hudson River."

"That whole area's torn down now," said Jack. "Good riddance."

"The place had a lot of character," said Eve. "But the *real* characters lived next door. A bunch of men, although you couldn't tell how many actually lived there, because so many of them showed up at all hours."

"Just men?" asked Melissa. "Were they gay?"

"How do you know about gay?" asked Jack.

She rolled her eyes. "TV. Movies. My friend Douglas. And my other friend Kai is trans, but their parents won't admit it."

"Well, they might have been gay," said Jack. "There was one fat guy who hardly ever came out, but when he did he dressed like he was ready for a Halloween parade in Greenwich Village. A cowboy hat and a fur coat, plus a big walking stick."

"Fur? Ooh, gross."

"It wasn't a fur coat," said Eve. "Just the collar."

"Still gross."

"Anyway, the young one was definitely not gay," said Eve.

"How do you know?" asked Melissa.

"Because he gave me the eye." She winked.

Jack frowned. "You never told me that."

"You had a temper in those days. I didn't want you to get beaten up."

"By that clown? I could have taken him."

"Oh no, you couldn't."

Melissa grinned. "Was he cute, Grandma?"

"Very, sweetheart."

Jack snorted. "Cute, hell. He barely had a nose."

"Oh, he had one." Eve winked again.

"Something wrong with your eye?" asked Jack.

"And they had the most amazing visitors. I'd see movie stars coming by. Politicians. You never knew *who* would show up."

"God only knows what was going on in there," mumbled Jack.

"One day, I remember like it was yesterday, our doorbell rang, and guess who was outside?"

"Not *this* story again."

"Who, Grandma?"

"J. Edgar Hoover! He was as close to me as you are."

"You did not see Hoover," said Jack. "Back then, you thought everybody you saw on the street was a damned celebrity."

Eve put down her cup, a little harder than necessary. "It was him. You couldn't mistake that piggy face."

"Come to think of it, maybe it was. Didn't I hear he liked ladies' clothing?" Jack sipped coffee thoughtfully. "Maybe *that's* what they were doing in there."

"Anyway," said Eve, "I saw him. As I recall, you weren't home that day. You were at the racetrack."

"My boss invited me. What was I supposed to do? I was bringing in the only income—"

"I've heard of Jay Hoover," said Melissa. "Didn't he help impeach Richard Nixon or something?"

"Or something," said Jack.

"Google it when you get home, sweetheart." Eve took a breath. "Now, where was I? Oh, Mr. Hoover asked if he had the right address, but he didn't."

"That happened a lot. Sometimes the damned doorbell would ring four or five times a week. Like your handsome friend couldn't give out the right street address."

"Anyway," said Eve, impatiently, "Hoover apologized, nice as could be, and went next door."

"What did he want with the men next door?"

"I don't know, but they must not have been home, because he never got in."

"The fat guy hardly ever went out," said Jack. "They probably just wanted nothing to do with him. If it *was* Hoover."

"So why did these guys make you move?" asked Melissa, reaching for a second scone.

"That was years later. Your grandmother's business had gotten off the ground by then, thanks to her talent and my business acumen."

Eve muttered something.

"And we had bought our brownstone. Your father was a bouncing baby boy. Then, one day—"

"Stop," said Eve. "You're skipping the best part."

"Here we go again." Jack stood up. "More coffee? Milk?"

Everyone agreed.

"What's the best part, Grandma?"

Eve smiled. "I saved their lives, that's all."

Melissa's eyes went wide. "No kidding! How'd you do that?"

"Well. My office was on the second floor, in the back. When I sat at my desk, I looked out at this sad little garden they had next door." She shook her head. "They had a French cook—"

"He wasn't French," said Jack, back again with a full tray. "Belgian, I think."

"Whatever. Anyway, there was a fence with a gate in it, and he would come out to pick up deliveries. And, oh, there were a lot of them!"

"Because of Fatso," said Jack. "The guy must have eaten like the Green Bay Packers."

"You shouldn't body-shame, Grandpa."

"Anyway," said Eve, "I used to watch deliverymen come by with cases of all kinds of food. I would try to guess what was in the boxes that weren't labeled. They must have been gourmets, next door."

"Ha," said Jack. "That's what you thought."

"Go on, Grandma."

"So, the deliveryman I saw most was from Parsede's. They're long gone, but they used to be a major liquor company in New York. And at least once a week I would see one of their big blue trucks pull up to the gate in back. The driver would come out in this nice blue uniform with a hand truck stacked with cases of beer."

“Those clowns must have drunk like fish,” said Jack.

“Anyway, one day the truck arrived and the cook came out to let him through the gate, and I just happened to look down and thought, *Hey, there's something wrong*.”

Melissa's eyes were wide. “What do you mean? Wasn't it the usual deliveryman?”

“Oh, there were several different men. It was a big company. But, remember, I design fabrics for a living.”

“Used to,” said Jack. “You've been retired for, what, two decades? You sound like you still drive into Manhattan every day.”

“*Anyway*, I finally realized what was wrong. The Parsede's deliverymen always wore cotton uniforms, but *this* man was wearing polyester!”

“You could tell that from the window, Grandma?”

Eve nodded. “The way it reflected the sunlight. Fabric was my life, back then.”

“That and your darling son,” said Jack. “And your beloved husband.”

Eve sipped coffee, letting them wait. “Anyway, I worked for another few minutes, and then I thought about all those people I had seen going into that brownstone next door over the years. Police. Celebrities. And suddenly I just knew I had to tell them. Little Tommy was napping—your dad must have been about two—and I picked him up and ran down the stairs. I remember I was just wearing slippers, but I went outside and climbed up their stoop. The young man answered the door—”

“The cute guy,” said Melissa.

“Old Stubby Nose,” muttered Jack.

“I told him that the guy who just delivered their beer was a phony.”

“Wow! What did he do?”

“Slammed the door in her face. Neighborly.”

Eve scowled at him. "That was because he took me seriously, unlike *some* people around here. He wasn't going to endanger me and the baby by letting us inside until he saw what was up."

"So what did *you* do?"

"I took Tommy home and tried to get back to work. A few hours later, when Grandpa returned from the races—"

"I was not at the races that day. You're going to have our granddaughter thinking I was a character from *Guys and Dolls*."

"What's that?"

"Never mind. The doorbell rang, and there was the nice young man with a big tray covered by a linen napkin. He said somebody had tried to poison his boss—"

"Fatso," Jack explained.

"And this was a thank-you. It was a whole meal, cooked by their French chef."

"He was Danish, I think."

"All kinds of fancy stuff. It looked beautiful."

"Wow," said Melissa. "It must have tasted amazing."

"Ha," said Jack. "It was awful. There was this disgusting goo—"

"Caviar, I'm pretty sure."

"And everything was covered with these nasty sauces. They were so rich, I spent half the night sitting on the damned—"

"That's enough," said Eve. "I admit it *was* a little strange."

"Needed some ketchup, in my opinion."

"Well, it was a nice gesture."

"So is that why you moved out?" asked Melissa. "Because someone tried to poison them?"

"Nah," said Jack. "We were willing to let that slide. But a couple of years later, there was an explosion that shook our house, damn near threw me out of bed."

"We thought a gas main had blown up," Eve said. "That was

around the time the city almost went bankrupt, and they weren't big on—what do they call it?—interstructure?"

"Infrastructure," said Melissa. "What happened?"

"It was our neighbors," said Jack. "They had a late-night visitor"—he harrumphed—"and the guy decided to blow himself up in their guest room."

Melissa turned her head from one grandparent to the other, as if she were trying to catch a sign that they were making things up. "Really? Was he a terrorist?"

"We never heard the whole story. It got hushed up. But the fat guy paid for an engineer to come check our house for us."

"He said everything was fine," said Eve.

"Yeah," said Jack. "Of course, Tubby was paying him, so how much could we trust him? You could buy off any city inspector, back then, so who could believe a private contractor?"

"But that wasn't the end of it," said Eve. "A couple of days later, there was another explosion, right on their front stoop. If we'd been going out, we might have been killed!"

"Grandma! Really? Another terrorist?"

"Nah," said Grandpa. "As I understand it, it was some ex-employee of theirs who went postal."

"But that was the final straw," said Eve. "We put our place up on the market and decided to move to New Jersey."

"Did you ever hear from them again?"

"We did, once. When they saw our ad, the nice fellow came over and invited us to have dinner with him and his boss."

"Wow! Did you go?"

"For more of that awful food?" asked Jack. "You kidding? Plus, for all we knew, a whole street gang might have come in with machine guns while we were having dessert."

"That's some story," said Melissa. "Do you have any, like, souvenirs from those people?"

"Not a one," said Eve.

"Ha!" crowed Jack. "And you're always claiming my damned memory is going."

"What do you mean?"

He bent over the tray and started shifting things onto the coffee table. "We do have one souvenir, kid. This is the very tray your grandmother's pug-nosed boyfriend brought the food over on."

"Really?"

Eve frowned. "That's right. I'd forgotten that."

"Yeah. You're slipping."

Melissa bent over to examine it. "It's beautiful! And engraved. Are those initials in the middle?"

"They must be," said Eve. "I wonder what they stand for?"

"Miserable Neighbors?" guessed Jack.

His wife sighed. "You're reading it upside-down, Grandpa."

Acknowledgments

Many people provided invaluable assistance in the preparation of this book. I thank them, one and all, especially:

Lawrence Block, Jon Breen, Loren Estleman, Marvin Kaye, and Dave Zeltserman for providing copies of their stories and permission to include them here.

Robert Goldsborough and John Lescroart for granting permission to include chapters from their novels, and Joseph Goodrich for permission to use an excerpt from his play.

Michael Bracken and Robert Lopresti for taking on the challenge of writing original stories especially for this volume.

Janet Hutchings, Jackie Sherbow, and Deanna McLafferty at *EQMM* for tracking down some of the hard-to-find material.

Ira Matetsky and Jane Cleland of the Wolfe Pack for invaluable suggestions and other assistance.

Rémi Schultz in France for providing a copy of Thomas Narcejac's "*L'Orchidée rouge*," Rebecca K. Jones for translating it into English, and Editions Denoël in Paris for obtaining the reprint rights from Narcejac's heirs.

Virginia Brittain for granting permission to include her husband Bill's story, and Bill's daughter Susan Brittain Gawley for her kind assistance. Scott Mainwaring for granting permission to include the excerpt from Marion Mainwaring's novel. Carol Demont at Penny Publications for granting permission to include the story by Norma Schier. Vaughne Hansen of the Virginia Kidd Agency, Inc., for granting permission to include the story by Mack Reynolds.

Otto Penzler and Charles Perry at the Mysterious Press for instantly recognizing that *The Misadventures of Nero Wolfe* was a book that needed to be published, and for shepherding it through the publication process.

Rebecca Stout Bradbury, the late Barbara Stout Selleck, and the Rex Stout Literary Property Trust, faithful guardians of the literary legacy of Rex Stout, for their enthusiastic support, and for granting permission to use the Nero Wolfe name and characters.

And, most of all, thanks to Rex Stout, whose creation of Nero Wolfe in 1934 inspired the authors of the stories and other material contained in this volume.

Copyright Information

"The Sidekick Case" is copyright © 1968 by Patrick Butler and originally appeared in *The Saturday Review*. Every attempt has been made to contact Mr. Butler and/or his heirs. Anyone with information regarding the current copyright holder is encouraged to contact Josh Pachter regarding compensation for this use of the story.

"Who's Afraid of Nero Wolfe?" is copyright © 2008 by Loren D. Estleman. First published in *Ellery Queen's Mystery Magazine*. Reprinted with the permission of the author.

Murder in E Minor is copyright © 1986 by Robert Goldsborough. This excerpt is reprinted with the permission of the author.

Might as Well Be Dead is copyright © 2017 by Joseph Goodrich. This excerpt is reprinted with the permission of the author.

"The Purloined Platypus" is copyright © 2017 by Marvin Kaye. First published in *Sherlock Holmes Mystery Magazine* and reprinted with the permission of the author.

Rasputin's Revenge is copyright © 1987 by John Lescroart. This excerpt is reprinted with the permission of the author.

"The House on 35th Street" is copyright © 1966 by Frank Littler and originally appeared in *The Saturday Review*. Every attempt has been made to contact Mr. Littler and/or his heirs. Anyone with information regarding the current copyright holder is encouraged to contact Josh Pachter regarding compensation for this use of the story.

"The Damned Doorbell Rang" is copyright © 2020 by Robert

COPYRIGHT INFORMATION

About the Contributors

LAWRENCE BLOCK (1938–) has been widely regarded as a man who needs no introduction, and that's exactly what he's going to get here.

MICHAEL BRACKEN (1957–) is a novelist and prolific short-story writer. He has received the Edward D. Hoch Memorial Golden Derringer Award for lifetime achievement in short mystery fiction as well as two additional Derringer Awards. He is the author of the private-eye novel *All White Girls* and several other books. More than 1,200 of his short stories have appeared in *AHMM*, *EQMM*, *Mike Shayne's Mystery Magazine*, *The Best American Mystery Stories*, and many other anthologies and periodicals, and he has edited six anthologies of crime fiction, including the three-volume *Fedora* series. He lives and writes in Texas.

REBECCA STOUT BRADBURY (1937–) is the daughter of Rex and Pola Stout. She has worked for *Good Housekeeping* and at Marshall Field and Company in Chicago and currently serves on the board of the Colonial Dames, volunteers for various community groups (including the USO), and is a Stephen Minister at the La Jolla Presbyterian Church.

JON L. BREEN (1943–) is the author of eight novels (two of which were short-listed for Dagger Awards), over a hundred short stories, and two Edgar Award–winning reference books, *What About Murder?: A Guide to Books About Mystery and Detective Fiction* and *Novel Verdicts: A Guide to Courtroom Fiction*. His first story, a parody of Ed McBain's 87th Precinct books, appeared in *EQMM* in 1967, and he wrote *EQMM*'s "Jury Box" book-review column for about thirty years. His critical work also appears in *Mystery Scene*.

WILLIAM BRITTAIN (1930–2011) was a prolific author of short crime fiction, contributing more than sixty stories to *Ellery Queen's Mystery Magazine* and *Alfred Hitchcock's Mystery Magazine* between 1964 and 1983. From 1979 to 1994, he wrote fourteen children's books; in 1983, *The Wish Giver* won a Newbery Honor Award. In 2018, Crippen & Landru published a collection of all eleven of his "Man Who Read" and seven of his Mr. Strang stories as *The Man Who Read Mysteries: The Short Fiction of William Brittain*.

PATRICK BUTLER contributed half a dozen miscellaneous pieces to *The Saturday Review* between 1967 and 1970, mostly to Martin Levin's "Phoenix Nest" feature—beginning in the September 9, 1967, issue with a poem titled "Memo: Rand" and reading, in full, as follows: "An iron fist in an iron glove / Is Miss

Ayn Rand's response to love. / The Rands, I think, were once more pally; / Or so it seemed when I saw Sally."

LOREN D. ESTLEMAN (1952–) graduated from Eastern Michigan University in 1974, and his first novel was published two years later. He is the author of the Amos Walker detective series, the Peter Macklin hit man series, the Valentino film detective series, the Deputy US Marshal Page Murdock series, and many other books in the fields of suspense, historical western, and general fiction. The winner of more than twenty-five national writing awards, including three for lifetime achievement, he lives in Michigan with his wife, author Deborah Morgan.

ROBERT GOLDSBOROUGH (1937–), the official continuator of the Nero Wolfe mystery series, also is a longtime Chicago journalist, having worked in writing and editing capacities for the *Chicago Tribune* (21 years) and the trade journal *Advertising Age* (23 years). In addition to being the author of thirteen Nero Wolfe mysteries, he also has written six Chicago historical mystery novels (five from Echelon Press) that feature *Chicago Tribune* police reporter Steve "Snap" Malek. His most recent Nero Wolfe novel, *Death of an Art Collector*, was published by Mysterious Press and Open Road Integrated Media in 2019.

JOSEPH GOODRICH (1963–) is a playwright and author. His adaptation of Ellery Queen's *Calamity Town* received the 2016 Calgary Theater Critics' Award for Best New Script. His adaptations of *The Red Box* and *Might as Well Be Dead* marked Nero Wolfe's stage debut. *Panic* won the 2008 Edgar Award for Best Play. He is the editor of *People in a Magazine: The Selected Letters of S. N. Behrman and His Editors at "The New Yorker"* and *Blood Relations: The Selected Letters of Ellery Queen, 1947–1950.*

His fiction has appeared in *EQMM*, *AHMM*, and two MWA anthologies. A former Calderwood Fellow at the McDowell Colony, he lives in NYC.

REBECCA K. JONES (1986–) is a practicing attorney in Arizona, specializing in criminal law. Her first short story, "History on the Bedroom Wall," was published in *EQMM* in 2009. She translated another Thomas Narcejac pastiche, "The Mystery of the Red Balloons," for *The Misadventures of Ellery Queen* (Wildside Press, 2018).

MARVIN KAYE (1938–) is the author of nineteen novels, the editor of *Sherlock Holmes Mystery Magazine*, and the editor and copublisher of *Weird Tales*, America's oldest supernatural horror periodical. A native of Philadelphia, he is listed in *Who's Who in America* and received the *Who's Who* Lifetime Achievement Award.

JOHN LESCROART (1948–) is the author of twenty-eight novels, eighteen of which have been *New York Times* bestsellers. Libraries Unlimited places him among "The 100 Most Popular Thriller and Suspense Authors." With sales of over twelve million copies, his books have been translated into twenty-two languages, and his short stories appear in many anthologies.

FRANK LITTLER, like Patrick Butler, contributed a number of pieces to *The Saturday Review* in the late 1960s, primarily to Martin Levin's "Phoenix Nest" feature, Goodman Ace's similar "Top of My Head," and Jerome Beatty Jr.'s also similar "Trade Winds." A decade later, Thomas Middleton made several references to "a gentleman named Frank Littler" in his "Light Refractions" column, still in *The Saturday Review*, but it's unclear whether or not that was the same Frank Littler.

ROBERT LOPRESTI (1962–) lives in the Pacific Northwest. His most recent novel, *Greenfellas*, is the comic tale of a mobster who decides to save the environment by any means necessary. His seventy-plus short stories have appeared in *EQMM*, *AHMM*, *The Strand*, etc., and have been reprinted in *Year's Best Mystery Stories*. In 2013, the Wolfe Pack and *Alfred Hitchcock's Mystery Magazine* gave him the Black Orchid Novella Award for "The Red Envelope."

MARION MAINWARING (1922–2015) was a scholar, writer, and translator. She held a PhD in English from Harvard, was fluent in French, Russian, and Greek, and lived much of her life in London and Paris. She wrote two murder mysteries—*Murder at Midyears* (set at a fictionalized Mount Holyoke College) in 1953 and *Murder in Pastiche* in 1955—and translated the Russian writer Ivan Turgenev for fun, in part to overcome writer's block. Her talent for pastiche led to her most well-known project—also done for fun, as a break from her decades-long detective scholarship into the life of Edith Wharton—a seamless completion of Wharton's unfinished novel *The Buccaneers* (1993).

THOMAS NARCEJAC (1908–1998) was the pseudonym of Pierre Ayroud, who wrote collaboratively with Pierre Boileau as Boileau-Narcejac. Their best-known work was *D'entre les morts* (1954), which was filmed by Alfred Hitchcock as *Vertigo* in 1958. A collection of Narcejac's pastiches of famous fictional detectives was published in France as *Usurpation d'identité.*

JOSH PACHTER (1951–) is a writer, editor and translator. His short fiction has appeared in *EQMM*, *AHMM*, and many other periodicals, anthologies, and year's-best collections; *The Tree of Life* (Wildside Press, 2015) collected all ten of his Mahboob Chaudri stories. He coedited *The Misadventures of Ellery Queen* (Wildside Press, 2018) and *The Further Misadventures of Ellery Queen* (Wildside Press, 2020) with Dale C. Andrews, edited *The Man Who Read Mysteries: The Short Fiction of William Brittain* (Crippen & Landru, 2018), and coedited *Amsterdam Noir* (Akashic Books, 2019) with Dutch writer René Appel. He lives in northern Virginia with his wife, Laurie, who was reading a Nero Wolfe novel in a coffee shop when they first met in 2007.

OTTO PENZLER (1942–), proprietor of the Mysterious Bookshop in New York City, founded the Mysterious Press in 1975, now an imprint at Grove/Atlantic, and publishes classic crime fiction as ebooks through MysteriousPress.com. Penzler has won two Edgar Awards, MWA's Ellery Queen Award and the Raven. He has been given Lifetime Achievement awards by Noircon and *The Strand Magazine*. He founded two new publishing companies in 2018, Penzler Publishers, reissuing American Mystery Classics in hardcover and trade paperback, and Scarlet, which publishes original psychological suspense novels. He has edited more than 60 anthologies.

MACK REYNOLDS (1917–1983) was a science-fiction writer, credited with almost two hundred short stories (primarily in the 1950s and 1960s) and almost seventy novels (primarily in the 1960s and 1970s). Born Dallas McCord Reynolds, he wrote as Mack Reynolds and under numerous pen names, including Maxine Reynolds. His *Mission to Horatius* (1968) was the first original novel set in the *Star Trek* universe.

NORMA SCHIER (1930–1995) contributed ten unusual pastiches to *EQMM* between 1965 and 1970. In each case, her byline was an anagram of the name of a noted crime writer, and all the proper names in the stories were also anagrams. In 1979, the Mysterious Press collected all ten of these stories—plus five more—as *The Anagram Detectives*.

DAVE ZELTSERMAN (1959–) is the award-winning author of twenty crime, horror, and thriller novels, and numerous short stories. His novels have been named by the *Washington Post*, NPR, WBUR, the American Library Association, and *Booklist* as best books of the year, and his crime novel *Small Crimes* was made into a Netflix original film starring Nikolaj Coster-Waldau. He also writes the Morris Brick crime thrillers under the pseudonym Jacob Stone.

MYSTERIOUSPRESS.COM

Otto Penzler, owner of the Mysterious Bookshop in Manhattan, founded the Mysterious Press in 1975. Penzler quickly became known for his outstanding selection of mystery, crime, and suspense books, both from his imprint and in his store. The imprint was devoted to printing the best books in these genres, using fine paper and top dust-jacket artists, as well as offering many limited, signed editions.

Now the Mysterious Press has gone digital, publishing ebooks through **MysteriousPress.com**.

MysteriousPress.com offers readers essential noir and suspense fiction, hard-boiled crime novels, and the latest thrillers from both debut authors and mystery masters. Discover classics and new voices, all from one legendary source.

THE MYSTERIOUS BOOKSHOP, founded in 1979, is located in Manhattan's Tribeca neighborhood. It is the oldest and largest mystery-specialty bookstore in America.

The shop stocks the finest selection of new mystery hardcovers, paperbacks, and periodicals. It also features a superb collection of signed modern first editions, rare and collectable works, and Sherlock Holmes titles. The bookshop issues a free monthly newsletter highlighting its book clubs, new releases, events, and recently acquired books.

58 Warren Street
info@mysteriousbookshop.com
(212) 587-1011
Monday through Saturday
11:00 a.m. to 7:00 p.m.

FIND OUT MORE AT:

www.mysteriousbookshop.com

FOLLOW US:

@TheMysterious and Facebook.com/MysteriousBookshop

CPSIA information can be obtained
at www.ICGtesting.com
Printed in the USA
BVHW072234150320
574347BV00001B/1